EVERLIFE

by Gena Showalter

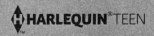

ISBN-13: 978-1-335-47043-0

Everlife

HARLEQUIN®TEEN
www.HarlequinTEEN.com

Printed in U.S.A.

To God, my Helper, Healer, Redeemer, Defender, Shepherd, Provider... my everything.

To Natashya Wilson, whose keen insight never fails to amaze me. Thank you for your incredible feedback as I worked on the Everlife series, for asking questions that needed to be asked and helping me reach a new level.

To Vicki Tolbert, Shonna Hurt, Michelle Quine and Christy James, for the prayers I so desperately needed. Also, a special thanks to Vicki for feeding me while I was working!

To Jill Monroe, who gets a thousand emails anytime I'm writing a rough draft. Most of those questions go a little something like this: "What do you think of this? Yes, but what about this? But, but, but what about this?" I am blessed to know you!

And last but not least, to the incredible animals who inspired some of the furry characters in this book: Biscuit, Mary Ann, Ginger, Nemo, Thor, Pepper, Boots, Noel, Peanut, Athena, Boomer, Riggs, Murtaugh, Milo, Goldman, Mya, Barney, Bailey, Champ, Lucy, Roxi, Lefty, Righty, Suzi and Dixie.

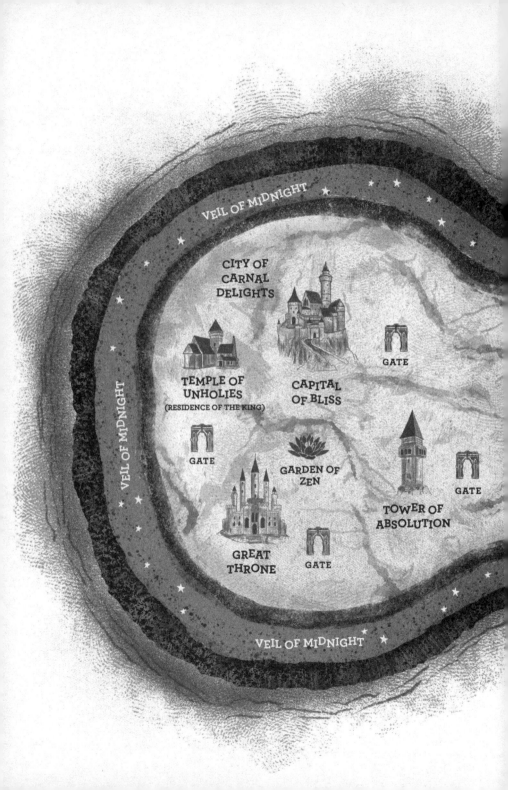

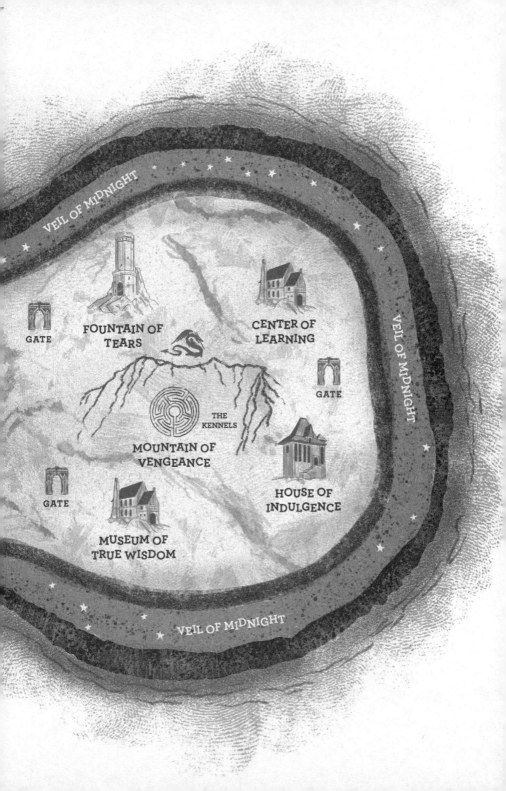

"The time will come, the time will not be long in coming, when new ties will be formed about you—ties that will bind you yet more tenderly and strongly to the home you so adorn—the dearest ties that will ever grace and gladden you."

—CHARLES DICKENS, *A TALE OF TWO CITIES*

The End of a Nation

All hope has been lost. Our armies have been defeated, our spirits crushed. We are helpless as night smothers day, choking out Light. We have nothing. We *are* nothing.

Or so our enemy would have us think.

If seeing is believing, they would be right. But we must trust the promise in our hearts. We are like a tree firmly planted by a riverbank, our roots so deep no storm can blow us down. We might bend, but we will never break.

Through trial and tribulation, victory will be ours.

After all, diamonds are made with pressure.

Soon a time will come, a time for every man, woman and child to make a choice. When you've been beaten down—physically, mentally and emotionally—when you've been betrayed, all hope gone, where will you find the strength to stand, and march on?

How far will we go for the sake of our realm?

Darkness may descend, but our Light can forever shine. Though we fall one by one, we can rise together. One body. One heart. One purpose.

One eternity.

Glossary of Terms
excerpted from Myriad's
Book of Evernight

Abrogate—
In the darkness, greatness is born.
* The highest rank of General in Myriad.
* Once rare, their numbers are now growing exponentially.
* Those who extinguish the Light in Troikans as well as in humans.

Conduit—
In the Light, destruction awaits.
* The second-highest rank in Troika, accountable only to the Secondking.
* Currently on the verge of extinction.
* Someone with the ability to harness sunlight and share its power through the Troikan Grid.

Covenant—
The solid foundation on which we stand.
* Any blood oath agreed upon between two separate

parties (i.e., a human and an Everlife realm), legally voided through court or loopholes.

* If terms are broken illegally, a human can be put to death and a spirit enslaved.

Everlife—
The end will always justify the means.
* The afterlife, where Myriad and Troika are at war.
* Also known as the Unending.

Firstking—
He that shall not be named.
* Creator of the realms, spirits, humans and the Land of the Harvest.
* Father of the Secondkings: Ambrosine, the Prince of Ravens, and Eron, the Prince of Doves.
* Let the name Eron forever be a curse.

Firstlife—
Let the countdown begin.
* A human life (i.e., a spirit encased inside a body).
* Dress rehearsal for the Everlife, when a human soul should be won by any means necessary.

Firstdeath—
What was shall no longer be.
* The demise of a human body.
* Occurs the moment a spirit cuts ties with its body.

Fused—
And two shall become one.
* When a spirit experiences Second-death, it joins to another—brand-new—spirit (or even multiple spirits) to be reborn in the Land of the Harvest.
* A fact disputed by Troikans.

General—
A dragon with ten heads cannot be defeated.
⋆ Accountable only to the Secondking.
⋆ One of ten individuals who oversee teams of Leaders,
Headhunters, Laborers and Messengers.
⋆ Responsible for planning battle strategies and leading
armies into war.

Grid, the—
One for all, and all for one.
⋆ A spiritual bond between every citizen of a realm and
the realm's Secondking.

Kennels, the—
Betray your realm at your own peril.
⋆ Prison for Myriadians convicted of crimes.

Laborer—
Work hard, play harder. Always win.
⋆ One of six main positions within a realm, overseen by
a Leader.
⋆ Responsible for returning to the Land of the Harvest to
convince humans to make covenant with their realm of
choice.
⋆ ML: Myriadian Laborer.
⋆ TL: Troikan Laborer.

Land of the Harvest, the—
They cannot run. They cannot hide.
⋆ Earth, home to humans.

Leader—
Only the strong survive.
⋆ An assistant to a General.
⋆ Females are known as "Madame," males as "Sir."
⋆ Responsible for delegating assignments to all other sub-

positions within the realm, while also meeting specific quotas (i.e., recruiting a certain number of souls).

Many Ends—
Where happiness goes to die and nightmares come to life.
* The realm where the Unsigned are imprisoned after Firstdeath.

Messenger—
Let the worlds know the horror that is Troika.
* One of six main positions within the realms, directly under Laborer.
* Responsible for teaching humans about the realms, protecting others from the enemy and chronicling exploits inside and outside the realm.

Myriad—
Autonomy, bliss, indulgence.
* The dark realm, ruled by the Prince of Ravens.
* Magical forests whisper enchanted tales, and secrets await you in every corner; self-indulgence is revered, and the party never stops; victors are adored and failures are abhorred; emotion always trumps logic.
* Motto: Might Equals Right.

Penumbra—
In the dark, the Light is easier to extinguish.
* A sentient darkness capable of draining Troikans of Light.
* Must be a Myriadian General to access more information.

Realms—
The only home that matters.
* Kingdoms in the Everlife: Myriad and Troika.
* Sub-realms: Many Ends and Troika's widely disputed "Rest."

Rest, the—
Deception cloaked in hope.
⋆ Troikans believe a spirit enters into a state of absolute tranquility after Second-death, forever separated from the realms...with one exception.

Resurrection, the—
A promise without merit.
⋆ Once every year, the people of Troika hold a vote, allowing one spirit to leave the Rest.
⋆ A trick—there is no Rest.

Second-death—
Another end, another new beginning.
⋆ When a spirit is drained of Lifeblood.
⋆ The moment a spirit is Fused to another spirit(s) in order to return to the Land of the Harvest.
⋆ Troikans foolishly believe a spirit enters into "the Rest."

Secondking—
Bow or break.
⋆ One of two sons of He Who Shall Not Be Named.
⋆ Ambrosine, Prince of Ravens, rules Myriad.
⋆ The Other Who Shall Not Be Named rules Troika.
⋆ Ruler of a realm.

Troika—
Self-proclaimed leaders of justice, equality and freedom of choice.
⋆ The realm of Light, ruled by the Other Who Shall Not Be Named.
⋆ Supposedly untouched by gloom, where hard work isn't an expectation but a way of life, equality isn't an ideal but a standard and fear isn't a treasured friend but a hated foe; "logic" always trumps emotion; people are

governed by a strict set of rules, never allowed to play,
and violators are punished.
★ Motto: Light Brings Sight.

Unsigned—
Punishment rides the wings of the damned.
★ A human who fails to make covenant with a realm
before Firstdeath.
★ Cursed to spend the Everlife inside Many Ends.

Veil, the—
Choose us and enter in.
★ A doorway leading into one of the realms.
★ The Veil of Midnight protects Myriad.
★ The Veil of Wings protects Troika.

Message Directory

MYRIAD:
Laborer Sloan Aubuchon: S_A_5/46.15.33
Sir Zhi Chen: Z_C_4/23.43.2
Abrogate Javier Diez: J_D_2/43.3.19
Laborer Killian Flynn: K_F_5/23.53.6
General Hans Schmidt: H_S_3/51.3.6
Laborer Leonard Lockwood: L_L_5/19.36.2
Laborer Dior Nichols: D_N_5/62.4.1
Laborer Victor Prince: V_P_5/20.16.18

TROIKA:
Laborer Raanan Aarons: R_A_5/40.5.16
General Jane Adamson: J_A_3/19.37.30
Messenger Clayton Anders: C_A_6/53.1.4
General John Blake: J_B_3/19.23.4
General Tasanee Bunyasarn: T_B_3/19.30.2
General Shamus Campbell: S_C_3/50.4.13
General Spike Jones: S_J_3/62.5.5
Conduit Ten Lockwood: T_L_2/23.43.2
General Chanel Moreau: C_M_3/5.20.1
General Marcos Pereira: M_P_3/45.10.9
Laborer Archer Prince: A_P_5/23.43.2

General Luciana Rossi: L_R_3/51.3.15
General Bahari Sekibo: B_S_3/51.3.13
General Agape Stavros: A_S_3/42.6.31
General Alejandro Torres: A_T_3/23.40.29
General Mykhail Vasiliev: M_V_3/54.5.8
General Ying Wo Li: Y_L_3/59.1.2

PART ONE

Troika

TROIKA

From: A_T_3/23.40.29
To: L_R_3/51.3.15, J_A_3/19.37.30, S_C_3/50.4.13,
C_M_3/5.20.1, Y_L_3/59.1.2, A_S_3/42.6.31, T_B_3/19.30.2,
B_S_3/51.3.13, M_V_3/54.5.8, J_B_3/19.23.4, S_J_3/62.5.5,
M_P_3/45.10.9
Subject: Tenley Lockwood

Fellow Generals,
We have two orders of business to discuss. The first: animals.
Because of the recent bombings inside our realm, our Secondking has issued a decree. Every citizen will be appointed a
guardian, whether four-legged or winged. However, we all
have the right to decline. I suggest you do so, and encourage your people to do the same. We haven't trained with
these animals. There's a good chance they'll be more of a
hindrance than a help.

The second order of business is the most important. For
the first time in our realm's history, the Prince of Doves has

decided NOT to hold a vote for the Resurrection. I don't know why, only that protests will not change his mind. Instead, Tenley Lockwood is tasked with selecting which of our fallen soldiers will leave the Rest.

No doubt she plans to choose one of the following (in order of rank):

General Levi Nanne, her trainer

Leader Meredith Cordell, her grandmother

Laborer Archer Prince, her friend

Laborer Elizabeth Winchester, her teammate

We have twenty-four hours to plead the case of our revered brother, General Orion Giovante. While I love and respect the others, Orion is the one we need. The war with Myriad is heating. We are outnumbered and outgunned, and Orion is a warrior among warriors, our greatest hope for victory. He has what Levi doesn't: a killer instinct. Toward the end, Levi softened. He worked with Killian Flynn, known by our Laborers as the Butcher. Mr. Flynn is also Miss Lockwood's biggest weakness. Their romantic relationship puts us all at terrible risk.

Orion will deliver Mr. Flynn's Second-death without pause or concern for Miss Lockwood's feelings. He will help us focus on the only thing that matters: Myriad's annihilation.

First, we must find Miss Lockwood. Second, we must convince her to do what will help us but hurt her. For some reason, I'm unable to find her in the Grid.

Jane, do you see her in the Eye?

Light Brings Sight!
General Alejandro Torres

TROIKA

From: J_A_3/19.37.30
To: A_T_3/23.40.29, L_R_3/51.3.15, S_C_3/50.4.13,
C_M_3/5.20.1, Y_L_3/59.1.2, A_S_3/42.6.31, T_B_3/19.30.2,
B_S_3/51.3.13, M_V_3/54.5.8, J_B_3/19.23.4, S_J_3/62.5.5,
M_P_3/45.10.9
Subject: Foolish girl!

Miss Lockwood has disabled her comm. Does she *want*
Myriad to kill her?

Worry not. I'll find her. I just need time.

General Shamus, gather your army and await further word
at the Veil of Wings. The moment I've located Miss Lockwood, I'll transport you to her side.

Light Brings Sight!
General Jane Adamson
PS: I have rejected my guardian.

TROIKA

From: S_C_3/50.4.13
To: J_A_3/19.37.30, A_T_3/23.40.29, L_R_3/51.3.15,
C_M_3/5.20.1, Y_L_3/59.1.2, A_S_3/42.6.31, T_B_3/19.30.2,
B_S_3/51.3.13, M_V_3/54.5.8, J_B_3/19.23.4, S_J_3/62.5.5,
M_P_3/45.10.9
Subject: I'll be ready

However, I doubt I'll be gentle. But then, I have a feeling "gentle" isn't necessary or even desired. Why else would you assign the Brute to retrieve her? You'd like someone to teach her the error of her ways, perhaps even scare her into doing what we desire.

Consider it done.

Light Brings Sight!
General Shamus Campbell
PS: I was appointed a guardian poodle. You did not misread. I said POODLE. If you want to be insulted on my behalf, feel free. I turned her down—of course.

TROIKA

From: L_R_3/51.3.15
To: S_C_3/50.4.13, J_A_3/19.37.30, A_T_3/23.40.29,
C_M_3/5.20.1, Y_L_3/59.1.2, A_S_3/42.6.31, T_B_3/19.30.2,
B_S_3/51.3.13, M_V_3/54.5.8, J_B_3/19.23.4, S_J_3/62.5.5,
M_P_3/45.10.9
Subject: I'll go with you, Shame-us

And I'll hear no protests on the matter. Anger has clouded your judgment; it is Myriad, not Troika, that deals in fear. Also, if we punish the girl, we risk alienating her. We cannot make her feel as though she has no allies, otherwise she'll vote for someone other than the General she's never had the privilege of meeting.

Do us all a favor and think before you speak, General Campbell.

Light Brings Sight!
General Luciana Rossi
PS: I was assigned a grizzly bear. Suck it.

TROIKA

From: S_C_3/50.4.13
To: L_R_3/51.3.15
Subject: Admit it

Your concern isn't for the girl or even our great realm. You've always lusted for Orion, and you'll do anything to bring him back—even pander to a Conduit too ignorant to pick a good decision in a lineup.

I'm sure Orion's wife will thank you for your efforts, eh. Or not. Yeah, probably not.

If ever YOU stop acting like a Myriadian and want to tup an *un*attached male, all you have to do is beg me. I'll do the dishonors, you have my word.

Light Brings Sight!
General Shame-on-you
PS: I guess Eron thinks you need a stronger guardian... because you are weaker.

MYRIAD

From: S_A_5/46.15.33
To: K_F_5/23.53.6
Subject: Penumbra

I know you're in hiding, Killian. I know you're in trouble. But you have to come back to Myriad. After Dior's court appearance, I overheard something I shouldn't have. We knew the Penumbra had begun to spread but we didn't know our realm had found a way to mass-produce the infection. Thousands of humans are going to be affected—and soon.

Killian, please! You have to come back. I can't fight this alone.

Might Equals Right!
ML-in-training,
Sloan Aubuchon

MYRIAD

From: Mailer-Erratum
To: S_A_5/46.15.33, K_F_5/23.53.6
Subject: THIS MESSAGE HAS BEEN DEEMED UNDELIVERABLE

Report to Zhi Chen for debriefing.

MYRIAD

From: Z_C_4/23.43.2
To: S_A_5/46.15.33
Subject: Your loyalty is rivaled only by your stupidity

Your devotion to Killian Flynn would be admirable, if he hadn't made the grave mistake of siding with a Troikan and disgracing his realm. The moment he's found, he'll be placed in the Kennels or killed. There are no other options.

Get your priorities straight, Miss Aubuchon, or you'll join him, whatever his fate.

Now, on to more pleasant news. I'm assigning you a mentor to help steer you in the right direction. His name is Victor Prince, and he's an exalted son of our Secondking.

Years ago, Victor made covenant with Troika in order to spy for us. Just last night, he managed the impossible. He defected and returned to our midst without having to go to court. Unfortunately, he lost both hands in the process.

Side note: As new as you are, you might not know spirits regenerate limbs. In time.

Until Mr. Prince is whole again, he'll remain inside a Shell. You'll remain inside one, as well, since he is now responsible for your training. Yours, and your new partner's, who is rising through our ranks. His name is Leonard Lockwood, and he is Tenley Lockwood's father.

I know you'll treat him with respect, because you know what will happen if you don't.

Might Equals Right!
Sir Zhi Chen

MYRIAD

From: H_S_3/51.3.6
To: Z_C_4/23.43.2
Subject: Javier Diez and Dior Nichols, among other things

Yo! I heard from one of our queens, who heard directly from our Secondking. Ambrosine wants the spirits of Javier Diez and Dior Nichols in Myriad, el pronto. No more waiting. Find someone to do the honors. I'm busy managing a warehouse full of ticking time bombs.

Speaking of, I flagged all messages about this particular topic, and came across one sent by a Laborer under your command. Sloan…something. Abadabado? Whoever she is, send her my way. I'm ensuring Troikans find the warehouse later today. Considering she's a sympathizer, she'll make excellent bait.

You might be willing to pardon her for her loyalty to Killian, but I am not. She can no longer be trusted, but she can be used.

Get ready. The war is about to take a drastic turn—for our better!

Might Equals Right!
General Hans Schmidt

chapter one

Ten
Present day

I peer up at the indomitable Killian Flynn, my heart thudding against my ribs. Every breath I take fills me with hope, wonder…and dismay.

Our relationship is about to change. *Everything* is about to change.

Earlier, we snuck out of our realms to meet in the Land of the Harvest. A secret cave in Russia's Ural Mountains, to be exact. Now we stand face-to-face, hand in hand. Jagged rocks create the perfect frame for Killian's wild, ravaging beauty and the unwavering strength he wields. Strength forged on the bloodiest of battlefields.

There's no other warrior I'd rather have at my side.

Our people might be at war, but we are going to usher in peace. One step at a time.

I drink him in, this boy I'm trusting with my present—and my future. His skin is a magnificent shade between bronze and gold while his hair is jet black. His eyebrows are thick, masculine, and his nose sharp as a blade. His mouth is soft and lush. Pure temptation...

A shadow of a beard dusts his triangular jaw. Under his T-shirt and jeans, his deliciously muscled body is covered in tattoos. Skulls, stars, roses and other images, all connected by lines, creating some sort of map. That map appears on both his spirit and his Shell—an outer casing made to resemble a spirit—but he's never told me where it leads.

One day, he'll share all. We both will.

But it is his eyes that draw me in and hold me captive. His eyes are a soulful gold with flecks of electric blue. Always those flecks strike a chord inside me, different songs piercing my soul. Some are fast and erratic, eliciting passion, while others are slow and dreamy; always they are haunting.

Today I hear a seductive melody that sets my blood aflame *and* chills me to the bone. Makes sense. I am fire, he is ice, yet we fit. After all, the warmth of a fire is best enjoyed on a frigid winter's day.

So many differences. Too many, most would say.

Just enough to rock the entire world.

I am day. He is night.

I strengthen in Light. He is unrivaled in darkness.

I like rules, structure. He thrives in chaos.

I believe our worst emotions should never dictate our actions; we should help, forgive and care for others. Emotions are fleeting, after all, and subject to change. Why let one ruin your life? He believes emotion should drive us every moment of every day, and caring for others is foolish. Those you help now will stab you in the back later.

To me, today's choices dictate tomorrow's reality. To him, Fate decides for us.

I'm a Troikan Conduit. He's a Myriadian Laborer. We are Lifeblood-born enemies, and yet he is the love of my Everlife.

As different as we are, we are also the same. Painful pasts shaped us, made us stronger. We hold on tight whenever something—or someone—threatens the people and things we love. We fight for what we believe is right, no matter the obstacles in our way.

I'm one of only two Conduits responsible for lighting Troika, and I'm supposed to kill Killian, our enemy. I'm going to marry him, instead.

Chemistry doesn't care about expectations. I love and adore this boy, and I hold on tight, remember?

Even if I despised him, I would say "I do." There's more at stake than our hearts.

Once we unite our spirits, we will have the opportunity to unite our realms and facilitate the peace we so desperately crave. Together, we will enter Myriad and slay Ambrosine, Prince of Ravens. The realm's corrupt Secondking.

A corrupt leader corrupts his people absolutely.

Then Killian will take the crown, and command, and order his armies to stand down. He will accept the truce Troika once offered. A truce Eron, Prince of Doves and the Second-king of Troika, has wanted for centuries.

Finally the war will end.

Once that is accomplished—or maybe before, we haven't decided on an order yet—we will save the poor souls trapped inside Many Ends, the hellish sub-realm connected to Myriad.

Many Ends is home to the Unsigned who experience First-death, as well as monstrous beings with a single goal: *kill everyone.* Spirits are hunted and killed in the most horrific ways.

Again…and again. Because, once a spirit "dies" in Many Ends, it comes back to life, ready for round two…three…four…

Four, the number for stability, order and justice. A strong foundation, considering there are four sides in a square. Four cardinal directions—north, south, east, west. Four seasons to complete a year—winter, spring, summer, fall. Four winds, and four phases of the moon.

Four is the only numeral spelled with the same amount of letters as its numerical value.

Focus. I *believe* the spirits trapped inside Many Ends come back to life, but my theory hasn't yet been proven.

Another uncertainty? Killian's mother, Caroline, and my friend Marlowe could be there. But here's the thing. Neither Caroline nor Marlowe were Unsigned. Caroline made covenant with Myriad years before, only to experience Second-death within days of reaching the realm. Marlowe made covenant with Troika, only to void it when she committed suicide. Different people, different policies.

Myriad claimed Caroline's spirit Fused with the spirit of a newborn infant the day of her death, but I think they lied. I think all Myriadians wind up in Many Ends, like all Troikans wind up in the Rest.

If people knew, they might not sign with Myriad. False-hoods and propagandas keep business booming.

I *need* to save the damned, and I can. I know I can. Not because I'm special. Please. I'm just a girl who can navigate Many Ends' treacherous labyrinth better than most, because I've been there.

A shudder of dismay rocks me.

"I hope you weren't thinkin' of me just then, lass." Killian lifts my hands to his lips and kisses my knuckles, sending tingles down my spine.

"Are you kidding? The great Killian Flynn only ever makes girls shiver with desire."

"Or vibrate with anger."

I'm smiling as I nod. "That's fair."

The ring on his thumb glints in the firelight, warming my heart. After my grandmother Meredith experienced Second-death, I was presented with a token of remembrance. A gun-ring with six-round cylinders, 2mm pinfire. A gorgeous piece of weaponry *and* a fashion statement. My most prized possession.

I could think of no better gift to give to Killian when he gave me a hand-carved pendant in the shape of pi. Infinite possibilities rest within the ratio of a circle's circumference to its diameter; every possibility for every life. A number without end. Convert letters to numbers, and they, too, can be found within pi. Meaning, every number with any meaning—from our birthdays to the date we die—and every word ever spoken, every word that *will* be spoken, exist within pi.

"I love you" becomes $9 + 12 + 15 + 22 + 5 + 25 + 15 + 21 = 619$.

Or as Killian says:

I = one letter.

Love = four letters.

You = three letters.

143, 10.

Even now, the pendant hangs from a string of leather around my neck, both beautiful and useful. Whenever I'm in trouble, I can press the center, and my location will be sent to Killian's comm. He can find me in an instant and help.

Now, we're going to help each other and intertwine our futures with an unbreakable covenant.

What if, despite this, I'm unable to enter Myriad?

Zero! The doubt devil surfaces, and swarms of others follow. Will my Light hurt him? Will his darkness harm me? Will we weaken or strengthen each other? Will our covenants to the realms be voided? What if, after this, neither of us can return home?

Firstlife was a dress rehearsal. Now the curtain is up, and we're performing in front of a live studio audience. Every word, action and decision comes with a consequence. There are no second chances to right our wrongs. No do-overs.

I've been told I'll turn the tide of the war, somehow, some way. What if my bond to Killian turns the tide in *Myriad's* favor?

Maybe I should back out. Except…every fiber of my being suddenly screams in denial. Both realms have reached a boiling point. Every day innocents are slaughtered. Something has to change, and fast. This is our best shot at peace. Our *only* shot. And really, I want to save Myriad just as much as I want to save Troika. I shouldn't put one realm above the other.

Face it. If I back out now, fear wins and *everyone* loses.

I will not make decisions based on "what if." I will do what's right, always. Because, in the end, I'm the only one who has to live with my regrets.

Doubt devils can suck it.

Killian squeezes my hands. "Yer paler by the second, lass. There's still time tae back out." His accent—a mix of Irish, Scottish, and I have no idea what else—is thicker than usual, his voice low and husky, and irresistibly sexy. "I doona want you feelin' pressured."

"I just… I wish we could speak with other inter-realm couples. We aren't the first Troikan and Myriadian to fall in love.

We can't be." Though we've searched high and low, we've found no one else. Either the others are in hiding…or dead.

He stiffens, as if he's expecting a devastating blow. "We can put this ceremony on hold and continue searchin'."

And end up right where we are, perhaps far too late. "We're doing this. I'll share my Light with you, and you'll share your darkness with me. I'll pass through the Veil of Midnight." The doorway that leads into Myriad freezes Troikans to Second-death. But I'm about to become half-Myriadian. Maybe. Probably. Fingers crossed.

He is far from comforted. "If yer only doin' this for your mother…"

Mom is locked in the Kennels, a prison in Myriad. I'm going to find and free her, so she can defect to Troika to raise my little brother, Jeremy. "She's one of many reasons," I say.

He relaxes, but only slightly. "Yer only seventeen years old. We can revisit the bond in a few decades, yeah?"

Decades? I inhale deeply, drawing in the familiar and beloved scent of peat smoke and heather. His scent. A new wave of calm flows over me, as warm and sweet as honey. "I'm almost eighteen, and you're only nineteen. So what? We've lived, died and lived again. I'm not going to wait to fight for what's right, and I'm certainly not going to wait to claim you."

"I doona want ye doin' something you'll regret."

His accent has reached maximum thickness. Aka sweet, mouthwatering molasses. Meaning his emotions are engaged and running rampant, and I'm melting as my blood heats. "How could I regret a miracle?" I ask.

One dark brow arches as his incredible eyes glitter. "Explain."

"There are over one hundred billion galaxies. And counting! There are incalculable universes, two realms in the Unending, two sub-realms, nine planets in our solar system, one hundred and ninety-six countries, seven seas and over seven hundred islands. The fact that we found each other—miracle."

He laughs. "You tryin' tae seduce me, lass? 'Cause it's workin'."

This boy. Oh, this boy. He's the one seducing me. Heart, mind, body. I love him.

But go ahead. Remove love from the equation. It doesn't matter. Still I trust him. Time and time again, he's defied the orders of his Secondking in an effort to protect my family. He's helped me when he should have harmed me.

"It's working, but it hasn't carried you to the finish line yet?" I mock-growl. "I can't believe you're making me talk you into this. It was your idea. Maybe I should wait until you get down on one knee to beg for the honor of becoming my husband."

His good humor fades in an instant, his features tight with tension. "I willna beg. I had tae beg for scraps as a child, simply tae survive. Now I'd rather die than beg for *anythin'*."

"Hey, hey." Amusement gone, I gently cup his face. Tenderness wells inside me. There's so much I don't know about him. So much I'm eager to learn. "I was only teasing, I promise."

He releases a shuddering breath. A second later, his lips curve in a slow smile full of promise, and tendrils of heat unfurl inside me. He is beautiful beyond imagining, though every chiseled line is cut by cruelty, as if pain lives and breathes inside him. I look at him, and I want to kiss him, hug him and shake him all at once.

"I'm sorry," he says. "You get I'll be cherishin' you every day of my Everlife, aye?"

Just like that. I'm undone. One smile—and I fall deeper in love with him. One moment of time—and I can't imagine a single day without him. One sentence—and I'm happier than I've ever been.

I rise on my tiptoes and press a soft kiss to his lips.

"Will *you* be cherishin' *me*? I mean, yer wearing Troikan armor. Think yer marriage is goin' to be a battlefield?" His irises glitter with a teasing light, but his tone is serious.

I give the collar of my black catsuit a self-conscious tug.

"I kid, I kid." Killian brushes his knuckles across my jaw-line. "You look good in anythin'. And I canna imagine a more beautiful bride." His voice takes on a husky timbre. "Later, you'll look even better in nothin'."

Heat blooms over my cheeks.

His smile returns, and it's full of mischief, wonder and adoration. He brushes his thumbs over the rise of my cheek-bones. "Yer eyes are like mini-TV screens. They broadcast yer emotions."

Others have told me I'm *impossible* to read. But then, Killian knows me better than most, and he wants me anyway. Not because I'm a rare Conduit, but because I'm me. Tenley Lock wood. A girl who's messed up, time and time again, but continues to get up and keep fighting the good fight.

"Today, a new future will be forged," I say. "Enemies become family."

"The first step toward concord between our realms."

Wind whistles outside our cave, snow billowing, while a fire crackles inside. My gaze snags on the far wall, where the numerical equivalent of our names is carved. 68 + 39.

Killian: 11 + 9 + 12 + 12 + 9 + 1 + 14 = 68

Ten: 20 + 5 + 14 = 39

68 + 39 = 107

"Sonnet 107" by William Shakespeare.

Not mine own fears, nor the prophetic soul
Of the wide world dreaming on things to come,
Can yet the lease of my true love control,
Suppos'd as forfeit to a confin'd doom.
The mortal moon hath her eclipse endur'd
And the sad augurs mock their own presage;
Incertainties now crown themselves assur'd
And peace proclaims olives of endless age.
Now with the drops of this most balmy time
My love looks fresh, and Death to me subscribes,
Since, spite of him, I'll live in this poor rhyme,
While he insults o'er dull and speechless tribes;
And thou in this shalt find thy monument,
When tyrants' crests and tombs of brass are spent.

In other words, love is not subject to time, or even death.

In the back of my mind, the Grid ripples with approval and delivers a new surge of confidence. I *am* doing the right thing. We *will* succeed in our endeavors.

Once, I lamented my invisible link to other Troikans. Now, I rejoice. Support can mean the difference between victory and defeat. But who would approve of this union? No one but me knows about it.

"Whatever happens next," Killian says, "doona forget I love you." The brawler capable of any dark deed leans down to rub his nose against mine. "All right?"

"All right." I'll never forget, and I'll never tire of hearing those words. "I love you, too."

His smile reignites, and oh, wow, it's like Cupid's arrow through my heart. Killian is more than beautiful. He is life. The crystalline flecks in his eyes...there are eight. Eight is the atomic number for oxygen. Killian is my oxygen, the reason I breathe.

"Ready?" He lifts my hands to his mouth once more and traces his tongue between my knuckles.

My stomach flips over. If not for Shells, Myriadians and Troikans would be unable to touch without agonizing pain. Usually Shells mute sensation. Today I feel *everything*.

"Tell me what to do," I rasp.

"Our word is our bond. Speak, and it's done. We'll pledge our lives tae each other. Simple, easy."

As simple and easy as pledging our Everlife to one of the realms. Okay, I can do that. The simplicity doesn't negate the difficulty, however. I'm giving my life—my future—to another person.

He raises his chin. "I'll go first."

My heart thuds against my ribs as I nod.

When he releases my hands, panic invades. I've lost my anchor. Then he cups my face, holding me as if I'm more delicate than glass. "Tenley Nicole Lockwood, you've given me life beyond the grave. Until you, I never knew the power of bein' connected tae another person. You saw the best in me even when I showed you my worst. You trusted me when all evidence pointed tae my guilt. For that, I give ye my Everlife. Everythin' I am, everythin' I have, is yers."

Be still, my heart. How am I supposed to match such a glorious pledge? Well, I have to try.

Nope. Troikans do not try. Troikans do. "Killian—" *Zero!* "I don't know your middle name."

"Niall."

Killian Niall Flynn. Five Ls. Four Ns.

$5 + 4 = 9$

Killian Niall Flynn + Ten = 5 Ls and 5 Ns.

$5 + 5 = 10$

10 = existence. $1 + 2 + 3 + 4 = 10$. (1) the FirstKing (2) the Secondkings (3) human life (4) the four elements: earth, air, fire and water.

Ten is completion: the end of one cycle, the beginning of another.

Concentrate!

Oops. My bad. I tend to lose myself in number trivia when I'm nervous. But there's nothing to be nervous about, right? This is Killian. *My* Killian. Together, we can handle whatever comes next.

"Killian Niall Flynn." I wrap my fingers around his wrists as I peer into his eyes. "You found me before the grave and taught me how to live. Until you, I'd known only disappointment and betrayal, but you picked me up every time I fell. You carried me when I was too weak to walk, and you put me first, even when it meant torture and possibly Second-death. For that, I give you my Everlife. Everything I am, everything I have, is yours."

His expression softens, and I wish, so badly I wish, that my family and friends could witness our union. While my mother is in the Kennel, my father is training to be an ML. He hates me, anyway. My aunt Lina, his twin sister, is missing. No one knows where she is.

Lina can see into the future. As a child, she taught me a rhyme that aided my escape from Many Ends. Only a few weeks ago, she taught me a second rhyme, saving my life when a supposed friend—Victor Prince—attempted to kill me.

My life has taken so many wrong turns and hits, but things are finally on the right track. Except... I frown. "I don't feel any different."

"We are no' done." Killian steps back, his arms falling to his sides. "Out of yer Shell, lass."

I'm confused by the command, but still I obey. He steps from his Shell, as well, gifting me with the sight of two potential husbands. The inanimate Shell, and the spirit man—the *real* Killian. Usually darkness surrounds him, his own personal veil of smoke. Now the darkness is muted, but there's no Light emanating from him, either.

He's so much taller than me, I'm forced to look up, up, up. Scars circle his neck, proof of the pain he's suffered throughout his Secondlife.

I reach out, intending to trace a fingertip along the raised flesh, but stop myself just before contact. "You've been a spirit all your life. Why didn't you regenerate after you were injured?"

"A spirit is unable to regenerate fully until reachin' the Age of Perfection. What you receive as a child, you carry with you always." He crooks his finger at me. "C'mere. I'm goin' tae kiss you now."

A kiss. Of course! A wedding always ends with a kiss.

I move toward him, eager, and he enfolds me in his muscular arms. His lips descend, claiming mine in our first spirit-kiss, no barriers between us, and he isn't gentle about it. He's demanding and possessive, pure masculine aggression, and I love every second.

Everything about him makes me think of forbidden nights and carnal indulgence.

I'm burning up rather than freezing as usual, pleasure consuming me, the pain I'm used to feeling nothing but a distant memory.

Realization: We can touch without consequence!

I melt into him, the rest of the world is forgotten as I luxuriate in the sweetness of his flavor.

Now the deal is sealed. This boy is now my husband. And this, our first kiss as a bonded pair, is everything I've ever dreamed and more. It's—

A bolt of ice slams into me, tossing me across the cavern. I collide with the wall and slide to the ground, fighting for breath. Agony sears my right arm. Panting, I look down. Double take. An image appears in my flesh, as dark as ink and in the shape of...a horse?

The animal rests under the words *Loyalty, Passion, Liberty.*

Loyalty to my realm. Passion for the truth. Liberty for all.

The words appeared immediately after my Firstdeath. Actually, numbers appeared. The moment I figured out what those numbers represented, the words took their place.

Why a horse? There has to be a reason. There's *always* a reason.

I rack my brain, but all I can come up with—Killian once likened me to a warhorse.

The warhorse paws fiercely, rejoicing in his strength, and charges into the fray. He laughs at fear, afraid of nothing; he does not shy away from the sword. The quiver rattles against his side, along with the flashing spear and lance. In frenzied excitement he eats up the ground; he cannot stand still when the trumpet sounds. At the blast of the trumpet it snorts, "Aha!" He catches the scent of battle from afar, the shout of commanders and the battle cry.

He...or she. But I'm not here to fight. I'm here to make peace. Unless...

The moisture in my mouth dries. Ready or not, a new battle is headed our way.

My vision goes hazy, and I moan. I am Light, and I've never needed to see more! Blinking rapidly helps, allowing me to search for Killian. The same terrible phenomena must have bombarded him, because he's slouched against the opposite wall. When our gazes meet, he reaches in my direction, the numbers tattooed on his wrist visible.

143, 10. *I love you, Ten.*

Beneath the numbers I spy a new image. A horse. A match to mine, though his is white and mine is black.

His eyes are alight with… No, impossible! The flecks I so adore cannot be doused in literal flames, flickering with both light and shadow.

I need to get to him, *now*, but my muscles are like frozen blocks of ice. And the Grid—

The Grid! My connection to Troika, and a reminder that there is so much more to the world—to my world—than what I can see and feel at any given time.

Shadows dance along the Grid, where multiple doorways loom. Those doorways lead to rooms. In some, I've stored extra Light. Others provide a link to the conscious minds of different citizens. One in particular opens up to the Rest, where our dead spend eternity at peace.

A pang of homesickness strikes me. Meredith, Archer and Levi are there. I miss them desperately.

Radiating hatred, the shadows try to sneak into one room after another. I fight to keep the doorways closed as information bombards me. Darkness is measured by the absence of Light. These shadows, whatever they are, must have come from Killian, and our bond, and yet they are so familiar to me…as if they are old friends. How is that possible?

Doesn't matter. Must…do…something. Now!

Left with no other choice, I change tactics and open a door to one of my storage rooms. In a vivid, dazzling rush, bright Light escapes. Shadows hiss, some dying the second they come into contact with a beam, others slithering away, and, oh, zero, sharp pains explode through my head, and I scream.

Can't give up. Strengthen in the Light, die in the darkness.

Between one breath and the next, the pain leaves me, and a scene opens in my mind. A memory that is not my own.

I'm standing in a doorway, watching a young couple walk down the center of a hallway. There are thirteen children lined up beside me, all under the age of ten. The couple stops to question a little girl before dismissing her and moving on to a little boy. He, too, is dismissed. The next three children are ignored, but the couple pauses to inspect the teeth of the fourth.

Closer to me by the second…

I'm nervous. I would kill to have a family of my own—literally—but no one will look at me twice. What's wrong with me? What do I lack?

Easy: Absolutely everything.

Once, my superiors thought I was destined to become a General. Everyone wanted me, then. When I failed to develop the necessary skills, the want turned to disdain.

I try so hard, and I train harder than everyone else combined. I learned how to use a sword and every type of gun. Even the Stag and the Oxi, the most dangerous weapons in a Laborer's arsenal. One day I'll kill more Troikans than any General in our history. I vow it.

Just give me a chance. Please!

The couple is on the move again…so, so close to me… the woman looks me over and gives an almost imperceptible shake of her head before passing me, silent. My heart sinks, tears threatening to spill down my cheeks.

Me? Cry? Never! I keep my head high. If this family doesn't

want me, fine, I don't want them, either. They aren't good enough. I'm better off at the Learning Center, anyway.

The scene goes blank, and I—Ten—blink open my eyes. I'm back in the present, back in the cave, panting and drenched in sweat yet shivering with bone-deep chill. I was wrong. The pain didn't subside; it ramped up.

The memory...it came from Killian. I know in my heart. Having died soon after his mother gave birth to him, he spent his childhood inside the Learning Center, a Myriadian orphanage.

Humans—both in flesh and spirit form—could be ugly in so many ways. Rotten inside. Vile and cruel. But they were also layered. Pull back the ugliness, and you might see a hurt. Pull back another layer, and you might see a child who used to crave approval, affection and acceptance.

A child like Killian had been. My husband has seen the worst the world(s) have to offer. I want so badly to hold him in my arms and comfort the boy he'd been, and praise the man he'd become.

My gaze seeks him. He's on his back, pulling at his hair. Like me, he's panting and drenched in sweat. But he's muttering, "Kill. Kill. Kill."

Kill...who? Is he seeing into *my* memories?

"I'm here," I tell him. "I'm—"

My heart stops, stealing my words as a man and woman storm into the cave.

chapter two

"Life is about what you gain. What you don't have, you can't enjoy."
—Myriad

Ten

The identity of our intruders clicks. Two Troikan Generals: Shamus Campbell and Luciana Rossi. Behind them, four Laborers I've never met. A total of six invaders.

6: symbolizes beauty and high ideals. The sixth sense: ESP. The sixth astrological sign in the Zodiac: Virgo.

Focus! A soft pitter-patter of footfalls echoes outside the cave. More TLs?

Killian isn't safe.

Panic claws its way up the ridges of my spine, and my blood flash-freezes. I strain with all my might, desperate to move, but my body refuses to cooperate. Every attempt to raise my arms threatens to pop my shoulders out of joint. I don't care. Nothing will halt my efforts.

"Kill, kill." Between each command—desire?—Killian snarls like a wounded animal. "Kill!"

Shamus, a big, barrel-chested redhead with pale skin and

countless freckles, slams a fist against his armor-clad chest
to gain my attention. His dark eyes are narrowed, a muscle
jumping in his jaw. "What did you do, Miss Lockwood? And
do no' tell me *nothin'*." His accent is similar to Killian's.

Luciana, a slender brunette with lovely brown skin and
startling gray irises, backs away from me, horror contorting
her expression. "I'll tell you what she did. She doomed us all."

Doomed...

Is she right? She can't be. She just can't.

I look down at Killian. My new husband is pulling at hanks
of his hair.

Hopes, falling from the highest of highs to the lowest of lows.

"Out," Shamus snarls at the TLs. "Now."

All four soldiers rush from the cave without protest.

I stiffen. The General has evened the odds. Two against
two. A foolish move for a war-seasoned veteran. Unless he
got rid of any witnesses...

Willing to use my body as a shield, I push through the
pain—*snap*. My shoulder *does* pop out of joint. Or maybe back
into joint. Air wheezes from my lungs. Worth it! Finally, I can
move. I crawl toward Killian, every inch I gain only adding
fuel to an already blazing fire of agony.

Can't stop. No, won't *stop.* Determination drives me. I only
wish it gave me wings.

"Kill. Must kill." Killian is lost in a world of his own.

"You won't be killing anyone, you son of a Myriad troll."
With a hand curled around the hilt of a sword, Shamus stalks
toward him.

"Stop! He doesn't know what he's saying right now." My
voice is barely audible, my gaze locked on my love. So close,
yet so far away. Desperation slams a spike straight through
my heart.

Any other day, I would have used the comm built into the forearm of spirit and Shell. With the press of a few buttons, it could transport me to Killian's side and, as long as some part of me is touching some part of him, whisk us both somewhere else. Somewhere safe. Like a fool, I disabled the device to hide from fellow Troikans while meeting with Killian.

I should have known they'd find me one way or another.

"Stop," I repeat, even as I gain another inch. "That's an order." As a Conduit, I outrank the Generals. As a newbie to the Everlife, however, my exalted rank doesn't really mean squat.

"We *can't* hurt him," Luciana grates. She extends her arm, stopping Shamus in his tracks. "You've effectively tied our hands, Miss Lockwood."

Though the shadows are no longer slithering through my mind, I'm not exactly thinking straight. I struggle to make sense of her words, finally throw in the towel. "I don't understand."

"You bonded to him, did you not?" She spits the words, as if they taste foul in her mouth. "That bond forces us to spare Myriad's favorite butcher and watch as you, one of only two Conduits, slowly descends into madness."

Madness? No. Absolutely not. But…

Maybe? Those shadows… They might not be threatening the Grid right now, but I can still *feel* them. A cold, dank presence I can't shake, hiding in the back of my mind.

With acceptance comes whole-body tremors.

"Do you think the Butcher is the first Myriadian to wed a Troikan?" She rests a hand on the Dazer strapped to her waist. One shot, and the weapon can stun a target into hours of immobility. "I've lived a long time. Every so often, a Troikan and Myriadian decide to risk everything and bond. The union puts our entire realm at great risk, so both parties are eliminated as quickly as possible, their names scrubbed from our databases."

My eyes go wide. I'll deal with everything she said—I hope. "Don't you dare shoot me. You'll stop my Light from reaching the citizens of Troika." If I can't move, I can't project.

"I won't shoot you, you have my word." She lifts her chin. "Though you aren't projecting much, are you, Miss Lockwood. The Butcher's shadows have dulled you and have the power to damage our Grid, harming *all of us*."

No. Absolutely not. Yes, there are shadows. But I won't let them hurt others. I'll keep fighting.

Not every fight can be won, a new doubt devil whispers.

"Stop calling him the Butcher," I say. Searching for calm, I begin to count. *One. Two. Three. Four. Five.* There are five rings in the Olympic symbol. Five fingers on each hand, five toes on each foot. *Take five* means *take a break.* Deep breath in, out.

"But you..." Luciana's eyelids slit. "We can't eliminate you or the B—Mr. Flynn. What happens to one happens to the other."

Jolt. The information hits me like a punch to the chest, sending me stumbling back.

In my current state, I struggle to make sense of what I'm learning. So I'll be wounded if Killian is stabbed or shot, and vice versa? It's not an ideal development, but it's manageable. What I cannot tolerate is the danger to my realm. I would rather die a thousand deaths than cause innocents to suffer.

"Why wasn't I warned about the bond's effect on others?" I demand.

"You were told consorting with Myriadians is dangerous," Shamus snaps. "You should have needed no other warning. Only a fool would pledge her life to an enemy."

Ouch. His words are the equivalent of a shame bell, trailing me everywhere I go.

"Did you forget how many Troikans Mr. Flynn has murdered?" Luciana anchors her fists on her hips. "Or did you simply not care?"

How dare she go there. "He fought and killed during battle, while at war, not in cold blood. There's a difference. And let's be honest. You have no right to cast stones. I bet you've murdered just as many Myriadians, yes?"

Thanks to the Grid, I know she's considered a peacekeeper in Troika. After a year and a half of torture inside Prynne Asylum—where my parents sent me to live when I refused to sign with Myriad—I know a sword is sometimes the only way to facilitate that peace.

Luciana flushes. With anger…or shame? Perhaps even a smidge of pride?

Shamus notches his chin. "I don't want to believe our Conduit is so stupid that she bonded with a Myriadian determined to ruin us from the inside out. I would rather eat glass."

Double ouch. Telling him, *You had better believe it*, doesn't really strike me as the proper response. "It's done. It can't be undone." I don't *want* it undone. "Trust me to have our best interests at heart. Let me move forward, full steam ahead."

"I don't trust you with *your* life, much less mine." Luciana drags me to my feet, then winds an arm around my waist to hold me up.

Anger blisters my insides, and I scowl. I despise weakness in any form, which is probably why I was drawn to Killian from moment one. He is a torrent of energy and ambition. Nothing stops him.

The General's grip on me tightens. "Centuries ago, a friend of mine fell for a Myriadian."

"By *friend* she means *mother*," Shamus interjects.

Luciana flicks him a narrowed glance. "Ultimately she bonded to him. He used their bond to navigate the Troikan Grid. And guess what? He let his friends in. Their shadows spilled into our Grid. To stop them, I had to kill my mother—and everyone she'd tainted. Everyone *they* tainted. Don't you see? We're *all* connected. What affects one has the power to affect us all."

My stomach twists, only to quickly settle. If—when—I share the shadows, individuals have the option to resist, like the General, and remain unaffected. There's hope, even if I fail.

"A bond forged in love cannot be a mistake," I tell her, my tone steady with conviction.

"You know nothing about love," she says, *her* tone hollow. "Love isn't a feeling but a choice. Feelings can change in a blink, as today has proven. You chose to turn your back on Troika, all for a pretty face."

In some ways, she's right. Love is a choice. "He's more than a pretty face." Far more. "In the end, we're *helping* Troika. You'll see. There are good Myriadians just like there are bad Troikans. We deserve a chance to live in peace."

"They deserve death," Shamus snaps.

"If you think you're better than someone, guaranteed you're better than no one," I snap back.

"You think this is about simple prejudice, little girl?" He sneers at me. "You haven't lived in the realm long. Haven't seen what I've seen. Haven't endured betrayal after betrayal at the hands of liars and thieves."

"Kill." Killian pulls at his own hair. "Kill, kill."

Breathing is suddenly a little more difficult. Forget the war. Right now, my husband matters most. Voice breaking at the edges, I ask, "What's wrong with him?"

"Only everything." Luciana gives me a little shake. "Of all the inter-realm couples I've hunted, observed and killed, the Myriadian half always has a harder time adjusting to the bond at first. Our Light forcibly attacks their shadows while their shadows gently seduce our Light. However, Troikans have a difficult battle in the end."

The heat drains from my face, then my torso, before evaporating from my feet. What fresh horrors await me in the future?

"You shouldna be surprised." Shamus glares at me. "Since the beginning of time, shadows have crept, and Light has exploded."

Whatever happens, we will overcome this. We'll do more than survive; we'll thrive. To believe less is to accept defeat.

"Kill, kill."

"Enough of that." With a scowl, Shamus closes in on Killian once again.

Though I fight Luciana's hold, I get nowhere fast. "I told you to stop, General." The boy who was rejected by family after family—even the one that eventually adopted him—is mine to protect. I'm his family now. "Killian is one of ours now. He's going to defect."

"Good intentions aren't guaranteed action." Rather than grabbing hold of Killian, Shamus circles him and plucks a dagger from the sheathe anchored to his waist. "But I'm neither a liar nor a fool. I merely plan to collect the boy. He'll be comin' with us to Troika."

I go still, inside and out. "Killian can pass through the Veil of Wings without harm?"

"Yes," Luciana hisses. "Congratulations. You've ensured the Butcher can walk among us without hindrance."

"Are you certain?" I won't take any chances with Killian's life. And I won't respond to Lucian's *the Butcher* comment. Not again. One, she won't believe my protests. Two, I comprehend the reason for her distrust. Killian *has* killed our people and recruited hundreds of humans to his side, if not thousands. But the past is the past. Like feelings, people change. Only time will prove her wrong.

She nods and says, "I am. Unfortunately."

Relief crashes over me, cool and sweet. At some point, one of those bonded Myriadians must have entered Troika, not just the Grid.

"We'll keep Mr. Flynn safe," Shamus says, "and you'll vote to Resurrect General Orion."

That is a thinly veiled threat, I'm sure of it. I'm supposed to pick which of this year's fallen soldiers rises from the dead. "Why Orion, and not Levi?"

"Our reasons do not matter." Luciana flexes her grip. "A bargain is a bargain."

Exactly. "I never enter into a bargain lightly. *Any* bargain. I never agree to terms until I know all the ins and outs."

Still in the process of disarming Killian, Shamus crouches and snags a gun holstered at his ankle. A quick snatch and grab. In and out. "Orion will put Troika first. Nothing else matters."

Wrong. Something else matters greatly. We need someone who will put *all* people first. But I make no mention of this fact right now. "I'll vote for the person who shares my vision for a better tomorrow." So far I think I've narrowed my choices down to Archer, Meredith and Levi. *I'm sorry, Elizabeth.*

But no pressure, right?

Killian's eyes blink open. He stumbles to his feet and backs away from us, shaking his head before banging a fist into his temple. Then, moving with lightning fast speed, he palms a hidden dagger, one Shamus missed, and points it—at me.

"You live," he snarls, and his accent is gone.

I almost despair. Every word he utters now comes with an edge sharp enough to cut through steel.

The problem is, my heart isn't made of steel but something akin to silk. If this keeps up, the organ will be shredded, leaving me raw, vulnerable.

"What happened to your accent?" I ask. I know him. He hides it only when he wants to keep someone at a distance.

"Why do you live?" he continues, as if I haven't spoken. "You were supposed to die."

Supposed to die? As in, he planned to kill me with the bond all along?

Yep. Shredded.

I must be mistaken about his meaning. My Killian would never do such a thing. Never! His love for me was—is—genuine. Something is very wrong here.

The madness...

I tremble as Shamus gives me a look: *Told you.*

He expects me to crumble, doesn't he? Determined, I lift my chin and focus fully on Killian. We'll get through this. We must. "What you're feeling right now is—"

"Shut up. Just shut up. You are... I can't..." He gives a violent shake of his head, then bangs the dagger's hilt into his temple once, twice; pain lances through *my* temple, and I wince. "I'm going to kill you."

Five minutes ago, he kissed me as if he couldn't breathe without me. Now he hates me and wants me dead?

Still mistaken, Lockwood?

Surely. Life cannot be this cruel.

Who am I kidding? Life can be far crueler.

"He doesn't remember you," Luciana says, and sighs. "They never do."

No, no. Killian would *never* forget me. But okay, say she's right. Knowledge is power. I need to learn more. "Will he *ever* remember me?" I swallow the barbed lump growing in my throat. "Will I later forget him?"

"I don't know." Now she shrugs, and it's obvious she doesn't care. "We had to ensure no couples survived more than a few weeks together."

Meaning, what? She murdered the couples?

Oh, zero. That's exactly what she did.

I suck in a mouthful of air, but my lungs constrict, refusing to accept the breath. If I wasn't a Conduit, she would murder me, too. That much, she'd already made clear.

Stomach churning, I meet Killian's narrowed gaze. "Remember me. Please." *Help me. I'm not sure I can do this on my own.*

"I'll kill you," he says, and frowns. "But I don't want to kill you."

Well, thank the Firstking for *that*. My Killian is still in there. "Fight this," I tell him, relief giving me strength. "Fight for me. For us." For our cause. There's so much left to do.

"Fight for a target?" He sneers at me, as if I'm not just an enemy but a *foolish* enemy.

Wait. He considered me a target? He truly doesn't remember me.

I struggle to maintain my composure, every nerve ending frazzled. The bond was supposed to bring us closer together, not rip us apart.

Shamus uses Killian's distraction to his advantage and tries to kick the weapon from his hand. But Killian kicks back. Unprepared, Shamus hunches over even as he stumbles.

Killian is a skilled fighter. The best I've ever seen. Whatever weapon he holds at any given time becomes a part of him. But he's in no condition to fight, a fact made clear when

Shamus gains his bearings, leaps at him and whales. *Jab, jab, jab*. Meaty fists hammer at Killian's face.

I gasp with shock, horror and pain, feeling as if *I'm* the one being pummeled. Stars wink before my eyes, though they fail to obscure the glittering Lifeblood pouring from Killian's nose. A warm gush of Lifeblood pours down *my* chin.

Huffing and puffing as if I just ran a marathon, I wipe my face with a shaky hand. In the crackling firelight, the liquid on my fingers is as breathtaking as it is priceless. Every drop ensures my survival. The more I lose, the weaker I become. At least Luciana's warning has been verified. Whatever injury Killian sustains, I will experience, too.

As Killian stumbles backward, Shamus finishes disarming him. But I know Killian, and I know what he's capable of— does he let the General do this?

I manage to wrench free of Luciana's hold and rush between the combatants with my arms extended.

Shadows cackle with glee, and I cringe. Does close proximity to Killian strengthen the darkness?

Flames still glitter in his eyes—eyes wild and crazed. Does close proximity to me strengthen his Light?

"Please, stop this," I say. "You're hurt." He needs to eat ambrosia, Myriad's version of manna. He'll heal in seconds. "Do you have—"

He lashes out his arm and wraps his hand around my bicep. If I'd been human, the force of his grip would have broken my humerus.

Shamus and Luciana rush toward us, but Killian spins me, putting my back to his chest as he places the dagger at my throat. But what is worse? He does it without pause. Cold metal meets warm flesh, and both Generals freeze.

My heart pounds with erratic fervor as I circle my fingers

around his wrist. "You don't want to hurt me, Killian. We're bonded. We plan to—" I zip my lips. Every word I speak will be relayed to other Generals and even my Secondking. No matter what happens here, I'll have to attend a debriefing at some point to explain my words and actions. I'll be judged by a jury of my peers.

Judged, convicted of a crime—and punished?

"You love me," I say.

"You're wrong. I know better than to fall for a Troikan."

But I don't know better than to fall for a Myriadian. "Fine. If you won't trust your love for me, at least trust our determination to—" Argh! Again, I have to proceed with caution. If others learn about our plan to invade Myriad and Many Ends, they might erect obstacles.

There are too many obstacles already.

Praying he understands, I recite,

You cannot trust me.
I'm lying when I say
"Today, tomorrow, forever, I will put you first."
And
"You are my everything."
I admit
Without hesitation
I will let you go.
You must know sweet lies flow from my lips when I say
"We will get through this."
Listen. Hear me now.
I love you not.
Never, ever believe that
I love you.

During tough times, I play with numbers, yes. I also craft poems. This one can be reversed, proving there are two sides to every story. Good versus evil. Light versus dark. Blessing versus cursing. Let the Generals and everyone else assume I hate Killian and I'm working some sort of Troikan agenda, but *please, please, please* let Killian understand the truth.

He doesn't. I know he doesn't when the tip of his dagger pricks my skin, and a bead of Lifeblood trickles down my throat. At the same time, he hisses, forced to endure a similar injury.

Our bond remains intact, at least, despite his memory loss.

"Inter-realm couples always turn on each other." Shamus sighs. "I expected you two to last longer than *immediately.*"

I would rather die than betray Killian. Too bad my hubby doesn't currently feel the same.

"I'm going to walk out of this cave with the girl," Killian says, "and you're both going to—"

Whoosh!

A flash of azure lances him, and he grunts. He's been Dazed, no longer able to move. I try to step from his hold—and fail. *Zero!* I've been Dazed, too.

I glare fire at Luciana.

"I kept my word," she says, unrepentant. "I didn't shoot you. I shot the Butcher."

Semantics.

My stomach begins to churn with broken dreams and promises. Killian and I, we're anchors to each other now. If Troika decides I'm no longer worth the hassle, they can take both of us out with a single blow. Same with Myriad. Kill one, kill the other.

I don't want to die, but I'm not afraid of my end. What terrifies me? The thought of Killian's end. I want him to have a chance to live the life he's always been denied.

"Take the boy to a safe house inside Troika," Luciana tells Shamus. "Tell no one where he is, least of all Miss Lockwood."

What? No. I won't be separated from Killian while he's inside Troika, and definitely not while he hates me. If we're apart, that hatred could fester and grow. Together, I can remind him of all the reasons he loves me.

"What happened to your desire to finesse the situation, eh?" Shamus asks her. "What about the vote?"

Her gray eyes narrow on me. "If she wants to learn the location of her beloved, she'll vote for Orion."

Are you freaking kidding me? I'm being *blackmailed* by *Generals?* Love and honor are supposed to be prized; revenge and deceit are not supposed to be a viable option, ever.

There's another way, a voice whispers along the Grid. A voice I've never heard before, and yet I recognize it as my own. Temptation wrapped in desire, too good to be true, yet too dark to be good.

The voice comes from deep, deep inside me. A place now mired in shadows. A place I didn't know existed...the worst part of me. There I find rage, hate and a thousand other things I thought I'd dealt with.

The shadows didn't come from Killian, I realize. They came from me. For years, they've been hiding, waiting to strike. Ready.

Despite this, I find myself replying. *Tell me.*

Make her pay. Make them all pay.

chapter three

"You cannot free a fool from the chains he reveres."
—Troika

Killian

Pain. Heat. I'm consumed! Flames engulf me from head to toe. If my skin melts from my bones, I'll scream and I'll curse and I'll probably beg for mercy, but I won't be surprised.

Might not even resist.

Part of me is ready to die. Death will be a relief. I'll wake up Fused to someone else. Two will become one. But the other part of me fights to live *now*. The enemy is here. Two Troikan Generals want me dead. I'll do them no favors. I won't just survive; I'll thrive.

As I fight for every labored breath, the Generals talk amongst themselves.

The female: "From what I've observed in the past, he'll revert to the worst version of himself. The more he fights his dark impulses, the better he'll become...but *she'll* begin to deteriorate."

The male: "Basically, they're screwed either way. And so are we."

I focus inward, searching for answers. Where am I? How did I get here, in this condition? I'm a blank slate, and the answers elude me. Emotions do not. A tide of misery, sorrow and grief rises, as if they've seethed for months, held back by a dam that no longer exists.

Anger joins the deluge, sparking a fall of acid rain inside my chest. Who can I trust, if not myself? I need my memories.

What did the General say earlier? *Myriadians always have a harder time adjusting to the bond. Our Light forcibly attacks their shadows while their shadows gently seduce our Light. However, Troikans have a difficult battle in the end.*

Bond?

Truth or lie?

Rays of Light burrow through my skull, shining, shining so brightly. In contrast, shadows wind and twine through my thoughts, memories and even the Grid to…protect me? Maybe, maybe not. Either way, those shadows are quite literally keeping me in the dark.

Bar me from what's mine? Die bloody.

Kill. Kill! A demand from the shadows. *Kill the Light, kill the girl.*

Some part of me protests. **Embrace the Light, trust the girl.**

There are only three people I trust right now. Me, myself and I.

Usually I avoid any hint of illumination. In the Light, destruction awaits. In the dark, indulgence is the name of the game. Today, I rush toward the brightest beams, determined to chase the shadows from my memories. Desperate times, desperate measures. To get something different, you must do something different.

Shadows disintegrate. Not all of them, not even close, but enough. Information unfurls. I have a name—Killian

Flynn. An occupation—Laborer. A goal—to please my king. A purpose—save my mother, whatever the cost.

The anger heats, quickly turning to rage. That rage races through my veins, my muscles seeming to plump and tighten on my bones. My skin pulls taut, threatening to rip at the seams. How can I not know more about myself? Why does the information seem...wrong?

On my wrist are the numbers *143, 10* and I have no idea why they're there. What else has been wiped away with mental Windex?

I need to know more. All. Ignorance isn't blissful, but dangerous.

Embrace the Light.

The words drift along the Grid, spoken by...me? A softer, gentler version of me, anyway. Confusion plagues me, and my brows furrow. Only a Troikan would suggest I embrace Light rather than fight to extinguish it, but I'm no Troikan. However, my affiliation doesn't matter right now. I obey.

The risk pays off, new facts crystalizing.

Once an orphan, I became the best ML ever born—it's not bragging if it's true. I have won souls no one else could reach. Ice queens, narcissists, the damaged.

For some reason, females like being seduced by me. I like seducing. Give me a challenge, watch me excel.

One of my last assignments was Tenley Lockwood, one of the damaged ones. Used for her station, rejected by her parents. Locked inside an asylum and abused.

I must have failed to win her. I—

Tense up. I remember. I *did* fail. Miss Lockwood made covenant with Troika, forsaking me, and choosing to be with Archer Prince.

Misery, sorrow, grief—now I know where they come from.

Never good enough…
Kill her!
Be at ease. Resist the darkness.

The chorus inside my head is maddening. A constant tug-of-war. Now, at least, Miss Lockwood is trapped in the circle of my arms. Wait. Miss Lockwood is trapped in the circle of my arms? The real girl, not her Shell. We're touching, skin to skin, and there's no pain.

How is there no pain? She's Troikan. The enemy. I'm Myriadian.

Perhaps we *are* bonded…

Her back is pressed against my chest, her head twisted to the side, her eyes staring up at me. Are *shadows* dancing in her irises?

If we were truly bonded, I wouldn't be resting my blade against her throat. Part of me wouldn't want to kill her.

Part of me really wants to kill her.

The other part of me…just plain wants her. She's soft where I'm hard, perfect where I'm flawed, and her beauty takes my breath away. Azure hair cascades around an exquisite and deceptively delicate face. She has a pert nose, angelic cheek-bones and a stubborn chin. Her lips are lush, like a ripened apple, and kissable—lickable. What does she taste like?

I force my attention to return to her eyes. The shadows are gone. Perhaps vanquished. Unless I imagined them?

Right now? Anything is possible.

Losing track of my thoughts… Don't exactly care… One of her eyes is blue and one is green, but both are luminous with love. An emotion never directed at me. It is *exquisite.*

A pang of…*something* sears my chest, branding me. Affecting me deeply. Anger, perhaps. Or irritation. *Not* a deeper attraction and a sharper awareness. We mean nothing to each other, and I won't have her or anyone thinking otherwise. But anger and irritation fail to explain the intensity of the burn…or the accompanying ache of *yearning.*

Can't be yearning. I live by a code: Want nothing, need nothing.

I look away from the girl, and finally, blessedly begin to breathe with more ease.

Must maintain emotional distance. Only moments ago, she said, *You cannot trust me. I love you not.*

But…why would she warn me of her disloyalty? She strikes me as foolhardy, but not foolish.

"Even I know blackmail isn't the answer, Luciana," the big redheaded male says, cutting into my thoughts. His volume is no longer tempered.

"Do you have a better idea?" the brunette demands.

A pause. A sigh. "No, but what happens after Miss Lockwood renders her vote?"

"I'm not sure. We'll figure it out."

No longer caught up in the girl, I look over the Generals. Their identities click, for *all* MLs learn to recognize all Troikan Generals. Shamus leads the strongest, most bloodthirsty army of TLs in Troika's history. Luciana and her crew are tasked with keeping the peace inside the realm.

Not so good at your job, eh, Luce?

There's a price on each General's head. Kill one, and you will earn more credits than you can spend. Credits—Myriadian money. Kill both Generals, and you'll earn the eternal respect of Ambrosine, Prince of Ravens. My Secondking, and hero. His power is legendary. His strength, unparalleled. He doesn't wield darkness; he *is* darkness.

I should have attacked the Troikans while I had the chance. Instead, I acted the fool and focused on Tenley.

I love you, too.

Her voice echoes in my head, as if a memory has slipped free from the shadows. The words aren't just a declaration, but also a response—to *my* declaration? A kernel of unease ghosts through me.

Did I once tell her I loved her, even though I believe love is an illusion?

Always be the first to walk away.

Perhaps I lied to her. I'm rotten to the core and not above such trickery. But why can't I remember? And why bother to go to so much trouble? The enemy you allow to live today is the one who stabs you in the back tomorrow. I have the scars to prove it.

Kill!

Trust.

A growl vibrates in my chest. The tug-of-war inside my head needs to end. Now!

I close my eyes, searching the Grid for— I go cold. In the back of my mind is a small tendril of Light that is radiating from her... This girl is more dangerous than most.

The Light connects us, forming a bridge between us. Once, a bridge stretched between Myriad and Troika.

We are truly bonded, then. I willingly pledged my Everlife to her, giving her power over me. Why? This makes no sense. And why would one of my targets willingly wed *me*? Why pretend to love me?

Unless she thought to control me, staying my hand from delivering a killing blow? As the General stated, I can't hurt her without hurting myself.

The rage returns, redoubles. *I will not be controlled!*

Killkillkill.

The shadows writhe with new purpose, sharp pains shooting through me…then seeping out of me and trickling onto the bridge that binds me to the girl. Agony contorts her features, the color fading from her skin. If I have damaged her irreparably, I'll—

Nothing. She's fine. She must be. Her Light hasn't damaged me.

Is it possible the bond has made us both Troikan *and* Myriadian?

—*Killian! Remember me. Please.*—

A new voice whispers inside my mind. *Her* voice. Miss Lockwood. Tenley. This isn't a memory. I know it with every fiber of my being. Somehow she's speaking inside my head, and every word ignites a new spark of Light.

The shadows writhe faster, lashing at my Grid. Sharp pains stab at my temples.

I attempt to push the question that plagues me most along the Grid, speaking to her as I would a fellow Myriadian. —*Did you wed me in order to protect yourself from my wrath?*—

Her eyes widen with surprise. —*Are you kidding? Protect myself from your wrath? I hate to break it to you, soldier, but I'm more powerful than you are. I wedded you because I love you.*—

It worked! She heard me, and responded. The fact that she thinks she's more powerful than me… I snort. As for her supposed love… I gulp.

Must stop harping on her supposed feelings for me. They do not matter. She *does not matter.*

Shamus peers at Luciana, clearly trying to mask his feelings for the other General and failing. "All right. We'll do this your way, Ana."

She hisses with displeasure. "Call me Ana again. See what happens."

Mental note: *Luciana Rossi has a temper.*

Tempers can be exploited.

"What, you'll start ripping off my clothes? Thanks for the warning." Shamus vanishes, only to reappear behind me.

I can sense him, though I'm unable to resist as he forces my arms behind my back, then binds my wrists with a band of…fire? Though I strain every muscle in my body, the effects of the Dazer hold strong.

"No," Luciana says, "I'll start ripping out your guts."

Shamus snorts and rips a small vial of ambrosia from my neck and pockets it. "Mr. Flynn's comm is disabled, and he has no way to heal." He plants a hard hand on my shoulder, and despite my link to Tenley, a waft of cold seeps past my shirt, not as potent as usual but still noticeable.

Tension emanates from Tenley as she struggles for mobility. Like me, she gets nowhere fast.

Part of me wants to shove her behind me—**will protect her with my life.**

Fool! The other part of me still wants to kill her. She's the reason I'm in this sorry state.

Yesssss. Kill her. Kill. Finally!

Trust.

Shut up, both of you. Or me. Whatever! Let me think.

No time. One second we're in the cave, the next we're standing on a crystal bridge, a crimson waterfall in front of us. Cool mist billows, rising above walls of layered sediment interspersed with ruby geodes, topaz, jasper and beryl; together the stones create the illusion of multicolored wings.

The infamous Veil of Wings. The only entrance to Troika.

Beads of sweat pop up on my brow. Myriadians have tried to enter the waters before only to burn to death. No one has ever survived.

Unless the Generals lied, my bond to Tenley will protect me.

All of Troika should pray the Generals are wrong. You don't escort a wolf into a herd of unsuspecting sheep without suffering the consequences.

As Luciana said, I can destroy the realm from the inside out. And I will.

chapter four

"Rules made by others are chains. Govern yourself."
—Myriad

Ten

I'm unable to protest, fight, *something*, *anything*, as Shamus carries Killian through the Veil of Wings. A desperate need to rush after him—my husband—bombards me, but my Dazer-frozen legs refuse to cooperate.

Can't let him out of my sight. Inside Troika, he'll be a target. I will be his only shield.

"Unless you assist us," General Luciana says, "you won't see your Myriadian again."

No. Unacceptable. And yet, her words have the desired effect. Panic sets in, seeming to turn my spine into a block of ice, and my limbs into icicles.

Emotions are fleeting, remember? They are changeable; Luciana was right about that. Just because my mind and body feel a certain way, well, that doesn't mean I have to let the emotion into my heart, as well.

I focus on the one thing I can control: my will. I won't

give up. I might have failed to stop this from happening, but I'll keep fighting.

Fail: First Attempt In Learning. Always try again.

If you can't save a world, save a city. If you can't save a city, save a block. If you can't save a block, save a family. If you can't save a family, save a person. One person and problem at a time.

Forget Luciana, and her scheme. Forget the vote. Today, I'll do whatever I can to protect Killian, even if I have to do it from afar.

Levi, my mentor, once told me the key to overcoming every problem is tattooed on my wrist. Loyalty to my realm, passion for the truth, liberty for all.

The horse… I still don't know what it means. Horses can be ridden, raced. They can pull cargo. They are strong, sometimes stubborn.

How does that help me now?

Liberty: the effects of the Dazer will wear off in time, or when someone feeds me manna.

Truth: I can find Killian through our bond. No one, not even a General, can keep me from him.

Loyalty: true loyalty stems from love, and love empowers.

Loving a loved one is easy. Loving an enemy is where the true battle lies. If I can bring myself to act in love with Luciana, perhaps I'll be unstoppable.

Even still, rage crackles inside me as I glare at her. Part of me feels like I'm back at Prynne, under the thumb of a cruel dictator. Too many things have gone wrong. I've been forgotten by my boyfriend/husband/whatever. I've been blackmailed by two Generals, and goaded by a voice in my head.

At least the voice—*my* voice—has gone quiet. As I'd peered

up at Killian, a bolt of strength hit me. I managed to lock the worst part of myself inside a room in the Grid.

See? Love empowers.

"Our turn." Luciana wraps an arm around my waist and drags me forward, as if I'm a mannequin.

Crackle, crackle.

Usually my troubles melt away under the crimson spray of water. Today I experience…nothing. No change whatsoever. Why?

Ahead, sparkling mist dusts a massive archway carved from a single pearl. A Troikan symbol is etched on top and on each side, making three in total.

Three is considered the number of perfection. Spirit, soul and body. Father, mother, child. Omniscience, omnipresence, and omnipotence. Loyalty, passion, liberty.

One can be a fluke, two can be a coincidence, but three is evidence.

Yesterday, no guards patrolled the wall. Today, different animals prowl from one end to the other. More than I can count. Dogs, cats, wolves, even lions, tigers and bears, oh, my.

Miracle of miracles, no one is fighting.

My gaze snags on a dog—pit bull?—and energy arcs between us. I gasp, startled. He must feel the energy, too. He blinks at me, shakes his head, as if disbelieving, then smiles.

Smiles? But why?

He must weigh over a hundred pounds. His fur is white and brown, matted and clumped with dirt. He has a serious under-bite that saves him from looking over-the-top ferocious. In fact, it makes him downright adorable. One of his ears is missing—bitten off?

My chest constricts with compassion. Spirits regenerate. Do dogs?

In the Everlife, animals can talk. Maybe I'll ask him. Later.

"Earlier, Eron decreed every citizen of Troika will be paired with a four-legged guardian," Luciana says. "You may choose to dismiss your guardian, as the majority of us have. These are the rejects, I believe."

My eyes glare my response: *What makes you think I'll ever take your advice?*

Her attitude shreds against my nerves. These "rejects" are living creatures, with thoughts, feelings, hopes and dreams. I will cherish my guardian, thank you very much. If I'm still allowed to have one, after bonding with Killian, that is.

I hope so. I didn't have a pet as a child, but I wanted one. A dog, cat, bird, fish. I had no preference, only longed for a companion.

My gaze returns to the big brown-and-white dog. Maybe he's my—

Nope, he's gone.

Disappointment sets in. As I force my attention past the animals to the heart of the city, sadness joins the deluge. This. This is the price of war. Armies of MLs invaded our outer borders. At the same time, Myriadian spies—people who had made covenant with Troika while remaining loyal to Myriad—set off bombs inside our cities. We have yet to recover. Our once-bustling metropolis is now a pile of rubble.

Only a handful of crystal castles remain, once the envy of any Disney princess. Woodland cottages extend from the base of trees. The ones that haven't collapsed, that is. Though there were once countless chrome and glass buildings, only three remain standing; they look ready to fly to another planet at… any…second. A copper structure rises from the center of the debris, beautiful and tragic all at once.

I search for Killian and Shamus, but they are nowhere to be found.

Crackle.

Lightning spears the crimson sky, and colorful flower petals rain. The waterfall surrounds the entire realm, allowing a garden to grow overhead.

"Don't worry," Luciana says. "Shamus messaged me. Your butcher is alive."

Alive, but not well?

CRACKLE.

Where is Killian being kept? The realm is divided into seven cities. The Temple of Temples, the Baths of Restoration, the Museum of Wisdom, the House of Secrets, the Garden of Exchange, the Tower of Might, where I train, and the Capitol of New, where I live.

Though each city covers hundreds of thousands of square miles, Gates and Stairwells allow us to travel at the speed of Light from one to another in seconds. Gates take us from one city to another, while Stairwells take us to different areas within any given city.

"You and I, we're going to have a chat." Luciana shocks me by prying open my mouth and pouring a vial of manna down my throat. "You're going to be a good girl, aren't you."

The sweetness coats my tongue, and suddenly my muscles unlock, permitting movement.

Is Killian free, too?

Let's hope. "Sorry," I tell Luciana, "but I think I'll be a bad girl today." With no more warning than that, I strike, slamming my fist into her face.

The dark part of me I thought I'd locked away has escaped.

The General stumbles back but quickly regains her bearings. As a bead of Lifeblood trickles from the corner of her mouth, her eyes narrow. "Hurting me won't help your cause, Miss Lockwood."

"No, but it will make me feel better. You threatened Killian's life. You hope to blackmail me into voting for General Orion. You deserve what you get."

She runs her tongue over her teeth. "We do what we must for the people we love."

"Exactly," I say, and stalk toward her. So she's older and has had more training, and I'm still fighting the effects of my bond. So what. I don't care. Rage drives me.

Override it!

Nope. Don't think I will.

When I throw my next punch, she's ready. She blocks and nails me in the eye. My vision blurs as I topple.

"Now the Butcher's eye is throbbing, like yours," she says, a little smug. "What other damage would you like me to do to him?"

With a snarl, I leap to my feet.

"I'm surprised you're so upset about this," she says. "You told the Butcher you didn't love him and couldn't be trusted. Why is that, I wonder. Did you lie to him? Your actions speak louder than your words."

I take another swing at her, then another, but she easily dodges both times.

"You don't want to take me on, Miss Lockwood. I trained Levi, who trained you. There's nothing you can do that I can't do better."

Not true. She can't share Light. I can. Or could. I pause as comprehension slams into me. I'm absorbing Light, but no longer sending the beams to the citizens of Troika.

Don't cave to panic. Don't you dare.

At least I'm strengthening. And I can find a way to fix this. I can, and I will.

"Perhaps you buy into the hype that you are somehow special? So precious, so unique." She sneers at me. "Myriad wanted you because they wrongly believed you were Fused to nine of their fallen Generals. We know better. And guess what? We tell *every* recruit they are special to us—that they are the chosen one—and that their actions will affect the war, because it's true. Everyone must work together, with the same goal. We must be one body. *The* body."

Mind—blown.

I knew it. I'm not any kind of chosen one. Although… "By your logic, I *am* special, because *everyone* is." Together, we are the chosen one. Together, we can win or lose the war. "If no one is special apart from the whole, how did I become a Conduit? How did you become a General?"

"Birth doesn't dictate our station, Miss Lockwood. Hearts do that. Yours happened to be more open and receptive to Light than most, more willing to share."

Her answer doesn't jibe with the things I've been taught. "I was an infant when my status as a Conduit was detected." Perhaps a better word—*decided*. By Eron? "How could my heart be open and receptive to things I didn't yet understand? I had no concept of anything outside hunger or—"

"Wrong," she interjects. She adopts a cool mask, hiding her emotions. "Humans understand less than they think, but spirits are far wiser than anyone realizes." Her head tilts to the side, her eyes like lasers. "I've watched you with your brother. I'd venture to guess he's able to speak into your mind."

She's right. Jeremy is only a few months old, has no concept of language, and yet he *has* spoken to me telepathically. The rest of my objections wither. I have other questions, of course. I always have questions. Knowledge is power. But this woman is not the person I want teaching me. She might have trained Levi, but she isn't half the warrior he was.

"Other infants speak to their loved ones, too." She spreads her arms wide, all *I'm the smartest woman in the universe.* "Just like I told you. Wise."

"I will *not* be blackmailed." A promise from the depths of my soul. If she knew me, even a little, she would understand I always mean what I say and say what I mean. Those who are weak, lie. Those who are strong, defend the truth, whatever the cost. "I told you. I will vote for the one I think is best. You won't change my mind."

The color drains from her cheeks, the cool mask slipping away. There's no hiding the desperation in her eyes now. Desperation I've seen reflected back at me more than once, when I stared into a mirror, wondering how I could get myself out of whatever mess I'd fallen into.

"Please, Miss Lockwood. Tenley. How you feel about Mr. Flynn is how I feel about General Orion."

Oh, *now* she calls him Mr. Flynn?

"He means *everything* to me," she continues. "When my family died, he was there for me. Let me be there for him. And he will save us from Myriad. He will. You just give him a chance."

The darker part of me—my Myriadian side?—laughs. **Such a fool. She's handed us the key to her destruction.**

Us? No, oh, no. "He didn't save us before. What makes you think he'll succeed with a second chance?"

She opens her mouth, snaps it closed.

I'm not done. "If you know the love I have for Killian and took him away from me anyway, if you are using him to blackmail me, you are worse than I realized." Even still, I focus on my Troikan side, where compassion holds my heart in a vise grip.

She's hurting. There's no need to kick her while she's down. And really, Luciana isn't the first person to ask me to vote for Orion. Levi did, too, right before his Second-death.

I know two facts about him. (1) He was a war hero who led his troops into battle with vigor and cunning, and (2) his return *would* be good for Troika. But so would Levi's. And Meredith's and Archer's. But I care about Myriadians, too. I want what's best for *everyone*.

"You love Orion the way I love Killian?" I say. "Even though the General is married to another woman?"

She flinches, as if I landed another punch. "I didn't say I was proud of my feelings, only that I have them. And I'm not asking you to pick him simply because I miss him. I'm truly concerned for our home, Miss Lockwood. Mere days ago, Myriad almost destroyed us. One second we were happily working as usual, the next we were fighting for our lives. If Myriadians aren't stopped, they'll come at us again, and again. Our children will be hurt. Or worse! Just…think about all I have said." She taps her wrist. A Light shines from her forearm, a keyboard that is an extension of her comm. As she types, she says, "Your choice could ensure our victory. Or our defeat. If we lose, everyone you love will perish."

"So I'm the chosen one, after all? Or perhaps you mean Orion is the chosen one, all on his own."

She scowls. Then, having no response, she transports away.

Zero! I'm not done with her—or Shamus! But first things first.

As I rush through the next Gate, no animals follow me. A flicker of disappointment burns my chest, but I quickly tamp it down. I make my way to the House of Secrets, where the

Eye is located. The portal will allow me to see anyone in the Land of the Harvest or Troika.

I exit the Gate onto a circular sidewalk about the size of a football field. Along the outer edge of the sidewalk looms one skyscraper after another, as well as two piles of debris, courtesy of the bombings. In the center is an island, connected to the sidewalk through multiple bridges, and in the center of the island is the Eye, a massive oval of glistening mist, surrounded by a cluster of jagged, unpolished diamonds.

Throngs of people meander in every direction, some coming, some going. Four-legged animals—everything from dogs to donkeys—trail a few of those people. The smart ones who accepted Eron's gift.

Something I've noticed: Whatever our Secondking does, he has a good reason, and that reason is always beneficial to us, his people. Take the Exchange, for instance. On the surface, it seems cruel. If we do something wrong, either inadvertently or on purpose, we are forced to trade places with the one we harmed; just for a moment, we experience the past through the other person's eyes. We feel their pain, learn their thoughts.

Honestly, a whipping would be easier to endure. Physical wounds heal. The ones on our hearts scar, and last forever.

"Excuse us."

The voice pulls me out of my head. A massive wolf with snow-white fur looms just in front of me. Eyes the color of emeralds stare at me, expectant. His teeth are long, sharp and as white as his fur. *The better to eat you with, my dear.*

I reel. "Um. Hi." I've never had a conversation with a wolf before.

Is he my—

"My human would like to speak with you," he says.

Oh. I look behind him, and spot a guy who is vibrating with eagerness, sadness and hope all at once. He's covered in soot, his clothing torn. Clearly he's been working to clean up the mess.

"Please," he says. "My wife died this year." He speaks Swahili, a language I've never learned; even still, the Grid translates every word in an instant. "I know you haven't met her, and that most of the realm wants one of the Generals to return, but please. *Please!* Consider my Fahari. She was the kindest, sweetest, most loving woman ever born."

Someone else I've never met pushes him out of the way, vying for my attention. "You must vote for—"

The wolf turns and growls at the newcomer. Newcomer's eyes widen as his mouth snaps closed.

Then, tone as calm as can be, Wolf says, "Allow my human to finish his conversation, *then* you may speak."

Guardian animals are *amazing*.

Unfortunately, the ferocity of the growl draws everyone else's attention. Suddenly, those others issue pleas of their own. Well. Word has certainly spread. Tenley Lockwood is the one who will decide who comes back to life, courtesy of the Resurrection.

A stray thought arises: *Am I Tenley Flynn now?*

"I'm sorry," I announce. I doubt anyone hears me. "I'm in a hurry."

I push through the masses. Once I'm standing before the Eye, I search the portal for any hint of darkness inside Troika...with no luck. Zero! I whisper Killian's name...still nothing. *Foot stomp.*

Maybe I'm supposed to do more than look and speak? But what?

Ugh. I can't ask anyone for help. If a Troikan discovers

a Myriadian currently lurks in our midst, mass panic could ensue.

Okay, so. Coming here was a fool's mistake. Noted. But where can I go? My apartment was destroyed in the most recent attack, and anywhere else, I'll be inundated with citizens just like these, desperate to influence my vote.

I'm tempted to open the door to the Rest and ask Archer, Meredith and Levi for advice. But the shadows...

Luciana's warning rings in my head. What if the shadows now taking up prime real estate inside my head somehow use the bond I share with my friends to sneak into their sections of the Grid?

Can't risk it. Not until I erect some sort of block.

Once again I fight my way through the crowd. A little more difficult this time around. No matter. I manage to slip through a Stairwell, then a Gate, and finally end up in a scorched—abandoned—manna field, no workers nearby. Raindrops join the flower petals, gently falling from the Veil. Before my eyes, little green buds break through the soil.

I lie upon the earth, the rain a light pitter-patter against my skin, mixing with a warm cascade...of tears? Ugh. I'm married, but I've never felt more alone. I'm—

Welcoming pity. A shudder rocks me. I will not feel sorry for myself. If I do, I'll weaken. Pity will only drain my hope and leave me empty.

Now is the time to rise and shine and fight for what's right. I have too much to do to sulk.

First up, *Killian's* liberation. End goal: freedom from war. Loyalty, passion, liberty.

Strength. Clarity.

Light.

Yes! I close my eyes and open a door in the Grid, unleashing a flood of Light. As shadows hiss and run, I do my best to erect a mental block before concentrating on my bond to Killian—

Suddenly I'm six years old. I'm perched on my knees, my stomach empty and twisted with hunger, my skin caked in dirt. I ran away from the Learning Center weeks—months?—ago. No one wants me, fine. I can make it on my own, and I'll prove it.

Or so I thought.

I gasp, realizing I'm in Killian's head, reliving one of his memories.

Two men stand behind him, ensuring he's locked in place as a well-dressed man paces directly in front of him, back and forth, back and forth. One of those men is holding a wafer of ambrosia and yelling at Killian, furious that he tried to steal food from him. Him, an exalted General.

Finally the General stops and glares at Killian with cruelty and calculation in his dark eyes. "You want this, boy?" He shakes the ambrosia in Killian's direction, making sure he smells the sweetness. His mouth waters, and his gums ache.

"Beg me for it."

Killian shakes his head no, refusing to beg. Even now, pride rules him.

Motions exaggerated for effect, the General takes a bite of the wafer. Little crumbs fall to the floor, and Killian whimpers. When he reaches out, the man on his left stomps on his hand.

A cry of pain from Killian—and me. Hot tears continue to pour down my cheeks.

The memory plays on, the General reaching for the whip hanging on the wall. Killian stays put, still staring at the crumbs.

With a nod from the General, the guards rip away Killian's shirt.

"Soon," he says, unfurling the whip, "I'll take you back to the Learning Center, where you belong. Until then, you're going to beg me, as ordered. That, I promise you."

The scene goes dark, and, even as I sob, I question why I'm not allowed to witness what happened next.

No doubt the answer is simple. It would have broken me.

I had tae beg for scraps as a child, simply to survive. I'd rather die than beg for anything.

So badly I want to wrap my arms around him, around the boy he used to be and the man he became. I want to protect him from the past, present and future. I want to know why he's forgotten me, but I'm learning more about him.

Something Luciana said nags at me. *Love is not a feeling, but a choice.* In that, I agree with her. But I wonder...

What if Killian lost his memories because he must choose to be with me *without* having feelings for me?

Will he?

More determined to find him by the second, I brace and pursue our bond...

A new memory takes shape. Killian stands in front of a mirror, naked. Gloriously, exquisitely naked. He's only seventeen years old, yet muscle sculpts him. His skin is bronzed, mostly free of tattoos but littered with scars.

Why didn't those scars heal? He should have regenerated.

A girl crouches behind him. She has short, dark hair, pale skin, elfin features and a slender build. She's wearing a black tank top and a pair of barely-there panties, and it's clear the two have just had sex.

Envy pricks me. Envy and anger, with a dash of hurt. This boy is my husband, and this girl is seeing him at his most vulnerable. Seeing him in ways I haven't. Not yet, anyway. Her memories of him belong to me!

At least I recognize her. Erica used to Flank Killian, chronicling his exploits. Then she helped him help me, and Myriad locked her in the Kennel.

Another item for my To Do list. Find her and set her free.

I turn my attention to the small but luxurious room. The bed is covered by a plush black comforter while a fuzzy white blanket drapes the foot. A matching circular rug surrounds the bed. Softness when you lie down, softness when you stand up. The walls are painted black, except for the mirrored one. Several frames hang throughout. *Empty* frames. Once they contained holographic images of Killian and Archer, but Killian deleted them after Archer defected, then saved the frames as a reminder. *You can count only on yourself.*

The dresser is hand-carved in the shape of a dragon, wings extending from the sides to act as bookshelves.

"Let me get this straight," Erica says as she tattoos his calf. "You want a map of Myriad to cover your entire body—just because. Isn't that taking realm loyalty a little too far?"

"There is no such thing as too far, baby. Besides, the tattoos will cover my scars," Killian replies, accent-less.

Doesn't feel comfortable enough to be his true self with Erica? And *baby*? Gross!

I have a direct line to his thoughts, but he isn't thinking about the accent. Only about using the map to keep track of all the things he plans to hide inside the realm, how Erica will never know. *No one* will know, no matter how hard or often they study the images inked into his skin. *Can't read a map without a key.*

His mind is the key.

He'll hide weapons, money used in Myriad, Troika and even

the Land of the Harvest, and extra supplies of ambrosia, just to name a few. That way, if ever he loses his home or earns a punishment that strips him of his possessions, he won't have to start over. Not again.

My heart clenches in my chest, seeming to bump against broken ribs. The other tattoos he's asked Erica to add… He's lost so much, and wants to honor what he loves and misses with the whole of his being. His mother, his friendship with Archer. The car he'd kept in the Land of the Harvest because he'd never gotten to drive in Firstlife, until some punk kids had stolen it from him. Ashley, the foster sister who died. Even Madame Pearl Bennett, Ashley's mother.

Pearl adopted him, offering him a family, only to return him mere days after Ashley's death.

What he mourned most of all, however, was his chance to become a General. When he failed to develop the proper gifts, he received a demotion and the Secondking's disappointment.

"Scars are sexy," Erica says. "And unique. So few of us have them."

"Most children are protected, their vulnerability carefully shielded."

I hear bitterness in his tone and realize he received his scars the day the General caught him stealing ambrosia. The whip…

Acid fills the pit of my stomach.

I've always speculated about Killian's scars and tattoos. While I'm grateful I now have answers, I would have preferred to learn the truth from present-day Killian. To know he trusted me with his secrets and pain.

But even if his memories were intact, why should he trust me? When I sided with Archer, choosing to live in Troika, I abandoned Killian, just like everyone else. At least, that's how he must have felt. Yes, he pushed me to let my heart lead the way, knowing I would never be happy in Myriad, but it cost him more than I ever realized.

Maybe he forgot me because he *wanted* to forget.

Sadness overwhelms me. Between one blink and the next, my link to Killian's past is disrupted, and the scorched manna field whisks back into focus. The rain has stopped falling, the sun shining brightly. I remained in the memory all night long?

Zero! The vote!

I jackknife to a sitting position, my thoughts whirling. Once I had a choice to make: Troika or Killian. I chose the realm over the boy. Today, with the vote, the same choice is set before me.

I'd already decided to put Killian first; now my determination solidifies. Today, I pick the boy. There is nothing more important than a life. A single life is priceless.

I will help Killian. I will save him from those who think to harm him. I will build a new life with him, and for him. A better life. Two realms united, one people. Starting with us.

Firstking help *anyone* who gets in my way.

MYRIAD

From: K_F_5/23.53.6

To: Z_C_4/23.43.2

Subject: **Here are the facts, short and sweet**

1. I've bonded with Tenley Lockwood. Yes, I'm that good.
2. I'm a prisoner inside Troika. ←Yes, I said Troika.
   (a) I successfully traveled through the Veil of Wings.
   (b) If you want more soldiers inside the realm, bonding is the way.
3. I had ambrosia hidden in a secret compartment in my boot, as I was trained.
   (a) I drank it, of course, so I'm now out of ambrosia.
   (b) No one has realized my comm is currently working.
4. I'll be returning to Myriad soon—with cargo. Be ready. This particular package bites, hard.
5. I don't have a fifth point, but I felt like using an entire hand. We must stay true to our feelings, right?

If you have any instructions for me, now is the time to send them. Let's win this war!

Might Equals Right!
ML, Killian Flynn

MYRIAD

From: Z_C_4/23.43.2
To: H_S_3/51.3.6
Subject: Killian Flynn

My dear General Schmidt,

First, I must admit it is an honor to fall under your leadership. Though you are only fourteen, you have been with us since birth, and I have watched you grow into the General of generals.

Second, Killian Flynn contacted me only moments ago. He says he's bonded with Miss Tenley Lockwood, that he's in Troika, and that he will soon return to our midst with the girl at his side.

He protected the girl yesterday, yet he's willing to harm her today? Something is off.

How would you like me to proceed?

Might Equals Right!
Sir Zhi Chen

MYRIAD

From: H_S_3/51.3.6
To: Z_C_4/23.43.2
Subject: Check it

Dude! Killian Flynn is the man. He nailed the babe no one else could score, yo.

Okay, so I just had a meet and greet with our queens and they—legit—almost crapped themselves. In fact, I've never seen them so excited. To celebrate Killian's victory, they are throwing a party tonight, and you and yours are invited. BYOB. (Bring your own babes. The queens will supply the beer!) Oh, and they say the K-man is hereby pardoned from all his crimes.

Our Secondking showed up for the last part of the meeting, and he says K doesn't even remember those crimes, that he's now on our side, totally and completely.

Side note: If you aren't ready to die from envy, something's wrong with you. I'm STILL high on Ambrosine's power. The intensity, man. My knees literally buckled. I dropped and couldn't move until he walked away. But the best part of it all? One of his shadows ghosted inside me—and freaking stayed put.

I carry a part of our king!

Chicks have been throwing themselves at me ever since.

Anyway. Alert me the moment the happy couple crosses into Myriad, you dig. K-man will need a Healer to purge him of Light. We'll use his link to Troika to destroy the realm. His wifey-poo will probably die, so, that's another plus.

Stick a fork in this war—it's over!

Might Equals Right!
General Hans Schmidt

MYRIAD

From: Z_C_4/23.43.2
To: V_P_5/20.16.18
Subject: New developments

I've spoken with Killian Flynn, as well as General Schmidt, who spoke with our queens, and even our Secondking. Mr. Flynn has been pardoned for all his crimes, and he will soon be returning to our midst with the infamous Miss Lockwood in tow. By some miracle, he was able to convince her to bond with him.

Victory will be ours.

Now, were you able to deliver Miss Aubuchon to General Schmidt, as requested? And how is Miss Lockwood's father doing? Update me.

Might Equals Right!
Sir Zhi Chen

MYRIAD

From: V_P_5/20.16.18
To: Z_C_4/23.43.2
Subject: Get your facts straight

He's not my Secondking, he's my father.

As for Sloan Aubuchon—yes. I delivered her to Hans. (You know him by the name General Schmidt. *I* know him on a more personal level.) By the way, his plan for her is spectacular. Just wait.

You'll be happy to know Leonard Lockwood hates his daughter with every fiber of his being. He blames her for his early Firstdeath, and he's eager to settle the score. He'll help us any way he can.

Here's the thing, though. I want to be the one to end her.

Might Equals Right!
ML, Victor Prince

MYRIAD

From: Z_C_4/23.43.2
To: V_P_5/20.16.18
Subject: Be patient

Once Mr. Flynn has served his purpose, Miss Lockwood—Mrs. Flynn now?—will have served hers. I'm sure your father will be amenable to giving the pair to you as a gift. They can die right along with Troika.

Might Equals Right!
Sir Zhi Chen

chapter five

"Wise counsel is an invaluable treasure."
—Troika

Ten

Electric impulses race through my comm, jolting me. One second I'm in the scorched manna field, the next I'm in a private room at the Baths of Restoration, standing in the middle of a pool.

The change of scenery is startling, and I struggle to catch my breath as I orient myself. Four stone walls surround me. Above, there's no ceiling, allowing me to peer up at the beautiful crimson sky, so peaceful it taunts me.

"It freaking worked." Clay Anders steps into view. He's flanked by three others: Reed Haynesworth, Raanan Aarons and Clementine Vickers.

Happiness overtakes me. My friends are here. I met Clay in the Prynne Asylum. He's the kind of friend others dream of having. Rock solid, loyal and 100 percent dependable.

Reed, I rescued from Many Ends. Raanan and Clementine experienced Firstdeath on the same day as me, so we went through Troikan initiation together. We haven't always gotten along, but we've been through hell and back. Bonds formed. Trust was forged.

Everyone but me is wearing a ceremonial robe. White with green trim = Laborer-in-training.

While Clay is my age, both Reed and Raanan are a year older. All three boys are tall with black hair, but that is where their similarities end. Clay is lean and tanned with wavy locks that frame a classically handsome face, and navy blue eyes. Reed is wider, more striking, with lighter skin, hair that is straight as a board and brown eyes with a beautiful uptilt. Raanan is dark from head to toe and packed with muscle, with midnight eyes filled with the smoldering heat of a desert sun.

Clementine is the youngest, her pale skin covered in adorable freckles. She has pink hair, big hazel eyes and charming features. To me, she looks like a living doll.

Normally my friend Kayla Brooks would be here, too, but she's currently recovering from a bullet to the face. My hands fist. The shooter? Victor Prince. He convinced her to betray Troika, told her they would bring about the end of the war and when that happened, they could be together. A lie, all a lie. Victor hadn't wanted the war to end; he'd wanted Troika laid to waste.

He is responsible for the most recent attack. When he failed to win me over to his cause, he tried to assassinate me.

Truth is, even if Kayla were recovered, I doubt she'd be here. Her actions hurt innocent people. *A lot* of innocent people. Yes, she realized her mistake, and she's been forgiven by the majority, but no one trusts her. Including me. I love her dearly, but even I have limits.

The muscles in my shoulders bunch into hard knots. I'm the worst kind of person in the world right now—I'm a freaking hypocrite. Again and again, I've sided with Killian. How easily my situation could have been like Kayla's.

If ever Killian had used me...

But he hadn't. He won't. There's a big difference between our boyfriends: Victor sees no value in life other than his own, and Killian does. Or he used to. I don't know the man he's become.

I need my old Killian back. Killian 1.0. There's no beating the original.

With my friends at my sides, I can do anything. Even bring Killian 2.0 into the Light.

The knots unwind, and my tension fades. "How am I here?" I ask. "Better yet, *why* am I here? And where are your guardian animals?" Dang it, where's mine? *Gimme!*

"One question at a time," Raanan says. "We heard you'd returned from a secret meeting and the first thing you did was visit the Eye. We needed to speak with you, so we had Clem retrace your steps. And I'm still waiting to meet my guardian."

"Me, too," the others say in unison.

"Tell us about the secret meeting," Clay says.

What to admit, and what to hold back? "I'll tell you, but can we backtrack a minute? Did you say Clementine worked the Eye?" Only Leaders train at the Eye. Last I heard, Clementine was a Laborer.

Grinning, she fluffs her hair. "Didn't you hear? Lots of people got a promotion, and I'm one of them. Thanks to the Grid, skills were downloaded straight into my brain."

"While you were gone, announcements were made." Reed sits at the edge of the pool, and draws one knee up to his chest. "The bombings killed so many, massive restructuring had to be done. Clementine, Rebel, Winifred, Hoshi and Sawyer are to become Leaders."

"What about you? What about Nico and Fatima?" They are the other newbies who experienced Firstdeath on the same day as me. Fatima is the youngest at six years old.

Reed rubs two fingers over his jaw. "I turned down a Leader position, and Fatima's training has been delayed. She's not coping well with all the disasters. As for Nico, I don't know. No one's heard from him since the bombings."

Zero! What if he's trapped underneath the rubble?

"I got a promotion, too, only information wasn't downloaded into my Grid." Raanan levels a hard gaze on me. "Probably because *you're* the one who promoted me."

Frowning, unsure I heard him correctly, I thump my chest. "Me?"

Nod. "What did you do to me?"

"Nothing?" I honestly have no idea what he's talking about.

"Wrong." He points a finger at me. "After the bombs were set off inside the realm, you touched me. Lightning arced between us. Ever since, I've been burning up with fever, though I'm not sick. I'm stronger. And I know, I know. I was hot already. Now I'm scorching." He winked.

As suspicions dance through my mind, I chew on my bottom lip. Is it possible…? "Has the Grid expanded inside your mind?"

His eyes widen. "Yes. New doors keep popping up."

I chew *harder*. Somehow I must have turned him into a Conduit, the way Myriadian Generals can turn humans into Abrogates. Except, he's not as radiant as before, and Conduits *glow*. Or maybe the problem with that is, well, me? Maybe *I* can't see Light the way I once did, my mind too clouded by shadows. "I have an idea, but I'm not sure I'm right. Let me do a little digging before I—"

"Tell me," he demands.

Oookay. How can I deny him? I'd want to know, too. "I think you may or may not—maybe, probably, hopefully—be…a Conduit." Before he has a chance to respond, I rush to add, "I don't know how, and I don't know why. Like I said, I don't even know if I'm right."

At first, he has no reaction. Then excitement pulses from him, and the corners of his mouth quirk up. "I've always known I was special. This proves it."

"All right. Enough of that." Clay gives Raanan a little shove before jumping into the water. Cool droplets splash my face. He closes the distance and gives me a hug. "Do you know what's odd?" he asks.

"You mean there's more?" I sigh. "Tell me," I demand, just like Raanan. See? I have to know.

"Every other number," Clay says.

I snort, taking comfort in the familiar. Whenever we're together, he tells me a number joke.

Now he tweaks my nose. "Don't take this the wrong way, but you kind of look like the grim reaper without a cape."

Seriously? "There's a right way to take that?"

Raanan rakes his gaze over me and shrugs. "He's wrong. You don't look like the grim reaper. You look like his evil twin."

Great! I absolutely refuse to lie to my friends, or anyone. I'm not weak. "I'm…" *Just say it.* "That secret meeting I attended? It was with Killian. We…bonded."

To my amazement, no one is surprised.

Raanan slaps Reed on the shoulder. "Knew it. Pay up."

Grumbling under his breath, Reed digs into the pocket of his robe and hands over a small vial of manna.

"Flavored with whiskey," Raanan says while wiggling his brows. "A rare mannskey."

I do a little glaring. "You guys bet on my relationship?"

"We experienced a ripple of absolute darkness through the Grid." He shrugs, all, *What else were we supposed to do?* "I figured you had something to do with it. And if you're involved in something, the Myriadian is involved."

Well. He isn't wrong.

"So you're married?" Clementine asks, and claps.

"I am." Happily…almost. Maybe. Hopefully!

Grinning, she jumps up and down. "Have you guys had sex yet?"

My cheeks heat, and I nearly choke on my tongue. "Um…"

"Hey. You aren't supposed to ask a girl that kind of question. You're far too young." Raanan flattens his hands over her ears. "Well?" he asks me. "Have you? And has anything bad happened because of the bond? Besides you looking like Death's evil twin, I mean. We're told to stay away from Myriadians, so…huh huh have you? Has it?"

I roll my eyes, and say, "I plead the fifth on both counts."

"You also suck." His hands fall away from Clem.

We haven't had sex, no, but I kinda feel like I acquired an STD anyway. Shadows Too Dark. How can I get rid of them permanently?

"Two of our Generals hid Killian inside Troika." I dunk into the crystal-clear water, ripples brushing against me, cleansing me from the inside out. Even my breath is freshened.

What the water doesn't do? What its name promises. My strength is not restored. I think I'm more tired than before. My limbs are shaky, and my stomach is a mess. What if I fight the Generals and lose? My frustration mounts. "They're blackmailing me, trying to control my vote for the Resurrection. That means finding Killian is priority one. Freeing him is priority two."

"Let me guess," Reed says. "You're supposed to vote for Levi."

"Nope." I shake my head. "Orion."

Clay thinks, frowns. "Why? Levi is the one we need, no doubt about it."

Everyone else nods. And I get it. I do. Levi trained us. He's smart, kind and determined. But…I'm not sold. Does no one see the merits to having Meredith or Archer returned to our midst? Meredith is a Leader and open to peace between realms. Archer is a Laborer with the heart of a lion. He's willing to die for his loved ones—and has!

How much am I willing to sacrifice for my realm…for peace?

How far am I willing to go for Killian…for love?

If we are truly to be one body—the chosen—the members of our body matter more than ever.

"We have an hour until the vote," Clementine begins. "I can return to the Eye and—"

A vibration rides across the Grid, arresting me. Arresting *all* of us. In unison, we go still.

"The Secondking has issued a summons," Raanan says, decoding the message that accompanies the vibration. "Due to murmurs of discontent, the Resurrection ceremony has been moved up. We're to head to the Garden of Exchange *now*."

Zero! What about Killian?

Deep breath in, out. Right now, he's safe. So I'll go to the Garden of Exchange. I'll cast my vote. As long as the Generals need me, he's going to be fine. Afterward, I'll find him. Perhaps with the help of the person who is Resurrected.

In a blink, my To Do list changes. *Decide who will come back from the dead. Find and save Killian.*

No pressure.

As Raanan helps me out of the water, Clay taps his wrist

and a bright Light appears directly over it. He type, type, types. A towel appears in one hand, and a purple robe in the other. Purple = royalty. I gulp.

Definite pressure…

Argh! When there is pressure, do not panic—sow and reap. Life is a garden. Plant a seed, and grow a blessing…or a curse. The harvest depends on your seed, for like gives life to like. If I want love, I must sow love. If I want to help my goals, I must help my realm.

Which of the slain will help my realm if Resurrected?

Clay tosses me the towel. After I dry off, I hand the towel to Clementine, and she uses it to shield me as I change into the purple robe. Then I braid my wet hair.

"Drink up. You're a Conduit, special and we need you well. I'm sure you could use a boost." She places a vial of manna in one of my hands, and heads for the exit.

I follow her, and everyone else follows me.

"I'm not special," I mutter, and drain the vial.

"You saved us during the invasion," Clay says. "Trust me. You're special."

The manna is sweet on my tongue, but for the first time, it burns going down. Sharp pains shoot through me, but thankfully they fade in a hurry.

Do I now need a mix of manna and ambrosia?

I'll figure it out. Later. Ahead is a Gate, an archway that looks to be made entirely of diamonds. Our group enters two at a time, the diamonds vanishing as fireworks explode around us. We remain on our feet, even continue walking, while we're shot to a new location.

There, we enter a Stairwell. Then we enter two more Gates before reaching our destination. The Garden of Exchange. Thank the Firstking, this city is untouched by the bomb blasts, its hanging wisteria, honeysuckle and ivy vines as lush as ever. Fruit trees are in full bloom, branches heavy with peaches, oranges, apples and every other kind of treat you can name. Wild strawberries and blackberries intermix with a maze of colorful flowers, sweetly scenting the air while leading to the heart of the city, where millions of citizens have already congregated, everyone decked out in some kind of robe.

There are children, teenagers and adults, though no one looks older than thirty-five. That's to be expected. When a spirit reaches the Age of Perfection, the outward appearance freeze-frames, no matter how old a physical body becomes or used to be.

Different animals are present, as well. Dogs. Cats. Deer. Wolves. A handful of zebras. Horses. Birds fly overhead. Despite the number of living beings amassed here, not a single conversation is taking place. Not a roar, growl or purr can be heard. Silence reigns, and it's eerie.

As we approach, the crowd parts down the center for the one who will be rendering the only vote. My heart thuds against my ribs. We motor forward, sweat dotting my palms. I catch sight of Nico and breathe a sigh of relief. Until his eyes narrow and fill with hate.

Hate? I stumble. Does he know I married Killian?

Someone steps in front of him, blocking him from view before I can speak with him. My gaze lands on my great-grandmother Hazel, and my mind trips along after it. Such a precious woman! Beside her is my great-grandfather Steven. If I fail to vote for Meredith, their daughter, they'll be hurt.

I swallow the lump growing in my throat. Next I see Millicent, my little brother's nanny, and Jeremy. My heart squeezes. As he wiggles and giggles, I pause to caress his soft cheekbone.

—*Ten!*—

His voice drifts along the Grid, filling my mind. This isn't the first time he's spoken to me this way, but I'm still startled.

—*Hey, baby bro. I love you so much.*—

—*Love, too.*—

"Get him out of here," I whisper to Millicent. "Keep him safe." If there's a riot after I render my vote, I don't want an infant caught in the chaos.

Her jaw drops, and she blinks rapidly. Then she nods and works her way through the crowd, heading in the opposite direction.

Keep moving. Get this done. A royal palace is ahead, with walls made of diamond, sapphire and ruby, emerald, topaz, and beryl, onyx and jasper. Every gem is flawless, breathtaking.

Before the palace is a bridge. Before the bridge is a dais.

Tremors flood me. On the dais stands the Secondking. The majestic Eron, Prince of Doves, is wearing a spectacular violet robe with gold seams and a hem that glitters as if it's been soaked in Lifeblood. He's tall and leanly muscular, with dark skin and eyes bluer than a morning sky, brighter than a sapphire and lovelier than a blue jay.

Despite the majesty of those eyes, his face is plain. A fact that always astounds me. He should be a showstopper.

Who am I kidding? He *is* a showstopper. Appearance means nothing. Heart, everything. Love and power radiate from him. So much power. Too much for one person to bear. Well, an ordinary person. Eron is far from ordinary. Light shines from his pores, radiant and pure, warming me.

In the back of my mind, the shadows shudder with fear. I grin.

Behind the Secondking stands each of our thirteen Generals. They represent a mix of nationalities and hail from all over the

Land of the Harvest. Today they are dressed in turquoise robes with metal links sewn into the shoulders to denote their exalted station.

My grin fades. Do the other Generals know that Luciana and Shamus are holding Killian hostage?

The shadows seize upon the rage that sparks inside me, and dip their toes in the waters of my mind…ripples flow along the Grid. Threatening to invade other doors?

Careful. In an effort to control the emotions, I breathe deeply and turn my focus to the others. The handsome Alejandro gives me a nod of greeting. I've always liked him, and I hope beyond hope that I have an ally in him—no matter what. Jane and Spike give me a nod of greeting, as well, while the others implore me with their gazes.

I can almost hear the chant inside their heads. *Choose Orion. Please.*

Tremors shake me. With my head high, I ascend the steps, the pitter-patter of my feet almost as loud as a scream. I walk onto the dais, stop a few feet from Eron and kneel, at the same time crossing my arms over my chest to form an X. As I raise my arms, they uncross to form a V. A show of my fealty.

Just like that. The rest of the world vanishes. I'm alone with Eron, surrounded by Light and fluffy white clouds.

"Rise," he tells me, his voice like music and thunder and rain all at once.

I obey, my mind whirling. "Where are we? *Why* are we here?" Whoa. *Bring it down a notch.* This is my king. *Be respectful or be quiet.*

"Consider this today's briefing."

Great. Wonderful. Hesitant, I say, "You know about my bond with Killian."

"I do."

He offers no protests. "You support us?" I suspected, but confirmation will—

"I do," he repeats. "Love never fails."

Confirmation will *thrill* me. I stand taller. "Some would argue I don't know real love."

"Some are deceived."

He says no more, and I don't press my luck.

"Would you like to know why I gave you the sole vote in this Resurrection?" he asks.

"Yes." The word leaves me so quickly, it's almost a hiss.

"After the bombing I realized a startling truth. You, Tenley Lockwood, are not a Conduit."

I gape at him, certain I misheard. "I'm not?"

"You are the first of your kind. A Conduit *and* an Architect."

"A what now?" I've never heard the term in association to a position here.

"You possess the amazing ability to *make* Conduits."

Part of me wants to argue with him. The other part of me accepts the knowledge without reservation. Look at Raanan. I suspected this. And really, in Troika, nothing is impossible.

"How?" I ask. And, wow. Wow, wow, wow. Being one of only two Conduits capable of cleansing Penumbra had come with tremendous responsibility and pressure.

Without pressure, there would be no diamonds.

Now there is another, and there will be more.

The ferocity of Eron's gaze intensifies, nearly drilling me to my knees. "Do you know what *apocalypse* means?"

I nod, even as my stomach churns. "The destruction of the world."

"That is one meaning, yes. But the other? A revealing. The end of the war nears, and with it, change comes." He mo-

tions to the horse branded on my wrist. "Change rides his—
or her—warhorse. You are the first of many. There will be
others, on both sides."

My mouth goes dry. Killian bears a horse on his wrist, as
well. Is he on our side—or Myriad's?

"How do I make Conduits?" I've touched others. Killian.
Clay. Luciana, even. Only Raanan has made the transition.

"When you find a candidate who is ready," he says, "your
Light will know, and do the work for you."

That…makes sense. But I'll have to ponder the pros and
cons later. I'm not sure how long I'll have Eron's undivided
attention. "I still don't understand why you gave me the vote."

"Don't you?" He offers me an indulgent smile. "I value
life. All life. Like you, I crave peace."

Nice to know I'm on the same page with someone like
Eron. He is a good king and a great man. I can't—no, I
won't—let him down. And not just him, but everyone; even
those who do not fully comprehend. My baby brother has
to live in the world we create. I can fight to give him something better, or let him wade through whatever crapstorm
we allow to rage.

"What if people are disappointed with my choice? Or in-
furiated?" I ask. "Will you stand with me?"

The look he gives me can be described only as indulgent.
"I'm always with you, even during the most trying times.
Especially during the most trying times. Just because you can't
see me, doesn't mean I'm not there. Just because things go
badly one day, doesn't mean I'm not working to make them
better the next."

That's fair.

"You've read the Book of the Law," he says. "My mission
statement has never changed, never will. Trust that we are

working together for the good of all. While I am the head, you—the people—are my body. Trust that I want what is best for everyone, no matter their allegiance. I believe my actions have proven this, again and again, even if some of my people have strayed."

The clouds vanish as quickly as they appeared, the rest of the world coming back into view. We're back on the dais, the crowd overflowing the Garden of Exchange.

"Have you decided who will rejoin our fight?" Eron's voice booms for one and all.

Here it is, the moment of truth. What am I going to do? Is the right choice for Troika the right choice for Killian? What about the right choice for facilitating the end of the war?

Half of the crowd begins to chant. "Orion. Orion. Orion."

The other half chants, "Levi. Levi. Levi."

Well. The masses want a General, no doubt about it.

But I cannot forget—these people are stuck in negative flow. A rushing river pulls us one way, and too many are content to be swept along. I'm fighting my way upstream, even though I'm tired, unsure and plagued by darkness. I can't stop. The second I do, the very second, I'll drift down the river alongside everyone else—and I'll suffer the same end.

Gotta get them in a different body of water.

My gaze meets Hazel's, then Steven's. This time, they silently plead with me. *Vote for Meredith, the woman who gave her life to save yours.*

My heart squeezes in my chest. I love Meredith. I want her back. I really do.

"Tell us, Ten." The Secondking waves in my direction. "Speak the name, and I will do the rest."

Shadows writhe with more force. People chant. Animals

call out. The Generals stare daggers into my back. My nerves fry. Inside me, pressure builds.

"I…" Deep breath in, out.

I had already tentatively removed Elizabeth from the equation, but I do so with surety now. She's with her boyfriend, Claus, and she'll have no desire to leave him. That leaves Orion, Levi, Meredith and Archer. Who's it going to be?

Loyalty, passion, liberty.

Sow, reap.

There's a name in my heart. The person I've wanted to pick from the beginning. The person I believe will most help this realm. Someone I would have picked already, if my mind hadn't gotten in the way, obsessing about the consequences of a wrong choice.

Heart and mind might not agree, but I'm done worrying. I'm going to take emotion out of the equation, and let my heart lead the way—the true Troika way.

For better or worse, I announce, "I vote for…Archer Prince."

chapter six

"The only advice you should heed is your own."
—Myriad

Ten

Behind me, the Generals give a collective gasp of shock and disappointment. Except for Luciana. With a scream of rage and horror, she falls to her knees. Beyond us, the crowd goes wild, a handful of people cheering, most others booing.

My decision remains unwavering. With Archer at my side, peace between the realms isn't just a possibility but a probability.

Approval glows in Eron's eyes, and I'm certain I made the right decision. Relief nearly buckles my knees. But mixed with relief is a tingle of dread. I'm still going to be punished by my haters, aren't I?

Eron speaks into my mind as clearly as if he's addressing the entire realm. —*Doing what's right isn't always supported by those around you. Even the most well-meaning people can stumble into darkness. Show your adversaries the Light, Architect. Show them you are willing to fight for what you believe. Show them you will not back down. You will not cower. That is how you win.*—

The reminder jolts me: I'm an Architect. What does that mean, exactly? —*Help me.*—

A soft laugh. —*Not a day goes by that I don't.*—

"The choice has been made. So she has said, so it shall be done." This time, the Secondking's words resound throughout the entire city, drowning out every other decibel of noise. "Behold. The Resurrection of Archer Prince."

A bright Light shines, blinding me. My world goes dark, but only for a second.

As the Light fades, the world comes back into focus. The Secondking is gone. At least, gone according to my eyes. Eyes do not always tell the full story.

Across the dais, a doorway forms from air, as if one layer has been peeled away from another, revealing a whole new world. Through that doorway, I see the fantastical land of the Rest, where a rainbow-colored sky glitters with thousands of stars, dinosaurs roam and peace isn't a hope but a way of life.

Is this really happening? Will Archer, a boy I've missed with every fiber of my being, walk through that doorway and join the living? Will he receive a second chance at Secondlife?

For a moment, one perfect, stolen moment of time, I think I spy the others in that small doorway. Elizabeth, a tall, slender brunette, smiles at me, content. Meredith, a petite blonde, beams at me, as if she's *proud* of me. Levi, the tallest, all tanned and chiseled, nods in support.

Tears scald my eyes, threatening to fall. I miss these guys, so, so much. Then Archer steps through the doorway, and my heart stops thudding only to flutter with happiness. He's as tall as Killian, as packed with muscle, tanned like a surfer and blond with copper eyes. While Killian is raw seduction and rugged aggression, Archer is flawless beauty and tempered steel.

I used to think of the two Laborers as sinner and saint, but I was wrong. Like everyone else, both boys have their strengths and their flaws.

Both deserve the best life has to offer, and both want what's best for their realm.

They will choose love over war, and love will not let them down.

With unsteady knees, I trip forward, my speed increasing until I'm running. Then I'm throwing myself into Archer's open arms, hugging him tight. He hugs me right back, and he's trembling just as violently.

I breathe in his scent—clean cotton warmed by the sun. I love this boy like a brother. Since his death, a piece of my heart has been missing.

Finally he pulls back and shakes me. "Why?" he demands, his English accent slight but noticeable. "I mean, I know why. I just think you should have—"

"No," I interject, the word little more than a croak. His eyes are different. The same color, just…deeper, wiser, fathomless. "I did what I should have done."

"The war—"

"I want peace between realms, Bow. You're going to help me." The first time we met, his gloriously masculine self was encased in the Shell of a short, pink-haired girl he'd called Bow. The nickname stuck. "I need to catch you up on everything that's happened."

"No need. I caught myself up before the Vote. We all did. We watched playbacks of your life in the Rest."

"So you know I'm an Architect." Just saying the word gives me pause. I clear my throat. "And that I'm kind of a married woman now. Oh, and that I also expect you to help save my husband." I drop each point all casual like, as if, hey, no big deal. Meanwhile my brain is shouting *huge deals!*

"Yes. On both counts. I knew about the promotion before you did." As he leans down, his eyes narrow. With his mouth at my ear, he whispers, "I also know your husband is here, in Troika, and I'd like five minutes alone with him—and a baseball bat."

I straighten with a jolt. "Do you know where he is, exactly?" When he doesn't respond right away, I grip his shoulders to shake him. He's wider than I remember, and more solid. But he's also weaker, the forced movements causing him to stumble. Ugh.

"Well, do you?" I ask, dropping my arms to my sides. Mental note: Archer has just come back from the dead. He might not be in tip-top shape yet.

"No. I tried to find him, but he's been expertly hidden."

Zero!

Frowning, I say, "Why do you want to hurt him? I thought you two were getting along before your death."

"Hey!" someone shouts, drowning out Archer's reply. "What's wrong with our Conduit? Where is her Light?"

—*Tenley.*—

Killian's voice suddenly rings inside my head. I jolt, air hissing between my teeth.

"What?" Archer demands.

I hold up one finger, asking for a moment.

I attempt to push my voice at Killian. —*Can you hear me? Are you all right? Do you know where you are?*— The words glide along the bridge between our Grids. At the same time, my shadows writhe all over again, paining me. No, not *my* shadows. I won't claim them. *The* shadows.

The question I most want to ask, but don't? *Do you remember me?*

—*I need you. Find me, baby.*—

Baby? The same non-endearment he used with Erica? My stomach twists into a thousand little knots, each leaking acid. He *never* calls me baby, a generic nickname any guy can use with any girl—as he's proven. What's more, my Killian never gently, tenderly asks me to find him. He demands I get my butt in gear but also stay safe.

So. Unasked question answered. No, he doesn't remember me. Now I wonder… Is he hoping to seduce me with this *baby* crap? Once upon a time, he had a routine he used on every target Myriad assigned to him.

Welcome to my web, said the spider to the fly.

What does Killian hope to gain from this?

The words he spoke to me after our bonding rumble inside my head. *Why aren't you dead?*

My stomach does that horrible twisting thing. Does he still want to kill me?

No matter. Whatever his goal, I'll deal. —*I'm on my way.*— Once again, for better or worse.

Disappointment chills me when one second bleeds into another, and there's no response.

"All right. I've given you enough time. Tell me what's going on," Archer says. "Wait. Never mind. Let's put a pin in that topic of conversation. Why do the Generals look like they want to murder you?"

"You know I decided who would be Resurrected, right? Half the crowd wanted me to choose Orion, the other half wanted me to choose Levi."

"*They* were using common sense," he mutters.

Man, I'm taking hit after hit today. *I could really use your help, Eron.*

Luciana leaps to her feet and closes the distance between us. Shamus keeps pace at her side, menace in their every step. Alejandro stops Shamus, but no one makes a play for Luciana.

Either her rage fuels the crowd, or the booers feed off each other, growing more incensed by the second. Soon, they're going to lose control and rush the dais.

Eron's words play through my head, and I receive a boost of strength. *Show them you are willing to fight for what you believe. Just because you can't see me, doesn't mean I'm not there.*

"Do we not prize wisdom over emotion?" I call. "Allowing our feelings to direct us will only lead to mistakes."

Aggression levels spike. Tension thickens the air.

A suspicion lurks… What if *I'm* responsible for their upset? Not because of the vote, but because the shadows found a way into the Grid?

Raanan, Reed and Clay leap onto the dais to form a protective circle around Archer and me. I hate that they're in danger, and I do my best to protect them with a beam of Light. Once, I could have used a single beam to carry us to safety. But no longer. Ugh! What little Light I have remains trapped inside me, held hostage by the shadows.

"What should we do?" Clay's eyes are wild as the crowd stalks closer. "How do we get out of here?"

Good question. Logic failed. I've got one other card to play. My exalted position. "Everyone—calm down and be still," I shout. A command from a Conduit. "Now."

I'm ignored, the crowds continuing to surge toward us.

"I sent Clementine to the Eye," Raanan says. He palms two short swords. "If we can keep everyone offstage for three minutes, eighteen seconds, she can get a lock on us and transport us into another city."

"First, put your weapons away." We can't hurt our own people.

Um, we might have to hurt our own people.

The first wave of protestors begin to climb onto the dais.

Oh, wow! The first line is knocked to the ground as a pack of animals leaps forward. A pit bull is at the helm. The one I saw patrolling the area just beyond the Veil of Wings. He still looks like he's smiling.

"We go now." His nails click-clack against the dais as he prowls inside the circle. "We go to safety."

He's talking to *me*? "Take my friends to safety. I need to find—"

"Your man. I know." His dark eyes fill with…admiration? "I also know where he is being held. Had one of my pups follow General Shamus. So we go now?"

"Yes, yes. We'll go now."

"Flankers!" he shouts.

In seconds, the pack of dogs, wolves, lions and tigers surrounds us, blocking *everyone*, including Luciana.

"What the—the *animals* are helping you now?" Archer gasps out.

"Maybe?" Or we're about to be mauled. "Eron assigned everyone a guardian."

"Hop on," the pit bull says.

Whoa. "Hop on to *you*?"

"No, silly hooman. *Les cavaliers.*"

Even as he speaks, a pack of zebras fights through the crowd and jumps on the dais. Six zebras, to be exact.

Six. Three letters. 3 + 3 = 6. Black-and-white beauties, wild yet tame.

"Pony express to the rescue?" Archer mumbles as he mounts the zebra closest to him. "Okay. I'm game."

Raanan, Clay and Reed each mount a zebra of their own. I'm the only one to hesitate. I've ridden a horse—once—but not bareback. Maybe I should—

Zero! Second-guessing this plan of action costs me. The zebras race forward, leaving me behind.

"Wait!" I call.

"I've got you." Archer turns his zebra around, comes up beside me, and hauls me up.

We jump from the dais. The gasping crowd parts, allowing us to land without causing or sustaining injury. The crowd continues to part as we gallop away. No one wants to be mowed down.

Wind in my hair, a friend at my back. What a rescue! In front of us, Clay, Reed and Raanan are sitting atop zebras of their own. One after the other, we blaze through a Stairwell, then a Gate and end up in the Tower of Might, where destruction from the recent attack is rampant.

One of the riderless zebras turns and enters the Gate we just exited.

—*I'm on my way, Killian.*—

I wait, tense, but no response comes in. Did something happen to him?

The dog keeps pace beside us. "Message your Clementine, tell her to hide us in the Eye. The one who left us, he is erasing our tracks."

"First things first. Why are you helping us?" Archer asks.

I don't need a reason. I obey, sending the requested message.

The dog's tongue is hanging out as he pants, and yet, he looks like he's smiling again. "The girl. Number ten who should be number one. I'm her guardian."

He's mine? Truly?

His gaze flicks to me. "You're overwhelmed, I know. You accept me. I get it. No need to gush."

I'm the one smiling this time. "Maybe I can gush a little? It's clear I got the best of the bunch."

He preens. "You did, didn't you?"

"No question," I say. "What is your name? And how did you get all these other animals to aid us?"

"I'm Biscuit." He flashes his teeth in the most mischievous expression I've ever beheld. "The others volunteered. That'll teach the citizens to reject us."

Yes. Yes, it would. "Is it rude of me to ask about your breed? I'm guessing pit bull, but I want to be sure."

"Why?" he snaps. "So you can tell me I'm too dangerous and—"

"So I can wear the right *I heart my dog* T-shirt."

He snorts. "I sneaked a smell of your butt when you weren't looking, so we're past rude, I'm thinking. I'm a mutt. A mix of everything, but mostly pit bull, shitzu and...poodle." He grumbles the last, as if it's a shameful secret.

I press my lips together. *Do not laugh.* "Poodles are the worst of the worst, huh?"

He snaps his teeth at me, and I can't stop my laugh this time.

"I'm foaming at the mouth with envy right now," Archer says, and I swear he's almost pouting. "I want a guardian animal."

"You have one," Biscuit says. "She's waiting for you at our destination, guarding the Myriadian."

He rubs his hands together with glee. "What is she? A bear? Lion? Cheetah?"

"No, she's worse. Her name is Beast."

My dog—mine!—says no more, but no other words are needed. Archer is vibrating with eagerness.

As we whiz past a pile of rubble, my amusement fades, and sadness swells inside of me. All this debris... How many citizens did we lose? At least I can stop wondering about Nico. He may hate me, for whatever reason, but at least I know he isn't trapped.

I also ache for the realm itself. The Tower of Might used to be a treasure trove of skyscrapers and arenas. A blend of futuristic and ancient Rome.

General Levi Nanne trained me in this city. He taught me how to enter and remain inside a Shell, which is a lot more difficult than it looks. He forced me to run for hours at a time, building my stamina. Mostly, he showed me that it's okay to ask for help. Knowing your limits doesn't make you weak—it makes you wise. And here...here is where Killian saved my life.

Myriad armies surrounded the realm, their shadows obscuring our outer Light. Victor—Archer's younger brother—lured me here in order to kill me. If Killian hadn't fought his own men outside the realm, allowing a beam of Light to shine through, strengthening me, Victor would have succeeded.

Poor Archer. He must know about his baby bro, and oh, it must hurt.

"Archer—" I begin.

"Tell me about Killian," he demands. "About the bond."

I'd say I can't catch a break, but I'm currently on the back of a zebra, escaping an enraged mob. "I thought you knew everything already. And what's your new beef with him? I asked before, but you never got a chance to answer."

"I learned some things while I was in the Rest. Things he did to hurt others."

Should have known. "He isn't that boy anymore."

Great! Now I feel like a broken record.

Archer ignores me, saying, "Indulge me. I'd like to hear about the bond from your perspective."

Very well. As I tell him about the bonding ceremony and Killian's loss of memory, he grows stiffer and stiffer.

"Before you tell me how foolish I was," I say, "don't. I followed my heart."

"No, you followed your feelings. The *Myriadian* way."

The old Archer would never speak to me so forcefully. But then, he isn't the person he used to be. He's grown a little harder, a little harsher.

"So I'm not allowed to be happy?" I demand.

"At the expense of others? No. You've put us all in danger, Ten."

"No risk, no reward. I'm fighting for a better life. For *all* of us. I plan to—"

"That's just it," he interjects. "*You* plan. But you've allowed no one else to make plans—protections—of their own. For all we know, you've kicked off a new Penumbra attack with your bond."

Ice crystalizes in my veins. Penumbra is a disease that infects humans and kills Troikans. Darkness invades the human body, and the more humans who are affected, the more Light that is sucked from Troikans. If an infected human dies after making covenant with Troika, they are hooked to our Grid.

Maybe he's right. Maybe there will be a new outbreak of Penumbra, and I'll be the cause. Maybe not. Either way, my bond to Killian *was* the catalyst for the crowd's upset. I'm sure of it now. I welcomed the darkness into our midst, and because I project Light to other Troikans, I now project darkness, too.

"I'm sorry," he says, and sighs. "I didn't mean to upset you,

only wanted you to see there are risks beyond your control.
What's done is done and can't be undone. I know it, you know
it. We can only move on from here. Hope for the best, prepare for the worst, right?"

He's using my own words against me. Words I'd spoken in
my Firstlife, after Myriad had hired men to shoot me down,
and Killian had killed the assassins. To save me, yes, but mostly
in retaliation. Threaten his stuff, pay the price.

Not that I was his "stuff." No, you know what? I *was* part
of his stuff. Proudly. Just like he was part of mine.

"I'll figure something out." I will. I must. "I'll die before
I let harm come to someone else."

"Pretty words. A soothing balm for your soul, nothing more."

He's wrong. He is!

But my tasks are mounting. Free Killian—get him out of
Troika unharmed. Help him get his memory back. Protect
my people. Facilitate peace between the realms.

"Tell me about Dior," he says.

Dior Nichols. A human med student and once the love of
Archer's life. Oh, and I can't forget she's the reason the feud
between Archer and Killian reheated. A feud that began years
before. Two boys ended up in Myriad as infants, and though
they grew up in different parts of the realm, they met and
fell in bro-love. Killian reached the Age of Accountability
first, and made Myriad his permanent home. Then, the worst
happened—in Killian's mind. Archer reached the Age of Accountability, and opted to make covenant with Troika, leaving Killian behind. Killian had felt betrayed, and lashed out.

Archer was Dior's TL, and he did everything in his power
to convince Dior to make covenant with Troika. Meanwhile
Killian did everything in *his* power to sabotage Archer's

efforts. He manipulated, lied and even issued threats against her loved ones.

Terrible of him, yes, but his tactics worked. Only, he did more than gain a new recruit. He gained a new enemy. Archer's love for Killian died that day.

Recently, Myriad decided to use Dior against Troika, and me specifically, by infecting her with Penumbra. With the help of Princess Mariée, Troika's only other Conduit at the time, I kicked butt and took names, cleansing Dior.

Of course, you can't help people if they won't help themselves. Despite putting my life at risk to save Dior, she allowed her boyfriend—the guy she'd started seeing after Archer died, in an effort to mend her broken heart—to infect her all over again.

That boyfriend? Javier Diez. The first Abrogate in decades. My evil counterpart.

"What do you want to know?" I ask. Levi would have told him all about Dior's attempt to defect to Troika.

Blood for blood. To go to court, one life must be offered in exchange for another. Hoping to save Dior, Levi risked everything for her...and paid the ultimate price. She forsook us and remained bound to Myriad.

"Have you seen or heard from her since court?" Archer asks.

"No."

"What about the boyfriend?" He sneers the last word.

"No." I wish I had more information for him, but I've been busy facing one disaster after another.

"What *can* you tell me about them?"

"They're alive."

He releases a heavy sigh. "That's something, I suppose."

After several twists and turns, we reach a neighborhood

of small homes. Most were reduced to rubble, but a few are still standing.

"I've never been this deep in the city before," I say. "Had no idea people lived on the fringes."

"Every city has guards that live on site." He hops down, sways as if dizzy, then helps me to my feet. "Their homes always surround the city's edges, creating a wall of protection."

A Chihuahua bounds over, growls at me, and races around Archer's feet. "Hello, hello, hello. You're here. You're finally here. I'm Beast, though I prefer Bea. Guess what? I'm yours, and you're mine."

Archer's gaze is as wide as saucers as it zooms to mine. As I cover my mouth with my hand to hold back a new round of laughter, Bea growls at me.

Biscuit sighs and taps her head with one of his meaty paws, quieting her. "Go inside." He nudges me. "My crew will fortify the outside of the home. Fair warning, though. Despite our efforts, we will be found sooner rather than later, and we'll have to fight our way out."

"Killian is inside?" I ask, and I can't disguise the tremor in my voice. "We should get him and go."

Biscuit's wagging tail slaps my leg again and again. "Freeing him will take time and patience."

Well. "We'll stay, then. Just…do me a favor and wait out here for a bit, okay?" I want a little privacy with my—with Killian.

Archer's nod is stiff, and Biscuit looks as if I kicked him in the ribs.

I'll make it up to both of them. Somehow. I rush past Raanan, Clay and Reed, who are arguing about their guardian animals, and soar toward the house. I need to talk to Raanan about *his* promotion. Need to confirm that he is, in fact, a Conduit. Later.

My heart thuds against my ribs. Anticipation propels me faster and faster. I jump onto the porch and burst through the front door. Eagerness and dread join the emotional deluge.

Ignore. Focus. Where is—

There. My gaze finds him, and I nearly melt with relief. At the same time, I come alive with awareness, every cell in my body aflame. He's alive and well, seated on the floor, surrounded by metal bars. His expression portrays boredom.

Icy eyes look me over and heat. "There's my sweet baby," he says.

chapter seven

"Anger lasts but a moment. The things you do while angry can hurt others forever."
—Troika

Killian

I'm beyond frustrated. I'm trapped in a home with a ceiling made of glass. Light streams into my eight-by-eight cage, which occupies a single corner. Normally, standing in sunlight while in spirit form brings pain. Today, I can tolerate the beams with only mild discomfort.

Another perk of my bond to Tenley.

As she looks me over, her relief is quickly replaced by a blend of fury and horror, her mismatched irises haunted and haunting all at once. What I expect to see but don't? Fear.

In the small house furnished with only a couch, two chairs and a table piled high with study guides, she is a treasure. Basically, she's my only source of hope.

"I hoped Biscuit was mistaken, but no," she says. "Shamus caged you like an animal." At her sides, her hands fist.

Biscuit? I know of no one by that name.

Tenley seems genuinely upset on my behalf, and I'm not

sure what to think of that. Girls desire me, or obsess over me, determined to win what I refuse to give. Truth, commitment. Affection. But no one has ever truly cared for me, because no one has ever truly known me. Not the real me, anyway.

She must think she has a handle on my deepest, darkest secrets and desires. I don't need my memory to know she doesn't. She can't. One, I can barely handle them myself. If *I* struggle, well, she's definitely not strong enough. Two, she's no different from other girls. If you've been with one, you've been with them all. The very reason it's always so easy to walk away.

"Are you all right?" Tenley asks.

"I spent the last however many hours locked in a cage," I reply, my tone sharp. "What do you think?"

"I think you'll recover just fine."

I've been scouring my mind, fighting my shadows. Fighting to recall who I am. More and more of my past has surfaced, though no interactions with Tenley.

What is truth, and what is lie? Who has my best interests at heart? The shadows or the Light?

The two war. Always they war. What one loves, the other hates. What one wants, the other opposes.

One fact needs no clarification. "I'm not a very nice person," I say. It's not like she hasn't figured out that particular gem. I'm rude when I want to be, charming when I need to be and always self-serving. If I won't look out for my best interests, who will? "Why are you here, helping me?"

"You're a good guy," she says, sounding confident. "You just haven't figured it out yet."

No, she's wrong. Not only have I seduced women and lied about my feelings, I've also killed in battle just for grins and giggles. I've tortured countless Troikans for information and for vengeance. I've convinced humans to make the worst possible covenants with Myriad. For a bonus, yes—whatever a Laborer is able to cut from a human's covenant, he can keep—but also for bragging rights.

I've turned negotiation into a blood sport.

I am no prize.

Tenley Lockwood should have run from me at our first meeting and never looked back. But here she is, flying through the door of my prison, and my body's reaction is immediate. I feel as though I've been hooked to a generator. My heart races, my blood heats and my muscles vibrate over bone. I'm tense, waiting for some sort of blow to the solar plexus.

I hate it, almost as much as I love it, but at least I don't have to wonder why. The bond. Always the bond.

I have no doubts about its validity now. Forget everything else. We can push our thoughts into each other's minds. A Troikan and a Myriadian. Should be impossible.

So. For some reason I haven't yet decided on, I pledged my Everlife to this girl. Even more astonishing, she pledged her Everlife to me. Why? And why did she come back for me? Earlier I threatened to kill her. Anyone with half a brain would stay as far away from me as possible, even if I called her baby and asked for help, as if I'm without other options.

"This brings back memories," she says.

I arch a brow, doing my best to hide the depth of my curiosity. *Must know!* "Do tell."

"You've been kenneled many times in your Everlife, and you despised every instance."

I...remember. Yes. Kenneling is a custom in Myriad. Cage is stacked upon cage. Punishment is given for breaking the realm's only rule: putting personal desires above the good of

Myriad. A few times, my jailer told me he would release me if I begged. I broke his nose instead.

I beg for nothing. Not even my freedom. Helplessness is the one feeling I've never embraced, but I will never compromise my pride. I'd honestly rather die.

Wait. There is another emotion I abhor. The worst of the worst: Love. Love involves trust, and I trust no one. I realized it before, but with the few memories I've regained, I'm more certain now. People never stick around. Everyone bails, because selfishness is ingrained at birth and only gets worse with age.

Tenley steps to the side, allowing a ray of Light to shine upon me. An image suddenly flashes through my mind. Chains string her up, and crimson blood leaks from her nose, mouth and ears. Sweat drenches her, and her clothes are torn. She's being tortured, but she isn't breaking. Fire still crackles in her eyes.

All right. She might be stronger than I thought.

Admiration sneaks in. I fight it, even as I say, "How about you come over here..." I keep my tone light, my voice husky, almost seductive. "And free me. Conversation is overrated. I can think of better things to do with our mouths."

"Freeing you *is* the plan," she says. "Even though I kind of want to throat punch you right now."

I blink with shock and disappointment. Not about the threat. Bring it. "What is wrong with you? Care about your realm, at least a little. Do not loose a wolf among sheep."

More shock. More disappointment—in myself. I'm warning her now? What's wrong with *me*?

"I can handle you." She makes a gesture that is one hundred percent dismissive and zero percent acceptable. "Where's my ring? And what happened to your accent?"

Her ring? She must mean the small, antique five-shooter that General Shamus took from me, despite the lack of bullets.

I wanted to kill him for his daring...and thank him. My head and heart had threatened to change places every time I looked at that stupid ring. Good riddance.

"What do you think happened to the ring?" I smile a cruel smile. "Shamus removed it, along with my daggers and the garrote wire that was hidden in my leather wrist cuffs. Leaving me armed would have made him a fool." I ignore the question about my accent. No need to tell her about my lower birth, or how my speech patterns are proof that I spent most of my childhood inside a Myriadian orphanage, nothing but a drain on society.

Her lush red lips purse. "Right now you remind me of the boy I first met. I bet you even trust the lies Myriad has fed you, right?" She doesn't wait for my response. "Once again, you believe Fusion is legit."

Once again? Try always. "I do. It is."

She smirks. "I'm about to prove spirits that experience Second-death never return to the Land of the Harvest."

I roll my eyes. "Let me guess. The vote everyone is talking about. Someone has come back to life. Hate to burst your smug little bubble, baby, but just because Troikans enter into the Rest doesn't mean Myriadians do the same."

Her head falls back, and she pushes a heavy breath at the ceiling, as if praying for patience. Facing me, she says, "Forget the Light and shadow thing. Our people are the same. And stop calling me baby."

"You're right. We are the same. *Baby.*" I motion to my cage with a wave of my hand. "Troikans praise love and forgiveness, and yet they keep prisons inside their homes. How very Myriadian."

Up goes her chin. "We have rules. When those rules are broken, measures must be taken. Punish the guilty, protect the innocent."

I arch a brow. "Are you protecting innocents now? I mean, you plan to free me." *Shut up. Shut up, shut up, shut up.* Am I *trying* to stop her? But I can't halt my next flood of vitriol. "Why are you really here? You claimed you love me not, and told me not to trust you."

Shame tightens her exquisite features, and *I* experience a jolt of regret. What is wrong with me? I *never* regret. But…

I want to see her smile.

I don't know her, not really, but between one blink and the next I remember she has three different types of smiles. The one reserved for her friends, genuine and open, rare; a cold facsimile for those who have pricked her temper; and the special one for me alone that is soft and plaintive, inviting me to taste.

That one. I want to see it *now*. I feel as if my life depends on it, something searing my chest, branding, burning, just like before. This time, there's no denying the truth. The culprit is absolute, utter yearning.

I want to see that smile because… My reasons do not matter! I want only what I need.

Want nothing, need nothing. I gnash my teeth.

"I couldn't let the Generals know how much you mean to me," she says softly. "They were trying to use my feelings for you against me. As for the poem…my Killian would have known there are two sides to every story, and the order could be reversed."

Her Killian. As if I belong to her. Or rather, the old me. A version I'm suddenly not sure I want to be ever again. "You're lying. No way the order can—"

"I love you," she interjects, starting with the last line of her poem. She's flipping the order, I realize. "Never, ever believe that I love you not. Listen. Hear me now. *We will get through this*. You must know sweet lies flow from my lips when I say, I will let you go, without hesitation. I admit, *you are my everything*. And *today, tomorrow, forever, I will put you first*. I'm lying when I say, you cannot trust me."

My throat tightens, and my lungs constrict. This girl *isn't* like others. Not even close. She's not like anyone I've ever known.

How am I supposed to deal with her?

She kicks into motion and stops at the door to my cage. I haven't moved from my perch in back. The part of me that I no longer understand longs to stand up, close the distance and sift her fall of azure hair between my fingers. The other part of me comprehends the absolute ridiculousness of such a desire. What good will contact do?

As she fiddles with the lock for a bit, learning it, I can see the wheels in her head turning. She thinks she can find a way to bypass Shamus's blood and fingerprint.

A sharp pang lances my chest. How is she even more beautiful than before—even a second before? It's maddening. But it doesn't matter. My comm is functional, and I've already made contact with my Leader. My mission is clear: get Tenley Lockwood inside Myriad.

What the Powers That Be have planned for her, I don't yet know. Don't really care. Yeah, yeah. I know whatever befalls her will befall me as well, but I don't care about that, either. There's no fighting Fate. If I die, I die. My spirit *will* Fuse with a human, and I *will* be reborn.

Maybe this time I'll live past infancy and actually experience Firstlife. Maybe I'll Fuse with a Leader or even a General, and better my station.

Once, the Prince of Ravens believed I *was* Fused with a General. But as weeks passed, I failed to control the darkness in myself, as well as others. I let him down. I let *everyone* down.

Victors are adored, failures abhorred.

Maybe, if I have a better station, someone will be obligated to care about me. Perhaps my new mother. Out with the old, in with the new. I'll finally have a family of my own. Not that I want a family that is obligated to care for me. No, I'd rather have what so many others take for granted: unconditional acceptance.

An impossible dream most likely. We are what we are, whatever our form. Still, hope can be stronger than reality.

Tenley grips the bars of my cage, her knuckles quickly leaching of color. "I wasn't going to ask but I can't help myself. No, that's not true. We can always help ourselves. We simply choose not to. So. I'm asking because a part of me is desperate to know. Have you remembered *anything* about me yet?"

Yet. She considers a successful reboot of my brain inevitable. I wish I had her confidence. I *need* the return of my memories, even if I don't want to be the boy I once was. I need to know why I did what I did, exactly, what I had planned— surely I had something planned—and what I deemed as my endgame. Myriad's salvation...or my own?

Myriad's, surely. How many times have I tried to impress my Secondking? I've pushed myself hard, won more spirits than most, but I'm still one among millions. A simple cog in the wheels.

A part of me would like to impress *Tenley* instead. What would it take?

In the past five minutes alone, she's proven to be honest and raw, refusing to wallow in self-delusions about her motives while accepting the consequences of her words and actions. She's flawed…human, and yet everything others should strive to be.

Ambrosine isn't human or flawed. He is power. When he glides into a room, carried on a cloud of darkness, spirits drop to their knees unbidden, no longer able to stand. Shadows continually rise from him, his constant companions. One look into his eyes—deep, fathomless pools—and you are forever entranced.

"I haven't remembered anything about you, no," I tell her, knowing she'll see through a lie. I lower my voice, letting it become a husky rasp once again. A voice meant to seduce. The ridiculous thing? *Every* part of me is on board, longing for her capitulation for reasons that have nothing to do with war. The only thing I have to force is my accent-less speech. "But I'm determined to remember *everything*."

I'm given that cold facsimile of a smile. "You can be *such* a jerk sometimes."

Well, that certainly isn't the reaction I expected. "How am I being a jerk right now?" Especially when I pretended to be nice.

Pretense is never the answer.

I grind my teeth.

"You think I don't know you, but you are *so* wrong." She crouches, pulls a dagger from a sheath anchored to her waist and stabs the edge of the lock. "Before our bond, you looked at me like I was a meal and you were ravenous. Right now you're looking at me like I'm an experiment and you're hoping to take home first prize at the science fair. It hurts, Killian."

My darker side: *Play on those hurts. Win her to your side— use her.*

My new lighter side: **Ease her. Help her. She is your ally.**

The two sides of me war, shadows dancing with my synapses, sending bolts of pain through my temples, Light fighting back, marching forward to cover more ground.

I decide to go with the familiar, calling on the determination I've been praised—and cursed—for possessing. "I can't *no'* look at you, baby."

Unfortunately, the statement is true on more levels than I'm comfortable with. And why is my accent trying to come out to play?

She scowls, somehow more beautiful than ever. "Call me *baby* one more time," she says, "and I'll remove your testicles to make a coin purse. And by the way. You don't remember this about me, *obvi*, but I never make threats. I make promises." Her tone is pure sass—and I like it.

For a moment, a suspended blip of time, the corners of my mouth twitch as if I'm about to smile. *Am I?* Threats—or promises—are not something I take lightly. Ever. Kill or be killed. That is my wheelhouse.

"What's your problem with being called *baby*? It's a sweet endearment."

"It's generic, and it implies I can't survive without my big, strong *daddy*." She sneers the word, as if it tastes foul in her mouth.

She has daddy issues—got it.

But she's not the only one. My father killed himself weeks before my birth, ending his Firstlife. With the terms of his covenant, he made it into Myriad rather than Many Ends. Though he'd been a trainee in Myriad—a Laborer just like me—he had the option of taking me in. I'm told he refused and signed away all rights to me.

Later I repaid him in kind. We were part of the same army, under the command of Madame Pearl Bennett, who later experienced Second-death. He desperately needed my help during a particularly nasty battle. Instead of acting as his shield and stopping his opponent's lethal blow, I turned my back and focused on a target of my own.

Payback hurts.

I sometimes wonder what my mother would say about my actions.

She met my father in some kind of Myriad-based, get-happy program, while battling depression. I've visited the Hall of Annals countless times to read about her life, and, according to her files, she considered her dalliance with my father a mistake, but a mistake she could not regret.

Even before my birth, she loved me. For the first time in her remembrance, she wasn't sad but overjoyed, excited. Because of me, she had hope for a better future.

But Fate had other ideas for her.

Caroline Flynn died within minutes of giving birth to me.

My chest constricts, breathing a little more difficult. I've watched the video of my birth...watched her nuzzle my cheek and coo to me as she bled out.

Before a child reaches the Age of Accountability, parents decide his or her fate. Caroline had a covenant to Myriad, ensuring I would follow her to the realm. And I did, two days later. The medication she'd taken while pregnant affected my heart. Or so I've been told. Deep down, I think I'd known I lost something—someone—precious, and my heart broke.

I know beyond a doubt Caroline would have taken me in, but again, Fate had other ideas. Even in the Everlife, her spirit was too weak to sustain her, and she experienced Second-death within days of her first.

"Killian."

Tenley's gentle voice invades my mind, causing the memories to scatter. I focus on her, wanting to lash out and hug her at the same time.

What is this strange pull she has on me?

"Be honest," I say, unable to mask the croak in my voice. "Tell me how you convinced me to bond with you. What leverage did you have?"

"Me, convince you?" She snorts. "Baby, you practically begged me."

I run my tongue over my teeth, not liking the *baby* endearment, either. "You lie. I would never beg you or anyone for anything."

A glimmer of sadness appears in her mismatched eyes, only to vanish as she rallies. "No, you wouldn't." Gaze pointed, she adds, "You asked, and I said yes because you are one of the best people I know. You are strong, and you are kind... sometimes. You fight for what you want, never back down. Your courage astounds me. The lengths you'll go to for the ones you love amazes me."

My heart thuds against my ribs. She's lying. Of course she's lying. I can't be one of the best people she knows.

But every fiber of my being wants to believe her.

"We married because we love each other, but also because I need to get inside Myriad," she says. "Trust me, you want me there, too. We *must* dethrone Ambrosine."

Myriad is all I have. I'd rather die than lose my place. "I would never agree tae dethrone—"

"And we *must* get inside Many Ends," she continues, quieting me. "Many Ends is connected to Myriad, and we both believe your mother is trapped there. We plan to rescue her, together. And we can. I know we can. I've been to Many Ends before. Three times, to be exact. On my final trip, I rescued two spirits who now live in Troika." She pauses, chews on her bottom lip and looks up at me through the thick fan of her lashes, hopeful. "Any of this ringing a bell?"

Breathing becomes a little more difficult. My mother, trapped in Many Ends. The equivalent of hell.

Truth? A falsehood?

Falsehood, definitely. Anger froths inside me. I must have told Tenley about my mother's First- and Second-death. Or she did some digging and learned all on her own. Either way, the result is the same. She used the information against me.

And I let her.

Tenley Lockwood thinks to manipulate me. Because she has power over me. Power that has nothing to do with the bond.

What if she finds the human fused with my mother? What if she *hurts* my mother?

The anger heats, turning into fury, my cells becoming bombs and exploding. With a snarl, I leap to my feet. Menace in every step, I approach her.

She straightens, but she doesn't back up. When I reach the bars, she raises her chin, stubborn to the core, and I almost admire her.

Who am I kidding? I do. I admire her.

But I won't stop. Though I'm without a single weapon, I'm far from helpless. I can kill an entire contingent of soldiers with my bare hands—and have.

Silent, we stare at each other.

Shadows protest such close proximity to her, my bride. The bond warms and tingles, empowering the Light inside me. I don't care. Tension crackles in the air, so thick I can feel tendrils of it brush against my skin, sensitizing my nerve endings. She feels it, too. Her inhalations grow shallow, her chest rising and falling in quick succession.

She's tall for a girl, but I dwarf her. I have a good hundred pounds of muscle on her, too. I could easily overpower her. And yet, just then, overpowering her isn't what I crave…

The fact that she doesn't back down, well, I'm impressed.

"Before our bond, someone in Myriad told you the identity of the human your mother's spirit is supposedly Fused with. A teenage girl," she says, her voice as calm and steady as before. "You tracked her down, and decided she couldn't possibly be the woman who had given birth to you. Couldn't even be half of her. So I told you my suspicion—Fusion is a lie Myriadians tell to cover up the fact that they wind up in Many Ends after Second-death."

Please. "I would know if Many Ends was connected to Myriad."

"Because you know everything? Because you're never wrong? Because no one in Myriad has ever been dishonest for personal gain? Which is it, Killian? One, two or three?" She grips the bars of the cage, and shakes. "Maybe all? A lie cannot stand forever, because its foundation is fundamentally cracked. When a storm comes, the lie will crumble and fall, and only the truth will remain."

I don't want to answer her questions or respond to her analogy, but for some reason I don't want to lie to her or hurt her, either.

Wanting her off guard, I reach out and place my hands over hers. She gasps, but still she doesn't back down. Her gaze zooms to my wrist, to the horse branded there.

"Have we had sex yet?" I ask with enough sneer and leer to enrage a saint.

Her gaze jerks back up, meeting mine. Twin pink circles

stain her cheeks. The blush quickly spreads to her neck, covering the pulse hammering at the base, and along her collarbone. How I would love to strip her, find out just how far that blush travels.

"No," she snaps. "We were waiting until we could touch without our Shells."

As we're doing now? "Interesting, considering I've never waited for anyone."

"You said you'd wait forever for me."

Another lie. Except...

I've never wanted anyone this intensely.

Slowly, so slowly, giving her time to avoid me if that is her choice, I lift my hand toward her face. She merely lifts her chin another notch. The closer I get to contact, the tenser we both become. Then my fingertips are on the rise of her cheekbone. A tremor rocks her at the same time that white-lightning arcs through me.

White-lightning...pleasure.

Undiluted bliss.

With a grunt, I drop my arm to my side to sever contact. I'd wanted to tease her, as well as put her on the defensive by saying something smarmy like, *We can touch now. How about you hit your knees, baby, and drink me down.* At the moment, I can't work a single word past the lump growing in my throat.

The front door of the house suddenly bursts open, and a new snarl leaves me. Archer Prince, a boy I despise with every fiber of my being, stomps inside, a massive white-and-brown dog at his side. A tiny Chihuahua trails behind them.

My mind locks on a single thought: Archer was dead, and now he's alive. I watched him die. We were in the middle of a battle and—

Shadows sink their claws into the memory. Distorting my view of it? I wince.

"I said I would prove spirits that experience Second-death never return to the Land of the Harvest. Well, here is my proof." Tenley sounds almost smug. "Fusion is a lie."

"For Troikans, at least."

Now she sputters for a response.

Not by word or deed do I reveal she's set my mind on a new path. *Could* Fusion be a lie for Myriadians, too?

A bolt of Light slams into the shadows. Hisses erupt. Darkness scatters. Despite a flare of pain, a memory clicks into place. I've heard rumors that Troikans can be resurrected; Light is life. That Myriadians cannot be resurrected because shadows are, supposedly, death.

Perhaps Myriadians could be resurrected, as well, if our Secondking would let us? But in order to preserve the illusion of Fusion, the dead must stay dead.

Not that Fusion is an illusion. Truth...lie... Suspicion niggles the back of my mind.

If this is true, the other might be true as well, and more than the Unsigned go to Many Ends.

Unease slithers through me.

Archer's copper gaze skips over me to land on the girl. For some reason—that treacherous bond, no doubt—I'm not happy that another guy is looking at her, and she's looking back.

Can't get her to Myriad soon enough. Will use her against Troika, lock her away and finally wash my hands of her.

Blue flashes from Tenley's comm. With a single tap, a glowing message appears just over her wrist. I'm unable to read the words, but she hasn't received good news. Her color fades. She frowns.

"We've got problems," Archer says.

"Tell me about it," Tenley mutters.

"The army…it's already here."

TROIKA

_____

From: Unknown
To: T_L_2/23.43.2
Subject: Hi

Did I tell you I died? I'm sorry I killed Killian.

I cried. You cried. I cried some more. I'm glad my husband made it up to you.

Light was the answer. Light was always the answer.

TROIKA

From: T_L_2/23.43.2
To: Unknown
Subject: Aunt Lina?

Let's face it: If anyone could find a way to reach me in the Everlife, it's you. But I need clarification about, well, *everything* you said. You died, or you will die? Are you in Myriad, or will you wind up in Myriad sometime in the future? Please—PLEASE—help me understand.

And what do you mean, you killed Killian? Tell me every detail! You have to know I won't let you hurt him. I will stop you—wait. Is that why you die? Do I kill you? (*If* you aren't already dead, that is. Ugh, I'm confusing myself.)

Second to last question: If Light is the answer, what is the question?

Lastish query (on my part): Who is your husband? You and Uncle Tim are divorced, and you've never remarried.

Light Brings Sight!
Conduit-in-training,
Ten Lockwood

chapter eight

"Make others fear your anger now, and save yourself heartache later."
—Myriad

Ten

Anger and frustration mount as Lina's message plays through my mind. Neither of which will do me any good right now. Lashing out will make a bad situation worse.

My emotions cannot dictate my actions. Right. I block the message and all its implications—for now—and focus on the matters at hand.

Bea growls at Killian, the cutest little bundle of ferocity I've ever seen.

Killian growls right back, though there's no heat to the action.

Unable to trust my husband at my back, I step away from him and toward Archer. Bea goes quiet, but turns her focus to me, as if daring me to make a move against her charge.

"How many soldiers?" I ask him. "How many Generals?" A sense of urgency kicks my heart into a gallop that would put our zebras to shame. "Where are they?"

"Two hundred soldiers, led by Luciana and John," he replies. He's pale, little tremors shaking him on his feet. "They—"

"Hey. Are you all right?" I ask, fighting concern. Leaving the Rest couldn't have been easy for him. There, he'd had peace. Here, I've tossed him straight into war.

He continues as if I never interrupted. "—just exited the nearest Gate. I'm guessing they want to capture you and lock you up until they can find a way to break your bond with Killian without killing you."

John Blake. I don't know much about him. Considering the current location of his army, I have roughly five minutes to learn everything I can. "What do I need to know about John? And was there any sign of Shamus?"

"No sign of Shamus." He thinks for a moment, frowns. "There's a back entrance to every city, one only Generals are supposed to use. Shamus could be sneaking in from the other side."

Or he's staying as far away from me as possible, because he fears what I'll do to him the next time I see him.

"As for John," Archer continues, "you should know he's—"

"The one who's called upon when capture rather than death is the desired result," Killian interjects. "That's why your boyfriend thinks the army plans to capture you."

I scrub a hand down my face and mutter, "Archer isn't my boyfriend. Unfortunately."

"Unfortunately?" Killian glares daggers at me, as if I landed a powerful blow. "What does *that* mean?"

A romantic relationship with Archer would have been easy, even effortless. Too bad I feel only sisterly toward him.

Archer's gaze is unreadable as he glances between Killian and me. "John's soldiers will do their best to split us up.

They'll want to capture one of us, at least. Once they succeed, they'll torture the captive in an effort to control the rest of us."

"If they fail, will they try and use Jeremy against me?"

"No. Never. Not for any reason." Archer shakes his head, adamant. "He's a child, an innocent, and he's off-limits."

Inhale…exhale…

Will I sacrifice my friends to save Killian?

Will I sacrifice Killian to save my friends?

Yes and yes. Sacrifice anything and anyone. Save yourself.

No and no. Sacrifice yourself to save the others.

Ugh! There are two sides of me. Troikan and Myriadian. Those sides will never agree. Not exactly a news flash, I know, but come on! The constant tug-of-war leaves me floundering.

I'd go with what I know, but any sacrifice I make will be in vain. Archer is right. The Generals hope to sever my bond with Killian. I can't let them. I *must* get into Many Ends.

One of the reasons I choose to live in Troika? The people (supposedly) support each other in the best and worst of times. The people (supposedly) *love* each other. Didn't take me long to learn that people are people, and no matter their realm, they are flawed. They make mistakes. Even Troikans sometimes let their emotions get the better of them.

Sow and reap. A harvest *will* come in. Sow support, receive support. Sow dissent, receive dissent. Today, I will sow support—for the innocents who need me. I will not let the shadows win.

"Here." Archer tosses me two short swords, his aim off. "You don't want to hurt our people. I know. I get it. But you can't remain weaponless while armed soldiers approach."

I have to jump to the left to catch both swords by their hilts. "You just came back from the dead, and I've thrust you into the middle of a war with people you love, respect and admire. If you want to ride the pine for this battle, I will—"

"Ride the pine while you risk your life?" If looks could kill, *I'd* be dead. "Never!"

"—knee your testicles into your throat," I finish.

A moment passes while he absorbs my words. Then he snorts, and the reaction is pure Archer. He's always appreciated my snarkier quirks.

"A little obsessed with balls, wouldna you say?" Killian asks me.

His accent has emerged a couple of times, thrilling me. Even better, his words are classic Killian, his snarling tone suggesting he's upset that I dared to threaten another male's genitalia. Like I'm supposed to threaten his, and his alone.

I turn, hoping to see a glimmer of recognition in his eyes. However, he isn't focused on me but Archer, and it's safe to say he's forgotten the truce he and his former bestie once shared. Killian's expression is cold and dark, and his hands are twitching, as if he wishes he clutched his own pair of blades.

Boys!

His life matters more than his feelings.

The house begins to shake, only to stop…shake again. Stop. Shake. Stop. My heart thuds in time. "Bombs?"

Archer smiles with genuine amusement. "Nah. I think the elephants have arrived."

Elephants? Seriously? Well, why not?

Killian looks at me, one brow arched. "Perhaps you're Fused with Tarzan. Or some kind of Disney princess."

Fusion again. Before this day ends, I'm going to slap him. As a favor to us both. Maybe I'll knock some sense into him.

Ignoring him, Archer says, "I placed inter-realm Bucklers

around the house. No one but us will be able to transport inside. On the other hand, none of us will be able to transport out, either. We'll have to walk."

A small price to pay for a safe haven. "Where are the others?"

"Here." Raanan's voice blasts through the house.

He appears, with Clay and Reed at his sides. Clementine and a blonde Healer named Dawn are quick on their heels. Dawn has patched me up on numerous occasions.

Different animals trot in behind the group, and introductions are made.

Raanan's guardian is a donkey named Pop Tart. Spot, one of the zebras, is working with Clay. Paco the parrot stakes his claim on Reed by perching on his shoulder. A black Lab named Frank remains glued to Clementine's side. Gloria, a deer, is paired with Dawn.

I wish Kayla were here. Forget any trust issues. She would understand me better than most. And she's part of our crew. She's valued. Where is she? Last time I saw her, she was inside a makeshift hospital, recovering.

Dawn looks me over, and clicks her tongue against her teeth. "What have you done to yourself?" When she's standing directly in front of me, she checks my vitals and pulls a small syringe from her pocket.

"Whoa," I say. "Hold up." A sedative? What if she's here to knock me out and make me easy prey for the Generals?

"So suspicious." Again she clicks her tongue against her teeth. "This is concentrated manna. You have my word, Conduit. I'm a Healer. I've never hurt *anyone*, never will."

Deciding to trust her—because she's never lied to me before—I relax, allowing her to inject my bicep annnnd yes. Warmth seeps inside me, trailed by strength. Definitely concentrated manna.

The shadows kick up a fuss, malevolence spewing from them. They crave death and destruction—not just mine, but everyone's.

These shadows...

Ambrosine and his people revere them. But...but...why? I don't understand. Why is Ambrosine like he is? He has the same father as Eron. The two had the same upbringing. How can one brother be so good and the other so evil?

Choice.

The single word whispers across the Grid, and I suck in a breath. New Light floods me, the Grid suddenly glowing like a tree at Christmas, sending the shadows fleeing, desperate for cover.

Relief nearly buckles my knees, and yet, my mind remains on the quandary. Ambrosine versus Eron. Always everything comes back to choice.

Something I know firsthand: Every downward slide begins with a single thought.

Troikan history claims Ambrosine envied—envies—his brother. When the first vine of envy grew in his heart, he must have fed and watered it, rather than yanking it up by the root and destroying it. Eventually he would have reached a point of no return, his mind completely overshadowed by a garden of jealousy, resentment and rage.

Now he is obsessed with the idea of besting his brother.

And Killian is currently his staunchest ally.

My husband has *de*volved into the person I first met at Prynne, doing everything in his power to intimidate me. Or seduce me. With him, there's no middle ground.

How am I supposed to deal with him?

When he touched me moments ago, the shadows inside my head quieted, but only for a few seconds as pleasure assailed me. I'd begun to hope. Surely we can make this work. Then he backed away as if I'm the equivalent of toxic waste, and the shadows erupted all over again.

I'm floundering. I want to hug and kiss him, then shake and slap him.

Actually, there's no need to deal with him right now. Lives are at stake. I've got to take my relationship out of the equation. And really, no relationship is going to be a fifty-fifty give-and-take every day. Some days—some weeks and even months—someone is going to need their partner to pick them up and carry them.

Dawn uses a second syringe on me. Warmth...a river of new Light...a new tide of information from the Grid...

When the first human spirits arrived in Myriad and bonded to Ambrosine, their Secondking, his shadows had new hosts. Mere playthings. New darkness was conceived, and the vilest emotions quickly spread.

Ambrosine can't just be dethroned; he must be killed. No ifs, ands or buts about it. Although, the notion goes against everything I've come to believe. All life is precious.

How can I justify murder?

In war—on the battlefield—I protect the weak, the innocent, even the not so innocent, those who can't or won't defend themselves. An enemy who attacks us must be dealt with, plain and simple. Otherwise we'll be enslaved or slaughtered.

When Ambrosine dies, his shadows will die with him. At least in theory. Myriadians could be freed from his evil influence, able to live life on their own terms.

Yes! This! This is what I want.

Since no one else seems willing to do the deed, the burden falls on me. But how am I to accomplish it? Ambrosine isn't human or spirit; he's something else entirely. Like must fight like. Flesh to flesh. Spirit to spirit.

And what about *my* shadows? How did they come to be? At first, I thought they came from my bond with Killian. Then I suspected they'd been with me for years. Now I'm certain. We all have a garden in need of tending. I failed to uproot hatred for my father and fury directed at my mother. I fed and watered both in the bowels of Prynne Asylum.

Upon my escape, I buried my emotions, but I didn't eradicate them. They've been with me for years.

I shudder. I need a complete overhaul, but oh, wow, there's so much to do.

One mission at a time. Right now, I choose to focus on the emancipation of Myriadians. They *can* be saved. And, no matter who they are or where they come from, they are worth saving.

A warm hand settles on my shoulder, startling me from my thoughts. "Check your messages," Archer says, his voice taut with grief.

Acid churns in my stomach. "What happened?"

"Check," he commands. "Tell me he's wrong."

Churning faster. I type into my comm and find a message from General Alejandro.

We need you, Miss Lockwood, more than ever before. Word has just come in. Our soldiers discovered a warehouse in the Land of the Harvest, with an army of potential Abrogates inside. These humans are infected just as Dior Nichols was. They are strapped to gurneys, asleep, and hooked to machines. We need your Light to cleanse them before these people awaken and escape. I don't have to tell you the devastation they could cause to us—to the world.

My blood chills in my veins. I haven't fully digested the ramifications of this development before another message catches my attention. Drawing in a deep breath...hold, hold... I read it. Alejandro again.

The bad news keeps coming. Dior Nichols and Javier Diez were killed in a car accident. Myriad's doing, I'm sure. They must be planning another strike against us, and building their forces. We have to act fast, before it's too late. Please, Miss Lockwood. Let me help you so that you can help our realm. Shamus told me what he did to Mr. Flynn. I will take over the boy's care. I will guard him with my life. You have my word. All you must do is sever your bond to him. If you are plagued by shadows, how can you aid those who need your Light?

All the air leaves my lungs in a single burst. My gaze flips up, landing on Archer. "I'm so sorry. He's right. Dior experienced Firstdeath. She's now in Myriad."

His nostrils flare as his attention whips to Killian. "Did you know what they planned?"

Merciless, Killian spreads his arms, all *what do you think?*

"Don't pretend ignorance." Archer points at him, the action spurring Bea into another round of snarling. "Dior is no longer human, able to right the wrongs committed against other humans. Yesterday's actions led us to today's destination. She is stuck on the wrong path!"

Guilt darkens Killian's features only to vanish a second later.

"Just think. If you'd stayed in Myriad, where you belonged, you'd be with her."

How cold and callous he sounds.

With a curse, Archer bangs a fist into one of the bars. "If I find out you were involved in her murder..."

"You'll forgive me," Killian snaps. "Because you're a Troikan. Isn't that right? Or can you take the boy out of Myriad but not take Myriad out of the boy? Would you like to let your dark side out to play and wreak havoc against me? Would you like vengeance? Go ahead. *Feel* your rage, Archer. Act on it. I dare you."

Tremors rock Archer. He's like a powder keg about to blow.

Zero! What should I do?

By slaying Dior and Javier, Myriad has upped their game. They have an Abrogate in their realm rather than the Land of the Harvest, and that Abrogate is a major threat to my friends. He must be fought by a Conduit at the top of her— or his—game. More than that, the potential Abrogates must be stopped. Alejandro is right about that. Where he messed up? Suggesting I sever my bond to Killian and give him to the Generals.

Can the bond between an inter-realm couple be severed? Surely. A bond between a spirit and a realm can be dissolved in court. Perhaps we simply need to disavow each other.

My mind whirls as my gaze meets Killian's.

He frowns. "Your thoughts," he says, frown deepening. "I can hear them."

What?! No way. Sweat beads my brow. "I'm not pushing my words into your head." Am I?

"Oh, really? You're thinking about severing our bond. We simply need to disavow each other." He smiles coldly as I struggle to breath. He *had* heard my thoughts. "How about this? If you don't meet my list of demands, I'll disavow you here and now."

Okay, I *had* unconsciously pushed my thoughts into his head. I'd been thinking about him, and must have activated the link. I summon beams of Light around my mind, just in case, sending the shadows into a tailspin. Pain shoots through my temples, but I continue to let the Light shine. Killian winces, as if burned.

I think: *If you tell me what I'm thinking now, I'll strip naked.*

His expression never changes, and I nearly drop with relief. Okay, then. My thoughts are now shielded. No way a hedonist like Killian could resist such bait. Not because he wants to see me naked—maybe he wants to see me naked—but because the act will embarrass me.

I'll have to be more careful in the future.

"What are your demands?" I grate.

"For starters, Archer Prince will leave the house. On his hands and knees."

Anger sparks. Around me, my friends sputter. I hold up my hand in a bid for silence, and return to my musings. If I'm right, and Killian lost his memories because he must choose to love me, the enemy, without the aid of emotion—effectively embracing his Troikan side—his Myriadian side would make him *inclined* to disavow me as soon as possible. But. By willingly sticking with me, he's going against the urge to drop me like a hot potato, unwittingly embracing Light.

Maybe I'm off base. Shall I force the issue, as he has done, and find out?

You want to be rid of me? Fine. Disavow me.

I will be taking a big risk. Huge. He could respond without hesitation: *Boom. You're disavowed.*

Beads of sweat pop up across my brow. I can't lose my way into Myriad, and Many Ends.

But no risk, no reward, right? And I can't let him hold our bond over my head, continuing to use it as leverage every time he wants something.

"I'm not meeting any of your demands," I tell Killian. "Neither are my friends. If you want to disavow me, do it."

His eyes narrow to tiny slits, his breathing a bit more labored.

"Do it," I shout. My hands fist. "Say goodbye to your ticket into Troika and disavow me."

Though anger glitters in his eyes, a slow smile blooms. A wicked one. "How could I *ever* let you go, baby? I have plans for you…"

I run my tongue over my teeth. I'm sure he does. But three cheers for me! I'd defused a tough situation. The risk had paid off.

"Just as I have plans for you," I tell him. I won't lose focus on my endgame. Peace between the realms. Freedom for the spirits in Many Ends.

One mission at a time.

The smile fades in a hurry. He didn't like hearing that I might be using him. Good!

"I'll help Dior," I promise Archer, getting us back on track. I'll enter Myriad with Killian, as planned, find and hide her so that she can't be used against us, then go full steam ahead toward my endgame.

I face the others. "You never asked to be part of my personal war, and I don't expect your support." Amid twitters of confusion, I add, "I intend to find Shamus, free Killian and enter Myriad…and Many Ends. The two are connected. Ask Reed. I intend to—no, I *will* save the spirits trapped inside. It can be done. Reed and Kayla are proof of that. But.

While I'm there, I need your help in the Land of the Harvest. There's a warehouse full of humans who are infected with Penumbra."

Penumbra is a big, bad boogyman, and only a select few citizens know about Dior's and Javier's infection. We've held our silence, hoping to avoid widespread panic.

My friends are part of the few.

"I'm proof spirits can be saved from Many Ends," Reed says, "but you forget. I never experienced Second-death while there. Others were not so fortunate. I witnessed countless murders. There, spirits vanish." He snaps. "Just like that. What if they are dead for good?"

"They could be, but I doubt it. You remember the screams as well as I do, I'm sure." From the moment I awoke in Many Ends till the very second I left, a chorus of pain and agony rang out. "There *are* survivors, and whether those people died once, twice or a thousand times, they are suffering unimaginable horrors."

Eyes closed, he shuffles from one booted foot to the other, huffs out a breath. When he faces me once again, he's pale, as if a soundtrack of those screams is now playing inside his head. "You're right. I'm in. Whatever you need me to do."

One down. Five to go. The majority.

"What about the people infected with Penumbra?" Raanan asks.

"I doubt I can cleanse anyone. The bond to Killian...it's changed me. Shadows fill my head. What if I share shadows instead of Light? I won't weaken Penumbra but strengthen it." Time to drop a few truth bombs. "Raanan, you *are* a Conduit, and I *did* change you. Apparently, I'm a Conduit *and* an Architect."

Murmurs of confusion arise.

"Before the vote," I say, "Eron told me I have the power to make Conduits. Well, my Light has the power. It decides who's ready and who isn't. Raanan, you were ready. You can go to the warehouse. You can cleanse the infected." I've had trust issues for as long as I can remember, but I'm not letting them dictate my actions anymore. I'm letting others help.

I can't do everything on my own, and neither can they. We need each other. One body. One heart. Working together.

"Not on your own, though," I add. "Okay? All right? Without help, you could drain yourself to death. Through the Grid, I can be with you." The way the princess was there for me. "I will help you every step of the way. All you have to do is contact me when the time comes."

Silence greets me, thick and oppressive.

Finally Raanan draws in a deep breath. Bright, bright Light glows from his pores. "Yes, I'll go to the warehouse. I'll cleanse the infected."

Thank the Firstking.

Wait. Back up a sec. I see his Light?

I do, I really do. Three cheers.

One is lonely. Two are necessary for war. Three is the minimum number of examples needed to explain a concept efficiently.

The shadows must be losing their hold on me.

"I'm with you," Archer announces with a nod.

"I'm insulted you don't already know my answer," Clay says. "You're my Number Girl, and I'm on your side. Always."

I'm grateful beyond measure. Absolutely overcome. "Why are you guys so loyal to me? So far, I've given you nothing but trouble."

"You're honest, brutally so," Archer says. "I'd rather help an enemy who tells me truth than a friend who tells me lies."

During my Firstlife, I read an amazing series of books by Kresley Cole. *The Arcana Chronicles*. In it, a character says lies are curses we place on ourselves, and I wholeheartedly agree.

"You always do what you believe is right." Raanan crosses his arms over his chest. "You inspire me to do the same."

Clay smiles at me. "You never back down. No matter the obstacles in your way, you forge ahead."

"You consider peace, not the destruction of an enemy, a worthy goal." Dawn withdraws another syringe and fills the vial hanging around my neck. "As do I."

Clementine nudges my shoulder. "I firmly believe you could hit eleven out of ten targets, with only nine bullets."

I snort-laugh.

"What?" she says. "It's true. I also believe you could cut a knife with butter."

This time, *everyone* snort-laughs.

A pulse of annoyance flows along the bridge that connects me to Killian, and I frown. What's his problem now?

"While Raanan visits the warehouse and I hunt Shamus," I say, "I'd like the rest of you to stay here and defend the house—and Killian." I bat my lashes, all *pretty please with a cherry on top.* "I know he's your enemy, but we Troikans embody love, and it's time we acted like it. It's time we loved everyone, rather than those it's easy for us to love."

Agreement doesn't come quickly, but it does come.

Relief pours through me. "For the coming battle, there's only one rule. We do not kill or irrevocably harm a Troikan."

"In that case," Killian says, "you will fail. Free me, and I'll win the battle for you."

"You mean you'll slaughter everyone," I mutter, and again I feel the pulse of his emotion along our bond. Frustration this time. The need to act—to destroy. "Look past the shadows. You'll be surprised by what you find."

Biscuit barrels inside the house before Killian can respond, knocking down Ranaan, Clay and their guardians. "Who's ready to do this? Me, me, me! Don't worry, you don't have to catch me up on the latest developments. I gots me some super hearing! And looks who's with me. Deacon!"

"A talking dog." Killian moves his gaze over the other animals, and I realize the pack has remained quiet during our conversation. "In Myriad, dragons fly at all hours, but to my knowledge they've never deigned to speak with lowly citizens."

Head high, Deacon strides inside the house, claiming center stage. My first reaction: dismay. He's a by-the-rule-book kind of guy, and I'm about to go rogue. My second reaction: surprise. How did he get past our Buckler? Unless the Buckler Archer erected includes Deacon as "one of us." Yes. That. My third reaction: joy. This is Deacon. We've had our differences, but my love for him has never faltered. He's here, and he's safe.

He nods at me before focusing on Archer, his best friend. The two close the distance to meet in the middle. Any lingering dismay that Deacon might blow up my endgame fades. He will never go against Archer. As the two embrace, a beautiful contrast of light and dark—unity—my eyes mist again.

No time for a break. "How many friends have you recruited to our side?" I ask Biscuit.

"Counting...counting. One sec, still counting. Okay done. Only *all* of them."

The exact answer I hoped to hear. "Can you escort me to General Shamus?"

His furry chest puffs with pride. "I can do anything. I'm amazing."

And mega humble.

"Anyone going to introduce me?" Killian asks. "To the dog, not the Laborer. He and I have met. Although, if I'm being honest—for once—I consider him a dog, as well."

Nice. My husband remembers everyone but me.

I'm not bitter—much.

The dog bounds over to press his face through the bars of the cage. "Hiya. I'm Biscuit. The best! You're Killian. You smell like you've been rubbing all over Ten." *Sniff, sniff.* "I like it."

My cheeks heat as I hug Deacon, then Archer. "By the way, I'm really glad you're here."

"I know." He tweaks my nose. "Because I'm invaluable to your cause."

"And as humble as Biscuit," I reply, my tone dry. "Though I'd love to stay and chat, there's a little business I must attend." I turn, intending to leave.

"Hold up," Archer calls, stopping me. "If you think you're leaving without weaving me a poem, you're sorely mistaken."

Ha! "Little Bow Peep, there's no time."

"If you're breathing," he counters, "there's time."

Very well. Knowing he prefers poems that rhyme—all others are crap in his mind—I sigh and say, "The worst happened and you were dead. I couldn't get your loss out of my head. I cried, I mourned, I longed to see you. It sucked, I tell you true. But here you are, back in my arms. Ready to battle—though you might be harmed. But listen well, you adorable piece of poo. If you die again, I'll forever haunt you."

He barks out a laugh, and I go soft as butter. With this boy, I'm basically mush.

Smiling, I reach out and pat his head. "You are the sister I always wanted."

Mock growl. "The poem sucked balls, sis. Work on it."

My smile widens. I soften further, but also warm. He is a bright Light in my life, our relationship as necessary as air. "I missed you, too, Ten," I say, mimicking him. I focus on Biscuit. "All right. Let's go, guardian."

I motor forward, the dog at my side. Just before I clear the door, I'm driven by a crazy impulse to look back at Killian. In the same way Archer is like a sibling to me, Killian is like an addiction. Resistance is futile.

Our gazes meet, and lightning arcs across our bond, startling me. It's bright, hot and unmistakable. A palpable hum of energy.

"Be careful." His body is drawn as tight as a bow, ready to snap. "Your death will cause mine."

Disappointment slaps me, but I say nothing as I head outside with Biscuit.

One mission at a time.

Different species of animal now surround the house. Six elephants at the helm, four giraffes directly behind them, then ten gorillas and two rhinos at the rear.

$6 + 4 + 10 + 2 = 22$.

Twenty-two, the atomic number for titanium.

I must be as strong as titanium right now.

On the sidelines of the neighborhood are countless dogs and cats, deer, alligators, bears, lions and tigers. I'm awed. The city has become a veritable zoo.

In the distance, hundreds of Laborers crest a hill. They are dressed in catsuits. Troikan armor. No more robes. They are ready for battle, even if destruction isn't the desired result. Swords glint in the Light that shines through the Veil of Wings. Red, red rose petals tumble from the sky, dancing and twirling toward the ground.

Leading the way are Luciana and John.

John is dark-skinned and muscled to the max. A warrior without equal.

Animals stand beside their soldiers. A blast of fear almost sends me rushing back into the house. What if someone gets hurt? What if—*No! Stop.*

I rub the brand on my wrist. I must be the warhorse. Fearless. Determined. Nothing will stop me from my goal: victory.

The Grid hums with approval, causing the shadows to writhe. Here, now, it doesn't feel like they've lost their hold on me. Not that I rely on my feelings. But either way, I know I'm going to have to battle those shadows. Soon.

One mission at a time. Focus. Right. My brows knit as the Grid guides me to push a ray out, Light *from my eyes.* Um, okay. But why?

Does it really matter? The Grid has never steered me wrong.

I close my eyes and concentrate on a ray of Light. Deep breath in, out. Then I shove the Light, and open my eyes. A ray shoots from me, zooming through the air like an arrow. My gaze follows it and—I gasp. I can see a great distance perfectly! Can see little details I might have missed otherwise.

Might have? Ha! Definitely.

Luciana is wearing a metal and mesh dress, a regal look, but also a deceptive one. I've worn something similar, and I know the design allows easier weapons storage, as well as more fluid range of motion.

I've met John once. We shook hands at my Welcome to Troika party. Though he is six-four, he appears tiny standing next to a massive steed. His shoulders are wide, his chest shaped like a barrel. John's, not the horse's. A thick golden beard covers the lower half of his face.

"I don't recall you looking so awed when you met me." Biscuit bumps into my leg. "The General isn't as cool as me."

"Oh, I was awed. Trust me." When John glances in my direction, I duck. Silly. The Grid informs me I'm hidden. The ray of Light I blasted has blinded others from seeing me. So cool!

Biscuit bounds off in the opposite direction, and I give chase.

We slip past the Buckler Archer erected with zero problems. Not that I expected any. We can come and go as we please.

We trek through row after row of the tiny homes. The deeper into the city we go, the cleaner it becomes, until we reach an area without any damage at all. A forest stretches for miles, only it's a forest like no other I've seen. A veritable rainbow. The trees have green trunks and blue leaves. Some of the bushes are pink, some red, some orange. Lush yellow grass carpets the ground.

Colorful birds fly from branch to branch, singing about love, love is always the answer.

According to Aunt Lina, *Light* is always the answer. Perhaps they are one and the same?

"By the way," Biscuit says. "I wasn't lying about your scent. Your butt is—"

"Hey!" I swipe up a rock and lob it at him.

He laughs as he ducks, then picks up the pace. A Stairwell looms ahead. I wonder where it leads, where we'll—

A twig snaps behind me. Whirling, I reach for a dagger. But a whip of Light lashes out, snags around the blade and yanks. Shock. Dread. Both consume me. A shadowed figure about fifty yards away. In one hand, he holds the whip. In the other, a rock. A rock he hurls—

No. Not a rock. A grenade.

"Bomb," I scream, diving for Biscuit to cover him with my body.

Boom!

chapter nine

"Believing is believing."
—Troika

Killian

The moment Ten is gone, Archer seizes the reins of control, certain he'll be obeyed.

"Everyone outside," he orders. "Subdue anyone who makes it past the animals, and remember—killing isn't an option. Dawn, you stay inside." He slaps a Dazer into her hand.

As one of ten legitimate sons of the Prince of Ravens, Archer grew up issuing commands, expecting and receiving absolute compliance. At one time, even I obeyed him.

When we were friends, I envied his confidence. Then he defected to Troika, leaving me behind, proving once again that no one sticks around and "love" can't be trusted. Now? The trait makes me see red. I grew up with nothing, had to work for every promotion, every scrap of admiration, yet still I am seen as less than nothing. He is looked upon as a savior.

I...envy him? I would rather die!

"Arming a Healer?" I sneer. "Why don't you shoot her in the head and save her the trouble of shooting herself."

Dawn grows pale.

Archer snaps his teeth at me, before saying to Dawn, "If anyone but the people in this room walk through the door, shoot first, ask questions later. And don't worry. You won't be causing anyone any kind of injury. If the prisoner threatens you, or hey, if he even breathes in your direction, shoot him, too."

Though she's trembling, she nods.

I swallow a curse, hating my helplessness. The urge to act, to rip those bars out of the way, bombards me. My hands twitch and my legs ready. But I remain seated, frustration mounting. I'll succeed only in entertaining the enemy.

Archer casts me a smug glance, all *game, set, match*.

Rage...so much rage burns and bubbles inside me. A volcano set to erupt. But I tamp it down, and smile. A cold unveiling of my teeth. His time will come; I have only to bide mine.

"Dear ladies, genitalmen and assorted faunae of Troika," I say, my tone smug enough to annoy, well, anyone.

"Did you say *genital*men?" Archer demands.

"Oh, good. Your ears are working." I continue just as breezily. "If you Daze me, you Daze Ten. Have you already forgotten we're bonded, and what happens to one happens to both?" As I speak, I rub at the brand on my wrist. The horse Tenley spent a good few seconds staring at.

She bears a similar mark. Meaning we have matching tattoos. Stab me, please. I must have convinced myself we'd last forever. *Idiot*. Nothing lasts forever. Not even truth, apparently. If Tenley is right and Fusion is a lie, my mother is trapped in Many Ends. My father, too. But who cares? My Secondking lied to me...like I once lied to so many others.

Sow and reap, as Tenley likes to say.

If she's right about one thing, there's a good chance she's right about the other. Many Ends could be connected to Myriad...and I have value. I'm strong, capable and brave. I'm worth something.

Her words still ring inside my head. To her, I mean something.

Focus on what matters. Right. How can I support the realm, if that's the case?

How can I not?

No realm, no future.

When Archer scowls at me, his little dog goes crazy, barking and growling. Finally she tells me the many ways she's going to hurt me if I continue to upset her human. Disembowelment is at the top of her list.

Archer cracks a smile, and the dog goes quiet. Danger averted.

"You won't prick my temper today," he informs me. "I learned a lot in the Rest. Namely the extent of your betrayal. You set me up. *You* are the reason I died in battle."

Am I? So badly do I want to remember, but the shadows clouding my memory are rooted deep. "What a neat trick, cooling the fire of your rage. Please. Teach me how to be dead inside, oh, wise one."

A pause. A sad smile. "Perhaps one day you'll turn your mess into a message." Dismissing me, he skids his gaze over the others. "All right. Get to work."

Everyone rushes to obey him without a single protest, the animals following. I'm envious. I'd love a pet of my own. Someone to look at me the way the dogs look at Tenley and Archer.

Speaking of, does Tenley find the resurrected TL attractive?

My hands fist, even though the answer doesn't matter. I'm

not going to think about her. I don't like the way I feel when I do, as if I'm trapped in a car, careening toward another, unable to stop the collision.

A distant *boom* sounds. The house shakes, and the furniture rattles.

"They're setting off bombs?" I demand, only to wince. My head feels as if it's been split in half by a hammer. Sharp pains erupt in my limbs. My stomach churns, threatening to heave. Gashes appear on my arms and torso, Lifeblood dripping. Understanding dawns, followed by horror. "Your people are attacking Ten." The words lash from me, an accusation as much as a demand something be done.

"No. They…" The color drains from Archer's cheeks, and he sways. This isn't the first time his body has betrayed him today. Sweat pops up on his brow, and he wipes it away with a shaky hand. "They would never risk hurting her or the realm."

"So what *was* that?" I demand. Worry screams: *Something terrible.* "Why am I covered in wounds when I never moved an inch?"

"I don't… I can't…"

"Are you feeling okay?" Dawn flattens her palm against Archer's forehead to gauge his temperature.

"I'm fine, thanks," I mutter, my tone dry.

"You're overheated," she continues, as if I haven't spoken.

"I'll be okay." Archer draws in a breath, holds, and exhales. "I just need a moment to catch my breath."

"No concern for Ten?" I spread my still-bleeding arms. "You are wonderful friends. The best."

"At the moment, there's nothing I can do for Ten," Dawn snaps at me. Well, well. The mouse can pretend to be a lion.

"Besides. You are well enough to cause trouble, which means *she* is well enough. I must focus my efforts where they matter."

"Doesn't look like your efforts matter much to Archer, either." His tremors are worsening by the second. This keeps up, and he'll soon drop like a condemned house. "Not that you've done anything but talk."

Pain and frustration have burned away any filter I might have had.

Hurt glimmers in her eyes. What, does she expect me to apologize for speaking the truth?

I need to leave, and I need to leave now. Someone has to look out for Ten. My life depends on it!

If I can lure Archer closer, I can expedite his nap and steal his weapons. Won't get me out of the cage, but at least I'll be prepared when I do break free.

Escape, weaken Troika, return to Myriad with Tenley.
Put the needs of others before yourself.

I press my tongue to the roof of my mouth to halt an irritated verbal response. Two voices, both mine. Dark versus Light. Light can shove off. I'll put the needs of others before myself *never*. Been there, done that, suffered for it.

"Anyone with half a brain could tell Archer needs water. He just rose from the dead. Maybe he's, I don't know, dehydrated." Why does my throat feel raw, like I swallowed acid? "While you're at it, you should probably get yourself a glass, too. Unless you *want* to pass out?"

Dawn glares at me, and I flash her my coldest grin. Then I blink—

Suddenly I'm running through a thick veil of black smoke. Even as I cough, it hurts. I wrap a strip of cloth around the lower half of my face. It helps, but not much. As I scale down a pile of rubble, hunks of metal cut my legs, making me wince.

The dog leads the way. He glances over his shoulder to ensure I haven't fallen too far behind.

Wait. I'm seeing the world through Tenley's eyes?

My eyelids snap open, and once again I'm standing inside the cage. The smoke is gone, though the air in the house now feels a hundred times hotter.

Archer has regained his bearings. He's standing in front of the bars, just as I hoped, though I never heard him move. The realization chafes. Still, I don't strike out. Yet. My concern for Tenley is back, and magnified.

"You need to understand something," Archer says. "That girl is one of a kind. She—"

"Shut up. Just shut up." I need to return to her. The moment I close my eyes, I'm connected to her once again. The smoke is back, and it's thicker, as if another bomb has been detonated.

Biscuit calls, "Hurry! He's going to catch us."

He? Who is chasing them?

Boom!

Directly behind me—her—something explodes. The ground rocks, and debris shifts. Directly beneath Tenley's feet, the pile slides in different directions. She plummets with a gasp. Impact jars her, emptying her lungs. I know, because I'm struggling to breathe, as well. Our minds are dizzy, our vision hazy as Lifeblood drip, drip, drips.

Panic settles in my bones, setting my marrow aflame. Must save her—I mean me. Must save *me*. She could be harmed *worse*, which means I could be harmed worse.

I don't want her—us—harmed.

A whimper draws her attention. One of Biscuit's legs is trapped underneath a fat marble slab. She crawls toward him, uncaring when a shard of glass slices her thigh.

Her biceps tremble as she fights to lift the slab.

"Go," the dog tells her. "I can't walk. There's no need for us both to die."

"No! I'm not going anywhere without you. Here." She yanks the vial of manna from her neck. "Drink—"

She goes still. A man with bright red curls ascends the pile, coming into view. She gasps, a name wafting over our bond. —*Nico*.—

Information follows the voice. Nico and Tenley died on the same day. Firstdeath. She considered him a good guy. They've had little interaction, and nothing turbulent. The One Who Shall Not Be Named must have considered him a good guy, too, because he found and locked up all the Myriadian spies, and Nico wasn't among them.

Ambrosine hates his brother so much, he doesn't allow his people to speak the name.

"Why are you doing this?" she demands. "How are you doing it?"

He motions to the hawk soaring overhead. "My guardian tracked you, figured out where you were heading and told me where to wait. Of course, he had no idea what I planned... Or maybe he did, and expected me to change my mind. Spoiler alert. I'm not going to change my mind."

Biscuit growls at Nico and then snarls at the bird, a promise of vengeance.

—*His reasons do no' matter. End him, end the danger to your life.*— I shove the command along our bond, my only means of supplying aid.

She gasps, and I know she's heard me. As stealthily as possible, she releases the vial of manna and reaches for a small, sharp shard of glass. Good girl. Going for her swords would be too obvious.

Nico says, "After you attacked Victor, he came to me, admitted his feelings for me. We were going to be together—until he had to defect. Because of you."

Another tide of information. When Victor Prince reached the Age of Accountability, he made covenant with Troika in order to spy for his father and ultimately lead the revolution to destroy the realm from the inside out. I'd had no idea, until too late.

Too late—for what? I scour my mind, but the shadows maintain a firm hold on the memory.

"Victor," she spits at the redhead. "He's a liar and a user."

"No!" Spittle sprays from the corners of Nico's mouth. "Troika voided his contract, allowing him to return to Myriad. I wanted to go with him, but I was denied. To be with him, I'll have to go to court."

—Throw the shard.—

She doesn't. She says, "He only loves himself, Nico." Her tone is soft, gentle. "He used you, just like he used Kayla. Probably many others."

"No. He loves me." He pulls a minigrenade from the pouch anchored to his waist. His hawk squawks in what sounds like protest. Clearly he—she—doesn't want the Laborer to murder an innocent girl. Good bird. "To void my contract, I must do as Victor did."

His message is clear. Victor tried to kill her, and Nico plans to finish the job. My rage returns, redoubles, a fever boiling in my blood, and this time, there's no tamping it down.

—Throw the shard. Now!— The moment Nico pulls the pin, all hope will be lost. Both Tenley and I will die.

Not ready… Haven't truly lived.

A deluge of fury, fear and determination vibrates along the Grid, and for a moment, I'm afraid she's going to try to talk some "sense" into herself and then the boy. Foolish girl. There's no time. When death comes for you, you don't try to reason with him. You fight hard, and you fight fast.

With a cry from the depths of her soul, she swings out her arm, hurling the shard. Her aim is true. The tip slices through Nico's neck, skin splitting open, Lifeblood spurting out.

His eyes widen with shock. He struggles to breathe as he reaches for the wound he will never be able to close. His knees give out, and he topples. The grenade falls from his grip.

The hawk swoops down to catch the grenade before it hits the ground.

Tenley rushes forward, too, her heart a riotous storm. When she realizes the hawk succeeded, she stills, unsure what to do, but the bird gently sets the weapon in her palm.

She expels a sigh of relief. Then she kneels beside Nico and whispers, "I'm sorry." Hands trembling, she sets the grenade aside, pushes the man to his back, and rips a vial of manna from his neck. "It didn't have to be the way. I wished you'd listened to me."

—*What're you doin'? Doona waste yer manna on him. You might need—Argh!*—

The foolish lass dispenses much-needed liquid directly into Nico's wound, wasting every precious drop. Because it's too late. He breathes his last as Second-death claims him.

Her shoulders roll in, and her head bows.

Now she mourns for him? I ground my teeth. Mourns the loss of the man who tried to kill her. How can her heart be so...soft? I'd like to kill the male all over again.

Perhaps she absorbs my determination through the bond. She straightens, and returns to Biscuit, swiping up the extra vial of manna along the way. The dog watches her with dark eyes filled with adoration.

She takes a drink. Only a sip, not nearly enough, and only for the boost of strength needed to push and shove the slab from Biscuit's leg.

The moment he's free, she empties the remaining liquid down his throat.

I *loathe* being a voice in her head, unable to force her movements, to ensure she does what's necessary to ensure her own survival. How can she help an enemy at a time like this? How can she take so little for herself when a battle looms, and give so much to a dog?

Frustration burns as deeply as my rage. Does she not understand weakness is her enemy? With every drop of Lifeblood she loses, failure moves from a possibility to a guarantee.

Part of me wants to shake her, and rattle her brain against her skull. *Come on, help yourself.* If she won't do it, I'll do it for her. Somehow, some way. She must be protected, whatever the cost. She needs me, and I think… I think I need her.

In the back of my mind, a memory arises. Just after our bond, she looked at me with absolute, utter acceptance. To her, I was family.

I'd never really had a family. The something from before… the something I couldn't identify but suspected was longing— it strikes again, pricking my hollow heart.

For the first time, that hollowness bothers me.

Like the big bad wolf, I huff and I puff with indignation. Family is an illusion. *Never forget.* Even if I forsook my realm to be with this girl, giving up my home, my job and the accolades I've earned in favor of the rancor I'll receive from Troikans, one day Tenley will leave me.

No one sticks.

"You stayed," Biscuit says, awe crackling in each word.

"Well, we're a team."

"Yeah, but you *stayed*."

Though she's panting and sweating, she takes time to scratch him behind the ear. "Are you feeling better?"

"Much." He leans into her touch. "But you're not."

"I'll be fine. Right now, we need weapons. And a place to store the grenade."

He bounces up and stretches, testing his agility. "I know the perfect place. Come on!" His limp lessens in severity as he bounds forward.

Tenley lumbers to her feet and follows after him. Sharp pains shoot through her legs. My legs, too. Muscles burn and tremble, and bones ache. This poor, sweet lass has it worse. Blood pools in her ankles, causing swelling, making every step agony.

I bang a fist into the cold, hard floor beneath me with enough force to crack the wood. While I lounge comfortably in a cell, she is fighting with every ounce of her strength to free me. Despite her aches and pains. Despite any consequences. Her tenacity blows my mind. Nothing stops this girl. Ever. Although...General Shamus might. If he's at full strength, and she's not...

Pang. I rub my chest. —*Return to the house, Tenley. We'll find another way tae set me free.*— I doubt she'll obey, but I have to try. Have to do *something*.

—*There isn't another way. I'll continue on, as planned.*—

PANG. Is this how she won me over and got me to bond with her? By keeping me on a mental carousel, always spinning, spinning, never sure what was up and what was down?

How can she care about my well-being, even now? —*There'll be no reason tae open the cage if I'm dead. Return, and we can have lunch at one, and two drinks at three. Eat petit fours at five, and be in bed by six.*—

—Well, well. You certainly have my number. But I'm going to pass. Don't worry, though. I'll do whatever it takes to protect you.—

—I'll protect my own life, thank you very much. Do us both a favor and see to yers.—

—Careful, Killian. It almost sounds like you care about my well-being.—

I sidestep that little land mine with a question, making sure my accent is undetectable. *—Why would my shadows want to hide memories of you?—*

—I think they want you to forget me so that you'll betray me. I also think the Light lets them hide those memories, so that you'll learn to trust me even without the aid of your emotions.—

—And why aren't you learning to trust me, hmm?—

—I trusted you long before this, against all logic, emotion and the advice of my friends.—

I...have no rejoinder. Guilt sidles up to me like an old friend. An old friend with a knife in one hand and a gun in the other.

Hurt sizzles over the Grid. *Her* hurt. My throat constricts, and my chest tightens. But I don't care. I won't care. I'd rather she hurt emotionally than physically.

I would? What is *wrong* with me? A girl is a girl is a girl, right?

Yes, but *this* girl is *mine*.

Stop. Just stop! Claiming her will do me no good. I'll never be able to count on her.

Count. The word gives me pause. Tenley Lockwood... count... A memory teases me, but shadows writhe, maintaining a firm grip on our past.

Screw the shadows. Screw the Light. Someone tell me something!

I slam a fist into the floor beneath me. I suspect Tenley and

I had a sizzling connection before her Firstdeath. Problem is, that connection must not have mattered to her. Not enough, anyway. She still chose Troika over me. She will *always* choose Troika, so I will do the same; I will choose Myriad.

Besides, nothing lasts, remember?

Escape the cage, weaken Troika, return to Myriad with Tenley.

Put the needs—

No. Stars whiz at her sides as Biscuit leads her through a Stairwell, then a Gate. We have a similar travel system in Myriad, only there are no bright illuminations to signify movement, just a moment of blinding darkness, where you can't even see your hand in front of your face.

The pair emerges into a busy metropolis, Laborers working alongside Leaders, Messengers and Healers, cleaning up debris.

I huff and puff with indignation. —*Don't just stand in front of these people as if today is an average day.*—

"Uh, Biscuit?" she says.

"Can't be helped, my little hooman. By the time word of your location spreads, you'll be long gone. Let's burn rubber. We gots a lot of ground to cover and very little time to cover it."

As the two hurry forward, Tenley receives smiles and waves from some of the throng, but glares from others. She scrambles for a distraction, asking the dog, "Why the name Biscuit?"

"I had a Firstlife, too, you know. In the Land of the Harvest, my owner named me, so you'd have to ask her."

"If you spent your Firstlife with her," Ten says, "why weren't you assigned to guard her?"

"She decided to go to Myriad."

"So why didn't you go to Myriad? Why didn't any of the animals?"

"Eron called dibs on everything with four legs and fur,

and fish. Ambrosine wanted dragons, snakes and creepers like that."

Suddenly a big bruiser steps in front of her and Tenley skids to a halt. "Hey!" he snaps. "You owe us an explanation, little girl. Why did you vote for Archer Prince? He's a Laborer. We need a General. Or do you *want* us to lose the war?"

"I want peace," she says.

Biscuit growls. "Take one more step toward my girl, and you'll lose a foot."

I'm impressed. And I'm jealous of a freaking dog. He's a hero, and I'm a zero.

Bruiser is lucky I'm not with her. I would have shut him up with my fists. And of course, Tenley would have been angry that I dared to hurt one of her precious people.

Paling, Bruiser backs off. The dog doesn't relax his I'll-chew-your-foot-off stare until Tenley runs her hand along his spine. The two hurry on without any more interference. Once they reach a more rural area, Tenley swipes a catsuit from a line of clothing drying in the sun. She discards her tattered robe and shimmies into the suit, careful not to look down.

—*Don't want me to see your curves?*— Adorable.

—*You can see them as soon as you remember me.*—

—*Suddenly I remember* everything. *Honest.*—

She snorts, and I experience a flicker of satisfaction.

Ignore it. Change the subject. —*Why do you protect people who don't like or respect you?*— I'm genuinely curious.

—*They dislike me now. They might grow to like me later.*— Her tone is sharp, defensive.

Interesting. I've struck a nerve. —*You* need *their approval, do you?*—

—*No. I wasn't saying… Look. Their feelings have nothing to do with anything. But. They deserve a chance to live in peace, whether they like me or not.—*

I'm beginning to understand why her friends follow her so ardently. *One of a kind. Fights for what she believes in, no matter the obstacles in her way.*

She is different. Okay. All right. There's no denying it any longer. She's different from other girls, boys and everyone in between. Part of me cares for her; I admit it. The other part of me recognizes the danger she poses to me. To my future. That part of me wants to cut all ties and run.

Embrace your feelings. Isn't that what I've been told all my life? If those in Myriad knew what I was feeling, they would change their tune.

—Rise above what you feel, good or bad, and do what's right.—

Tenley's voice drifts through the Grid, and I tense. Did I unintentionally project my thoughts, prompting her response? *Must be more careful.*

Biscuit leads her through another Stairwell and a Gate, through a vibrant manna field, where she plucks petals straight from the vine. Those petals aren't as strong as the liquefied version, but they provide a kick of strength.

The next Stairwell leads to a snowcapped mountain with skyscraper trees and wild, overgrown bushes teeming with the biggest flowers I've ever seen. A beautiful—and treacherous—landscape. Icy winds beat at her, worse than a thousand needles poking and prodding her skin. Her teeth chatter.

Biscuit enters a small, dark cavern. Muscles heavy as stone, Tenley trudges after him. As warm air envelops her, she whimpers with relief.

Two polar bears lounge on boulders...telling jokes?

"—call a cow that eats your grass?" one asks.

"Don't know," the other says. "What?"

"A lawn moo-er."

Laughter abounds.

When the bears notice Biscuit, they jolt upright, ready to attack. The moment his identity clicks, however, they relax.

"Hey, Biscuit. What you doing this far out?" one asks.

"And with a human." The other *tsk-tsk*s. "You broke the beast-code."

"Frick, Frack, this is Ten," Biscuit says. "Ten, Frick and Frack. Forget the code, guys. We need to borrow some weapons. And by *borrow* I mean *keep forever*."

In unison, the bears ask, "Why?"

The dog glares, the hair on his back spiking. "Because I said so. Why else?"

"Uh-oh," Frick says. "His poodle's about to come out, isn't it?"

Frack gulps. "Oh, yeah. Give him whatever he wants."

Frick, the bigger bear, lumbers toward the back wall. "We got Stags, Oxis and Dazers? Or you wanting something old school?"

A single dart from a Stag can trap a spirit inside a Shell, preventing any sort of mobility and rendering both incarnations defenseless. That dart can also incapacitate a spirit *without* a Shell, causing agonizing pain.

Oxis age a spirit and Shell until both are reduced to ash.

"Yeah," Biscuit says. "Those. All of those. New and old. Whatever the hooman can carry."

In the back of the cavern is the most beautiful arsenal of all time. I weep with envy. There are different types of guns, just like the bears said, but also swords, daggers and garrotes.

Tenley stores the grenade in a box before selecting a pair of short swords, wrist cuff garrotes like the ones I prefer to wear, two bejeweled daggers and a mini-Dazer. Doesn't take a genius to notice she avoids the most dangerous items.

Foolish girl. She hopes to avoid hurting others, even the temptation of it, but others might not hope to avoid hurting her. Doesn't she know? The enemy you allow to walk away is the enemy who will return to stab you in the back.

"Thank you so much for your help," she says.

Frick nods. "Any friend of Biscuit's an acquaintance of mine who is sometimes welcome."

Laughter bubbles from her, and I hate to admit it, but the sound of her amusement enchants me. *I'm* the fool.

Biscuit heads for the door. "One, two, three, time to move, my Ten."

Through another Stairwell, then another Gate they go. They reach what looks to be an abandoned warehouse. Inside, there are no furnishings. Dust motes dance, illuminated by bright red lasers shooting from every wall, blocking a large metal grate in the floor. That grate is shaped like the Troika symbol: a circle with three petals.

"We need to get to the symbol, but if we touch the beams, we experience instant Torchlight," Biscuit mutters.

Torchlight. For Troikans, Light is power. Like electricity. If a human is hit with too much electricity, his or her body shuts down. Torchlight is the spiritual equivalent. Only, a spirit doesn't just shut down. A spirit explodes.

Tenley shakes her head. "Not me. I'm a Conduit, remember?"

His eyes widen. "That's right! You can walk right through, push the lid out of the way, and descend into the tunnels, no problem."

"Shamus is down there?" Tenley asks.

"Yep. So is Princess Mariée. She is kept down here when danger is high."

Princess Mariée is Eron's fiancée. Maybe it's the Troikan in me, but I no longer feel a need to avoid the name Eron. Like Tenley, Mariée is a Conduit. And because there are only two Conduits in existence—three now, with Raanan—one must be protected at all times. If both are killed, other citizens will weaken and die, and the war will be over. Just. Like. That.

If I die, Tenley dies. Troika will weaken.

Am I willing to die for Myriad?

"There's a slight problem, however," Biscuit says, and cringes. "So minor I probably shouldn't mention it."

Tenley presses her hands against her stomach. "What? Tell me."

"Normally I can scent us through anything, but I still got smoke trapped in my sniffer. We're going to need a lamp. We won't be able to see the passages otherwise. But, if we use a lamp, Shamus will see us coming and we'll lose the element of surprise. If we lose the element of surprise, we'll lose, period."

She draws in a shaky breath…slowly releases it. "Well. It looks like we're going in without a lamp."

I swallow the words poised at the edge of my tongue. *Such recklessness will get us both killed, you fool!*

I've learned enough about Tenley to know she doesn't react to threats, dangers and warnings like anyone else. I'll only spur her on. Fuel to her fire. Besides, she doesn't need a rebuke. She needs help.

Though my mind is a jumble of contradictions, I make a decision. —*Don't worry, baby. The dark is where I excel.*—

chapter ten

"Seeing is believing."
—Myriad

Ten

I walk through the lasers, expecting no problems. Mistake! Shadows scream and hiss, clawing at my skull. My chest constricts, and my lungs empty.

Instinct demands I turn. Retreat. **Leave now, now, now. Destroy everyone, always.**

I grit my teeth and continue forward, my fingers remaining clenched in Biscuit's fur. I won't let him go for any reason. My dog will not experience Torchlight. And he *is* mine. A part of my family—just like Killian.

Biscuit contorts this way and that, avoiding the lasers. If he accidentally brushes against one, I will absorb and store the excess boost of Light. Light I can then share with Raanan when we cleanse the humans in the warehouse.

With every step, Killian's last words reverberate inside my mind. *The dark is where I excel.* Having him with me has been a blessing and a curse, a help and a hindrance. A comfort, but also a distraction. Does he have my best interests at heart?

No, no. Of course not. He has his own interests at heart.

New Killian sucks. Maybe if I punt his face like a soccer ball a few dozen times, I'll knock Myriadian-made screws loose, and he'll start to remember our past.

—*I'm sensing irritation.*— His voice is a caress along the Grid, causing tremors to rush down my spine.

Argh! Concentrate.

If there are rats down here, I don't want to know it. Or insects. During my time at Prynne, I had to eat bugs to survive. But...oh, zero! What if the rats and insects *talk*?

—Now *I'm sensing fear. Is the mighty Ten afraid?*—

—*I'm leery. There's a difference. I mean, what if I once dined on their family member?*—

His chuckle is genuine and husky, and it warms me. How I've missed his amusement.

Very few people have the ability to make him smile, and even fewer people have the ability to make him laugh.

"We did it!" Biscuit exclaims as we pass the final laser.

Thank the Firstking. Breathing is easier. And rewarded. The air is warmer here, and scented with manna, lavender and orchids.

The princess is nearby. I like her, admire her even, and do not want to hurt her. If she tries to stop me, however...

Determined to return to Killian victorious, I push aside the grate, revealing a small entrance to the tunnels. Light bursts free, pure and bright and warm.

I thought we were experiencing total darkness?

I scale down, down, Biscuit behind me. The scent of lavender and orchids intensifies as we inch forward, toward an open doorway, from which the Light seems to originate.

Looming outside the door, we see the princess inside. She's standing—no, she's levitating, her head thrown back, her arms spread. She is oblivious to the rest of the world. No longer does she appear to be a living being—she is the embodiment of a true conduit. I don't mean the job title, but a channel or instrument.

Awe renders me immobile. Light shines from her. Bright, bright Light, spilling from her pores. I'm astonished I'm able to see her, but I'm certain she can't see me. Beams of Light shoot from her eyes, as well. Glorious beams aimed up, up at the ceiling. *Through* the ceiling.

Around her, I hear… My ears twitch. A chorus of singing angels? The melody is haunting and gorgeous, a soothing balm. A promise that her royal highness is not alone. None of us are.

One of the voices stands out, capturing my attention, and the singer's identity crystalizes. Meredith. Our dead are serenading the Conduit?

Shock punches me. The spirits in the Rest are helping her as she…

She's powering the entire realm, isn't she? Sacrificing herself to save others.

My awe deepens, and my Light responds to hers, warming, growing, brightening. Shadows flee in terror, searching for new hiding spots. I'm witnessing a miracle, and I don't want to ever look away. This is beauty. This is life.

I've never exuded so much Light, even when I fought Dior's Penumbra. I absorb as much as possible, strength driving the last of my tremors away.

Zero! I might not be able to help Raanan cleanse the people in the warehouse, after all. We'll have to come up with a new plan.

There's no sign of Shamus.

I force myself to continue on, Biscuit at my side. The farther we get from the room, the darker the tunnel becomes, until *whoosh*, all Light is gone.

In an instant, I'm weakened. Which sucks more than usual, because the cuts in my legs have been steadily leaking Lifeblood, and I'm out of manna.

"I can do anything, absolutely anything...except see in the dark," Biscuit says.

"Today, thanks to Killian, I'll be *your* Seeing Eye dog." I unwind the thin metal belt from my waist, then loop one end through the other to create an all-in-one collar and leash. "I hope this doesn't offend you, but..." I lean over, patting the air until I encounter the softness of his fur.

"We'll tell no one of this," he mutters as I anchor the collar to his neck, and I want to smile. "Ever."

Killian's voice directs me. —*Close your eyes. Let your other senses take over.*—

I obey, knowing he needs me alive. Not because he loves me, but because he'll do anything to protect himself, just the way he's been trained. A stab of disappointment keeps me quiet.

—*Feel the breeze against your skin. Hear the sound of it drifting through the hallways.*—

A slight wind drifts from...the left!

—*Go against it.*—

Very well. With my arms extended, I move forward at a gradual pace. Encountering no resistance, I increase my speed, fueled by ferocious determination. Biscuit's nails *click-clack* against the concrete, blending with our panting breaths, creating an ominous soundtrack.

Exhaustion sets in, but I remain resolute. My mind is my worst enemy right now, a whirlwind I can no longer subdue, and a bramble of emotion I do not want to feel. Less than an hour ago, I killed a man. A friend of my friends.

Guilt threatens to burn my outward calm to ash. Sorrow picks off my excuses like a hunter who finally found worthy prey. *I had to kill Nico in self-defense—I could have found another way. I had no time to capture Nico and escort him to jail—There's always time to save a life. I had to choose, him or me, and I chose me—Could I not have chosen both?*

How am I supposed to tell my friends what I've done?

If Nico had survived, he might have realized his mistake. He might have gone on to do amazing things, perhaps even help save our realm. What if he was a key player, necessary for our victory? We'll never know, because he'll never have the chance, and it's my fault.

—Why am I bein' flooded with sadness? Whatever you're thinkin', stop.—

I sigh. Killian is right. In the past, I would have broken down over something like this. At least for a little while. I've never enjoyed ending a life. But. I won't break down, not this time. I defended myself, yes, but also Killian and Biscuit. I can bring myself to regret only the need to act.

Nico made his choices, and I made mine. What's done is done.

Now I wonder how many other lovers Victor left behind. Who else will attack in his name?

And, oh, zero! All this focus on death reminds me of Aunt Lina's message. I jolt before tensing from head to toe. She thinks she's going to kill Killian. Has she foreseen his death?

My stomach twists into those hated knots, wringing out acid. I've never had the power to change her visions, but then, I've never before known they were, in fact, visions. This time, I can take precautions.

—*So. What do you plan to do with Shamus when you reach him?*—

Good question. —*I'll Daze him and, with Clementine's help, transport him to the house. Boom. Done.*—

—*If the Bucklers are down, sure. You can use your comm to transport. Good plan. If Bucklers are still up, you'll have to drag the man across the realm. And we both know citizens will not be lookin' the other way when they see a General being hauled down the street like luggage.*—

Ugh. He just had to go and make a good point, didn't he. —*What do you suggest?*—

—*You already know the answer, you just don't want to do it. Now slow down. You're approachin' a fork, and I need to figure out which way you should go.*—

I ignore his comment about knowing what to do…because he's right. —*How can you tell? About the fork, I mean.*— The gloom hasn't thinned, is still all-consuming.

—*Subtle nuances in darkness. Trust me.*—

—*I did…once. Look what it got me.*— A groom with no memory.

Silence. And it's like poking a bear with a stick. The anger currently lying dormant inside me yawns and stretches, close to wakefulness. My hands fist.

When I reach the fork, as predicted, I pause, as commanded. I'm told: —*Go right.*—

—*How do you know?*—

—*You are bound to Troika, and I am bound to you. I feel what you feel. There's a charge when you shift right, but no charge when you shift left.*—

Right again.

My heart rate spikes as I round the corner. Up ahead, a spark of Light glows. More of the princess's Light? Like a moth to a flame, I surge forward. Must get closer. Strength awaits.

—*Stop!*—

Killian shouts the command, jarring me enough to stop me. Biscuit bumps into the back of my leg, and I stumble forward another step.

—*What's wrong?*— My heart is ready to pound its way out of my chest.

—*Look down.*—

My gaze drops, and I gasp. Through the Light, I spy a row of zigzagging spikes that extend from the ground, ready to rip me to ribbons.

—*Thank you.*— "Careful," I whisper to Biscuit.

Together, we tiptoe, hop and wind our way past the spikes.

—*In roughly one hundred feet, there's a room on the right.*—

—*I'm not going to ask how you know. Not again.*— No way he can miss the grumble in my tone. I palm the mini-Dazer, my finger hovering over the trigger.

Kill Shamus. He dared take Killian from you. He must learn the error of his ways.

Not Killian, not this time, but me. The darkest part of me. I stumble as the desire for bloodshed overwhelms me.

Resist! My teeth gnash. Must ignore her—or me. I'll Daze Shamus, nothing more.

Once again I surge forward, this time counting my steps. Two...ten...thirty...ninety...

At long last, I reach this newest Light. Killian claimed the room is on the right, but the Light shines from the left. I'm about to step in that direction when the tiny hairs on the back of my neck stand at attention. Electrical impulses. From the Light. A trick?

I turn to the right—

Something hard slams into my jaw. I careen to the side,

sharp pain exploding through my face, stars winking in the back of my mind.

Killian hisses. Biscuit growls.

A booted foot kicks my stomach, and I careen once again, stumbling toward the Light, then through it. Lasers! Shadows scream and claw at my skull, sharp pains shooting through my temples.

No time to recover. Another kick. The Dazer flies out of my hand and skids across the ground, and it *does* reach the Light. Oh, yeah. Definitely electrical impulses. A new kind of laser. The gun disintegrates.

—*Attack!*— A command from Killian, the white-hot burn of his rage crackling, inciting my shadows. —*He isn't allowed to hurt you.*—

Kill. End your enemies, end your problems… A true temptation.

With a grunt, I fling myself at my opponent. He reels backward, and we fall into a spacious and well-lit room. No time to appreciate the finer aspects of the decor. Or the fact that Biscuit can't pass the lasers on the door. In the Light, my attacker's identity registers. General Shamus. I'm not surprised, only disappointed he's willing to harm me in order to keep Killian behind bars.

We spring apart and face off.

Though Shamus is taller and stronger than me, and far more experienced, I refuse to back down. I've taken down bigger and stronger.

"You shouldna have come here. You'll never convince me to leave with you, and I'll never decide it's a good idea to free the Butcher." He pops the bones in his neck. "You're part Myriadian now, and it's clear Troika isn't, and will never be, your top priority."

"And you, the guy who broke Troika's law to love his fellow citizens—to do no harm to one another—are a shining example of putting Troika first?"

He flinches.

Unfortunately for him, I'm not done. "If you only love the lovable, you're no better than the Myriadians you hate. You know that, don't you?"

"They killed my wife. I have good reason to hate them." His dark eyes are wild, his body vibrating with rage of his own. Or is his darkness fueled by mine? "She was a Messenger, had no battle experience, and wanted none. Like you, she craved peace. One day, she was in the Land of the Harvest, helping a human, when an ML spotted her and…" His hands fist. "He beheaded her. She'd done nothing wrong. Nothing! And he killed her."

—*Enough conversation. Take him out.*—

—*You mean do your dirty work for you?*—

Argh! Push, pull. Why am I doing this? Why am I fighting so hard to free a boy who plans to betray me? And he *does* plan to betray me, doesn't he?

The answer fills my head, and it is as simple as it is complicated. Plans can be changed. I have hope. Hope that Killian will remember our past. Hope that I will reach him. Hope that we didn't destroy our futures but can strive for better.

"I'm sorry for your loss, Shamus." I hurt for him. I really do. "Tell me true. Is Killian her murderer?"

He blusters for a moment. "What does that matter? A Myriadian is a Myriadian."

"Do you really believe that? Is one Troikan the same as any other Troikan?" As his cheeks darken, I demand, "Is. Killian. Her. Murderer?"

"No," he finally snarls.

"Then your vendetta isn't against Killian. Stop this. You

are a General. The best of us. So be the best! Set an example
of love and forgiveness." I give my words a second to sink in,
pray they do. "Enough people have died. It's time for peace."

"As if we could ever trust Myriadians to keep a peace treaty.
We would merely set ourselves up for slaughter. Again! Do
you think we never tried your route in all these millennia?
We did, and we suffered for it."

Why are we not taught about the attempt(s)? Let me guess.
For the same reason we're not told about inter-realm bonding.
To weed out the fools. "The Prince of Ravens is to blame."
Everything I've learned about him tells me this. If he were a
tree, his people would be his branches, feeding off him. He
lies and cheats. Envies and steals. "When he's gone, the shadows will die." They must. You can prune the branches, but
to kill the tree, you must uproot it. "Myriadians will be free
of their influence." Killian will be free.

I will be free.

"*You* are supposed to be the best of us, Conduit, and yet
you gave a key to our Grid to the Butcher!"

Zero! It's like I'm punching at the wind, getting nowhere.
"He's lost people, too." His mother. Archer. And at one point,
even me. Having seen into Killian's past, the constant rejections from potential families, the General who beat him and
made him beg, I may never get over my guilt and remorse,
or my desire to hurt those who hurt Killian.

I know nine Myriadian Generals died the day of my birth,
his greatest tormentor among them. Deep down, I'm kind
of…glad.

"Your compassion has ruined us," Shamus informs me.

Where is that compassion now? "No." I shake my head.
"*Your* lack of compassion ruined you a long time ago."

My words push him over the edge. With a war cry, he

hurls his big body at me. We bang together and fall. I take the brunt of impact as we slam against a table, shattering its legs. Pain sears me. As I sprawl over the remains, Shamus's heavy weight shoves the air from my lungs. Empty.

Stars wink before my eyes. Fear mixes with anger and congeals, becoming a hard lump I can't swallow. I've lost the fight before it ever really began? Unacceptable!

In one seemingly fluid movement, he maneuvers to his knees, straddling me and cocking his fist, ready to whale. I hold up my arms, blocking him. At the same time, I anchor a finger through each of the metal hooks on my wrist cuffs and stretch the two wires across the open space between us. His fist tangles in the wires, momentum shredding skin and muscle. Glittering Lifeblood pours and splatters over my face as Shamus bellows with agony.

Guilt makes a play, trying to overwhelm me, but I resist. How can I hurt a General? Easily.

Before he can try to land another blow, I jerk upright and slam the heel of my palm into his nose. Cartilage snaps, and a new bellow assaults my ears. More Lifeblood pours down his chin.

Determined, knowing I have a very small advantage, I work my legs out from under him, flatten my feet on his chest and push. I expect him to soar backward, but he's too strong and merely tilts.

Frustration mounts. *Think, Ten. Think!*

No time. He snaps upright and throws a punch. I kick up my leg, his fist meeting my thigh rather than my face. A saving grace. When he draws back his elbow to throw yet another punch, I react on instinct, wrapping both my legs around his neck and squeezing with all my might.

Threat… Must kill…

Guilt and remorse return, redoubled, reminding me of my choices. Find another way or deal with the consequences.

Is there another way?

He strains and pulls at me, but cannot free himself, and I force him to the ground. Momentum lifts my upper body and, with a screech of aggravation, I release him at last, spinning away while on my knees. I kick out my leg, my boot slamming into his jaw.

Killian is silent, providing no distractions for me. *Appreciate it.*

Fast as lightning, Shamus grabs my ankle and yanks, planting me on my back, the short swords clinking. In seconds, he has my legs tied together. Once again, I jolt upright, but this time he's ready and punches *me* in the jaw. Pain! The bone snaps out of place, annihilating the joint.

There's a slight ringing in my ears, but I think I hear Killian roar. Again, the desire to kill bombards me.

Must resist!

As panic knocks on the door of my mind, I fall back, punting Shamus in the face with my bound feet. Hissing, bleeding, he reaches for my arms, probably intending to bind my wrists, too. But I kick up my legs again, blocking him, before contorting my body. I swipe the space between my ankles over the tip of a short sword, and the rope is rendered useless.

A cool tide of relief propels me to my feet. Problem: Shamus palms a gun. Not a Dazer, meant to stun me, but a revolver, meant to maim. He aims, fires. The bullet whizzes through my hand, cracking bones and tearing muscles, and a cry leaves me. The newest wound throbs. Other sore spots make themselves known. Warm Lifeblood pours from the wound, weakening me, and I drop the sword.

My relief is gone, wiped away as if extinct. Helplessness hurries to launch a coup.

—*Ten!*— Killian is a commanding presence in my head, and he refuses to be ignored. —*Kill him. Kill him* now. *Before it's too late.*—

I can see Biscuit prowling behind the lasers, as if he's considering risking his life to enter the room.

"No," I shout, my heart galloping at warp speed. "Don't. Please."

Shamus takes aim a second time. Target: right between my eyes. Decided he's better off with me dead?

Cold fingers of dread creep down my spine as shadows flicker inside his eyes. Because of me. Because I welcomed the darkness. He was right about that, at least. Or maybe he's always had shadows, like me, and they're just now coming to light.

Maybe we *all* have shadows.

"You doona yet understand the price of betrayal." He radiates fury. Letting his emotions get the better of him. "But I'm going to teach you. As a General, it's my job to teach you."

An eye for an eye, a hurt for a hurt. This is a recipe for disaster.

But even faced with defeat, I will not buckle. I will fight for what I believe is right.

"How can I learn anything if I'm dead?" Every word is agony, my jaw unhinged. I hold up my hands, palms out. Pretend innocence. "But go ahead. Do what you think you must." *Just as I will.*

Killian protests, loudly. —*What are you doin'? No! Accept nothin' but survival. Fight this. Fight* him.—

"Trying to spur me into killing you?" Shamus stalks to-

ward me. "Too bad, little girl. You're going to face a jury of
your peers and answer for your crimes."

—*If you doona take him down, Tenley Lockwood, I'll find a way
tae survive without you and tear this realm apart.*—

My eyes narrow, my lids heavy with fury of my own.
—*Isn't that your plan, anyway?*—

A pause. Then, —*Tenley. Ten.*—

His tone beseeches me. Seduction is his default, after all. I
ignore it—ignore him. I must.

The second Shamus is within reach, with every intention of
binding me, I swing my arm. I've learned from my mistakes.
With Nico, I hesitated and second-guessed myself. Too bad
for Shamus I'm all systems go now. Full steam ahead.

He doesn't see the shard hidden between my fingers. Then,
he doesn't see *anything*. The tip jabs into one of his eyes, then
the other. With a scream, he drops the gun to reach for his
face. Cold as ice, I act swiftly, hooking my leg behind his and
sending him to his knees. He hits the ground, and I press my
boot into his back, holding him down.

Kill him. My darker side. Again, I ignore it.

What will I do for my realm? For Killian? Anything.

"I meant what I said." Shamus is panting, and there's Lifeblood on his teeth. "I won't leave with you."

"That's okay. You can stay." I clasp the hilt of my other
sword and raise my arm. Then, not giving myself time to
second-guess my actions, I swing the weapon down, down,
and remove one of his hands.

TROIKA

From: R_A_5/40.5.16
To: T_L_2/23.43.2
Subject: Bad news/worse news

Check it. I'm outside the warehouse with Pop Tart, and we're peeking into the windows. We count roughly 100 humans. But there's no telling how many are inside the rooms *without* windows. Everyone is snoozing, and strapped to gurneys. Here's the thing that's got my Spidey senses tingling. There's no Myriadian Buckler up. Nothing to keep me from storming inside and going crazy on potential Abrogates.

Why aren't they protected to the max? Why aren't MLs here, acting as guards?

The only answer that makes sense: Myriad wants us to break in. This is a trap. I mean, they know we'll be desperate to sneak inside to pull the plugs before any of the humans wake up and spread Penumbra.

Okay, here's the worse news.

I know, I know. You thought you'd already heard it. Nope. Brace yourself.

Sloan Aubuchon is trapped inside. (I've never met her, but the Grid filled me in.) She's nailed to a pole, as if she's a Myriadian scarecrow. She's awake, and when she spotted us through the window, her eyes went wide and she flashed the number 6 (3 fingers from each hand, flashed 3 times, like Morse code or something). There's a gag in her mouth, so she can't call for help—or warn us about a trap.

Tell me what you think is the best plan of action. If I agree, we'll do it.

Light Brings Sight!
Conduit-in-training,
Raanan Aarons

TROIKA

From: T_L_2/23.43.2
To: R_A_5/40.5.16
Subject: 6...6...6

Do not enter the warehouse. I repeat, do not enter the warehouse. At least not until we figure out Sloan's message. As much as I want to help her, I don't want to lose you to an ambush. (And when you do invade, make sure she's protected.)

Now. Let's figure this out. Sloan and I go way back, spent more than a year locked in Prynne Asylum together. The number might deal with our confinement. But if that's the case, there are too many possibilities.

The sixth girl to die at Prynne...the sixth guard to die... our sixth class...my sixth roommate...our sixth fight...our six a.m. alarm...our sixth day together...our *sixty-sixth* day together... None of it means anything to me, though.

666—the universal sign for evil. Betrayal is evil.

6 + 6 + 6 = 18. Eighteen alarms. Eighteen bombs. Only eighteen Abrogates.

Argon has the atomic number 18, and is the third-most abundant gas in the Earth's atmosphere. Louisiana became the 18th state of the United States.

Whatever the answer, I agree with you. Myriad has set some kind of a trap.

Continue to watch the warehouse. Let me know if anything changes or anyone enters, leaves or even approaches. We'll design a game plan when we have more information.

Update: I've got the key to Killian's cage. I'm headed back to the house.

Light Brings Sight!
Conduit and Architect,
Ten Lockwood

chapter eleven

"You have a treasure hidden inside you. If you take it for
granted, you will lose it."
—Troika

Killian

My connection with Ten ends abruptly, my mind going blank.
I fight to reestablish the link to no avail.

Curses tumble from my lips. She was punched, kicked and
shot. She's in pain. I know, because searing pain throbs in *my*
jaw and hand. She's losing Lifeblood fast.

I shouldn't care about her sorry condition. The bond is
responsible for my concern, nothing more. Plus, with a little manna she'll be as good as new. But I do care, and it has
nothing to do with saving my own hide. The girl genuinely
likes me. She might be the only one in the realms who does.
I'm not yet ready to lose her.

Going to lose her, anyway. One day. Why not now?

Because…just because!

Be at peace. She is strong. Capable. She will return to you.

My voice, courtesy of my Troikan side. And that's exactly what it is. Troikan Light, a gift from Ten. Strangely

enough, I'm beginning to like him. Or rather, me. Like myself. Whatever.

My eyes flutter open. I'm crouched in the corner of my cage, my nose pressed into the wall. Must have given myself a time-out, to better block out the rush of activity that's taking place around me.

What if someone attacks Ten before she finds manna? Biscuit will guard her to the best of his ability, but what if his abilities aren't enough? How are they going to sneak past the armies to reach the house?

Forget peace. I worry.

As I try, again, to reach Ten through the bond, my fingers rub at the numbers tattooed atop the horse brand. 143, 10. Earlier I noticed Ten has 143, 11.9.12.12.9.1.14 tattooed on *her* wrist, and to my surprise, it doesn't take me long to decipher the meanings.

I love you, Ten

I love you, Killian

The knowledge steals the air from my lungs. I did. I loved her. *That* is why I bonded with her.

Numbers always tell a story, and they never lie.

Is this how I felt after meeting her for the very first time, all twisted up, like a vine wrapped around barbed wire?

Why remember the tattoo, though? Why now?

She thinks I need to learn to trust her without emotion.

The answer slams into me, stealing the air from my lungs a second time. I do trust her. Just a little, but enough. I trust her not to harm me. A little trust, a little memory.

If I want to remember everything else, I need to trust her fully, with the fate of my realm? No, sorry. Asking too much.

My ears twitch as the sounds of battle register. The growl of the dogs. The roar of the cats. The chorus of sounds from the other animals. Snorts, screeches, caws, bleats and brays. Marching footsteps—then racing footsteps. Shouts. Not a single gun goes off, however. The TLs must not want to shoot the animals.

"Fall back, fall back!" Deacon's bellow echoes from beyond the house. "They're using some sort of sleeping gas."

I stand, and scan my surroundings. Only a few feet away, a side table is overturned, an unconscious Archer splayed in front of it, his body twitching. Seizing? He must have been standing at the bars of my cage, trying to get my attention, when he passed out.

Bea is licking his face.

Dawn is crouched beside him, pale and trembling, staring at an empty syringe as if it has let her down in the worst possible way. Her deer waits beside her. "Whatever they did to him, he's not responding."

They? Troikan soldiers?

"What happened?" I demand.

"He went outside," she says. "When he came back in, there was a dart in his neck. I pulled it out and he collapsed."

Some type of drug then. "Give him more manna." The more severe the trauma, the more medicine—strength—a spirit needs. Every word agonizes my jaw. "Give me some, too." Maybe I'll heal. Maybe I'll strengthen Ten through the bond.

"I'm *out* of manna," Dawn says, her gaze tormented. "And I don't know if I'd give him more, anyway. The first dose made him worse, I think."

Some people thrive under pressure, like Ten. Some people fall apart, like Dawn. "The soldiers wouldn't do anything that would lead to the death of one of their own. They had to know we'd give him manna. Maybe they want you to think he's worse after with manna, so you won't give him any more. Do it, and see what happens. This is a soldier's quarters. Soldiers get injured. There's more manna, guaranteed." *Ignore the pain.* "Check everywhere."

"Everywhere. Right." She climbs to her feet and rushes around the house, her deer following her every move.

I waste no time, sitting and shoving my legs through the bars. With my feet braced on either side of Archer's neck, I pull him toward me. Bea lunges at my ankles, and bites. When I run my hands along every inch of Archer's body, finding only a single dagger—*will have to do*—she bites my wrists.

Kill him…no better time…

The urge bombards and overwhelms me, rousing the new Mary Sue side of me.

Harm a defenseless man, and you harm your soul.

Maybe I *don't* like the Light side of me. Troikan proverbs? No, thanks. But still I pocket the weapon and shove Archer back into place, Bea calming. Ten cut off a man's hand for me. In return, I'll let her best friend live.

Mistake! If I plan to raze this realm to the ground, I've got to start somewhere, with someone.

And I will. Maybe. Definitely. Just not with Archer Prince.

The healer and her guardian return with a first aid kit. Unaware of what's transpired, Dawn administers a second dose of manna. Archer begins shaking more. White foam forms at the corners of his mouth.

"What do I do?" she asks, her voice hoarse.

"Give him a third dose," I say.

"But—"

"Do it!"

The deer rams his antlers into my cage, rattling the bars. A warning, I'm sure.

Trembling, she obeys me. "You're not going to die—again!—on my watch." She slaps his cheek, hard. "Do you hear me? You're not going to die." Another slap.

Finally, a moan slips from him, and his terrible shaking stops.

As she expels a heavy sigh of relief, Bea dances atop Archer's chest.

With a trembling hand, Dawn offers me a vial of manna. "Depending on the strength of your bond to Myriad, this will hurt you worse or help you. At least, I'm assuming. I've never met someone bonded to both realms."

I accept the vial with muttered thanks and, after a slight hesitation, take a sip. Warmth. A twinge of pain. But my jaw does begin to heal.

Does Ten's?

As I drain the rest, the door bursts open. Deacon and a Messenger I recognize as Clay Anders rush inside, animals close on their heels. A pit bull and a zebra.

The house is basically a zoo.

"Reed was captured, so the troops are backing off. They are ready to bargain." Deacon spots Archer on the floor and rushes to his side. Bea offers no protests, turning her attention to the pit bull to lick his face. "What happened?"

Dawn chews on her bottom lip. "Archer was drugged. He—"

"What did you do?" Deacon's emerald gaze finds me and narrows.

For once I can honestly say, "Blame someone else. He went outside, and he got plugged. Now forget him. He'll recover. Probably. One of you needs to track down Ten. *Now*. Shamus injured her. As you can see." I motion to my body. My jaw is out of place, and there are cuts all over my torso and limbs.

As Clay pets his zebra, he looks me over and pales. "You could have hurt yourself just to hurt her."

Ignore the pain. And the accusation. "She has no manna, and no way to get manna without being spotted by angry mobs determined to punish her for choosing to bring Archy-boy back to life."

His stride long and strong, Clay closes the distance. Scowling, he shakes the bars of my cage. "If she's hurt because of you..."

"You'll what?" I ask. "Tell me I've been a bad boy?"

Deacon stands and places a hand on his shoulder, quieting him. "Don't listen to him. We can't trust a single word from his mouth. So, if he wants us to leave, we'll stay put."

No, they can't. I can't even trust myself anymore. And yet, still anger burns inside me. Their *inaction* hurts Ten.

Fools! If they won't go after her, I will. Even if I have to break every bone in my body in order to slip through the bars. Or, maybe I can claw through the metal. Either way, nothing will stop me.

This is my fault, not theirs. I've sown dissention. Now I reap it.

Argh! I'm 100 percent certain now. I loathe my Troikan side.

Deacon crouches to pat Archer's cheek once, twice, a gentle wake-up call. My former best friend moans as his eyelids flutter open.

"Hey, man." Smiling with relief, Deacon helps Archer ease to a sitting position. "You okay?"

Before he can respond, the house shakes, the foundation rattling. I tense. Another bomb blast? No, couldn't be. There wasn't an initial blast or ensuing boom.

"The soldiers managed to override our Buckler with one of their own," Clay says. "I bet they just lowered it."

Yes. Makes sense. Now that General John has his bargaining

chip, he doesn't need to force his opposition to remain inside the house. They'll stay of their own accord in hopes of saving Reed.

This. This is why having friends...or a bonded mate... makes you vulnerable. When you stand alone, no one can be used against you.

"Take posts at each of the windows," Deacon instructs the animals. They rush to obey.

In the center of the room, a flash of Light arcs from the ceiling to the floor. I tense all over again, expecting John to appear, ready to deliver his terms: Reed's life in exchange for everyone's cooperation. But it is Ten and Biscuit who appear.

My heart slams against my ribs; I'm hit by shock, delight and fear all at once. She's pale and trembling, but her jaw isn't out of place. Her clothes are soaked in Lifeblood. In her hand is *Shamus's* hand.

I jump to my feet, propelled by a surge of adrenaline; it's like rocket fuel has been poured into my veins. "Ten."

Her wild, mismatched gaze finds me. We share a stolen moment of relief: she's here, we're together again, and all will be well. Then she collapses, hitting the ground with a thud.

My own knees begin to quake. The manna I consumed did, in fact, aid her, but not enough. "Help her," I shout. "Or my new mission in life will be killin' every single one of you."

"She needs manna," Biscuit barks. "Get some, like, now, or get bit."

"I have more," Dawn says, her voice hoarse once again.

I curse my helplessness as the Healer removes the last syringe from the first aid kit. The rest of the group swarms her, crouching and blocking Ten from my view. Even Archer. With a moan, he lumbers to his knees and crawls to her.

My hands fist, and my teeth grind, but I say nothing. Must keep my cool. Perception is reality. To protest is to reveal my thoughts and emotions to my enemies, and that I will not do. Knowledge is power.

That phrase. It's familiar to me. I think... I think Ten has said it to me.

Are more of my memories returning?

I back away from the action and sit down, leaning against the wall, keeping my expression blank. No one who glances my way will suspect my heart is galloping as if I'm in the middle of a race. Who cares about my memories right now? I need to know if Ten will pull through.

She must. What's the worst that can happen? She dies, causing me to die? So what? I'll be reborn.

Doubt immediately flickers. What if Ten is right? What if I'm not reborn, but a prisoner of Many Ends?

Why do Myriadians go to Many Ends and Troikans enter into the Rest?

The shadows sink their claws deeper into my mind...hiding the answer from me? With a snarl, I slam my fists into my temples, attempting to dislodge the block—failing. The throbbing pain in my hands eases, at least, and my jaw aligns.

"She's responding," Dawn says, her tone now as bubbly as champagne. "She's going to be okay."

Cheers ring out. Everyone hugs everyone else.

I'm Ten's husband, but I'm not her family. Nor am I a part of this celebration. As always, I'm an outsider looking in. And that's the way I like it. Can't forget—I'm better off on my own.

So why do I feel like a fire poker is being shoved through my rib cage?

Easy answer: The manna must not have healed the bulk of Ten's wounds.

"Where's Reed?" she asks as she sits up.

Silence. The others look at themselves, clearly trying to decide what to tell her.

I strain my eyes to look past other people's limbs...think I see her profile. She appears strong, steady.

"Where is Reed?" she asks again. "Tell me."

"General John took him," I say. She deserves the truth.

Deacon slants me a death glare.

What? *Rip the bandage, TL, before she rips you apart.* "John hasn't listed his demands yet, but we can guess what he wants. Control over me, and therefore you."

Her shoulders droop. "You guys aren't the only ones with bad news. Nico is... Well, there's no easy way to tell you. He's dead. He attacked me, desperate to violate his covenant so he could defect to Myriad without the hassle of a trial. He wanted to be with Victor and I... I just... I'm sorry."

Archer scrubs a hand down his face. "I'm sorry. I should have seen my brother's evil heart. I know him better than most. Or thought I did. I should have stopped him before I died."

I've lost track of Ten, the others' movements keeping her well hidden, until she reaches out to twine her fingers with Archer's, offering comfort. Hell, no.

If realm covenants can be broken without court, marriage covenants can be broken without court.

Has she decided Archer is the better man for her?

—*Look at me.*— My heart projects the command directly at Ten, without permission from my mind. My Troikan side needs her within sight *now*.

To my relief, she stands and pushes through the crowd, leaving the severed hand on the floor—out of my reach. Her gaze seeks mine. *Everyone's* gaze seeks mine. The color has returned to her cheeks, her skin luminous. My hands itch to hold her, almost as if they remember her softness even though I do not.

My Myriadian side says, *Reveal nothing.* I force a yawn.

She takes a step toward me, stops. Head high, she asks, "Have I starred in any new memories?"

In an effort to drag a reaction from her, I pucker my lips as if I just tasted a lemon. She's taken a page from my book, her tone neutral, disguising her emotions. Tables, turned. It sucks.

The pulse in her neck pounds—with nervousness at what I might have recalled? Success! "Only our tattoos," I reply. "One. Four. Three. Ten." *I love you, Ten.* "The tattoos, and the reason for them, change nothing."

Hurt sizzles the bond, and my guilt flares.

Biscuit trots to her and shoves his nose where the sun doesn't shine, probably hoping to lighten the mood. Yelping, she jumps away. The dog grins and licks her hand.

All right. Fine. I admit it. I like him.

"Got you a present." Tenley tosses my ring through the cage bars. The one Shamus stole. I catch it, the sight and feel of it comforting me on a level I don't quite understand. "Try to take better care of it this time."

What I think she means: *Take better care of my heart.*

My guilt magnifies. "I willna thank you."

Shrug. She removes the wrist cuffs and tosses those through the bars, as well.

I reel. She's not just releasing me, she's arming me.

"Go," she tells the others, her gaze never straying from me. "Work with the Generals. Save Reed."

Protests erupt as I strap the cuffs in place. Only Biscuit remains silent.

"You guys have to turn your backs on me," she says. "There's no other way. Tell the Generals absolutely everything they want to know. The princess will help Raanan cleanse

the Abrogates and save Sloan. He's going to need more Light
than I can give him."

New protests ring out.

"I'll go with Raanan," Deacon says. "I'll watch over Sloan."

Ten nods. "I'll free Killian, and we'll be long gone before
they can stop us. Mostly, I'd rather you were as far away from
us as possible. If Killian were to hurt one of you—"

"All of you," I correct.

Her eyes narrow, the first sign of trouble. "I'd have to hurt
him, which would in turn hurt *me*."

"There's no way I'll betray you," Archer says, lifting his
chin. "Not now, not ever."

"You're not betraying me," she replies. "You're *helping* me."

"And now you're irritating me."

Their easy camaraderie irritates *me*. As my wife, she should
banter with me, and only me.

Archer rubs the back of his neck. "Killian could evade you
and turn his sights to the destruction of the realm."

"Yes. He's told me." She smiles at me slowly, coldly. "But
he's as bound to Troika as he is to me. He might fight the
connection, but it's there. Hurting our realm will weaken
him, and he will never purposely weaken himself."

She isn't wrong.

Frustration mounts. All right. New plan. *Escape without
harming Troika. Return to Myriad with Ten. Find a way to break
our bond. Give her to Ambrosine. Receive a promotion.*

Different pangs raze my chest. First guilt. Then remorse.
Finally loss.

Ignore. Focus on the prize. Maybe, when all of this is over,
I'll enjoy my life for once.

Or hate myself more than ever.

"Don't go," Deacon says. "You'll be on your own in Myriad,

surrounded by the enemy. I doubt you'll escape. What are we supposed to tell your brother then, huh?"

I bite my cheek to stifle a snarl. He's trying to manipulate her. I know, because I've often done the same thing to others.

"Someone has to stand in the gap," she says. "For those who won't, or can't. So you'll tell Jeremy I love him." Tears fill her eyes, but she blinks them away. "That I died fighting for what I believe in. Peace, and salvation for the damned. You'll tell him I regret nothing."

Her words shut down any other protests.

She hugs Clay, Raanan, Dawn and Deacon, then Archer. His hug lasts seconds longer.

I'm grinding my molars all over again. Jealousy has never been part of my playbook, and I'm not sure how to deal. Well, besides killing Archer.

The idea has merit. *Should have struck while I had the chance.* Ten would never forgive me, of course, so even if I continued to want her, I'd never be able to have her. Two birds, one stone. Or dagger.

Finally, everyone but Ten and Biscuit takes off. The dog hangs back, determined to stick to her side. "Protect my friends while I'm gone."

"Nope. Sorry. Where you go, I go." His tone is petulant.

How quickly the dog has bonded to her. I bite my cheek until I taste blood. How quickly *I* bonded to her.

Frowning, Ten presses a hand against *her* cheek. "Please," she says to Biscuit. "I'm begging you."

I jerk with astonishment. Begging. She's begging. Has no concept of the damage she's doing to her pride. I want to close my eyes, cover my ears. For a moment, my chest feels as if acid has been poured inside.

"You're so strong, Biscuit," she adds. "You can protect my friends while I'm away. Please. I need them protected."

A pause. Then a sigh. "Fine. I'll do it. But you had better return—or I'll go digging for bones *inside your friends*." He presses a paw against her before running out the door.

With a sigh of her own, Ten picks up the General's severed hand. Steps slow; a bit unsure, she approaches my cage.

"Shall we bargain for my freedom?" I ask before she can speak. She has conditions for my release, no doubt. If I seem eager to participate, she'll be more likely to believe I'll keep my word.

"No," she says with a shake of her head. "I can't trust you to keep your word."

Ouch.

She's not the first to say so, but she's the first I'm unwilling to charm out of her pique. An action that has always proven necessary in order to win spirits for Myriad. Necessary, and annoying.

Being free to act like myself is, well, freeing.

"You're right," I say. "You can't trust me."

"Right now, the only things you need to know about me are...I always tell the truth, and I never threaten. I promise."

"So you've told me."

"I know, but with your memory problems, a girl can't be too careful. So. Here's how this is gonna go."

"Do tell." I make a sweeping gesture with my hand, a royal prince demanding more information. I like this side of her, bossy and prickly but also vulnerable.

"I'll let you out. As we travel through Troika, you'll stick to my side like glue, or I'll shoot you and drag you to Myriad. There, I'll prove Many Ends is connected. We'll kill your Secondking and save...everyone. We'll find your mother, and my friend Marlowe. We'll free your friend Erica. Not too long ago, you told me she had been locked in the Kennels."

Erica Morales. One of my Flankers. She aided me when I asked, putting her eternal future at risk. I owe her.

I gulp as anticipation goes head-to-head with dread. If Ten is right, and Many Ends *is* connected to Myriad, my mother has been tortured every year of my life. Rescuing her will be priority one. I'll need Ten's help.

But helping Ten means betraying my king, a man I greatly admire.

Ambrosine is the epitome of power. Beyond ruthless. Savage when necessary. And yet, he took a chance on me when no others were willing. Every time I've won a new soul for our realm, he's praised me, given me boons. Once I asked for the head of the Myriadian General who tortured me as a child, and made me beg for every scrap of food—even beg for beatings I didn't want.

My body shudders. It amused him to break my spirit, I suppose.

While the Secondking refused to grant that particular wish, he *did* grant me time with the General. Time to mete vengeance. *He* begged *me* for mercy I refused to show.

I can't betray my king. Not even to save my mother.

Not even to save Ten.

"What happens if I betray you the moment we're inside Myriad?" *Heed my warning, beautiful girl. It's the only one I'll give.*

Her shoulders wilt a little. "Let's deal with one problem at a time."

TROIKA

From: J_B_3/19.23.4
To: T_L_2/23.43.2
Subject: Do not make me harm your friend

Miss Lockwood,

As you know, I have captured Reed Haynesworth. I also have Kayla Brooks in my possession. We had to drag her out of her sickbed, but desperate times…

I assure you, I don't want to harm the two. Violence is never my first choice. Over the centuries I have learned to make hard choices, and do what needs doing for the good of the people. Mr. Haynesworth and Miss Brooks will be released the moment you turn yourself in. You will stand before a jury of your peers and explain your actions these past few days. You will accept punishment, whatever it is, and help us cleanse the humans infected with—well, there's no need for me to say the word. You know it.

Until each of my requirements have been met...
I *will* harm your friends.

Light Brings Sight!
General John Blake

TROIKA

From: T_L_2/23.43.2
To: J_B_3/19.23.4
Subject: You don't know me very well

Dear General Blake,

When it comes to saving the humans infected by Penumbra, we're of the same mind. Although I'm not afraid to say the P-word. Penumbra. PENUMBRA. We are stronger than the disease. Let's act like it.

BTW. You have a new Conduit in your midst. He can cleanse the Abrogates in the warehouse. Yes, I said *he*. Raanan Aarons. He's ready to be of service. The princess can help him the way she once helped me.

And before you wonder if this is really Ten Lockwood talking/typing, don't. At one time, delegating work would have been the equivalent of stabbing myself in the heart. Now, not so much. I know my people, and they are spectacular.

You can break Reed's and Kayla's bodies, but not their

spirits. Or mine. Even if you hurt my friends, you will not change my mind. However, you will darken your soul. The concept is found in our *Book of the Law*. I suggest an immediate reread.

If you harm your own people, you are no better than the Myriadians you fight.

Face it. Your plan has been rendered moot. I'm leaving Troika today, entering Myriad—and Many Ends.

Don't worry about Killian. He's going with me. In fact, by the time you read this message, he and I will *both* be gone.

I'm led by three things, General. Loyalty to my realm, passion for the truth and liberty for all. You will not stop me.

Light Brings Sight!
Conduit and Architect,
Ten Lockwood

TROIKA

From: J_B_3/19.23.4
To: T_L_2/23.43.2
Subject: You put yourself in danger—and all of us

Architect? Never heard of it.

As for Mr. Aarons…what you want me to believe is impossible. A Laborer cannot become a Conduit.

Leave this realm, and I will break one bone in one of your friends' bodies every day that you are gone.

Actions have consequences, Miss Lockwood.

Light Brings Sight!
General John Blake

PART TWO

Myriad

TROIKA

From: A_P_5/23.43.2
To: T_L_2/23.43.2
Subject: Guess what?

Per your orders—when did you become so bossy, anyway?—
we told the Generals about your plan to free the spirits in
Many Ends. They're pretty sure you're going to die, but we
have faith in you.

Also, Biscuit rocks. He rallied Reed's and Kayla's guardians—
a parrot and a mountain lion—and bingo bango, they rescued Reed and Kayla. (Can I keep the dog, Mom? Huh, huh,
please, can I?)

Everything went down in a matter of minutes. No one
knew what hit 'em.

All the Generals are frenzied. Not about the prisoners
they lost, but about Raanan. He returned just long enough
to confirm his new Conduit status.

Oh, and you'll be happy to know the princess has agreed

to aid Raanan in his cleansing efforts. Three cheers. The first part of your plan worked. Let's just hope the next part does as well.

Deacon is determined to get in the warehouse and rescue Sloan, Myriad's version of a scarecrow, I guess. I'm not sure how much longer we'll be able to keep him out.

But. You'll be happier to know we're all fine, and so is the realm. (I probably should have led with that. My bad.)

Stay safe, or I will spank you till you scream for mercy. ←Not a joke. And I know I don't have to ask you to check on Dior, and keep me updated.

Light Brings Sight!
Archer Prince

chapter twelve

"The best treasure is total domination of your enemies."
—Myriad

Ten

I'm either the dumbest girl in all the realms…or the second dumbest. If I'm second dumbest, I feel sorry for the ditz ahead of me, because wow. She's a few clowns short of a circus. Let's be real. If she had a second brain, it would be lonely, her intellect rivaled only by her garden tools.

I armed a boy who practically guaranteed he'll betray me, all because I hope that he *won't*. Now, I'm going to free him.

See? Dumb. To achieve my goals, I'm willing to risk everything. So maybe I'm actually a genius. I mean, let's face it. Sometimes the world's definition of "foolish" is actually wisdom at work.

At least Reed is safe. And Kayla, apparently. All thanks to Biscuit. And, with the princess's help, Raanan is going to cleanse the humans afflicted with Penumbra.

I don't know the specific plan of action, or what's going on with Deacon and Sloan, the "scarecrow." Not going to the warehouse, not helping my former enemy-turned-friend-turned-enemy-turned-friend-again is tough. Tougher than tough. A little piece of my heart withers.

If anything happens to any of my friends…

It will be okay. It will *all* be okay. What I'm doing, I'm doing for everyone.

With a sigh, I pick up Shamus's hand from the floor. The fingers curl inward, like claws. Lifeblood is congealed at the tips of disconnected tendons and arteries.

Gearing for an attack, I press the thumb against the ID pad on Killian's cage. There's a whoosh as the lock disengages. Then my husband is free. He stalks toward me, every step measured and precise. He is a predator who's spotted prey…

Breathing becomes a little more difficult, the air electrified, crackling with awareness. His scent—peat smoke and heather, forbidden fantasies and midnight rain, as dark and mysterious as the boy himself—goes straight to my head, intoxicating me.

I back a step away, then plant my heels into place and still. I'm not weak, and I'm certainly not a coward. I face my problems head-on, whatever—whoever—they might be. And Killian *is* a problem. A very beautiful, seductive problem. Until he remembers me, I must resist him, my warhorse. Or rather, *Myriad's* warhorse. Who will he support in the end? In this, he cannot play both sides.

He's with me. We charge ahead together.

Loyalty to my realm—our realm. Passion for…Killian. Liberty for all.

My pulse points go crazy, hammering at warp speed. My blood burns as hot as fire, becoming a forge that melts the steel in my spine, remaking the bones into a weapon…of seduction. I tingle and ache.

Finally he stops, only a whisper away. So close our chests brush together every time one of us inhales.

"Are you trying to intimidate me?" I ask, breathing *faster*. The tingles expand.

"Tryin'?" He laughs, and the deep, husky notes caress me. "If intimidation were my goal, lass, I'd say mission accomplished."

Perhaps he needs a lesson or three about the girl to whom he pledged his eternal future. I slam my fist into his nose once, twice, thrice—and feel the cartilage in *my* nose shatter. In unison, we howl in pain.

"I'll never advocate spousal abuse, but right now, you aren't my husband, are you?" I raise my chin. "You're my enemy." Wait. Hold up. He called me *lass*.

Suddenly I want to grin. My Killian *is* in there.

He chuckles. "Shoulda known you would cut off yer nose tae spite yer face."

Shiver. His accent is back, and oh, do I love it. "I'll punch you every day for the rest of our lives if it means I get to hear your sexy brogue."

In a blink, his good humor is gone. He scowls at me. At least our noses heal, the manna I consumed only minutes ago still rushing through my veins.

I reach up, causing *Killian* to back up a step. But I follow him, determined, and flatten my palms on his chest. His heart is racing in time to mine. Despite his memory loss, he's still affected by my nearness.

A cool cascade of relief blends with a sizzle of excitement, but I fight to keep my reactions separate from the Grid. I don't want Killian to know how I feel. Let him wonder. Let wonder turn to obsession.

Whether he's onboard or not, I'm going to help him.

Pre-Killian, my life was a mess, my heart nothing but jagged pieces. I was dealing with my parent's abandonment and the fact that they'd paid Dr. Vans to torture me, all in a desperate bid to force me to sign with Myriad. I mourned the friends I'd lost in the asylum, and struggled to make a viable plan for my future. Killian helped me pick up the pieces of my heart and weld them back together. He made me stronger.

Now I will do the same for him.

Resisting him isn't the answer, I realize. No, I've got to help him the way he helped me. I've got to strap on my big girl panties and go for gold. His gold, to be exact. I've got to seduce him, the same way he's seduced me. I'll keep him off balance and guessing—and wanting more.

More…yes. The more he thinks about me, the sooner his memories will return. The sooner he'll trust me.

"Before we transport out of Troika," I say, my voice as low and husky as I can make it, "you're going to kiss me."

His breath hitches. "Am I, then? Because you always get what you want?"

"No." I nibble on my bottom lip and bat my lashes at him, all false innocence and temptation—I hope. "Because I'm giving you what *you* want."

Rather than deny my allegation, he stares at my lips, as if they hold the key to his salvation. White-hot desire smolders in his baby blues.

I've seen him in battle. I've witnessed his calm, his unwavering relentlessness. Now, he trembles—for me.

"Do you think I'll kiss you, fall in love and forsake my home?" he rasps.

Been there, done that, my love. "Are *you* afraid you'll fall in love and forsake your home?"

I expect him to balk, to rant about my daring, or perhaps even feign disinterest.

But he croaks, "Yes," and presses his mouth against mine. Gentle. Tender. Exploratory. Even still, a startled gasp escapes me. He's kissing me. Killian Flynn is kissing me.

He takes full advantage of my astonished delight, tangling his tongue with mine. Another gasp escapes me.

He's giving me a glimpse of the bliss to come. Teaching me to crave it—to crave *more*. And I do. Oh, I do.

Desire fogs my head. He's as sweet as manna and as potent as the wine we once shared inside of Prynne. Waves of pleasure roll over me, eroding any resistance I might have harbored.

"More," I say.

Muscled arms wind around me, yanking me closer, mashing my chest against his. I'm breathing his air and he's breathing mine. Touching him isn't just a want, but a need. I comb my hands through his hair. The strands are butter-soft and seem to melt against my fingers.

He's so strong and hard against me. Where he is stone, I am silk, and I can't get enough.

We've kissed before, and he's touched me far more intimately, but this is somehow inestimably...better. As if he's staking a claim, one he's determined not to forget. As if he's stoking a slow-burning fire with every intention of basking in the ensuing inferno.

How he can take my mouth so slowly, and make me drunk on him so quickly, is a true testament to his skill...or a revelation of the intensity of his desire for *me*.

A low growl rumbles deep in his chest as he jerks his lips from mine and lifts his head. Panting, he stares down at me, his eyelids hooded, his irises glittering, wild. His lips are red, slightly swollen. *My* lips prickle.

"The things I want to do tae you," he tells me, and he sounds drunk.

Don't stop. Don't give me time to think. "More," I beseech. "Please."

"Oh, aye." Once again he descends. But something has changed. The sparks between us have intensified. This time, he slams his mouth against mine and thrusts his tongue deep, taking, giving. *Demanding.* Hard hands settle on my backside, and knead.

This is a full-on sensual attack.

Shadows writhe against the Grid, agitated by our connection, paining me, and yet, the pain is diluted by the great storm of pleasure raining inside me.

So easily I could lose myself in this moment, forget the trials and tragedies ahead. I could be selfish for once; here, now, with him, I'm happy. We're a family. A family that chooses to be together. But selfishness, even momentarily, could cost other loved ones their lives and condemn the dead to their hellish eternity in Many Ends.

Somehow I find the strength to break the kiss. Though every cell in my body mourns the loss of him, and shouts in protest.

"All right," I croak, unable to catch my breath. The drugging taste of him lingers, nearly sending me straight back into his arms. "We need to go." *Now, now, now.*

The crystalline flecks in his eyes are like raindrops falling from a sunny sky. His hands fist at his sides. "Yer plan failed. I did no' fall in love, doona trust you fully and won't betray my home."

He doesn't sound certain, and I take heart.

"The day isn't over." Still trembling, I curl my hand around his shoulder. With my other hand, I type a message to Clementine into my comm. Thankfully, she messages right back to tell me she's ready.

A beam of Light slams into me and transports me to the cave in Russia. Through my physical connection to Killian, he's caught up in the beam, as well, and appears beside me.

Without the warmth of a blazing fire, the air is frigid. I'm wearing a catsuit, covered from neck to toe, but still I shiver.

My gaze seeks the numbers Killian carved into the wall. $68 + 39 = Love$

"Now it's your turn," I say. "Take us to the Veil of Midnight. And Killian? Don't betray me. I'm begging you. You reap what you sow."

He flinches, then runs his tongue over his teeth. "You don't believe in Fate, but you believe in karma, an extension of Fate?"

Ugh. His accent is gone again. "Actions equal consequences. And one way or another, in one life or another, we will face the consequences of our actions. That isn't karma but truth."

A pause as he absorbs my words. "You want me to believe Troika is perfect. You—"

"I never said Troika is perfect. Where there are people, there are problems."

He continues as if I haven't spoken. "What about your Secondking? He is touted as a leader without flaw while his brother is touted as a leader without valor. Yet, under Eron's command, bad things happen, same as they happen under Ambrosine's. Why?"

"*Why* is the wrong question because it makes the assumption Eron is responsible for all of our deeds. He isn't. We have free will. We alone are responsible for the things we do and say. Bad things happen because people make wrong choices, even good people." Always everything comes back to choice. Mine, Killian's. Everyone's.

Irritation radiates from him, and I'm not sure if it's directed at himself, or me. Then he shocks me, reaching out to frame my face with one beautiful, scarred hand.

Do. Not. Move. Impossible. How can I not lean in to his touch? For too long, physical contact was impossible for us. Now the warmth of his skin tantalizes me, a dream come true. A fantasy made flesh. Tremors overtake me.

"What is the right question, hmm?" he asks.

Easy. "What can we do to make things better?"

He peers at me as if he can't quite decide what to make of me. "You are a singular lass." Without disrupting our connection, he uses his other hand to type into his comm.

My gaze never strays from his. I'm ensnared, a song of hope and Light singing in my veins.

"Get ready." Even as he speaks, shadows rise from the rocky ground. Then, we're swallowed whole.

I lose sight of Killian—of everything. Panic threatens as bone-chilling cold invades, a cold far worse than the icy wind whistling along the mountain.

In a blink, the shadows fall away, leaving us standing—

Inside a home.

I hiss at him. "This isn't the Veil of Midnight. Where are we?"

"The Land of the Harvest. This is one of my safe houses. You're welcome, by the way. As recognizable as you are, you need a Shell. Otherwise you'll be captured or gunned down." His gaze roves over me. "And you could maybe use a shower. Okay, you could definitely use a shower. I could use one myself." One of his thick, black brows arches. "Want to conserve water? We're married, after all. Showering together is perfectly acceptable, even encouraged, considering this is our honeymoon."

Sweet temptation...

He's right. This *is* our honeymoon...

Shivers slip down my spine and spread to every limb. *Resist!* I'm supposed to seduce Killian, not the other way around. Not yet, anyway.

"Let's be wild and crazy and splurge for once," I say, my tone as dry as the desert. "We'll shower separately." Even though I would be wise to keep this boy in my sight at all times. But then, I've already established I'm a few cards short of a deck.

"Your loss." He shrugs, as if my answer mattered very little to him, though he can't stop the tingle of disappointment that arcs through our bond.

To hide a smile, I turn on my heel and study my surroundings.

If home is where the heart is, Killian's heart is empty. There's no furniture, only a backpack in the far corner. There are no pictures on the walls, no decorations of any kind.

Now *I'm* the disappointed one. I'd hoped my husband's decor style would teach me more about him and his turbulent past.

Learn the past, ensure a better future. True for both of us.

Killian stalks forward, leading me down a hallway, through the master bedroom—as empty as the rest of the house—and into a bathroom.

"Where are we, exactly?" I ask.

"Oklahoma City."

"And no one cares that the owner of this house is never home?"

"It's a ranch house on thirty acres of land. No one notices." He fishes a yellow towel out of the cabinet and tosses it my way. "When you're done, a new Shell will be waiting in the bedroom." He moves to the door, hand curled around the knob.

"Wait." What if he returns to Troika while I'm distracted? Or messages his Leader, and I emerge, soaking wet, to find the house overrun with MLs determined to capture me? Argh! I'm dumb, but I'm not *that* dumb. "I've changed my mind. We're showering together."

He turns so fast he might have whiplash in the morning. The crystalline flecks in his eyes flare with Light as he shakes his head. "I think I misheard. Did you say you had changed yer mind?"

Annnd we're back. I melt like butter.

"I did. Soon we'll be rushing headlong into danger. Why not enjoy the moment?" Wetting my lips, trembling with nervousness, I drop the towel and remove my catsuit. Head high, I stand before Killian in nothing but my bra and panties. A matching set, black, and just about as sexy as—zero! I can't think of a decent comparison. The circuits in my brain are fraying, connections misfiring.

Despite the plainness of my undergarments, his gaze heats as it slides over me, and I begin to tremble for an entirely different reason.

"Your turn," I croak.

"You got two more pieces tae remove."

No, oh, no. What little resistance I have, well, it will crumble. "Our underwear stays on."

Motions clipped rather than smooth, he strips down to his

underwear and the wrist cuffs. I'm utterly mesmerized. Every cut of muscle...every tattoo... Now that I know what the images mean—the treasures he'd hidden throughout his realm, the people he misses—they are even more beautiful to me.

I reach for the knobs in the stall blindly...there! Twist. Water sprays from the spout. Soon, steam fills the room, creating a warm, dreamlike haze. As Killian approaches, my tremors intensify. His hand brushes mine, and I jolt. My breaths go shallow.

"Yer in control, yeah," he says. "We do nothin' you doona want tae do."

I nod. He twines his fingers with mine and pulls me into the stall. The hot cascade of water rains over me, soaking my hair, my skin.

"Goin' tae clean you up now." He shampoos and conditions my hair, then picks up a bar of soap and lathers me up, his fingers traversing every inch of me, even beneath my undergarments... Such an intimate act. "Or am I makin' yer thoughts dirtier, hmm, lass?"

"You are." I'm aching and quaking, reduced to sizzling need. "But I will resist until you remember me."

"I remember what you *taste* like. Heaven."

Shivering, I take the soap to return the favor, driving him wild. "Our first time—my first time with *anyone*—will be a memory I relive again and again for the rest of my Secondlife. I have enough regrets, and don't want this to be one of them. Don't want to be vulnerable with a boy I can't trust. I want to give myself to a boy I love and who knows he loves me."

His muscles tense under my hands. My gaze chases the bubbles sliding over his skin, and I like my lips.

Temptation made flesh...

Stay strong!

He cups my jaw, and I lean into his touch. "I think you like bein' the giver as much as the receiver, lass." He sounds surprised.

"Why wouldn't I? Your body is a work of art. A true masterpiece."

Water droplets catch in his eyelashes as he smiles. "Wet is a good look for you, lass. Strike that. *Everything* is a good look for you."

Irresistible boy. I lift my lips to press against—

What are you doing? Stop! I can't kiss him a second time. I won't be able to stop again. Look how little control I have right now.

"We're clean," I say, my tone harder than I intend.

Bending down, he nuzzles his cheek against mine and runs his hands down my sides to clasp my hips. "Yeah, but *my* thoughts are still dirty."

A grin blooms. *Charming* boy. "I'm getting away from you before I decide to spend the rest of my life in bed with you."

"I know what gets *my* vote."

Laughing, I hop out of the shower and scoop up the towel.

Killian exits soon after, drops his soaked underwear, and grabs a towel from the cabinet. I catch a glimpse of his perfect butt before he anchors the white cotton around his waist.

He casts me an odd look before he stalks into the master bedroom. I follow just in time to watch him disappear inside the closet.

"Killian?"

"I'm dressing. You're welcome to watch if you'd like."

His accent is gone again. Not a good sign.

I probably should watch him. I mean, just to keep tabs on him. Got to protect myself, and all that.

Just as I step forward, he exits fully dressed in a T-shirt and jeans. Disappointment flares. He tosses a handful of garments my way, including a new bra and panty set. In neon pink. The tags are still in place, but my shadows do not care; they spring from hiding to prick me with jealousy.

This. This is why I don't want to be with him until he remembers me.

"You keep lingerie in your safe house?" I ask, one brow arched. "In my size."

"I keep lingerie in *all* sizes."

Ugh. The accent is still gone. "Why?" The same reason he has top-of-the-line conditioner in his shower, most likely. And I doubt it has anything to do with a dislike for split ends.

"Better question. Why not? I recruit women. Women like presents. I like women." For some reason, he won't meet my eyes, and his cheeks are flushed.

What's going on? He's not embarrassed. Or is he?

"You *used* to like women," I grumble. "Now you like me."

"And you're not a woman?"

"I—oh!" I've talked myself into a trap, and I know it. "I'm a woman, yes, but I'm yours."

He casts me another one of those odd looks, and I have no idea what it means. There's something almost...vulnerable about him.

My Killian is never vulnerable. Is he?

Silent, he heads down the hall. I hang back, exchanging one set of undergarments for another, then don the rest of the clothing. A tight, white T-shirt and equally tight leather pants. As soon as I'm decent, I comb my fingers through my hair and trail his wet footprints to a room on the other side of the house, where at least twenty Shells peer at me through empty eye sockets.

He motions to a female with shoulder-length white hair

and black brows. A silver hoop pierces her bottom lip, and the Myriadian symbol is tattooed on her neck. A black tank top molds to her very large chest, and a pair of short shorts displays the long length of her legs. Combat boots complete the outfit.

Prick, prick. "Why do you keep female Shells here? And don't tell me they're gifts, because you can't give the humans you hope to recruit a Shell that is intended for a spirit."

"Who said the gifts are always for humans?"

Right. *PRICK.*

He pops his jaw and says, "Just so you know, I've never brought a woman or girl or lover to this house. Human, spirit or otherwise. I've never brought *anyone* here."

"Not even Erica?" The former lover who'd given him his tattoos. "You used to work with her. Among other things."

"I remember. But she and I were never exclusive."

How wonderful. He remembers Erica but not me. "As your Flanker, she chronicled your successes."

"Also my failures. And yes, there were a few." There's a note of bitterness in his tone.

Am I one of those failures he regrets? "Victors are adored, failures are abhorred, right?" A motto he's chanted on more than one occasion.

He frowns, but nods.

All right. Enough chitchat. We've got work to do. "Which Shell will you be using?"

He points to a short, redheaded boy with freckles, and a laugh bursts from me.

My Shell could eat his Shell for dinner. "We're going to make an odd pair." We'll stand out. Big-time. At least I think. Maybe all couples are mismatched in Myriad.

"I've used the other Shells. These are the only two *not* associated with me. I'd give you the shorter male, but your walk is too feminine."

I snort. "If that's your idea of an insult—"

"At worst, it's a simple statement of fact. At best, it's a beautiful compliment."

"—then we're going to have a good life together. Once you remember me, that is."

He laughs, but sobers quickly. "Somehow, you always manage to surprise me."

Doesn't like that I can make light of our bonding, too? Good. "So no one will know it's you and me inside the Shells?"

"Exactly."

"Are you sure? In Troika, Leaders keep a log of every Shell. They know who owns each and every one."

"So do the Leaders in Myriad. But I made these, so there's no record of them anywhere."

He *made* them? Hidden talent alert! Guess I should have known, though. He's a creative soul. He made my pi necklace, after all.

"There are voice modulators in their throats, so even our voices will be disguised."

"What about our eyes?" Every Shell has empty sockets. Anyone who looks at me will see my unique, mismatched gaze, and anyone who looks at him will see those crystalline flecks.

"We'll wear sunglasses."

"In the dark?"

He shrugs. "We'll set a new fashion trend. Or bring back an *old* fashion trend."

Very well. I step into my Shell. I had to practice for days to learn how to anchor, and now I do it with ease. Just *boom*,

I'm part of the Shell and the Shell is part of me; the movement of my spirit directs the movement of the Shell.

This Shell has gun Whells—Shells for weapons. Meaning, I can go in armed. His Shell has Whells, too, even for his wrist cuffs.

"Do people walk around armed in Myriad?" I ask as Killian straps a gun on either side of my hips.

"Some of them. Most of them." Killian enters his Shell, anchoring just as easily, then holds out his hand.

The moment has come. One of the reasons I agreed to bond with him. To enter Myriad. After all the hardships we've endured...putting everyone we love at risk...

Was it worth it?

We'll find out.

Killian takes my hand, yanks me against him, and presses a kiss into my lips.

"Do not leave my side," he says.

"I won't."

A second later, he transports us to the Veil of Midnight.

MYRIAD

From: K_F_5/23.53.6
To: Z_C_4/23.43.2
Subject: I have the package

We're on our way. Give me a day, just a day, to show the girl our world. I can convince her to help us. I know I can. Just as I know that whatever you have planned for her will fail. She's too stubborn. Torture won't break her. But I can. Let me do this. Ambrosine will thank us both.

So. Here's the plan. I'll bring Tenley inside, and you'll give her a chance to fall in love with Myriad. If I fail—I won't fail—I'll return to Troika and personally end their Generals. War over, that easily.

Face it. I'm bonded to her. If you hurt or kill her, you hurt or kill me, too, and I'm the only one capable of getting inside Troika. You need me inside Troika. Betray me, and lose the war. Your choice.

Might Equals Right!
Killian Flynn
    PS: I want Erica Morales released from the Kennels by the end of the day.

MYRIAD

From: Z_C_4/23.43.2
To: K_F_5/23.53.6
Subject: Of course

I'll have one of my men follow you, just in case you need backup. Take the time you need. You are a valuable member of our team.

Once you've won over Miss Lockwood, we can visit the Kennels to free Miss Morales.

Might Equals Right!
Sir Zhi Chen

MYRIAD

From: Z_C_4/23.43.2
To: V_P_5/20.16.18
Subject: It's almost time

Mr. Prince,
You'll be pleased to learn I've received another message from Mr. Flynn. He's bringing Miss Lockwood into Myriad TODAY. You are to follow the couple in an unrecognizable Shell, and stay out of sight. Understand? I don't want Miss Lockwood to recognize you. Honestly, I don't want Killian to recognize you.

He wants his former Flanker, Erica Morales, released from the Kennels. Problem is, we executed her yesterday morning. I told him we'd do what he wanted, so, if you do end up in his crosshairs, continue the ruse.

He believes we're giving him time to convince Miss Lockwood to join our cause. In reality, we need time to test the limits of her Light, and the strength of our shadows.

The end justifies the means. You'll have your revenge soon enough.

Might Equals Right!
Sir Zhi Chen

chapter thirteen

"Our Light loses nothing when it is shared. Quite the opposite.
New Lights shine. The world grows brighter."
—Troika

Ten

I stand before the infamous Veil of Midnight, amazed.

I'm used to the Veil of Wings, a mountain of a wall with a very small doorway. This one has no wall, or doorway. The endless expanse offers a shower of ebony...water? No, it can't be. As citizens come and go, no one gets wet. Whatever the substance, it glitters with starlight as it flows from a sky of black velvet.

My mother and father are inside. So are Dior and Javier. Erica. My friend Marlowe. Perhaps my Aunt Lina. Many Ends is inside. Which means Caroline—Killian's mother—is inside as well, ever since her Second-death.

"Nervous?" Killian asks.

I hate fear with the heat of a thousand suns, but... "Yes."

"Don't be. I'll protect you the way you protected me."

I take no comfort from his words. Ever since our shower, he's been distant. I've begun to wonder if he messaged his boss while he was in the closet. Guilt has appeared in our bond more than once.

But, let's say he's telling the truth right now. *Did* I protect him? On my watch, he was Dazed and locked away. So. I kind of expect an army to be waiting for me the moment I exit this Veil.

A group of giggling girls races past us, vanishing under the Veil, paying us no heed. No one acts as if Myriad's enemy #1 is nearby.

Another comforting thought: Eron is on my side, helping me, even though I can't see him...or feel him...

Feelings mean nothing right now.

What's more, if Killian plans to betray me, Aunt Lina would have warned me. Right? She's warned me about almost every other disaster in my life.

Aunt Lina. My heart rate increases. She plans to kill Killian. Maybe. Probably. One of her past visions might just support her claim. The song she taught me as a child...

Ten's tears fall, and I call. Nine hundred trees, but only one is for me. Eight times eight times eight they fly, whatever you do, don't stay dry. Seven ladies dancing, ignore their sweet romancing. Six seconds to hide, up, up, and you'll survive. Five times four times three, and that is where he'll be. Two I'll save, I'll be brave, brave, brave. The one I adore, I'll come back for.

My mind locks on the last line: *The one I adore, I'll come back for.* I haven't yet come back for Killian—until today. My shoulders stoop. I'm back in Myriad. For him. For us. For everyone.

What if Lina *does* manage to kill him? If I'm right, and slain Myriadian spirits go to Many Ends...Killian could maybe possibly probably wind up in Many Ends. Does his final destination depend on which realm he most identifies with? His location?

Cold sweat beads on the back of my neck, but I pay it no heed. I used the song to navigate the sub-realm once, and I can do it again. Whatever happens, I can save him.

"Ready?" Killian asks.

Am I? "Wait!" I close my eyes to search the Grid. Shadows still writhe, stronger now, and Light still glows, but it's duller by the second. I'm tempted to use the Light I've stored. I'm *dangerously* low, weakened, and Light is my strength. But I resist. Before the bond, I could draw more Light to me whenever I wanted. Now, surrounded by darkness, I'll have nothing and no one to draw from.

Right now, I'm going to keep my reserves on reserve…and trust that Killian has our best interests at heart, if not at mind.

"All right. Yes," I say. "Let's do this."

He takes my hand in his, the "bones" in his Shell smaller than I'm used to, while mine are larger. But his eyes…those eyes…they are the same as always. Eight flecks. A song. Oxygen. The reason I breathe.

Loyalty to Killian. Passion for Killian. Liberty for us all.

How much stronger will we be when we are genuinely united?

He marches forward, determination in every step. I square my shoulders and follow on his heels, drawing closer and closer to the Veil of Midnight…

My heart is a drum, and the beat is pure rock and roll. Soon there will be no turning back.

For over a year and a half, I fought to avoid Myriad, enduring torture at the hands of Dr. Vans. Now I'm willingly walking inside.

Liberty for us all.

Finally we reach the fall of darkness, and I inhale a sharp

breath between my teeth. Icy cold encompasses me, making me feel as if I've jumped headfirst into a bank of snow. Next, different sensations invade. An increase of fear. Certainty I will fail, and everyone I love will die. *I'll* die. The exact opposite of what I used to feel under the Veil of Wings.

Then I'm stepping out of the darkness and into...deeper darkness. But it doesn't matter. Suddenly I can see in the dark. I have freaking night-vision, and it's kind of awesome. As Myriad greets me, my mind goes quiet. Eerily quiet. The Grid no longer hums with approval—or anything. Too many shadows cover it. More shadows than before. I'm comforted only by the knowledge that several of my rooms still brim with Light.

I'm sweating now, panting. But okay, all right. At least I'm alive.

I'm standing on a cliff that overlooks... Wow, just wow. The bustling city looks like a king's treasure chest. Buildings are made from precious gems. Diamonds, emeralds, rubies and sapphires. Moonstone, morganite. Opal, garnet, topaz. Crystal of every color. Amethyst, aquamarine, citrine. Pearls and peridot. Maybe even coral.

Absolutely breathtaking. In the distance, there's a towering fortress surrounded by a wall made entirely of skulls. Giant spiders climb those walls. Dragons fly overhead. I count one...five...ten...twenty...thirty. They spew fire, burning the clouds and lighting up the sky.

This is every gothic lover's wet dream, or sweetest nightmare.

I breathe deeply, taking in the scents of night rain, mysteries and carnal fantasies—if those things had scents. Heady, almost drugging. *Definitely* drugging. My head swims.

Close by, a cobblestone path winds around a wealth of

buildings. Some are sleek and sophisticated. Others are lavish and ornate. Some stretch so high that they knife through the sky—or rather the Veil. The Veil of Midnight circles the entire realm.

In Troika, flower petals fall. Here it's…stardust? I stretch out my hand to capture a few grains, but they absorb into my Shell and brush against my spirit. A sudden burst of cold leaves me shivering, and the sensation is not pleasant.

To distract myself, I study the flashing neon signs that adorn many of the buildings.

Party! Party! Party!

Companions R Us

Brew for You

Men and women congregate on balconies, catcalling everyone who walks by. Or flies by. A few spirits have metal wings strapped to their backs. Shirts and skirts are raised, body parts flashed. Laughter is plentiful. Everyone is smiling, not a frown in sight. Drinks are passed around. In dark—darker—corners, men and women kiss and touch…and more.

There's a little something-something for everyone, no vice left untapped.

The sheer number of people overwhelms me. There are too many to count.

"What do you think?" Killian ask. "Ever seen anything like this?"

"Reminds me of the Red Light District in Amsterdam, only on a much, much, *much* grander scale."

"You've been to Amsterdam?"

"I have. I used to travel with my dad." He is—was—a Senator for the House of Myriad, tasked with ensuring Myriad's rights are never violated by Troikans or humans. Once upon a time, he loved me, and took me with him. Now he hates my guts.

Will I see him? Do I *want* to see him?

"Let me show you more of my world," Killian says. "Tell me your wildest fantasy and greatest wish. I can make it happen."

Play now, work later? "I'm not here for pleasure."

Frustration floods the Grid. "We have time for business *and* pleasure."

"Every minute counts," I say. "I promised Archer I'd check on Dior." In the process, I'd like to avoid Javier. He's an Abrogate, and he has a home court advantage. "Then we need to head to the Kennels, free Erica, and proceed to Many Ends." That's why we're here, after all. Get in, get out.

He scrubs a hand over his face. "You hate the realm and I—"

"I don't hate it." Not at all. "I hate what the darkness does. It's evil. Once it's gone, this realm—"

"And," he continues, as if I'm not speaking, "I want you to see a side Troika doesn't talk about. I want you to know what you're fighting for, when you're fighting for peace."

No, he wants me to fall in love with his home. The realization shimmers inside me, and I gulp. "You're giving me the hard sell, but it's not going to work. I will never embrace darkness." I lift my chin. "If you can't leave it…"

Eyes narrowed, he angles his body toward me. "What did you think would happen when the war ended? I would defect?"

"Yes. Before our bond, you *already* planned to defect. We were—are—going to help both realms." Deciding to take a calculated risk, I add, "But if you'd rather sever *our* bond, as the Generals said, go ahead. It will break my heart, but broken hearts mend."

I'm not going to let him hold our bond, and our plans, over my head, as if they need to be ransomed. He needs to understand, and fast, that he has as much at stake as I do.

"Sever our bond." He scowls, as I'd hoped. "You'll let me go, just like that?" He snaps his fingers.

"Don't you see?" I grab and shake him. "I'm fighting to *stay* with you. Why don't you help me?"

A roar cuts through the night, and my gaze zooms skyward, just in time to watch a dragon the size of a Mack truck fly overhead. His black-and-green scales are resplendent, his wings magnificent. A spiked tail wags behind him.

"Only guards and prisoners are allowed in the Kennels," Killian says, picking up our conversation as if the argument never began. His grumbling tone tells a different story, however. "We'll be noticed the second we enter. But I have a plan."

"If you tell me we need to get ourselves arrested, I'll punch you again."

He rolls his eyes. "As you can see, no one can resist a good party. We'll spend the day spreading word about the one we're going to throw. Once that party kicks off, we'll convince everyone to walk through the Gate with us. As they're kicked out, we'll sneak past the guards."

It's…not a bad plan. "Will your friends help us?" The more people we have on our side, the better our chance for success.

"I have no friends," he admits. "None outside the Kennels, anyway."

How sad. A good support system matters. Everyone needs someone who will pick him up when he's down. Someone to laugh and cry with—someone willing to tell the truth when lies abound.

I squeeze his hand, offering comfort, but he quickly pulls from my grip. Hope fizzles. If he remembered me, I could ask what's wrong and how I can help. This stranger isn't interested in revealing his vulnerabilities to me.

Deep breath in, out. "Tell me what you want me to do."

"We'll walk around, telling everyone we meet about the party. Since this is our honeymoon," he adds, "I won't even charge you for my escort duties or party planning." Eyes glittering with amusement, he nudges my shoulder with his own.

"What's your normal fee?" I ask.

"You misunderstand. I've never given a tour to anyone else. But here, nothing is free. Everything costs." He leads me forward, and I gasp. Every time we take a step, a stone lifts from the ground to meet us, allowing a smooth descent to the land below. "We work hard for our money, and our time is valuable. We don't part with a coin or a single second lightly."

"The people of Troika work hard, too, but gifting is a way of life." In fact, the giver often looks more joyous than the receiver.

"Ridiculous. The more you give away, the less you have." We pass a group of teenage boys, and Killian nods in greeting. "Dudes. Party at the beach tonight. Clothing optional. Trust me, you don't want to miss this. Tell your friends."

The boys whoop, holler and high-five each other.

The next group we pass is made up of older women dressed in elaborate Victorian gowns. Killian bows and says, "I bid you good morrow, ladies. There's a gathering at the beach tonight. I hear Victor Prince is hoping to meet a bride."

Feminine twitters erupt as the ladies hurry on.

Unease pokes at me. He's telling everyone what he thinks

they want to hear. How many times has he done the same to me?

"Give me the lowdown on Myriad." Facts are facts, and there's no reason to lie. The more I know about enemy territory, the better chance I'll have of escaping when the time comes. Or hiding, if it proves necessary.

He nods, saying, "The realm is divided into ten territories. The City of Carnal Delights, or CCD, where we are now. This is also where most businesses are located. They're open 24/7. Then there's the Museum of True Wisdom, where dossiers are kept on every citizen, human and even Troikans. There's the Temple of Unholies, where the Prince of Ravens lives. Although he has a home in every territory."

"The fortress I saw when we entered…"

"Yes," he says. "Then there's the Tower of Absolution, where we train. The Garden of Zen, where speaking is forbidden. The Capital of Bliss, where I live. The Mountain of Vengeance, where the dragons reside, and also where the Kennels are located. The House of Indulgence, where official ceremonies are held. The Center of Learning, where orphans are raised. And finally, the Fountain of Tears, where people go to indulge every emotion to the fullest."

The differences between Myriad and Troika shouldn't surprise me. Not even a little. They are night versus day. Logic versus emotion. Ten versus Killian. But I'm surprised, I admit it. The self-indulgence…the carnality… How does anyone get anything done?

We reach a small beach with onyx sand and water the color of a sky at sunset. The scents of salt and coconut, so familiar to me, fill my nose.

Killian calls out another party invitation to the people in

the water—they're the ones with the metal wings. They fly in and out of the surf.

"Compared to Troika, you must have triple the population," I say.

"*More* than triple," he replies. "With every new arrival, the realm expands."

The name Myriad makes sense. Myriad = countless multitudes.

Having more soldiers doesn't necessarily equate to having a stronger army, clearly, or Troika would have been conquered long ago.

We walk along the cobbled path for over an hour. Killian continues to tell everyone he sees about the party, or gala, or cheese tasting—whatever seems the most desirable to the people involved—and no one says no.

In Troika, citizens wear either catsuits (armor) or robes, nothing in between. Here, citizens wear whatever they want. Or so I'm guessing. Besides the Victorian ball gowns, I spot scanty togas and punk rock leather. Some men wear kilts, some wear loincloths. Others wear slacks or jeans. A mix of cultures, traditions and fashions.

The party vibe never fades, however. The throng that meanders along the streets, or in the buildings, never thins. Voices rise and blend together; though the volume of all those conversations ebbs and flows, it's never less than a dull roar.

The skin on the back of my neck prickles. A warning. Something is wrong. Stiff as a board, I search the faces around me. No one seems overly fixated on me, but...my suspicions aren't laid to rest.

"Still nervous?" Killian asks. Something about his tone... And the flush is back on his cheeks.

"Yes and no." I check our bond, and find a mixture of guilt, shame, remorse and determination.

Zero! What did he do?

Anger sparks to vibrant life, burning my chest.

Betrayed, the shadows whisper, throwing fuel on the fire.

Stop, just stop. I don't know what he's done. Whatever it is—however big or small—there's still time to reverse it.

I must continue my course: Seduction. Maybe, if I make my husband want me, desire will prompt trust and trust will prompt his memory. I need him to remember me, need him on my side. Before it's too late.

Another dragon flies past us, casting a massive shadow. The shadows inside me moan with delight, loving it.

Ignore. Stay focused. "You're a wonderful escort. Totally worth the cost." I lean my head on Killian's shoulder and say, "Speaking of cost, how do you guys pay for things?"

He jolts, as if surprised, but he doesn't dart away.

One step at a time. I must take joy in small victories.

"Credits." He holds out his arm, and points to his wrist. "We have a chip implanted. Every time I convince a human to sign with Myriad, a certain number of credits are added to my account." His tone hardens. "When I *fail* to convince a human to sign with Myriad, I lose a certain number of credits."

A barbed lump grows in my throat. "How many credits did you lose when I made covenant with Troika?"

"Doesn't matter. Come on." He leads me to a small chrome and glass building. Near the closed—and locked—door, he holds his wrist under what I assume is a scanner.

Bingo! The scanner thanks him for paying a credit, and the door unlocks.

"Don't worry," he says. "We can't be traced." Now he leads me inside the building.

Well. He wasn't kidding when he said everything costs something.

I find myself in— A white-hot blush heats my cheeks. A small bedroom. There are mirrors on the walls *and* the floor. There's a vanity-slash-wet bar, complete with mirror and stool, a bed without sheets, and a cabinet filled with individual packets of sheets that are for sale. A desk occupies the far corner, a screen hanging on the wall in front of it. Beyond another door is a bathroom with a shower—and a scanner in order to turn on the water—plus a bin with a sign overhead that reads, *Dirty sheets go here.*

The door locks behind us.

"This is a love shack," I blurt out. "A place for a quickie on the go."

"Also a place to make inquiries. You want to see Dior, don't you?" He scans his wrist at the wet bar, and a shot glass slides from a cubby in the wall. A spout extends from a different cubby to fill the glass. He downs the shot before sitting at the desk, scans his wrist on a different scanner, and begins to type on the desktop, despite not having any kind of keyboard. Images appear on the screen. "I need to log on to the data system under an alias."

Interested in the exchange of money, I hold my wrist under the sink's scanner, but nothing happens.

"Chips are placed inside Myriadian comms," he says. "Scanners scan a spirit, even when a Shell is involved. But there are ways around it. There's a chip in my Shell that overrides the one in my comm."

"Are you using stolen credits, then?" I ask, realizing he

can't use the ones he earned while using a Shell that isn't linked to him.

"Only from the dead." Noticing my confusion, he adds, "When a spirit experiences Second-death, their remaining credits are wiped from the system. But not right away. Not until the bodies are collected and identified. See, when we go to battle, we lose soldiers. It's inevitable. I take note of who bites the dust. As soon as I return to Myriad, I break into the accounts of the fallen soldiers, take a small amount of credits, and assign them to a new owner."

"So credits aren't passed to family members?"

"Nothing is passed on to family members or loved ones. If you don't do something to help the realm—"

"You don't get," I finish.

He nods.

"What will happen if you're caught?"

"Depends. The number of credits you steal is the number of days you spend in the Kennels. But how will I get caught? The dead won't come back to tattle."

I detect a note of bitterness in his tone, that the system is so broken, and part of me wants to exploit it. *Think of all the times Myriad has punished you, let you down, or hurt you. You don't want to help the realm, do you?* Instead, I move to the doorway that separates bathroom from bedroom and lean against the frame, watching as he works.

He curses. "Dior's location has been blocked. I can't track her."

Disappointment flares, and I quickly tamp it down. "We'll find another way." We always do.

My thoughts travel another road, returning to the problem with his memory. Maybe seduction isn't the answer. Not on its own, anyway. People only ever take from Killian. By his own admission, everything he's gotten, he's had to pay for. I can give him access to my mind—my heart—free of charge.

"How long are we allowed to stay in here?" I ask. The longer we're here, the less time I can be watched by whoever is following us. And someone is following us, guaranteed.

He pauses, meets my gaze. Curiosity and interest glitter in his eyes. "One hour. Well, fifty-six minutes now. Why?"

A slow smile blooms. I walk toward him, stepping out of my Shell and saying, "Because I have plans for you."

TROIKA

From: A_P_5/23.43.2
To: T_L_2/23.43.2
Subject: Something strange is happening

You know how you're an Architect now? Well, so is Raanan. He's making other Conduits, Ten. Like, a lot. Deacon, Clementine, Clay and Reed and…drum roll, please…ME. Yes, you read that correctly. Me. Archer Prince. He touched me, that's all, and a bolt of lightning shot through me. Suddenly I could see—and absorb—Light like never before.

So yeah, I rock hardcore. The entire realm is going batcrap crazy over this. (Be honest. Are sophisticated Conduits like us allowed to use the word *batcrap*???)

I'm sure you want other updates, though I'm sure we can both admit I just gave you the most important one.

The princess: She's come out of hiding. Not just to help Raanan, but to train us. In fact, with so many Conduits, she has no reason to hide anymore.

Warehouse: We haven't engaged. Yet. Deacon figured out Sloan's code (you know, the flash of three fingers, three times.) She was warning us. There are eighteen warehouses just like the one we found. The moment we trip one of many silent alarms, the machines shut down and the potential Abrogates wake up. A new battle begins.

Kayla: She's doing well. She's on her feet, and standing with us.

Have you found Dior?

Wish you were here!

Light Brings Sight ←Especially to me! Because I'm a Conduit!
丅ㄴ Conduit Archer Prince

TROIKA

From: Mailer-Erratum
Subject: THIS MESSAGE HAS BEEN DEEMED UNDELIVERABLE

chapter fourteen

"There are no moral absolutes. What is wrong for one might be
right for another."
—Myriad

Killian

I have plans for you. As Ten saunters toward me, full of confidence and the embodiment of feminine wiles, her final words echo in my mind. I'm undone.

I look at this girl, and I want her. I scent her sweetness, and I want her. She has become the sun to my world, and I cannot help but gravitate to her. The loss of control enrages me, even as it thrills me.

The earth cannot touch the sun without being engulfed by flames. The problem is, I long to be engulfed. I'm as desperate as a man dying of thirst.

I should walk, no, run, from this room.

I'm trembling as I stand, my body thrumming with aggression, my blood hot. I step from my Shell, becoming myself again…and sit at the edge of the bed.

I'm not leaving.

The bond…it can't be blamed. Not fully. Not this time.

The bond isn't responsible for Ten's breathtaking smile, or the way her mismatched eyes light up every time she looks at me. The bond also can't take credit for her stunning wit and staunch determination...or the trust she continues to have in me.

Trust I do not deserve.

She has no idea I've already sold her out. After our shower, I was reeling more forcefully than ever before. Or *harder* than ever before. Yeah. That, too. In more ways than one. Touching her had been a *revelation*. The softness of her skin nearly unmanned me. The little mewls in the back of her throat delighted me. Everywhere they traveled, my fingers left a trail of goose bumps, and it thrilled me. When *she* touched *me*...

My world upended. I craved more, then and now.

The craving consumed me, and I freaked out. I shouldn't want her this much. Shouldn't want *anyone* this much. At some point, I'm going to lose her, either because of the war, or because of my own foolishness. I thought, *Why prolong the inevitable, making things worse for myself?*

Rip the bandage. Move on. Quickly.

Next I thought, *If I have to sacrifice myself and my desires to get this done, so be it.* For my realm, and my king, I will do anything. I believe in both—yes?

As soon as I entered the closet to dress, I sent a message to my Leader, Sir Zhi Chen. Because of me, an ML was waiting for us just beyond the Veil of Midnight. Took me a while to pinpoint who, exactly, but only one Shell followed us to every location.

The second I lost him, I darted in here.

We're at a serious disadvantage. Except for my cuffs, our weapons are bogus; they don't work.

What have I done?

My dark side provides an answer: the right thing. If I hadn't bargained for Ten's life, death would have been a real possibility, if not an outright inevitability.

Now, Ten will stay safe. And so will I.

The true shocker: When I made the bargain, I wasn't concerned about my future, only hers.

Right now, she's looking at me with the same intense longing and desire that is smoldering inside of me. When she finds out what I've done, she'll look at me with hatred.

"Mr. Flynn. Where are you? I demand a report."

Zhi's voice fills my head, unbeknownst to Ten, interrupting the moment, and I grind my teeth. I programmed my Shell to relay every incoming message via audio rather than text. Texts can be sent along the Grid, which is a danger while I'm connected to Ten.

Once again, Zhi speaks. "We have intercepted a message from Archer Prince to Miss Lockwood. There's been a startling development. Either that, or the Troikans have realized we've hacked into Miss Lockwood's feed and hope to trick us. But either way, something must be done ASAP."

I palm a dagger and stab my comm, ending any further communications. "I'm out of my Shell," I say, my voice roughened as I head off any questions she might have. "Doona want tae take any chances."

My time with Ten isn't up, and I won't relinquish another second.

She reaches me and climbs onto my lap, bracing her knees at my sides. Automatically my hands settle on her hips to hold her in place. She smells incredible, like a field of wildflowers on a warm summer's day. I breathe her in as if she's a lifeline. Maybe she is. Or maybe she's more than a lifeline.

Maybe she's *everything*.

"You make my toes curl." She rubs her nose against mine, and the soft contact is electric. "Tell me what you want, Killian."

I open my mouth to say, *Ye, only ye*, but an accusation escapes instead. "You make poems for Archer." As the words echo in my ears, I curse. I want a poem more than I want sex?

Who have I become?

"Are you jealous?" A tinkling laugh leaves her, her warm, sweet breath fanning over my chin. "Even though I made one for you, too. *Tsk-tsk.*"

"I have no' forgotten the one you made me, lass." It's getting more and more difficult to control my accent around her. And why bother, anyway? She knows I'm an orphan, and she doesn't care. "You doona love me. I canna trust you. Blah, blah, blah."

"Except now you know I do love you, and you can trust me." She studies my face, grinning a toothy grin and spinning my heart into a dangerous spiral. "But you still want a new one."

I hike one of my shoulders in a shrug, all *whatever*. Meanwhile, my mind is shouting, *Give me!*

She plays with the ends of my hair, tickling my scalp, and recites:

There's a boy named Killian Flynn.
The most handsome of all the men.
Each and every night
Girls melt at first sight
But he only has eyes for Ten.

One corner of my mouth lifts. "A limerick?"

"Archer would flip his lid over a limerick, yet I've never

created one for him. But. If you don't like it, we can pretend I didn't create one for you, either, and—"

"It's mine," I rush to say. "You can no' take it back."

Her grin returns full force. "Possessive of a poem. Could you *be* any more adorable?"

I shouldn't preen, but that's exactly what I do, like a once-dying rose suddenly opening to face the ever-brightening sun. This girl *likes* me, just as I am. She likes me enough to tease me, and she enjoys the time we spend together. To her, I'm worth something. I'm...family?

"Since you can't remember our past," she says, then pauses to chew her bottom lip. "What if I can let you inside my mind so that you can see our history through my eyes?"

Shadows take me by the throat, squeeze. "You know how tae let me in yer mind?"

"No. I mean, yes." Frowning, she tilts her head to the side. "My Grid is on the fritz, and yet I know exactly what to do."

I'm shaking my head before she finishes. "You shouldna make such a temptin' offer." *Not to me.* "You shouldna let *any-one* inside your mind, *ever. Especially* me. I'm no' a bad guy. I'm worse. People will always take advantage, learnin' your weaknesses tae use against you."

She's got to do a better job of protecting herself from preda-tors like me.

Again she rubs her nose against mine. "How cute. You as-sume I have weaknesses."

I want to smile and shake her at the same time. And I want to resist her... I do...should...but I can't. My curiosity is too great. Can I be blamed? With Ten perched on my lap, my brain isn't functioning at optimum levels; all of my blood has rushed elsewhere.

"Whatever memories you share, I'll see through yer eyes,

learn yer every thought and secret," I say, my final warning. "I might acquire information you wish tae keep private."

"You are priority one. Whatever you need, I'll give."

My mouth dries. I nod.

Nibbling on her lower lip, an action that only makes my blood descend faster, she frames the sides of my face with her beautiful hands. Skin to skin, female to male. Warmth to warmth, wife to husband. My fingers twitch involuntarily, my grip tightening on her hips.

Determined to maintain control of my memories, the shadows sharpen their claws, sinking their razor tips deeper into my mind. I flinch.

"Close your eyes." Ten kisses one of my temples, then the other.

Perhaps this is a trick meant to disarm me. When I close my eyes, she'll attack. For once, I don't care. I'm willing to take a chance.

No risk, no reward, right?

"Inhale…exhale… That's good," she says, her voice as soft as a caress. Every time I inhale, she exhales; when I exhale, she inhales, until we're breathing each other's air. I still taste the shot of whiskey I downed, but now the sweetness of her teases my senses.

As I wait for something, *anything* to happen, I'm tense, on edge. Then, oh, then, I *feeeeel* her. She's there, in my mind, standing in the middle of the bridge that connects us, smiling at me, everything right in a world gone wrong.

Light glows from her pores. Light she saved and desperately needs, yet still she gives it to me.

"Stop," I croak.

She brightens…grows brighter still…making my shadows shudder with fear, run and hide.

Between one second and the next, a nearly blinding flash of Light explodes between us. Agony sears me, and I grunt. Sweat pours from my temples.

Suddenly I'm trapped inside a small room. My—Ten's— arms are lifted overhead, wrists bound by chains that are anchored to the ceiling. She's human, a prisoner at the Prynne Asylum.

A thirty-something human stands in front of her, rolling up his shirtsleeves. Dr. Vans. Evil in the flesh. "You know, I've always admired your spirit, Miss Lockwood. It's a shame I have to damage it."

She's sick to her stomach, but determined to withstand whatever the male dishes. "Go ahead. Do your worst. Your best has only ever tickled."

Sickness churns in *my* stomach. How could anyone hurt her like this?

A big-boned nurse with frizzy red hair wheels a large tray inside the room. The door closes behind her. Two wolves. One sheep. No way out.

Ten does her best to remain calm. "You don't have to do this. You said there are no other options, but that's not true. You can give me the time I asked for."

Time... She hasn't yet decided where she'll live after she dies. Myriad or Troika. Stand with her parents, or against them. All she wants is the right to freely choose—what we *all* want.

"Time is running out." The doctor smiles at her, and it's clear he enjoys her pain. "No, we're going to do this. Money buys happiness, and anyone who says otherwise is lying. I want my money."

"Aren't you afraid of what awaits you in the Everlife?" she asks.

"I've never cared about tomorrow. Only today."

I bite the inside of my cheek. I've always been like Dr. Vans, taking care of now with no concern for tomorrow. Or the feelings of others. I despise the fact that we have something in common.

The two argue for a bit, and I'm amazed at Ten's strength, at her unwillingness to bend. She's willing to die, simply to use a basic human right too many take for granted. When have I ever felt so strongly about *anything*?

Then she says, "Living shouldn't be synonymous with surviving."

The doctor pops on a pair of latex gloves. "You have my permission to scream as loudly as you'd like. These walls are soundproofed."

What he does next fills me with such righteous rage, I'm nearly rent in two. Yes, he makes this brave, precious girl scream, over and over again. Despite the horrors he inflicts upon her, she never gives him what he wants: a pledge to Myriad.

A realization I reached earlier solidifies: Ten Lockwood will never betray Troika. Not now, not ever. And I... I...

The shadows do everything in their power to shut down the memory, but they are no match for Ten. Her Light forces those shadows to run and hide...and...

I begin to remember bits and pieces of my life... How I read Ten's file before I met her. How my Leader called her "hard-headed" and "foolish." Before me, Myriad sent a sleazy ML named James to win her over. While everyone else around her attacked her, he pretended to show her kindness; of course she fell for him. Only, she still didn't make covenant with Myriad for him, even under the guise of saving his life.

So I was sent in, because my specialty is romance, like James, only on the opposite end of the spectrum. He is (supposedly) the good boy a good girl can build a life with, and I am the bad boy those good girls hope to tame, (supposedly) exciting. I can show them the time of their lives.

At first, Ten wanted nothing to do with me. Not exactly a new experience. Many others have rejected me, too. Then, she softened toward me. How? I must know! But the specifics remain a blank.

Why does it matter? In the end, she rejected me, choosing Troika.

As she softened toward me, I softened toward her. I must have despaired, knowing I'd lost her. Wrong. Knowing I'd never truly won her.

I can't have Ten and my position in Myriad. One will always endanger the other.

She made her choice, leaving me in the dust. After our bonding, I had to do the same.

Ten moans, as if she's in pain, and my attention zooms to her. She's surrounded by darkness. My shadows didn't run away to hide. No, they zoomed along the bridge, entering *her* mind...strengthening the darkness already writhing inside her. She's fighting, but she's losing, growing weaker.

Protective instincts surge, and I curse. This girl and her memories have me twisted up. I make a decision, or think I do, and emotion rises up to change my mind.

Emotion—or trust?

I don't know, I can't tell. Up is down and down is up. If the shadows overtake her, I will win. Her Myriad side will take over. Maybe. Probably. She'll do what I considered impossible and betray Troika. Hopefully.

No, no, not hopefully. I like her, just as she is. I don't want to change her. She's—

Boom!

My eyelids spring open as the door to the rented room bursts at the hinges. Zhi Chen looms in the entryway, a Dazer in hand. Dark hair. Pale skin with a slight golden tint. Behind him are three men—that I can see. Knowing my Leader, I'm sure many others surround the building.

I stagger to my feet while shoving Ten on to the bed behind me, using my body as a shield. A sense of urgency bombards me. *Get rid of them. Now.* I need more time. I'm not ready to part with Ten.

She splays across the mattress, her eyes closed, her hands pressed over her ears. Little whimpers escape her.

"Go," I shout, but of course, Zhi remains in place. He's a Leader, my superior.

"We're here for the girl." His smile reminds me of Dr. Vans's. Cold. Cruel. "But don't worry, Mr. Flynn. You'll be coming with us. We'd like to…chat with you, too."

My hands fist, the bones so taut I fear my knuckles will cut through my skin. "The Troikans call me the Butcher, Mr. Chen. Do no' make me show you why."

He pales but remains in place. "You are outnumbered and outgunned."

I could beg for mercy—but I won't. Zhi knows nothing about my past. Few do. Before Archer's defection, he erased details about the abuse I endured from my files. As a beloved son of the Secondking, he had access to every building in every city, and no one dared question his actions.

At the time, I thought he had my back. He was the only friend I trusted. When he left, I figured the action was a parting gift, and I hated him all the more. He'd known he was leaving, but hadn't talked to me or warned me.

For years I wondered how Archer could give up glorious

freedom in exchange for the stifling rules found in Troika. I even asked him once, when he attempted to recruit me.

I desire the trust of my brethren more than the adoration of my father's people.

At the time, I considered him a fool. Now...

"Take us tae Ambrosine, then," I demand. I'll speak with the king directly. After everything I've done for Myriad, he'll agree to place Ten in my care. He must.

Zhi's smile only widens. "Who do you think ordered us to take her in early?"

My heart drops into my stomach. No. Absolutely not. But...

I know as well as anyone that the Secondking will do anything, betray anyone, to defeat Troika.

As Ten says, we reap what we sow. I sowed betrayal, so, I'm reaping betrayal. This is my fault in more ways than one.

"If she's hurt..." I stealthily reach for the dagger hidden in the waist of my jeans.

"Oh, she'll be hurt, and so will you." Zhi squeezes the trigger on the Dazer. "*That* is the only guarantee I can give you."

chapter fifteen

"If you do not work, you do not eat."
—Troika

Ten

Voices. Strange noises. Huffs and puffs. Grunts. One thud after another.

Fighting?

I pry open heavy eyelids. My vision is hazy. I think I see Killian dodge a stream of Dazer fire as he lunges at a group of soldiers. Intruders! He uses his wrist cuffs to disarm two men. Not just to disarm, but to arm himself. The hooks at the ends of the wires latch on to the weapons and fling them in Killian's direction. He catches both and fires.

Pop, pop, pop. Pop, pop.

Men bellow with agony.

Why would Killian need the soldiers' weapons when he has ours?

Unless ours do not work…

Darkness envelops me, pain sears me and I lose track of my surroundings. *My fault.* I gave my Light—my strength—

to Killian, and took some of his shadows. Only wanted to set him free.

His life has been a series of tragedies, and I hoped to give him peace. I want better for him—and I'll *be* better for him, even if it destroys me.

He comes first. *Love* comes first.

Darkness will not win.

Except, the shadows in my mind are thicker than before and only growing. Old resentments flare, no longer content to remain hidden, blending with a fresh surge of rage.

Killian betrayed me. With his shadows come more and more of his secrets. After our shower, he messaged his Leader, thinking he would win me over, convince me that there's no better place to live than Myriad. Zhi Chen promised to send someone to follow and "protect" us. What a joke. As if the powers that be would ever accept me. All along, they planned to hurt and use me.

Still, a part of me refuses to fault him for doing what he thinks is right, what is best for his people, and the realization makes me flinch. I'm Kayla, I realize. I thought myself different, thought my love stronger and my man nobler. Wrong! Killian taught me better.

Luciana said Myriadians go crazy after a bond, and Troikans suffer later. Now I get it. Because of Killian's actions, I'm going to suffer. I am suffering.

If there's a reason for his memory loss, there's a reason for this. What am I supposed to learn? How to forgive? I can do that. To trust him, anyway? I can't.

No, you won't. *Trust is a choice, like love.*

Fool! Look where love takes you.

Stop! What's done is done. Anger will lead me down the wrong path. I'll rant and rave, and do nothing but convince

Killian that he made the right decision, choosing his realm over me.

Punish them all. Make them beg for mercy.

A command from my deepest, darkest instincts. A desire to get even with the people who betrayed me. Tit for tat. I did nothing wrong, and yet I suffer. A tormentor deserves to suffer a thousand times worse than his victims, yes? Problem is, these instincts aren't always right. Fruit that grows on a poisoned tree is poison. If I give tit for tat, I'm no better than the one who hurt me. Actually, I'm worse. I'm a hypocrite.

And really, blame can be laid at my door, too. Sow, reap. Once, I put Troika first, Killian second. Today, Killian put Myriad first, me second.

The best response? Resist rage. Look beyond the moment to the eternal.

What future do I desire? One with Killian, or without?

$1 + 0 = 1$

$1 + 1 = 2$

There are two sides to every story. The positive and the negative. Some people say there's a third side. Neutral. But neutral isn't a side—it's an excuse.

Pain explodes through my head, disrupting my musings, drawing me back into the present. Killian hisses, experiencing the same explosion of pain. Perhaps he is the cause?

Then I'm floating, the softness of the mattress no longer supporting me. No, not floating. I'm…being carried? A heart beats against my temple, and an unfamiliar scent envelopes me—grapes not yet completely fermented into wine. Not unpleasant, but not welcome, either.

My darker side loves it, has never smelled anything sweeter.

"—to Killian?" a male voice says, catching my attention.

"He took out sixteen of my men before we were able to

subdue him. He *should* be headed for the Kennels, and soon he will be. *After* our interrogation of the girl."

There are sixteen ounces in a pound.

Abraham Lincoln was the sixteenth president of the United States, and he led during the Civil War.

Sixteen is the atomic number of sulfur.

Why did Killian fight his own countrymen? To safeguard me?

A trick. Only a trick.

Or my seduction worked, and Killian is beginning to trust me.

Too late.

"She's to be interrogated? Nothing more?" the male asks.

"Of course there's something more. We've never had a Troikan inside Myriad. We'll be running tests on both of the Flynns. Ah, but I love the sounds of screaming. Music to my ears." A chuckle of genuine amusement.

"She's only half Troikan, and we *have* run tests on others like her."

"Wrong. While we've run tests on Amalgams, we've never before had a Conduit in our midst. Which is why our new Abrogate is going to try to push our darkness through Miss Lockwood's Grid. If the darkness is able to invade Troika, the citizens will be weakened. If the darkness spreads and surrounds the realm, even better. We'll be able to enter just as Killian did."

Information hits me one bomb at a time.

Amalgams. Is that what inter-realm bonded couples are called?

New Abrogate. Definitely Javier Diez.

I can't let him do what is planned. Interrogation, torture,

sure, I can endure. I have before. But not the destruction of my home.

The two sides of me war, just like the realms.

The people of Troika do not love you. The Generals blackmailed you. Face it. You are hated, and now that your Light is partially extinguished, you are no longer needed or wanted. Why defend them?

You don't need to be loved by others to do what's right for them. Resist, and the darkness will flee. It must.

Then Killian's voice joins the deluge. —*I'm sorry.*—

—*Sorry doesn't change our current circumstances. You aren't the man I thought you were.*— The words slip from me, unbidden, my dark side striking out.

He flinches. —*I'm better.*—

—*Hardly. You lied to me.*—

He cuts me off. —*I know I'm nothin' like your precious Archer.*—

Jealousy? Now of all times?

Doesn't matter. Through sheer grit and determination, I listen to my Troikan side and resist the darkness. Anger, hurt and worry will only strengthen the shadows. Deep breath in, out. Happy thoughts. The end of the war. A peaceful future for Jeremy. No more friends dying too soon.

Good, that's good. I begin to calm, and the darkness begins to fade.

I suspect I haven't seen the last of anger, hurt and worry, but for now, they're hiding again, and I'm centered. Learn from misfortune and move on.

I focus on Killian. —*I've never desired Archer. He's my brother, and you're my...*— What?

Doesn't matter. Logic over emotion. *Escape with Killian. Enter Many Ends. Save...everyone.*

I'm tossed on to a cold, hard floor. Impact knocks my brain against my skull. Next, a storm of ice water splashes over me, and I gasp, sputter. My eyelids break apart, and I meet the gaze of the man I know is Zhi Chen. He is dark from head to toe, with a lean body barely strong enough to carry me however far we traveled.

Beside him stands a Shell. Masculine, rugged. Blond with the same nearly translucent skin of the Secondking and glittering green eyes. A face so beautiful that both females and males, young and old, have fallen for him. And killed for him.

I know those eyes. Here is Victor Prince, Archer's younger brother.

He likes to pretend he's some kind of angel. I know he's fallen.

Though he's not pretending today, is he? He's too busy glaring daggers at me.

I don't have to wonder why he's in a Shell. During our last encounter, he tried to force me to bond with him the way I willingly bonded with Killian, and when I refused, he then attempted to kill me. I cut off his hands, and they have not yet grown back. In the Shell, he can at least pretend to be whole.

"Oh, but the mighty have toppled," he says, his tone smug.

I'm barely able to move, my strength depleted, my Light gone, but still I blow him a kiss, taunting him. *Take your anger out on me, not Killian.* Although, hello, we're bonded. What happens to me happens to him. Double zero. "At least...you know...I'm mighty."

Victor decides to humor me. With a hiss of rage, he moves toward me. The guy beside him holds out an arm, stopping him.

That guy—Javier Diez. The enemy. He is an Abrogate, my total opposite. I supercharge in the Light while he supercharges in the dark. I can push Light into others; he can tamp it out and create shadows from nothing but air.

Although, with my dual citizenship, I wonder if I can transition from Conduit…to Abrogate. Scratch that. I'm certain I can. The knowledge rises up inside me, temptation wrapped in persuasion and sprinkled with enticement. I have only to embrace the shadows hiding in my mind. Then I can use Javier's powers against him. Shadow versus shadow.

Will be so easy…

Steel fuses to my spine, squaring my shoulders and lifting my head; the position of a soldier who refuses to back down. *Easy* doesn't mean *right*. How can I utilize darkness, then turn around and condemn Ambrosine and his followers for doing the same? How can I create darkness, stealing Light from my friends? *Hurting* my friends?

No! There's another way. A better way. The *Light* way.

What do I know about Javier? Kayla once called him the quintessential dreamboat. He's tall, with a golden tan, and handsome. But to me, he's the embodiment of evil. He gets off on the misery he inflicts. Death and destruction are his constant companions, and selfish is the name of his game. So, dreamboat or not, I'm not a fan.

Before Javier's Firstdeath, I received a small taste of his powers. He might as well have been a needle, and me a balloon. One moment I was strong, the next I was weak. Now that he's a spirit, we're on equal ground.

He's cocky, and he'll underestimate me.

I can take full advantage.

Determination tramples any lingering fear, but not by word or deed do I betray my newfound fight. Let him see me as weak. Let him act accordingly.

Javier extends one finger, only one, and not the middle one.

Surprise surprise. I think he's creating shadows. Yes. Oh, yes. Dread attempts an invasion as shadows seep from the ceiling and floor; they slither toward me and wrap around my wrists and ankles. Ice-cold. I gasp.

A second later, I'm yanked upright, my limbs stretched out as if I'm on a rack. My gaze is suddenly eye level with Javier's. He's smiling a smile as frigid as his shadows.

"As you might have deduced," he says, his tone even smugger than before, "I'm learning to use my gifts."

He expects me to cower. *Keep dreaming.* "Aw. You're going to make *such* a good puppet for your realm." Speaking while panting proves a challenge, but I manage it.

Rage contorts his features.

To prove he means nothing to me—less than nothing—I mentally dismiss him and scan the room. Between Zhi and Victor is a large dog crate—

Horror slaps me. Killian is locked inside the crate. He's on his knees, the diameters of the walls not allowing him to stand, and he's wearing an expression of pure boredom.

This is where betrayal leads you. Happy?

"I'm sure you remember when you cleansed Dior Nichols of Penumbra." Zhi is as smug and superior as a king. "Now Javier is going to cleanse you of Light, and you're going to help him. Let him into your Grid. Anytime you resist, Mr. Flynn will be… Well, there's no kind way to say this. He'll be deep-fried. Meaning you, too, will be deep-fried."

Deep breath in, out. I need help, can't do this on my own.

Desperate, I reach out to Archer through the Grid. Considering Raanan is an Architect, I reach out to him, as well. And the Conduits. The princess. And Biscuit. Clay. Deacon. Reed. Clementine. Kayla. Someone has to hear me, despite the distance between us.

One second, two. Three. Radio silence remains.

Zhi arches a brow. "Nothing to say, Miss Lockwood?"

My panicked gaze swings back to Killian. He's gripping the bars of his cage, his knuckles white, his calm slipping away.

Slap! Javier's palm makes contact with my cheek. The pain is sharp but fleeting as my head whips to the side. Lifeblood leaks from the corner of my mouth.

"Do yourself a favor, Miss Lockwood." Zhi tugs at the cuff of his shirt. "Pay attention."

Rage detonates along my bond to Killian—and it's not mine.

"Hitting girls now, Diez?" Killian *tsks*. He appears even calmer than before. So calm it's almost scary. "And bound girls who can't fight back, at that. Your bravery is inspiring."

"Keep talking. Please." Javier peers over his shoulder and smiles slowly. Then, still watching Killian, he slaps me harder. "Ten is the one who will pay for your crimes."

"You consider truth a crime?" I laugh. "I don't know why I'm shocked. The *truth* is, you're pathetic in every way. You're a coward with—"

His arm lashes out a third time. Third time is the charm. Rather than delivering a slap, he balls up his hand and punches me. Stars explode in my vision. My teeth cut my cheeks, and agony sears my mouth.

No longer can Killian maintain any type of facade. He rattles the cage and screams, "I'm going to do everything in my power to ensure you rot in Many Ends."

I use his outburst to my advantage, shouting again for my friends. —*Archer! Raanan! Biscuit! Someone!*—

—*Ten...*—

I suck in a breath. Archer! I'd recognize his voice anywhere, anytime. He may be in Troika, and I may have used up all my Light, but I'm still connected to him through the Grid.

"What happened?" Victor closes the distance, then reaches out to clasp my chin. Problem is, he's in the Shell and I'm in spirit form. His hand ghosts through me. Glaring at me now, he snaps, "Tell me!"

—*Archer. I used up my Light, and now I'm a captive. I—*

—*No need for a recap, Sperm Bank. I know the gist.*—

Sperm Bank. The nickname he gave me the day we met. He said I had lady balls and an explosive temper.

—*Listen up. I'm with Clay, Raanan, Clementine, Kayla and Reed. Earlier I sent you a message explaining everything, but it bounced back. So here's the condensed version. Our group has changed. We're ALL Conduits now. Well, not Kayla. Not yet. Raanan is an Architect, like you. Okay, okay, I'll tell her.*—

Maybe Javier's punch damaged my brain, because the last part of Archer's speech fails to compute. —*First, I'm so happy for you guys. There are no better people for the job. Second, I'm sorry, but I don't understand. You'll tell me what?*—

—*Biscuit is insisting I let you know he's with us. Anyway. We're going to send Light across the Grid. Maybe it will work, maybe it won't. We're new at this. Good news is, the princess thinks it will, in fact, work.*—

The princess has left the protection of the tunnels. Perfect! More Conduits means more safety for Troika. I can use whatever Light I'm given to fight Javier's shadows.

But what will happen to Killian? I stiffen. He reacted to Light so badly the first time.

Doesn't matter. Whatever happens, we'll deal. Without Light, we might not survive this encounter.

—*Thank you, Archer.*— All for one, and one for all. —*But be careful. I'm with Javier, and he wants to spread his darkness along our Grid. If you begin to feel drained, stop.*—

"Enough." Javier cups the sides of my face *annnd* the next thing I know, darkness is hurled into me.

Oh, the pain; it consumes me. Gritting my teeth, I summon every bit of my remaining strength to erect a block and keep it—him—away from the Grid. Sweat beads in different locations. Ice seems to spread over my spine. I can't breathe. I need to breathe.

Finally Javier pulls back, and the darkness vanishes.

The pain fades, and I begin panting. —*Archer!*—

—*Working on it, but...*— The words are gritted. —*We're blocked.*—

No, no, no. Is the block I erected against Javier also keeping out my friends?

"Well?" Zhi demands.

"She's resisting," Javier snaps. Glaring at me, he adds, "Now Killian will pay the price."

Killian will pay the price either way. This way, at least, there's a chance we survive.

"You were warned, Miss Lockwood." Zhi lifts a remote and presses a button. Volts of electricity flow through the metal bars of Killian's cage.

My entire body shakes. My vision goes dark, and in my veins, my blood begins to boil, muscle and flesh cooking.

Agony nearly rends me asunder, worse than anything I've ever before endured. One second, two. I scream. Or try to. Suddenly the volts die. I continue to quake, my teeth rattling against each other.

My gaze meets Killian's, his beautiful eyes reminding me of open wounds. He may not remember everything about our past, but he hates what's being done to me.

"Again," Zhi says.

Javier reaches for me only to still as multiple voices call out greetings from the hallway.

"Majesty."

"Your Highness."

"My lord." Distress tinges each and every voice.

Pulse after pulse of power hits the room. Hits *me*. My entire body shudders, my nerve endings buzzing.

Ambrosine has arrived.

While the people of Troika adore Eron, the people of Myriad fear Ambrosine. The contrast proves everything I've begun to suspect.

Ambrosine must die.

Zhi and Victor stiffen. Javier smiles. Interesting. He must see himself as prince's pet.

Then the door opens, and a man who can only be the Prince of Ravens glides into the room.

He is so beautiful, with pale hair and eyes that glitter like diamonds, that I can only believe my eyes are deceiving me. His nearly translucent skin is flawless, his muscles well-honed and displayed to perfection even though he's wearing a robe made of raven feathers and brushed with…stardust?

A crown of shadows rests upon his head, a hundred pairs of red eyes within its depths, glowing like rubies as they watch the world with undiluted glee. On his hands are strips of metal. One for every finger. Each strip arcs into a sharpened claw at the tip.

His power intensifies, his shadows growing darker, the hum of evil ringing in my ears. Zhi, Victor and Javier are forced to their knees. In the cage, Killian struggles to rise into a crouch, refusing to look as if he's begging.

Were I standing and at full strength…I don't think I would

have had the same reaction. When his shadows bump up against my Grid, they cringe and flee.

Hope ignites. There might not be a better time to kill this man. Scratch that. He's not a man. He's an otherworldly being. There might not be a better time to kill this other-worldly being. I've never been this close to him, may never be this close again.

Just…need…to…break…free. Argh! Though I struggle, my bonds hold firm.

Come on, come on. Fight harder.

Ambrosine destroyed the bridge that once connected Troika and Myriad. He promises a better life filled with excitement and untold pleasures, but he lies, cheats and steals. He can't be trusted to maintain a truce, has proven himself treacherous at every turn.

He claims he enforces no rule but one: Myriad comes first. And yet, he doesn't always follow his own rule. *He* comes first. His wants, his desires. He's selfish to the extreme, dooming his people to eternal war and endless torment in Many Ends.

"Majesty." Zhi lumbers to his feet as the Secondking's shadows thin. "We are humbled by your presence."

Ambrosine must control the intensity of power he exudes; he can crank it up or let it simmer. I highly doubt he revealed the true depths of his strength just now. Why show all of your cards at once, when I'm already captured and restrained? Why not save the best for last?

I'm not going to be able to kill him, am I?

Hope withers, and fury ignites.

No. No! I will not give up. This man—this being—is the epitome of hate. Hate will never be stronger than love.

Long ago, Ambrosine allowed envy to lead him, and chose to betray his brother. Over the centuries, he has grown worse.

Darker. In the end, his home mirrored his soul—a cesspool of jealousy and greed. He sends his own people to Many Ends when they experience Second-death. Just because he can. Maybe because he likes their pain.

A person like that—he will not defeat me. Even if I'm faced with pain and the loss of my life, I will still choose what is right.

I will choose love at the cost of *everything*.

Victor stands, and nods a greeting to his father. Javier beams with something akin to hero worship.

The Secondking glances at Killian—and nods with approval.

"Majesty," Killian says through gritted teeth. "I would like to speak with you privately about—"

"Be silent." The Secondking flicks a finger, and a shadow appears over Killian's mouth.

Killian's eyes go wide. He begins to shake, as if a new round of electricity is flowing. He's fighting against the shadow, I realize. But he's weak and soon deflates. His emotions do nothing to help. I feel the sting of rejection and dejection along the Grid.

My stomach sinks, even as my heart aches. He pinned all his hopes on his king, and this is his reward.

Ambrosine turns those diamond eyes on me, staring me down, but I refuse to cower. I'd rather die.

"Well, well," he says. My hatred for him is reflected back at me. "Finally I meet the little girl who's going to win the war for me. Let's get started, shall we?"

TROIKA

From: L_R_3/51.3.15
To: J_A_3/19.37.30, S_C_3/50.4.13, C_M_3/5.20.1,
Y_L_3/59.1.2, A_S_3/42.6.31, T_B_3/19.30.2, B_S_3/51.3.13,
M_V_3/54.5.8, J_B_3/19.23.4, S_J_3/62.5.5, M_P_3/45.10.9,
A_T_3/23.40.29
Subject: New Conduits

We've heard the rumors about Miss Lockwood and Mr. Aarons becoming something known as an "Architect." Now we've seen proof. Raanan Aarons has turned other Troikans into Conduits. Archer Prince, Deacon Williams, Clayton Anders, Reed Haynesworth and Clementine Vickers. I think Kayla Brooks—a known traitor—is on the verge of changing, as well. She grows brighter every hour.

Though Mr. Aarons has tried, he was unable to turn a single General into a Conduit. Why? I've reached out to Eron, but have not received a response.

If we're going to overcome this new Penumbra attack, we need more Conduits—we need *us*.

Light Brings Sight!
General Luciana Rossi

TROIKA

From: A_T_3/23.40.29
To: L_R_3/51.3.15, J_A_3/19.37.30, S_C_3/50.4.13,
C_M_3/5.20.1, Y_L_3/59.1.2, A_S_3/42.6.31, T_B_3/19.30.2,
B_S_3/51.3.13, M_V_3/54.5.8, J_B_3/19.23.4, S_J_3/62.5.5,
M_P_3/45.10.9
Subject: I disagree

For a Myriadian General, turning an ordinary citizen into Abrogate requires self-sacrifice. And the sacrifice might not even work. All they can do is infect a single person with Penumbra and hope for the best. (Like Miss Lockwood, I will name the disease without fear.) Yet, we must sacrifice no one for our advancement, and an Architect can turn more than one person. That is the difference between Light and dark. Light builds up. Dark tears down. And Miss Brooks is a *former* traitor. There's a difference. Eron has forgiven her. So should we.

We should be celebrating our victories rather than envying our members.

We are leaders. So, let's lead.

The people Raanan has succeeded in turning into Conduits? The people aiding Miss Lockwood. We have done nothing but hinder her. And before you ask—hinder her from doing what?—I'll tell you. She craves peace between the realms.

Perhaps we should consider the same?

I know. We tried to facilitate peace eons ago, only to endure one ambush after another. But at this very moment, I can almost hear Miss Lockwood screaming inside my head that the answer is simple. Myriad needs a new Secondking. The head directs the body.

Is this worth considering?

As for the warehouses, I have good news and bad news. I'll start with the good. We have unexpected help. Sloan Aubuchon managed to fight her way free of the pole. She's doing her best to deactivate the many alarms. If a single one is triggered, every potential Abrogate in all eighteen warehouses will wake, a Buckler will fall around the buildings, trapping our men inside while allowing the humans to leave.

Be ready to act at a moment's notice.

Bad news. Someone told Myriad about our Architects, new Conduits, and our plan to sneak inside the warehouses and cleanse the infected before anyone knows we've been inside. The Bucklers *we've* placed around the buildings will not hold much longer.

Light Brings Sight!
General Alejandro Torres

chapter sixteen

"Do not wait for what you want. Take what you want."
—Myriad

Ten

Hours pass. Perhaps days. One agonizing moment bleeds into another. If Javier isn't flooding me with darkness, Victor is electrocuting me. My muscles aren't just cooked; they're burnt to a crisp. The blood in my veins boils. I have no Light, no strength and I desperately need both, but I can't drop my shield. I just can't. Javier will flood *my friends* with darkness before they can fill me with Light.

Killian has fared no better. He's as soaked in Lifeblood and sweat as I am. His lips are gnawed to ribbons, and multiple bones are broken from the strain of clenching muscles.

Again and again he's threatened to murder every man in this room, each threat more brutal than the last. He kicked off with decapitation, then vivisection and finally ended with peeling everyone like an onion.

Now he's a panting, sweaty mess, and he's watching me. For a moment, only a moment, I think I see gut-wrenching guilt, soul-shattering regret and agony. Mostly he radiates determination. His nostrils are flared, and a vein is bulging in his forehead, as if he's exerting pressure. And yet, he's sitting perfectly still.

I wonder if he's attempting to help me? If he's the reason I'm able to hold the shield, despite my weakness?

Too little too late.

Love, always love, even in the face of the worst betrayal.

"How is she doing this?" Javier demands.

Perhaps he would have succeeded already, forcing his shadows along my section of the Grid, if not for his anger, frustration and embarrassment. He hates that he is failing in front of his new king, and his emotions are getting the better of him.

Though my jaw is nearly unhinged, my tongue swollen, I manage to slur, "Easily. You're weak. You can't—"

Slap.

"—win," I finish. If I can push him over the edge, he'll no longer pose a threat.

Slap, slap.

"If I link to her, she will die instantly," Ambrosine says, anger crackling in his tone. "She's of no use to us dead. Yet."

"Try harder," Zhi snaps at Javier.

"Don't be afraid to break her." Victor clenches his fists, and it's clear he wants to be the one tormenting me. "Break her!"

With a roar, Javier shoves his palms against my temples. He uses so much force, I'm pretty sure my skull cracks. Thousands more shadows flood my mind, each one beating at my shield. Every strike sends a lance of pain through my head, and I scream and scream and scream. Unconsciousness beckons, but even still, the shield holds strong.

But Archer's voice is stronger and fills my head. *—Ten! Drop the shield. Now!—*

—No. Can't.—

—*You won't.*—

Exactly. —*I won't risk you.*—

—*Trust us. Please. Let us fight him for you.*—

I…won't. Zero! I won't. If my friends fail, Myriad will prevail and Troikan will lose the war. I love them too much to risk them.

Will fight…on my own…

No, not alone. Eron is with me always, yes? And Killian is here. The shadows. So many shadows. I'm consumed by hatred for Ambrosine, and an icy determination to defeat him. I won't give in—won't give these men the satisfaction of defeating me. Revenge is sweet.

"Let. Me. In," Javier snarls.

"Die." I laugh in his face, knowing there's a fresh coat of Lifeblood on my teeth.

Hissing, he hits with another blast of darkness. Still I laugh. Oh, how I adore making these men shrivel up with frustration. Although, I don't know how much longer I can hold out. I'm exhausted, utterly drained. Without the shadows, I would have caved already.

"You," the Secondking says in a chilling tone. He glares at Killian, who is drenched in sweat, cut and bruised, and barely able to hold up his head. "If you want out of your cage, you'll gather what remains of your strength, break through her barriers and allow my Abrogate entrance. Do this for your realm. Do this for your king."

Oh, no. No, no, no. Swallowing my panicked pleas, I peer at Killian, beseeching him. I want to shout through our bond, *Don't do this. Please, don't do this.* But I remain silent. Strong or weak, he can use our link to orchestrate my doom.

The shadows laugh, gleeful, as fear squeezes my throat, and air wheezes from my mouth.

Killian's gaze remains glued to the Secondking. "You lied tae me and locked me up." His voice is raspy, as broken as mine. "*Of course* I trust you tae keep yer word now."

Ambrosine's features twist with disgust. "Must you sound so...*poor* when speaking to me?" He lifts his chin. "The end justifies the means. Lies are sometimes necessary to facilitate a desired result. You know this. If you put your realm first, as you once swore to do, you would understand—no, you would *welcome* the sacrifice I'm asking you to make."

Terrible silence. Killian flicks me an unreadable glance, and my heart sinks.

—*Please, Killian. Don't do it.*—

"Lies," Killian says, his voice roughened by abuse, "are never necessary. Trust is too important."

Seconds pass before his meaning clicks. My heart flies. He knows he picked the wrong team. He's going to fight for me, not against me. Unless this is another trick? Could be.

Must remain guarded at all times, with everyone.

I love him, but trust is another story.

"Enough." The Secondking's crown of shadows splits in two and slides down his arms, stretches past his hands and culminates into razor points. "You. Leader," he says to Zhi. "If your man cannot break Miss Lockwood, then we will kill the humans infected with Penumbra. Those who exhibit the traits of an Abrogate."

What, does he not know the names of his own people, and yet he knows mine?

"The warehouses are currently surrounded by Troikan armies," Zhi replies.

"Perfect." The Secondking smiles. "We'll use the Abrogates to kill them, too."

Cursing, Javier drops his hands to his sides. He's panting, unable to catch his breath.

—*Archer! Stop trying to give me Light. Tell our Generals that Ambrosine is sending men to the warehouses to kill the infected so they can try to infiltrate my Grid, harming everyone in Troika.*—

—*We aren't giving up, Ten. You…need…Light.*— He roars as he continues to push.

Then a gentle voice whispers through my head, startling me. —*Love my Ten.*—

Jeremy. For one moment, my defenses are down. A ray of Light glides past my shield, along the Grid and rains over me like ice-cold water on a scorching summer day. I jolt. The ray came from my little brother, didn't it? My *infant* brother? Not by force, but by love.

I can't let Javier get to him, and fight with every ounce of my newfound strength to fortify the shield. *Must protect Jeremy.* If Javier senses any vulnerability inside me…

"What just happened?" Victor demands.

—*What just happened?*— A demand from *Archer.*

Javier's eyes narrow on me. Leaning forward, he sniffs me. "Somehow, she received a bolt of Light."

"How?" Ambrosine walks a circle around me. He seems to glide, his grace unparalleled. "I have worked hard to ensure there are no sources of Light in this realm."

He has worked hard…meaning, there were once sources of Light for Myriadians?

"The Grid," Victor says. "Her friends. They *love* each other."

"Impossible," Zhi replies.

All three males stare at me as if I'm a rat in a lab. Though it strains already strained muscles, I keep my chin lifted high. Not by word or deed will I reveal my inner turmoil. Reveal a weakness, they'll exploit it—and more!

With the Light came strength, yes, but also knowledge. Knowledge is power. I fought too hard for control of my Secondlife, and I won't allow my future to fall to ruins at the hands of men who see no value in me, and no worth in anyone willing to break the cycle of darkness and pave a better path for a better future.

How often they disparage Troikans for their rules. Too restricting. All work, no play. But at the heart of those rules: love. Love fellow spirits, love humans, love yourself. While these men tout indulgence and self-love, they punish anyone who dares put themselves before the realm.

Hypocrites.

The Secondking stares at me for a long while, an obvious attempt at intimidation. Fear of any kind cranks his chain. Perhaps even strengthens him.

Shadows, feeding...

When I refuse to cower, he snaps, "Cage her and put her in the town square until our new Abrogates arrive. Let my people witness the weakness of Troika's strongest soldier."

My cheeks heat with humiliation, but I force myself to laugh, as if he's just offered me a tropical vacation. "Say goodbye to your PB&J." At his confused look, I add, "One day I'm going to knock your penis, brain and jaw right off your—"

Slap. Stars wink before my eyes.

Javier gets in my face, his nose pressed against mine. "Give me another crack at her." Though he's speaking to his Secondking, he's glaring at me. "I can get through. I know I can."

"If that were true, you would have done so already. Instead, you did nothing but waste our time." Ambrosine wipes an invisible piece of lint from his shoulder. "Admit it. The girl can't even stand without assistance, and yet she bested you.

You should be on your knees begging for your life, not demanding a favor."

A vein throbs in the center of Javier's forehead. He pops his jaw, but he says no more.

Zhi clears his throat. "And what would you have me do with Mr. Flynn?"

Victor steps forward, shoulders squared. "I would like to keep him. Consider him a gift from a beloved father to his loyal son."

I almost shout *No!* A thousand times no. Victor has a score to settle, and he won't hesitate to hurt Killian in order to hurt me.

For the third or fourth time, my gaze locks with Killian's. I've lost track—how unlike me. I'm not even sure how many seconds pass as I stare into soulful gold eyes flecked with electric blue; they are filled with hurt, so much hurt, all ingrained. In my mind I see the little boy who desperately craved a family of his own, who faced rejection over and over again. The nightmare of his childhood is being relived here today. Rejected and abandoned by his king, no friend at his back.

I have Archer, Clay and the others. Killian has no one.

He had me, but he threw my trust away.

"You hardly deserve a reward for your most recent failures," Ambrosine tells Victor. Then he sighs. "However, you did ruin several cities in Troika, so, you may have the caged boy for the rest of the day. Do what you will with him, as long as you do not kill him. He's still connected to the girl."

Having delivered his verdict, he glides from the room on a carpet of shadows.

Maybe I've been stripped of sanity, because the first thought I have? *Drama king.* A hysterical laugh bubbles from me.

On a mission, Zhi marches my way. "Do you think you've

won a reprieve, Miss Lockwood? Is that why you dare to laugh?" He reaches out, clasps my chin in his hand and forces my gaze to meet his. "You, girl, are a fool."

The moment his skin touches mine, a scene flashes inside my head, and I gasp. I'm not bonded to this man—or perhaps I am, through Killian. Or perhaps Zhi's actions against me formed some kind of twisted tie between us. Perhaps my new status as Architect comes with perks.

Again I see a dark-haired little boy, but this time, the image has nothing to do with Killian. This boy is no more than ten years old, perched at the edge of a bed, trembling. Like Zhi, he has dark eyes with a ring of ebony around the edge.

Realization: Not like Zhi at all—the boy *is* Zhi.

Tears slip down his cheeks, but he's careful to swallow his whimpers so that he never makes a sound. There's a cut on his lip, and drops of crimson blood drying on his chin, proving he's human. There's also a knot in his jaw.

His father paces in front of him, his fisted hands smeared with crimson. His blood, as well as his son's. The last time he punched, Zhi's teeth cut into his knuckles.

"We are Troikans," his father snarls. "Your visit to the Myriadian center has shamed us. Our loyalty will be questioned now. How could you do this to us?"

"Because...because I don't want to be like you," Zhi whispers. Then he raises his head, emboldened by hatred and defiance.

"Ingrate! Fool!" His father backhands him. "You would be so lucky."

Zhi withers under the new onslaught of pain, but as quickly as the scene manifested, it vanishes.

I stare at him now, at the adult he's become. Knowledge is power. I understand his hatred for Troikans. It was beaten into him.

Words are either seeds or water. What is spoken is planted in the rich soil of a human heart. What is spoken again is poured over the seed, and in time, that seed sprouts. Roots grow. A trunk. Branches, leaves. Fruit. Like produces like. Speak evil, reap a harvest of evil. Can't see the forest for the trees. Soon, if the tree isn't uprooted, the fruit will be eaten... and shared.

We must break the cycle. Help create a better path for a better future.

Whatever Zhi sees in my expression unnerves him. The compassion I can't help but feel? His hand falls away, and he steps back, widening the distance between us.

"There are good and bad Troikans." Every word scrapes my raw throat. "Same with Myriad. Good and bad. Though I'm still waiting to meet a good one." From the corner of my eye, I see Killian flinch, as if he's been punched. *Oops. Sorry.* But truth is truth. "Want to know what's similar between us? We all have baggage, even our enemies."

I get it now. Even when I don't understand why someone does what they do, or why they make the choices that they do, I must choose love.

Their actions cannot dictate my reaction. And that goes double for Killian.

"You, shut your mouth," Zhi snaps. "And you," he says to Javier, "let her down."

Javier glares at me before holding up one arm. The shadows release my wrists and ankles, and I topple to the floor. What little oxygen I've managed to draw in leaves me in a single burst.

Victor stalks to me, leaving his Shell behind. He is pale and sickly thin, with tiny nubs growing at the ends of his arms. Hardly matters. He doesn't need hands to hurt me. Now that

I'm on the floor, too weak to stand, he kicks out his leg, his boot nailing me in the stomach. My already empty lungs deflate, and another shower of stars winks before my eyes.

Just like that. My resolve to love and not hate is put to the test.

He draws back his foot to deliver another kick—

He topples before contact, his face smashing into the ground. I peer beyond him to Killian, whose arm is sticking out of the cage, the wire from his wrist cuff extended and wrapped around Victor's ankle. No time for Zhi or Javier to react. With another yank from Killian, the wire cuts through muscle, catching on bone, nearly removing Victor's entire foot.

A scream of anguish rents the air.

Zhi unsheathes a blade and hacks the wire in two. Panting, sweating, Victor reaches for me. I spin around and punt him in the face. Yes, I'm determined to love my enemies. No, I won't allow others to abuse me.

The muscles in my thigh quake and burn, the bones threatening to crack. Agony sears me, but I brace, ready to deliver another kick if necessary.

Snarling, he reaches for me again, but this time Zhi steps in the way.

"Enough," the Leader says, and motions to Javier.

Though Javier is vibrating with rage, he remains quiet as he helps Victor stand and hobble back to his Shell.

"You just made the biggest mistake of your life, Flynn." Victor smiles. "Did you forget? I own you now."

Killian doesn't pull his gaze from me, and through the bridge between us I feel a frisson of...strength? As if he's returning the Light I gave him. "*I* am the fool, Victor. I deserve what you do tae me. I only wish you were more like yer brother. Archer is—"

"Dead," Victor snarls. "In the grave where he belongs."

"You don't think he Fused with a human?" I ask, batting my lashes at him.

A slow smile curves Killian's beautiful lips. "He experienced Resurrection. He's alive and well."

In a blink, Victor is as stiff as a statue. "No. There were two Generals. The people would not vote for a lowly Laborer."

"The people didn't," I say, trying to stand. My legs are jelly and refuse to hold me, and I crash back to the floor. *Zero!* "The honor of the selection was given to me. And guess what? He's a Conduit."

Because of my predicament, the enormity of the development managed to escape me until just this moment. Now, I rejoice. Princess Mariée, Archer, Raanan, Clay, Reed, Clementine, Kayla, even Sloan—we are a team.

In a single day, Troika went from two Conduits to seven.

The rainbow has seven colors. Seven means completeness and perfection, both of the physical plane and the spiritual.

Now there is one Conduit for each city. Coincidence?

Coincidence shmincidence.

"Impossible." Victor gives a violent shake of his head.

"Even if it's true." Javier's chest puffs up before he bends downs and hefts me into his arms. "I will destroy them all. No one is my match."

I want to fight him, but don't. I must pick my battles. Here, now, I'm well aware of the fact that I don't have the strength to win. But. As soon as Javier leaves me in the town square, I can lower my shield to receive Light from my friends without reservation. A veritable *torrent* of Light.

I'll strengthen. I'll plot, plan.

Tomorrow, when—if—other Abrogates arrive, I'll be ready.

chapter seventeen

"Corruption happens gradually, a slow fade of Light as
darkness creeps in."
—Troika

Killian

Once, I considered myself pain. Today I am rage. It fills me,
consumes me and darkens every corridor of my mind. Most
of it is self-directed. I've done many despicable things in my
Everlife, but this is by far the worst.

My actions led to Ten's capture and torture.

While Javier Diez attempted to gain access to the Troikan
Grid, I could only lament my part in her pain. As I chastised
myself for not trusting her, a new memory assailed me. Just
one, not nearly enough. Ten stood before me, her back to my
front. She was human and on the verge of becoming drunk.
I was in a Shell. We were both prisoners inside of Prynne.
Unwillingly on her part, willingly on mine. I'd signed up in
order to spend time with her and convince her to make covenant with Myriad.

Erica was there, too, only she was in spirit form, so Ten
couldn't see her. Erica leaned over to whisper into the hu-

man's ear, *His towering height is a very good thing, there's nothing to be afraid of, and maybe you should hold on to his shirt. For balance.*

An effort to influence her. While Ten's ears failed to hear the words, her spirit picked up everything. That's how Flankers— a subdivision of Messengers—worked.

"Are you ready for me?" Ten asked me.

"Can anyone ever be ready for you, lass?" I replied, and even then, I'd been scared of the truth. I *wasn't* ready for her. "But don't worry. I won't let you get hurt. You have my word."

Finally she trusted me enough to fall into my arms. When I caught her, I spun her around. If Erica hadn't been there, I would have kissed Ten then and there. Even then, I wanted her. Craved her like a drug.

I might have kept my word that day, but I have broken it many times since.

I made a terrible mistake today. I trusted the wrong people, betrayed the wrong girl. An *innocent* girl.

Once, she saw something great in me. She looked at me with adoration and admiration, even hope. When Javier carried her out of the small room, she cast me a final glance, one laced with wariness and suspicion. That glance hurt in ways I never imagined possible.

The electricity might have burned my body, but Ten's look burned my soul.

I've lost something precious: her trust. And for what? Imprisonment, degradation and pain, all of which I deserve. But she does not.

My hands fist. Determination rises inside me, an undeniable tide. Those who hurt her will pay. I will make sure of it. And I will do whatever proves necessary to win back her trust.

First, I will escape. Then I will save her.

Firstking help Myriad then. I will torch the realm and never look back.

"Let's get you more comfortable, shall we." Victor Prince clutches the edge of my cage—a cage tangible to both spirits and Shells—and drags me through the door.

Despite the injuries his spirit sustained, his Shell is strong. The outer casing is meant to shield us through the worst of times. Like a type of armor.

Revenge might not be Ten's thing, but it *is* mine.

Forgive. Let the Light illuminate your path and order your steps.

The other side of me. A side I ignore.

As I'm hauled through a hallway, down an elevator, outside the building and through a Stairwell, my rage continues to blaze. Every step he takes only serves as kindling. I want to maim and kill him. I *will* maim and kill him. I will also maim and kill Zhi, Javier and even Ambrosine—after I save Ten.

In the town square, she'll be used as an example. Love Troika and suffer.

As if she hasn't suffered enough.

While Javier did his best to invade her Grid, she remained strong as a rock, astounding me. No wonder I once fell in love with her. She is the only ten in a world of ones. She endured excruciating pain in order to protect her people, and despite her distress—distress I, too, experienced firsthand, certain I would die at any moment—she fought, a warrior to her core, and she won.

Now *I* will win, or I will die trying.

Victor drags me through a crowded section of the City of Carnal Delights. The carnival. More dragons fly overhead, streams of fire like fireworks. There's a kissing booth, and even an orgasm booth. *Come one, come all.* Every game involves stripping. Lose the severed hand toss and you have to remove an article of clothing. Lose Whack-a-Prisoner, and you have to remove an article of clothing. So really, everyone wins.

Except the spirits in the Kennels, of course. They provide the severed hands, and they are the ones who get beaten with a barbed-wire-covered baseball bat.

There are rides: the carousel showcases Shell versions of Troikan Generals on their hands and knees, bumper cars fly around an arena smashing into replicas of famous Troikan landmarks and a zip line offers a tour of the entire realm.

Snacks are sold: cotton ambrosia, fried ambrosia, ambrosia corn and ambrosia cakes. Even ambrosia bacon.

As a child, I often snuck out of the Center of Learning to play here. No one paid me any attention then, and no one pays me any attention now. I don't bother shouting for help. I know these people; I won't be aided—I'll be mocked.

Victor takes me through another Stairwell, then a Gate, and we enter the Capital of Bliss. Also known as the Cob. The air smells of chocolate, champagne and sex. The most basic indulgences. Skyscrapers, cottages and pyramids are scattered throughout. For our poorer citizens—those who refuse to fight in the war—there are warehouses or communal living spaces.

Here, crowds stop and stare at us, everyone dressed in the era of their death. *Be you, be free.* Some people laugh at me, others look at me with pity. Once, both reactions would have sent me over the edge. I would have ranted and raved. Having been raised in the Learning Center, abandoned by my father, overlooked by other families, I craved the good opinion of others, desperate for acceptance. Now I see the truth.

I wanted to be admired, but I also wanted to make everyone who'd ever overlooked me sorry for doing so. Another type of revenge.

At this moment? The opinions of others—of strangers—mean nothing to me. These people have no bearing on who I am or what I'm worth. With my actions and words, *I* decide my worth. And after everything I've done to Ten, I'm not worth much. But I'm going to change that.

Escape. Save Ten, kill our enemies. Rescue the survivors in Many Ends, including my mother.

It's time to face facts. Myriadians lie. The end justifies the means, Ambrosine said. What he meant: Sometimes, for the greater good, evil is necessary. But he's wrong. Evil is never necessary. It will never help the masses, will only ever hurt. And lies *are* evil; the very language of malevolence.

If the Secondking will lie about little things, he will most assuredly lie about big things. Like Fate and Fusion.

Again and again, Ten has proven herself trustworthy. *That* is why I will follow her wherever she leads. *That* is why I will trust her, no matter what the circumstance might be.

If I had a team, I would ask others for help. Might even beg. Anything for Ten. But there's no one here willing to offer aid or watch my back. My fault. Like Ambrosine, I lied to the people closest to me to advance my own agenda.

Never again.

I will be the man Ten wants. The man she needs. The man she deserves.

Victor enters another Stairwell. In order to pass through this one, however, he must endure an ID test. He places his hand on a data pad, and a machine reads the chip embedded in his Shell's wrist. As soon as he's cleared, we enter the most coveted neighborhood in Myriad, hence its name: The Coveted.

All of the Secondking's children live here. This is where all Generals live, as well, and where all Abrogates will live, when they arrive. This is where I have wanted to live my entire life. Mansions, castles and palaces abound. There isn't a hut or a shack in the bunch.

Victor lives in a palace that makes the most exquisite building in the Land of the Harvest look like a hovel. A bridge leads to a towering golden statue of his likeness. On either side is a wild, rushing waterfall that flows into a rocky moat. Ambrosia trees fill the courtyard and sweeten the air. Myriad's emblem is carved in walls made of crystal.

Servants stand outside, opening the doors as he approaches.

"Leave us," he barks.

The pitter-patter of rushing footsteps sounds as guards and maids rush to obey, dodging opulent furnishings framed by a plethora of precious gems. A Florentine ebony chest inlaid with rubies. A table made entirely of sapphires. A diamond encrusted sofa with a solid gold frame. But the prince's most prized possession? An alabaster display case with a man-pelt inside.

I've heard the story about the pelt a million times. Everyone has. Over the eons, Ambrosine and his brother Eron have met twice to discuss a peace treaty. At least, Eron the Prince of Doves believed peace was the goal. The first time, Ambrosine betrayed and skinned his brother. The second time, after Eron's skin had grown back, Ambrosine rinsed and repeated.

He would have killed Eron if he could have, but Eron survived.

One pelt hangs in the Temple of Unholies as a display of Ambrosine's "strength." He must have given the other pelt to Victor as a thank you for bombing Troika.

Once, I bought into the hype, believing true strength came

from a willingness to do whatever proved necessary to achieve victory. No longer. If the means is unjust, *nothing* justifies it.

However, I'm not looking for justification right now.

Victor sets my cage in the center of the room, a loud clang assaulting my overly sensitive ears. I'm not yet healed from all those volts of electricity.

I search my surroundings and find one of my Shells stands next to the display case. On the coffee table rests a remote and a large metal tong—no question, it's for my neck. Like the cage, the tong is made for both spirit and Shell.

He prepared for this, I realize. He planned to take over my "care" all along.

With a smile, he lifts the remote and flips a switch. Suddenly the cage is electrified, one volt after another spearing me in place. Even when the volts die down, I'm unable to move. Tremors continue to rack me, and I know Ten is enduring the same.

Payback will hurt—him.

His smile grows ever wider as he opens the cage and uses the tong to drag me out. He forces my spirit to slip inside the Shell and there's nothing I can do to stop him. Some force greater than myself acts as a magnet, holding me inside.

When he releases the tong, a metal collar remains around my neck, and the magnetic charge intensifies, ensuring I'm stuck inside my new prison—a prison bound to the wall with the same kind of shadows Javier used on Ten. The dark bands wrap around the wrists and ankles.

"I'm having fun already." He unsheathes a knife—and stabs me in the stomach. "Are you?"

My lips part on a grunt of pain. While a Shell usually mutes the sensations a spirit feels, negative or positive, I'm overly

sensitized. I. Feel. Everything. Which means *Ten* feels everything, my poor, sweet lass.

Revenge…

"I will make yer brain leak through yer eyes until you cry
your thoughts," I tell him calmly.

As Lifeblood pours from my wound, weakening me further, he steps back to survey his handiwork. "You look good
with extra holes. Let's add a few more, shall we?"

"Go ahead. Do it. Just know I'll repay you a hundredfold
for every slice."

"Brave talk for a prisoner." He sinks the blade into my
other side, and as I hiss, Victor wipes my Lifeblood on his
leather pants. "You should lighten up. This isn't personal. I
have a lot of anger issues with your girl, and not a lot of time
to exorcise them."

"Poor baby. Are you angry because she kicked your ass?
Twice?"

Rage flares in his eyes—a reflection of my own? He
punches me in the chest, right over my heart, warping the
next beat. Then, deceptively calm, he asks, "What do you see
in her? You can find a pretty girl anywhere, any time, and
really, they all look the same in the dark. So what turns you
and Archer into fools whenever this one steps into a room?"

Easy. "She has proven loyal, selfless and kind." Three things
I never knew I admired, until now. "Things you'll never be."

He laughs a little. "You make her sound like a dog."

"Which is why dogs are often better than people."

Another flare of rage. Another punch in the chest.

Forgive. Win with Light.

Again the other side of me speaks up. This time, as I fight
for breath, I actually listen. I want to win. Obviously, fighting

fire with fire doesn't work. You must fight fire with water. Only Light can chase away darkness.

Right now, there's only one person who might share her Light with me.

Hating myself, I push my voice along the bridge that's connecting me to Ten. —*I need your Light, lass. Archer's, too. Actually, any Light anyone in Troika can spare. Please. I doona deserve it. I know this. But I'm askin' anyway. It's the only way I know tae save you.*—

Seconds tick by without a response, and I fear she's given up on me.

One more chance. I need one more chance. I won't mess up, not again. I'll pour everything I've got, everything I am, into this.

Finally her soft voice whispers over the Grid. —*Or you hope to weaken me further, and do what Javier failed to do: destroy Troika through me.*—

The accusation cuts deeper than Victor's blows. But just like Victor's blows, it is deserved. —*Please, lass. I know I've done you wrong, but I need the chance tae do you right. This is the only way.*—

—*Only Killian Flynn can be pervy and apologetic at the same time.*—

—*It's a gift.*— She's going to trust me? At least in this? I wait, hopeful, ready to be flooded with Light, but one minute ticks into another and the darkness remains as thick as ever.

Too weak?

Decided not to trust me, after all?

—*I'm not currently connected to Archer. I got my Light from—never mind. Ready?*— A moment passes in silence. —*Argh! This must be how Archer felt when he tried to send me Light. You're shielded. Drop the shield, Killian.*—

Shielded?

A fist slams into my jaw, my head whipping to the side. "Are you paying attention?" Victor demands. "Or are you going to tell me I'm hitting like a girl?"

"I would never lie so outrageously. I mean, you'll need to hit a lot harder if you want to be compared to a girl."

My words prick his pride, and once again rage explodes inside his eyes. Shouting obscenities, spittle spraying from the corners of his mouth, he whales on me, slamming his fist into my face again and again. With every new blow, my pain magnifies, more Lifeblood leaking from me, my skin shredding inside and out.

What's worse, I can feel *Ten's* pain. Almost my undoing.

"You want this to stop?" Victor runs his tongue over his teeth. "Beg me, then. Beg me, and I'll stop."

I…can't. He's read my file; I know he has. Even the parts Archer deleted. There's always a backup. Victor knows the General made me beg, then never followed through. He won't follow through, either.

Would Ten beg for *my* life, just for the chance to save me pain?

"You picked the wrong team, Killian. In Myriad, you could have become someone of means, who makes a difference. In Troika, you will never be accepted. You'll always be the Butcher."

Maybe, but maybe not. How will I know unless I give everyone a chance?

How will I know if I don't fight for better?

The truth is, people who are hurt oftentimes choose to hurt others, whether wittingly or unwittingly. Either way, it's a vicious cycle. By maiming and killing him, I will perpetuate the problem.

Perhaps Ten *did* manage to share her Light with me. Perhaps I possess a reservoir of Light and just didn't realize it. Miracle of miracles, my desire for vengeance has begun to fade. But then, darkness is never a match for Light. The two do not tangle up. As soon as Light comes, darkness cannot remain the sole focus.

My shields drop. Suddenly a beam of Light zooms across the Grid, followed by another and another.

Ten's voice fills my head. —*Thank the Firstking! I've opened the link with Archer. We're giving you all we've got.*—

Victor lands his next blow—and bellows with pain. He stumbles away from me. At the same time, the shadows in my head scramble, desperate to hide. The shadows around my wrists and ankles loosen, fall away. The collar around my neck clinks open and thuds on the floor.

For a moment, only a moment, I'm bathed in pure Light. Not just Light, but a rainbow of Light. More real than the Shell I'm housed in or the air I'm breathing. It is brilliant. Luminous. Glorious. Hope and beauty in vibrant Technicolor. Everything my life has been missing. Everything I never knew I needed.

The Light heals my wounds, strengthens my body and fades. Like one of my memories, it vanishes, all used up. I mourn the loss. Light is like food, I realize. One meal will never be enough to truly live.

My eyes narrow as I focus on Victor. Another gift of the Light—the magnetic charge is gone. I can move in and out of the Shell at will. I can move, period.

Before he can puzzle through what's happened, I yank the blade from his grip.

The old me would have smiled at him, the same cold smile he's leveled on me so many times. I would have stabbed him, gifting him with wounds similar to my own. But I'm not the old me. Because of Ten, I've been made new.

$1 + 10 = 11$

$1 + 1 = 2$

2 is better than 1. We are better together.

In a single, fluid movement, I pick up the metal collar and dive for Victor. As our Shells crash together, he's ready for me and throws a punch. A split second after I block, we land. He takes the brunt of impact, his skull knocking into the marble tiles, disorienting him.

Wasting no time, *I* throw a punch. Or four. My rings rip through his skin, Lifeblood seeping from him. I have forgiven him, yes, but that doesn't mean I have to let him go free. He must be stopped.

When he is sufficiently disoriented, I scramble up, my knees pinning his shoulders. Once again I hammer my fist into his face. With my actions, my rage attempts to resurface and overtake me, but I fight it off with the same fierceness I fight Victor, maintaining a clear head. Ten was right. Emotion clouds judgment. Alive, Victor can be used...

Now I grin, a plan beginning to form.

The change in my expression frightens him. Good.

"Please," he croaks.

Well, well. Look at him beg.

"You mean I should show you mercy when you showed none to me?" Teeth bite into my skin, cutting into my knuckles, but I never pause. He bats at my arms—at first. "Apparently you have no' heard of sowin' and reapin'."

And what are you sowing right now?

You chose to forgive him. Now act like it.

A curse spills from my lips, but I raise my arms in the air, ending the assault.

His body goes lax as his head lolls to the side.

Taking no chances, I hurriedly step out of my Shell, pull his spirit out of his, and switch places with him. That done, I snap the collar around *his* neck.

It's odd, enslaving a Shell with my face.

Next I wrap a cloth around his eyes to hide the color of his irises, hook a muzzle over his mouth to keep him quiet, and anchor his hands behind his back.

"Doona think tae blame me for this," I tell his unconscious form, no longer fighting my accent. Had he let me go with Ten, this would never have happened. "Yer need for vengeance drove you straight tae yer doom."

A sense of urgency propels me from my new Shell. I strip, thankful there are mirrors everywhere. I study my tattoos. Line...line...line. Image. A woman's face, gentle, serene, even as tears of blood drip down her cheeks. One of those tears splashes onto one of the lines...

A memory clicks into place. The location of a stash of Troikan-made weapons. Things capable of hurting fellow Myriadians. Forbidden items. The penalty for having one, much less an arsenal, is death.

I look over the rest of my body. *Click, click. Click.* All excellent items. Myriadian weapons. Extra ambrosia. Shells. But none will help me now. Then I turn, look over my shoulder and scan my back. Again, I discard one buried treasure after another—

Click. A universal key. Yes. That! I can use it to free Ten from the town square.

Firstking save the realm then. I won't stop until every inch of Myriad is laid to waste.

Forgive. Save.

A demand from the other side of me. The Light side. I forgave Victor, because I sympathize with his past. I know the pain hiding in his heart. Been there, done that. But I don't think I can forgive Ambrosine. Too much betrayal, on too wide a scale.

You must. Break the cycle of betrayal.

Can I? I'm a new man, but old habits die hard.

Jaw locked, I dress, return to Victor's Shell, and head off.

I have to choose, and I choose Ten. Though I've broken the fragile threads of her trust, I will make amends. I will be better. She is my family now, and I'll prove it.

TROIKA

From: A_P_5/23.43.2
To: T_L_2/23.43.2, R_A_5/40.5.16
Subject: We've got problems

First, I'm using a stronger wattage, so hopefully this will reach you. Second, try not to crap yourself. I'll do the same.

Remember how I told you that two Generals joined Raanan, Deacon and Clementine at one of the warehouses? And do you also remember how you told me that Myriad was sending people to kill the Abrogates? Well, Myriad sent more than a few people. They sent an army. A battle broke out at all eighteen warehouses.

We were winning…until Myriad decided to bomb the warehouses, killing their own people. Many of the Abrogates are dead, their spirits now in Myriad.

General Ying Wo is dead, as well. General Alejandro is missing.

Also—yep, there's more—Sloan was killed. I'm so sorry.

I know you loved her. Perhaps this will lessen the blow: She fought like a true warrior. The humans we managed to save, we saved because of her.

Or perhaps that *doesn't* lesson the blow. Death is death. Deacon is inconsolable.

What's worse—yep, there's still worse—Penumbra has already begun to spread among humans...and spirits.

I'm sorry, but I won't be sending you any more Light, just in case I'm tainted. You've got your own darkness to handle. And I don't want to risk contacting you Grid to Grid, either.

We're in crisis, Ten, trying to cleanse our infected. We're new Conduits, and we're struggling, even with the princess's help. We need you. Please, come home. In Myriad, you are nothing but a target.

Light Brings Sight!
Archer Prince, Conduit of Conduits ←Yeah, I said it, and I stand by it

PS: Biscuit says "Hi hello how are you I miss you like crazy where are you I want to be with you please come home soon or I'm going to start peeing on your friends."

chapter eighteen

"Be true to your desires—be true to yourself."
—Myriad

Ten

As Javier carts me through the town square, he calls, "Meet Tenley Lockwood, a Troikan Conduit. She's considered their best soldier. The one they believe will win the war—for them."

Snickers ring out first, followed by boos, hisses and curses. "Troikan trash!" Rotted ambrosia pelts me.

I'm too horrified by Archer's message to lament my treatment. No one bothered to disable my comm after his beam of Light healed me; either they didn't notice or they don't care, because no Troikans are able to enter Myriad to help me.

I need to send a reply, and I will, as soon as I'm alone.

Javier reaches through the bars of my cage to rip away my clothing, leaving me in my undergarments. Cool air slaps my skin, but my mind remains unresponsive to my current circumstances. Penumbra is spreading. Sloan is dead, her spirit most likely in Many Ends. One Troikan General is dead, too. Another is missing.

Perhaps Alejandro has been imprisoned in the Land of the Harvest. Perhaps he's being tortured for information that can be used against his realm.

Maybe I should have followed Alejandro's orders before this started. Maybe I should have gone to the warehouse and done everything in my power to save Sloan and cleanse the infected humans. Would Ying Wo Ling still live? Would Alejandro be with his people?

Would I be dead?

Instead, I insisted on accompanying Killian to Myriad, buoyed by thoughts of peace and the belief that we would rescue every spirit trapped in Many Ends.

Killian warned me not to trust him, but once again, I insisted on doing things my way.

I'm Ten Lockwood, after all. I know everything.

Don't cry. Don't you dare cry.

Where is Killian now? What's being done to him?

I know he was stabbed twice, because sharp pains cut through *my* sides, Lifeblood pouring from me. He wanted my Light, and at the first opportunity, I shucked my distrust, desperate to help him.

Clearly I haven't learned my lesson, because I kept no Light for myself. It's better to give than receive, right?

But soon after the transfer, we both healed, and no new injuries have appeared on my body. So…he must have escaped Victor. Yes?

Will he come for me? Better question: Do I *want* him to come for him? I still don't trust him, and I cannot wait for him. I need to escape *now*. My friends are in danger— because of me. Though I wanted peace between the realms, I might have ushered in Troika's defeat and Myriad's victory. It's time for damage control.

I might be defeated now, but this isn't over. While there's breath, there's time.

—*Love my Ten. Need more Light?*—

My heart leaps with joy. Jeremy again. The fact that he's sharing with me…

He *must* be a Conduit. —*Save your strength, sweet boy.*— The future is uncertain. No telling how much Light he's going to need. Plus, if I were to inadvertently drain him…

Nope, can't risk it.

I tell him, —*If shadows try to invade your mind, let me know right away. I'll help you fight them.*— Or die trying.

Jeremy giggles, a new ray of Light sneaking past every defense I have. Any lingering pain vanishes. Weakness subsides. My trembling limbs go still.

—*No more, young man. I mean it.*—

Another giggle before our connection fades.

Concentrate on the task at hand. Worrying about him won't help either of us right now.

Okay. Need a plan of action. First, I've got to open my cage in secret. But how? Men and women, young and old, surround me. This is the City of Carnal Delights, and I'm the main attraction.

The town square is nothing but a glorified circus, where degradation is an appetizer and humiliation is the meal. There are other cages nearby, all positioned on a dais; some are occupied, others are empty. The other prisoners have been stripped to their undergarments, like me. Vendors sell things to throw at the prisoners. Hail, rotten manna, buckets filled with creepy, crawling insects.

The younger members of the crowd laugh and jeer at me, enjoying my predicament. Some of the older members watch me with concern, reminding me that there *are* good people in Myriad.

Am I truly considering returning to Troika to help destroy this entire realm?

To save my friends...to protect my brother...

Yes. I am.

Ugh! Who have I become? And which of these people can I convince to aid me? My gaze scans the sea of faces only to zoom back to—

Aunt Lina?

Shock pounds a nail of dismay through my heart. She can't be here. No one told me she died, and someone absolutely, unequivocally, would have told me. Ambrosine would have used her against me.

But *she* told me...

Did I tell you I died in the Land of the Harvest?

Maybe Ambrosine doesn't know who she is. As a human, Lina had dark, graying hair and age-lined skin. Her eyes were often milky, a phenomena that happened every time her brain made the switch from Aunt Lina to Looney Lina.

No matter Lina's age, though, Looney Lina acted five years old. The milky film over her eyes blinded her, whether physically or psychologically, but only to the present. She saw far into the future, her head filled with tragedies that had yet to happen.

The woman meeting my gaze has a glossy mane of silvery-white hair. Her skin is pale but flawless, and her eyes are brilliant blue.

With all the changes in her appearance, I'm not sure how I recognized her. Not that the changes are surprising. After my Firstdeath, my black hair turned blue.

She shifts, disappearing in the crowd, and I have to tamp

down the urge to shout at her. The rest of her message plays
through my head.

Did I tell you I died? I'm sorry I killed Killian.

*I cried. You cried. I cried some more. I'm glad my husband made
it up to you.*

Light was the answer. Light was always the answer.

Obviously Killian hasn't died, and I haven't cried.

If Light is the answer, what is the question? Who was—
is?—her husband?

"Not so high and mighty now, are you?" A sneering Javier
runs a metal baton over the bars of my cage. "I'm told this
is where traitors and Troikan sympathizers end up. I'm also
told they're more than happy to prove their loyalty to Myriad
after a few weeks of confinement."

I focus on him even as I add "find Lina" to my To Do list.
"You were misinformed. The condemned want their freedom, not a chance to prove their loyalty. Guaranteed, former
prisoners hate this realm—they're simply too afraid to say so."

"Fearful is better than loyal. Loyalties can change, but fear
never dies."

"Wrong." People like Javier, heck, like Ambrosine, think
they need others to fear them in order to get what they want,
but that isn't true. Just the opposite, in fact. Finally I get what
Levi tried to teach me when my training began. If you want
results, make people love you. Love inspires love. If you want
a secret enemy, make people fear you. Fear inspires betrayal.
"Eventually, people do everything in their power to destroy
the things they fear."

He pales, but spits another curse at me.

Troika isn't perfect. The citizens might be spirits, but deep
inside they are still human, and where there are humans, there
are mistakes. But one thing we do not do is lock up "traitors"

and "sympathizers," strip them of their clothing and dignity, and hurl objects at them.

I'd call that a win.

Teach him *to fear*.

My darker side rears her ugly head, and I grind my teeth. No. Absolutely not. Fear isn't the answer. Fear is a symptom of hate. Hate isn't all-powerful. Love is stronger.

My eyes widen. That's right. *Love is stronger. Light is the answer.* The words reverberate in my mind, creating an equation without numbers.

Troikan Light comes from Eron, who powers the sun. Eron is love. "Light is love. Love is Light."

How else could Jeremy share his Light—love—with me?

"What did you say?" Javier demands.

I ignore him.

If shadows are born of envy, hatred and fear, then Light must be born of love. Fondness. Tenderness. Intimacy. Endearment. Attachment. Devotion. Adoration. Passion.

Closing my eyes, I center my attention on love. Despite everything that's happened, I love Killian. That hasn't changed. The hard times are better with him than the best times with others.

I love Jeremy. I love Archer, the wind beneath my wings. I love Clay, my loyal, faithful friend. I love Deacon, Reed, Biscuit and Kayla. I love Raanan and Clementine. My helpers. I love Sloan, who proved herself loyal in the end.

I love Troika. I love Meredith, Hazel and Steven. I love Levi and even Alejandro and the other Generals. They fight for what they believe in: truth, justice and equality for all.

My heart begins to warm as…yes! Light flickers.

Shadows claw at me, determined not to lose ground. I love my mother, a Myriadian.

The Light spreads, and warmth follows.

Javier sucks a breath between his teeth. "What are you doing?"

Shadows quake.

"She's glowing," someone in the crowd calls, and others boo. "Make her stop!"

Someone buys one of the buckets of insects, and boos instantly morph into cheers. The other prisoners scramble to the corner of their cage, but they needn't have worried. The insects are tossed on me, only me. I remain in place, refusing to react, even as a thousand little legs skitter over me, cutting me, biting me, stinging my skin, muscle and even bone. I'm filled with love, and there's no room for hate. And this? This is nothing.

I even love these people. They are deceived. Connected to Ambrosine, mainlining his hatred and envy. They need my help, not my censure.

My lack of concern disconcerts Javier. "Stop that." He slams the baton into my cage, causing the entire thing to quake.

"I feel sorry for you," I tell him.

His jaw drops and he sputters for a response. "*You* feel sorry for *me?*"

"When I return to Troika, and I will, I'll be reprimanded for disobeying a direct order, but I'll also be accepted back into the fold. My worth isn't based on what I do, but on who I am. A Troikan. Beloved. You will never be able to say the same. You've already been cast aside by your king, labeled a failure."

With a snarl, he reaches through the cage, and though he can't touch me, his shadows can; they extend from his fingertips to wrap around my neck and squeeze. As I fight for air, he smugly says, "How do you feel about me now?"

Love…love…do I love *him*? The worst of the worst.

"Stop this." A young woman pushes her way through the throng. "Please."

Dark hair frames a face I recognize. She has a small nose and adorable, Cupid's bow lips. Her skin is a few shades lighter than her jet-black hair while her eyes are a few shades lighter than her skin and ringed with gold.

Dior Nichols in the flesh. Or rather, spirit.

I cleansed her of Penumbra, only to find her re-infected the next day, all because she refused to cut ties with Javier. Bad company *will* corrupt.

In the Everlife, she is more beautiful than ever, but she is still suffering from the effects of Penumbra, black lines branching under the surface of her skin. Her clothes are wrinkled and dirty, as if she hasn't showered or changed since her Firstdeath.

Archer was right. Troikans are in danger. But so are Myriadians. The infection can turn an ordinary citizen into an Abrogate, but I've gone head-to-head with it, and I know what others don't. Penumbra obliterates everything good and right inside a person, leaving only the things that thrive in absolute darkness. Hatred, misery, violence, despair.

As I gasp for breath she looks me over and squares her shoulders. "Where is the key to her cage? I'm letting her go."

Do I love *her*?

She's the reason Levi is dead. He went to court for her, acting as her Barrister, and died trying to save her. I want to hate her, but how can I? She made a mistake; she believed the lies Javier, her boyfriend, told her.

"Leave," Javier snaps.

"Let her go or lock me up with her," Dior states bluntly.

He goes stiff, ready to tell her off. Maybe because he's embarrassed by her behavior. Maybe because he doesn't want the crowd to turn on her. Either way, I brush a spider off my shoulder and tell her, "Don't worry about me." If I die and wind up in Many Ends, I can escape, free the spirits trapped there...and ambush Ambrosine. Win/win.

"I don't want to lock you up." Through gritted teeth, he adds, "But I will if you stay."

"That's fine," she says. "I'm standing with her—and against you."

His eyes widen. "You don't mean—"

"I do. I'm done with you. I should have been done with you long before now. You're a liar and a cheat. But I'm no better. I've been a fool. I let you play on my fears, convince me to stay with Myriad, despite the awful things they'd done to me, because I was afraid of being punished by Troikans. A good man died because of my decision." Tears well in her eyes, and her chin trembles. "I punish myself more than any-one else could."

"Dior." He reaches for her, but she wrenches back.

"No. Don't touch me. I hate you, and I hate myself."

—*Ten? Lass?*— Killian's voice drifts along the Grid, and my heart races with a mix of emotions I can't name. —*I'm comin' for you. Almost there. You need tae know...*—

The wall of my distrust shakes, but in the end holds steady, cutting off his words. Silence reigns.

No time to reach out. "I'm sorry, Ten," Dior says, drawing me out of my head. "Your father...he's on his way."

My heart races *faster*. One, ten, twenty, fifty—counting the beats doesn't do me any good.

Daddy loves me. Daddy loves me not. Loves me. Loves me not.

Yeah. That one. He loves me not.

"What's worse," she adds. There's worse? "He's got your mom."

Javier laughs, overcome with glee at the first sign of my distress. Then, my dad is there, standing beside my tormentor. He's alone, no sign of my mother. Like everyone else, Senator Leonard Lockwood is young and beautiful, and in his prime. He's tall, as leanly muscled as pictures promised, with blue hair and mismatched eyes: one blue, one green.

How can we resemble each other so much but be so different?

He's shirtless but wearing black leather pants. His feet are tucked into combat boots. Women eye him appreciatively, as do some of the men.

His gaze meets mine—and he smiles. "You destroyed my Firstlife. It's nice to see you're finally getting what you deserve."

The words slice me to ribbons. Deep down, part of me has always yearned for his approval. His affection. Even when he paid Dr. Vans to torture me at Prynne Asylum.

A little girl is supposed to be her daddy's princess, not his nightmare.

"How adorable," I tell him, feigning nonchalance, acting as if I'm not sobbing inside. "You're a fool. You haven't realized you destroyed your own life. As for me, I wanted only what you'd already been given. A chance to make a decision about my future."

"You thought of no one but yourself."

"Hello, Pot. Meet Kettle."

His eyes narrow to tiny slits. "Watch your mouth, young lady. Speak to me with respect."

"Or what?"

"Or I'll punish your mother for your crimes."

When he jerks his arm forward, I notice a strip of leather in his hand. At the end of that strip? Grace Lockwood, my mother. A metal collar circles her throat. She's on a leash, I realize, anger threatening to detonate inside me.

My love for this man withers.

My mom's head is bowed, shoulder-length hair shielding her face. When she was human, the strands were auburn. Here in the Everlife, the strands are fire engine-red.

She sniffles, a glistening teardrop falling to the ground.

"Let her go," Dior says, stepping toward him, but Javier grabs hold of her, keeping her in place.

The anger bomb detonates. Fire seems to sear me. Debris rains. Shrapnel embeds, slicing my heart to ribbons.

"Let her go," I scream, launching forward to rattle the door of my cage. "Now!"

"Or what?" my dad asks, mocking me.

Breathing becomes more difficult, every molecule of air an inferno in my lungs.

Kill him. Teach him the error of his ways. He deserves pain, and not even you, Goody Two-shoes that you are, can deny it.

Dread overtakes me. Not my dark side. No, no, no. Not now. My resistance is weak...

I shake my head, hoping to dislodge the terrible urges bombarding me. Or maybe I'm holding on to those urges. I want to hurt my dad the way he has hurt me. The moment I do, however, the darkness wins. It will own me; I know it. With every fiber of my being, I know it.

I will do everything I chastised my dad and Killian for doing.

You can't preach the merits of love, then turn around and hate your enemy. Anyone can love a friend. It takes a warrior to love an enemy.

Deep breath in, out. "You won't hurt her," I croak.

"Won't I? She attempted to defect to Troika, a terrible crime. As punishment, she was placed in the Kennels until early this morning, when she was gifted to me. I'm allowed to harm her however I wish."

"Gifted to you? As if she's a pair of shoes?" Does any life other than his own hold any meaning to him?

"Had she supported her realm, she would have been punished but forgiven, eventually permitted to rejoin society. But she continued to push for a court date, determined to defect."

"Let her go. Please." I swallow my pride. What good is pride, anyway? The opinion of others matters little. "This is between you and me. Face me like the man you never were in Firstlife."

A new smile blooms, but it radiates fury. "Beg a little more. I like the sound of it."

I don't hesitate. "Please, Leonard. Dad. If you want to hurt someone, hurt me." I want what she and I were denied as humans: more time together. I want her to defect to Troika, as planned, and raise Jeremy. This. This is a true desire of my heart. "Don't deny your son the mother he so desperately needs."

Now my dad stiffens. "You mean the son she tried to hide from me?"

Mom lifts her gaze, finally meeting mine. We have the same pale skin, freckles and eyes too big for our faces, though hers are dark and filled with a storm of tears. I inherited her high cheekbones, small but pert nose and heart-shaped lips, as well. Jeremy, too. He is her masculine counterpart.

"I'm sorry," she whispers.

"The past is the past," I tell her. The bond between a parent and child is sacred, a gift as well as a responsibility. "Jeremy needs you, too, Dad. One day, there will be peace between the realms. We could be a—"

"Shut up!" His nostrils flare as he inhales sharply.

While my parents failed me most of my teenage life, my mother more than made up for it the day of her Firstdeath, doing everything in her power to break me out of Prynne. She sent Jeremy to Troika, even though she would end up in Myriad. There's still time for my dad.

"I love you," she tells me softly. "Tell Jeremy I love him, too. You two made my life worth living. You are my greatest accomplishments, and I—"

"I told you to be quiet," Dad snaps, yanking her leash.

I reach for her, intending to take her hand, but he wrenches her backward, out of range.

"Oh, daughter dearest," he says, and *tsks*. "You're supposed to be smart, but you haven't yet grasped the gravity of the situation. Though enjoyable, no amount of begging is going to save your mother's life. Either you let Javier do his job, or I kill her, right here, right now."

I gulp. I can't let Javier invade the Grid. I can't save one woman while condemning an entire realm to death. Not even *this* woman.

"Momma," I say, my chin trembling. Hot tears stream down my cheeks.

"I understand, my sweet girl." She offers me a brave smile. "I want you to do something for me, okay? I want you to fight. Fight for what's right and never stop. Never give in—"

Again my dad wrenches her leash, silencing her. Then he forces her to kneel in front of my cage. My tears pour faster.

"Perhaps you don't think I'm serious." He unsheathes a dagger—and presses the tip into her throat, where a bead of Lifeblood wells. "Last chance, Tenley."

"Don't do this." Dior struggles against Javier's grip to no avail. "Please, don't."

"I know you're serious, Dad, but I won't allow Myriad to poison my home. My family." I grip the bars of my cage and shake. "If you do this, *you* poison *yourself*, and I will—"

"You'll do *nothing.*" He jerks the blade across my mother's neck. As I go still with shock and horror, he looks me straight in the eye, and says, "You have no one but yourself to blame."

chapter nineteen

"The greatest expression of love is giving."
—Troika

Killian

A woman's scream rips through the City of Carnal Delights. Ten. I know it's her.

Frantic and panicked, I pick up speed, rushing through a crowd, holding a bound Victor by the neck and dragging him behind me. As long as I keep my gaze downcast, no one will know we've switched places.

—*Ten. Lass.*— I shout her name, even though I no longer sense her along the Grid. If something has happened to her...

No. She isn't hurt. If she were, I would know. Right?

Protests erupt as I continue to push through the masses. As soon as my identity registers, protests become mutters of awe. Apparently Victor Prince is a national hero.

Finally I reach the dais in the town square. I scan the cages for Ten...where is...there. She's on the other side. I'd recognize that fall of azure hair anywhere.

Still dragging my cargo, I round the dais, then stop abruptly. Ten's father stands in front of her, Javier and Dior at his side. Dior struggles for freedom. At their feet, Ten's mother. Lifeblood pools around the woman, her body motionless. A body that is disintegrating before my eyes, as slain spirits do. Before *Ten's* eyes.

Ten is still as a statue, her gaze remaining on the pool of Lifeblood. Her arms are wrapped around her middle, as if she's attempting to protect her vital organs.

My heart shudders and aches as I drop Victor. Rage returns, boiling inside me.

Calm. Steady. I can't ask questions about what transpired. Victor might already know the answers.

Frustration joins the deluge inside me, only fueling the rage. Whatever the reasons, the cruelty of Grace Lockwood's death leaves me floundering. How can a man do this to his wife? How can a father do this to his child?

Once, I would have justified the act, thinking Grace would be Fused to a human spirit and reborn. Why mourn her loss? But life is precious. Every stage of life should be cherished, savored.

If Ten is right and Myriadians appear in Many Ends after Second-death, Grace is now faced with an eternity of torture. Unless we save her.

Leonard points a Lifeblood-soaked dagger at Ten. "You won't have to mourn your mother's death long. You'll join her soon enough, little girl."

My hands fist, my biceps flexing; I'm ready to lash out. What would I do if Ten were killed?

I. Would. Unleash. Hell.

A bitter laugh congeals in my throat, but I swallow it. Actually, I'd do nothing. She would go to the Rest, maybe, probably, and I would go to Many Ends, maybe, probably, and be tortured just like every other Myriadian. Either way, our time would be cut short, and I'm not okay with that. I'm not okay with any of this.

But...isn't a life without her better than the alternative? What if Ten winds up in Many Ends with me? She wants to go, plans to go, and she knows the way out, but I hate the thought of her in more danger. *Worse* danger.

I flip up my gaze, hoping to meet her eyes, to reassure her—*I'm here, I'll help*—but she's staring down at the spot her mother died, tears pouring down her cheeks, leaving track marks. My chest constricts.

This isn't the first time she's had to watch her mother fade away.

Bits and pieces of memory are coming more frequently now, the shadows losing their hold on me. At the end of her Firstlife, Grace was poisoned by Pearl Bennett, my former boss. The woman who adopted me only to return me when her daughter died. Ten had just escaped the Prynne Asylum and rushed home in time for her mother's final breath. Only seconds later, Jeremy, Ten's brother, took *his* final breath.

Ten cried that day, too.

I offered to take her brother's spirit to Myriad, so that he could be with their mother, but Ten rejected me, giving the boy to Archer instead. At the time, the rejection had cut like a knife, reminding me of all the times I had been passed over at the Learning Center, never good enough, unwanted.

Then. That moment. A part of me had begun to resent her. The rest of me—the smarter part—never stopped loving her. Now, I understand her reasoning. See so clearly. Loving someone doesn't mean agreeing with their bad ideas—and my idea was very, very bad. Absolutely terrible. Here, Jeremy would be used against Ten. In Troika, harming the infant brother in order to bring the sister into line isn't an option, no matter the desperation of the need.

Without looking away from Ten, I toss "Killian" in Javier's direction. Careful of my speech patterns, I say, "Put him in a cage."

"Why?" Javier releases Dior and grabs hold of the prisoner. "I thought you were going to—"

"I don't recall asking for your commentary. I gave you an order. Obey it."

Dior steps up to Ten's cage and wraps her fingers over Ten's hands. "I'm so sorry."

Ten remains silent.

Javier stiffens, and so do I. Is he going to challenge my authority?

After a slight hesitation, he obeys.

"Leave the traitor bound and blindfolded," I tell him, and don't bother offering an explanation. I'm Victor Prince, right? I do what I want, when I want, and the rest of the world can deal.

Leonard Lockwood bows in my direction. "Good to see you again, Mr. Prince."

How easy it would be for me to rip the blade from his hand and slay him. But I cannot say all life is precious one moment and kill the next. If my actions do not align with my words, I am a liar, and I refuse to be a liar. Ten hates lies, and for the first time in my life, so do I.

"Everyone leave," I shout. "Now."

"I'll stay," Dior tells Ten. "I'll stay and—"

"Go," she croaks, finally speaking up. "Just go."

Greater tension steals over Dior, but finally she nods and stalks off.

"You, too," I tell Javier and Leonard. "Go."

Javier stares at me, hard. "What are you going to do to her?"

"Whatever I want." I step closer to him, my chest bumping up against his. "Do you have a problem with that?"

Now he bristles. "What's wrong with you, man? Why are you acting this way?"

Had Victor treated Javier as a friend? I'll have to tread carefully here. "Did you or did you not fail to invade Lockwood's Grid?" A question is not a lie. And casting blame, well, I figure Victor is very good at that.

He huffs and puffs, probably scouring his mind for an excuse, a way to cast blame to someone else. Then he says, "I'm new to this. There's no one here to teach me, so I'm forced to learn as I go."

"When *I* succeed with her, you can ask me how I did it, and I might explain." I make a shooing motion with my hand. "Now go."

Leonard pulls him back, and the two spin on booted heels to stomp off.

As soon as I'm certain we're alone, I attempt to speak into Ten's head, afraid she won't believe me otherwise. The words never leave my head. How I *despise* the wall between us.

"Ten. Lass. I'm Killian, and I'm goin' tae free you." I crouch so that we're eye level and press my thumb into the lock. A second passes, then another, but nothing happens. I curse. I'm in Victor's Shell. He is the king's beloved son; his print should open *every* cage.

"I know who you are." Finally her gaze lifts to meet mine. Those mismatched eyes are windows to endless pools of anguish. "A change of eye color isn't the only tell. You and Victor smell nothing alike. He's tart. You're sweet."

Thank the Firstking for—

"But I trust you as much as I trust Victor," she adds, her tone flat. "Meaning, not at all. I thought I'd found a well of love, one big enough for everyone. I was wrong."

A knife seems to twist in my chest. "I'm so incredibly sorry for betrayin' yer trust. I'm sorry for gettin' you into this mess. I'm sorry about yer mother. More sorry than I can ever articulate. I'm sorry...for everythin'. If I could go back—"

"But you can't. None of us can."

Twist. "You're right. But I will never stop trying tae make up for my actions." Without hesitation, I settle on my knees. I expect my mind to scream in denial, to demand I rise, something. Instead, I remain shockingly calm. Here I am, the Butcher, the boy who once refused to beg for scraps, now begging for forgiveness, and happy for the chance.

Her eyes go wide. "What are you doing?"

"I'm so incredibly sorry," I repeat. "You deserved—deserve—better, and I will give you better. I know I do no' deserve absolution, but I'm beggin' for it anyway." Some things are worth *any* sacrifice. "No one and nothin' means more tae me than you."

She gulps.

"I'll do more beggin' soon, have no doubt. As for now... let's take care of yer needs." I stand and yank off my T-shirt and toss the garment through the bars.

"Thank you," she mutters.

I remember the time I told her I wouldn't thank her for her aid, and I want to kick my own ass.

After pulling the material over her head, she draws in a deep breath and squares her shoulders. The sadness and sorrow seem to leave her, quickly replaced by determination.

I've seen this same transformation come over her many

times, as she shucked off emotion in order to turn her attention to her endgame. I'm staggered, and impressed.

I'm also proud. This is my wife.

"Did your memory return?" she asks.

I will not disrespect her with anything less than the truth,
because I would rather die than give her another reason to doubt
me. "Not fully, but I'm rememberin' more every minute."

Her expression doesn't change.

Twist, twist. I wish so badly she would look at me the way
she used to, with admiration and adoration. But even if she
doesn't? I'll never stop fighting for her.

"Do you have a key to my cage?" she asks.

"No, but I'll acquire one."

"Sow and reap, huh? I acquired one for you, now you acquire one for me."

"Not just sow and reap. You are the best person I know,
and I want you free. But, since Victor's print didn't work, the
cages will open only with the fingerprint of a Magister." The
men and women in charge of the Kennels. "I'll be payin' one
a visit and returnin' within the hour."

Her head cants to the side. "Do you think saving me will
make me trust you?"

TWIST. "I know my word means nothin' tae you right now,
but I'm not goin' tae rest until we've saved our mothers from
Many Ends. At the same time, I'll be doin' everythin' in my
power tae win you back." I *have* to win her back. I might not
know the full breadth of my past, but I know beyond a doubt
I need her in my future. Without her, I have nothing, no one.
"Even if it takes me forever, I'll consider my life well lived."

She is *my life.*

"You're right." She stretches out her legs in a deceptively

causal pose, as cold to me as I was to her. "Your word means nothing to me."

I flinch, rubbing away the sting in my chest. What I don't do? React to the rejection in typical Killian Flynn fashion. I refuse to lash out at her or try to protect myself from further hurt by distancing myself emotionally.

For the first time in my life, I have something worth fighting for. Screw my old memories. I don't need them. I'm making new ones.

I'm not proud of what I've done, but one day soon, I will be.

"I hate tae leave you, lass, but I'm gettin' you that key."

"Just…be careful out there," she says, and plucks at the frayed edge of the shirt. "There's a chance my aunt is lying in wait somewhere. According to the message she sent me, she plans to kill you."

I long to reach through the bars and touch her beautiful face, but I don't, because I don't want my girl uncomfortable. "I'll be careful. And I will be back for you. I will prove myself tae you. Nothin' will stop me."

TROIKA

From: Unknown
To: A_P_5/23.43.2
Subject: Hi

If you want to save Ten's life, you'll meet me at the Veil of Midnight. Bring only the core four. Also, I'm going to marry a General. Congrats to me!

TROIKA

From: A_P_5/23.43.2
To: Unknown
Subject: Lina?

Of course I want to save Ten's life. But how can I trust you to help her and not hurt her—and the "core four"? What are you talking about? And which General are you going to marry?

Light Brings Sight!
Conduit-in-training,
Archer Prince

chapter twenty

"Love is the only wasted emotion. It removes focus from your
realm—and yourself!"
—Myriad

Ten

So much to process...

My mother is dead. My father murdered her. Killian begged
me to forgive him. I don't...

Thoughts begin to fragment, different emotions surging
through me. At the forefront: horror. My mother is now inside Many Ends. At least, I think she is. My theory hasn't yet
been proven.

But let's say I'm right. How long until the monsters capture and torture her?

*I love you. Made my life worth living. Fight for what's right and
never stop.*

My forced calm is shattered as tears burn the backs of my eyes.

"Lass," Killian says, hanging back.

"Go," I say. "Do what you need to do." I rub my fingers
over the words tattooed on my forearm. *Loyalty. Passion.
Liberty.*

My fingers stray to the shadow of the horse, and I frown. The image is fading. Because my bond to Killian is fading?

Is that what I want?

The tears burn *hotter*. I don't know what I want. I don't know anything anymore.

With a last, lingering look, he rushes out of sight. Will he return? I don't know. He's acting like my Killian 1.0, but what is truth and what is lie?

Doesn't matter. I can rely only on myself, and I won't be a damsel in distress. No, oh, no.

I'm sniffling as I wipe the tears away with the back of my wrist. There will be no mourning. Not now. There's too much to do, too much at stake. I can fall apart later.

Determined, I stuff the pain of my mother's death deep inside my heart. Next I stuff the fury directed at my father. Maybe hatred, too. Then I stuff the hurt Killian caused. Using distrust and disappointment as brick and mortar, I erect a wall. Nothing gets in, nothing gets out. Good, that's good.

Feeling somewhat sane again, I lift my head. If my mother is trapped in Many Ends, I'll save her when I save everyone else. This? This isn't the last I've seen of her.

Now to get free. I reach through the bars of the cage to try and jimmy the lock, but it holds.

In the distance, I catch a glimmer of color. A man is peeking around a corner. Looking for someone specific? As soon as he deduces no one is nearby, he rushes my way. A woman follows behind him, a basket clutched to her chest.

"Here. Ambrosia." She shoves a small bottle in my direction. "Drink."

She's just like the others. She can't be trusted.

I realize I'm nodding, and I gnash my teeth.

How quickly circumstances can change. How quickly *feelings* can change.

Maybe she means to hurt me, or maybe she does intend to help me. Either way, Myriadian ambrosia—if that's what this is—will do me more harm than good, strengthening my dark side while weakening my Light side. After my tangle with the Veil of Midnight, I'm sure of it.

I return the bottle to the woman's waiting grip. She frowns but accepts, and hurries on to the next prisoner, who eagerly drinks. Color and tone returns to his pallid, sagging flesh. How long has he been locked up?

So, she *is* helping. Her willingness to put herself in danger reminds me that there *are* good people in this realm, the same way there are bad people in my realm.

"Hurry," her companion calls. He's keeping watch a few yards away.

"Can you open the cage?" I ask her as she feeds yet another prisoner. "Do you have a key?"

Her mournful gaze slips over me. "No, I'm sorry. I wish I could do more, but..."

She can't. I get it. She reaches through the bars of Victor's crate and tugs at the binding over his mouth.

Panic infuses me, and I shout, "You gotta go." I can't let her succeed. "Go now. Before the authorities arrive."

Panic infuses them, too, and the couple rushes away, desperate to avoid detection.

I *must* escape. And soon. No telling when Zhi and Javier will realize Victor isn't Victor and return.

Again, there's a glimmer of color in the distance. I turn my head to study the newcomer more thoroughly, and my heart slams against my ribs. A familiar face barrels toward me.

This *is* Lina. My heart soars; I guess it recognizes what my eyes do not. This is the woman who played with me when my parents were too busy. The one who helped me survive Many Ends the first three times.

I love her, I do. Despite the fact that she once stabbed me with the end of a paintbrush.

"This is for you." She tosses a vial of liquid in my direction. Manna. "Bottoms up."

"How did you die?" A lump grows in my throat as her message reverberates inside my mind. *Did I tell you I died? I'm sorry I killed Killian. I cried. You cried. I cried some more. I'm glad my husband made it up to you. Light was the answer. Light was always the answer.*

"Walked across the street at just the right time. Boom. Crash."

A crash was "just the right time"? I drain the contents of the vial. Strength plumps my muscles, fortifies my bones. The darkness wanes, the fog of dismay clearing from my head.

"I'm here to help you get into Many Ends."

Whoa. She's speaking in complete sentences, and present tense. "If you're here to hurt Killian—"

"I would *never* hurt your boyfriend," she says, adamant.

And yet you're going to kill him. Uh, how will that help him, Auntie dearest?

A group of people rushes behind her, startling me— *astounding* me. Surely my eyes deceive me. Archer, Raanan, Clay, Reed and Biscuit cannot be here, in Myriad. Cannot be perfectly *alive.*

"I don't understand." I shake my head, thinking the image will fade. Lo and behold, it remains, and elation consumes me. This is real. This is happening.

"Guess what, guess what, guess what." The words burst from Biscuit, as if he can hold them back no longer. "Lina contacted Archer, and we met her at the Veil of Midnight, and she snuck us inside. We're the rescue crew!"

Are you freaking kidding me? "Guys, you could have burned to ash. The Veil of Midnight is a death trap for Troikans."

"True," Lina says, "but that was a chance I was willing to take. You're connected to Killian, and the Troikans are connected to you. I figured they'd make it through just fine."

A chance *she* had been willing to take. Because she *figured*. Because my friends mean nothing to her.

Fury and gratitude mix and mingle inside me, leaving me reeling.

"Killian took the chance and entered Troika," Archer says.

"He was forced," I remind him.

"Well, *you* took the chance. How could we do any less?"

Lina steps aside, and Archer presses a severed thumb into the lock. *Click.* "Took a page from your book. Courtesy of a Magister," he says with a grin. "Had to hunt one down before coming to see you. Totally worth the hassle."

The lock opens without further ado, and my cage door swings out of the way. At that moment, I'm just appreciative. I climb out of my prison, my legs trembling, and straighten. I don't care that I'm in nothing but a shirt and undergarments.

Archer winds an arm around my waist to hold me steady, then places a second vial of manna at my lips. I drain the contents; sweet liquid manna pours down my throat. Fresh strength. Steady legs. In seconds, I can stand on my own.

"I don't know what to say." I scratch Biscuit behind his ears. "I want to yell at you for risking your lives, but thank you for saving mine."

"These are for you." Lina hands me a pair of jeans and a pair of boots, both in my size. Guess it helps to know the future before it happens, and everything your team is going to need.

As I dress, I say to Archer, "You defected, and your face is recognizable. Why weren't you stopped as soon as you entered the realm?"

"I'm no longer part of their Grid. No one ever thought I'd be able to return to Myriad. And I did my best to keep out of view." Sadness creeps over his expression as he scans the City of Carnal Delights. "I could have made a difference here, wanted to, but my efforts were always in vain."

Sometimes I forget he grew up here, a vital part of Myriadian society, at one with the darkness. Oh, how he's changed. Now he is the essence of Light.

"Killian," he says now, and motions to the cage across from mine. "We should—"

"That isn't Killian. It's Victor." And he's still trying to fight through his bonds.

"Deacon, Clementine and Kayla remained in Troika," he adds. "Kayla made the change. She's now a Conduit like the rest of us. They are all working with the princess, helping her cleanse the Abrogates. And our friends aren't the only ones who have made the change. There are others. Many others. Those who used to be everyday average citizens. The number grows by the hour."

Shock punches me. "More than seven?"

He nods. "Twenty-six at last count."

Shock! Asteroid number 26, Proserpina, was named after the Queen of the Underworld.

I'm pretty sure I'm headed to the underworld myself.

"Any other Architects?" I ask.

"Yes." Clay grins and spreads his arms, revealing a horse branded into his wrist. "Us."

My chest constricts with joy. The war *will* come to an end, and we *will* win.

"Soooo. How happy are you to see me?" Biscuit bounds in front of me, grinning and panting and vibrating with eager-ness.

"The happiest."

He has a full arsenal hanging at his sides, weapons stuffed into sheaths. I claim a Sunray, street name Light'erup. The gun shoots beams of Light, and—happiness unfurls inside me. My short swords are here. I tremble as I shove my arms through their harness, anchoring the weapons against my back. The familiar weight comforts me.

A furious male bellow suddenly pierces the air. "Sound the alarm. Someone! Anyone! Ten Lockwood is free."

Victor. He's unbound.

Hate, love? Let him live, kill him?

Clay unsheathes a Sunray of his own and aims at Victor. "Be quiet or die."

Still the traitor shouts. "Help! I'm Victor Prince, and I'm trapped in Killian Flynn's Shell!"

"Time to go, go, go," Lina says. "Got to get the belle to the ball, so I can rescue my husband."

Yes, she mentioned a husband before, but I'm shocked all over again. "You're married?"

"Yes. Of course. Or I will be? I've forgotten."

Okay. We're dealing with future tense again. "To whom will you be wedding?"

"Who else? My husband. The General."

Ugh! Can she not— Wait, *what?* She's wedding a *Myri-adian* General?

Can I really trust her?

As Victor continues to shout, I place my hand on Clay's shoulder. Tension radiates from him. "Daze him, but let him live," I say, my tone soft. Light equals love. Love is always the answer. "Murder is *his* forte, not ours."

"His death will save us a lot of trouble."

"His death will *cause* us trouble. Trust me on this. I've killed before. You haven't. Some actions you can't ever take back, and guilt follows you around like a boulder chained to your ankle. Are you ready to condemn someone to an eternity of torture?"

"Grace, grace," he mutters before exchanging the gun for a Dazer. One shot. He nails his target.

Victor goes still, and quiet.

Clay is a good guy, exceptional actually, and violence is never his first choice. I don't want that part of him tainted.

"Thank you," I say.

"Enough chitchat. Let's go," Lina says.

As we follow her through the darkness, Biscuit remains beside me. Killian will have no idea where I've gone, but that's okay. I don't want him and Lina near each other. I still don't trust him, but I don't want him dead, either. And not just because his death would cause mine.

We run, race, sprint for hours, or what seems to be. We skirt around skyscrapers, fly through alleys, and maneuver through a throng of people dancing in the streets. Above us, a group of boys bungee jump from the surrounding buildings to grab purses, hats and other items from the crowd. Shirtless muscle men swing from ropes. Half-naked women twirl from ribbons that are hanging from an overhead canopy.

Drunk people call out, "Is that a dog?"

"It is. It's a dog!"

"Dude. Are you hallucinating, too? I think I see a dog."

"Don't be fooled. It's a costume," someone else shouts. "So lame."

Is this Killian's party? The one that will get us inside the Kennels?

"Wait," I call, grabbing Archer's hand.

He stops and orders the others in our group to do the same.

I haven't believed in Fate for years. And I still don't. But some part of me is beginning to see divine intervention at work. I had nearly given up all hope, only to be surrounded by friends. We rushed to escape capture, only to stumble upon the very party that can lead me where I want to go? A party Killian planned, even though he'd betrayed me and never expected to enter Many Ends.

Some part of him must have been on my side.

Lina's visions... No matter which way I slice it, she is the reason we're here, together. But where do her visions come from? The Troikan Grid?

She must have had access all her life. But to whom was— is—she connected?

Only one person would have the power...

Eron, I realize. Eron is helping us through Lina, and others. Through his body.

My heart races toward an invisible finish line. How else has he helped? And there are other ways, I know it. Even if I can't see them. He's been teaching us, preparing us for our futures. We've learned to work together, to rely on each other. To see our enemies as people like us, with hopes and dreams, rather than insects in need of extermination.

"Your costume sucks," someone sneers to Biscuit. Then adds, "Hey, want to give me a ride?"

Biscuit chomps his teeth in irritation.

Around us, laughter and cheers blend together. Bodies bump and grind to a fast pulse of music. Anyone who acci-dentally touches my group hisses in pain. Archer pulls me out of the mob, using his big body to shield me from slapping hands and kicking feet as couples grind together. Clay and Raanan herd Lina to my side and take up posts beside Archer.

I should be shielding *them*. They are bright, too bright, like night-lights. But booze and drugs are flowing freely—from one kiss to another—and everyone seems too inebriated to understand what's truly happening.

"What are we doing here?" Archer asks. "We won't be able to blend in for long."

"We're not blending in now," Raanan says, his tone dry.

"We need a plan." I explain Killian's idea to use the party to get inside the Kennels.

"Very well. We'll head for the Kennels. But first, we're disguising you. You're the one they're looking for." Archer steals a hat from a guy standing nearby. When the guy growls in protest, Archer puffs his chest, ready to throw down.

The guy rushes off. A grinning Archer tucks my telltale hair under the hat. This boy is a priceless treasure. Brave. Strong. Fierce. And weird as heck.

"A hat won't hide me for long," I tell him.

Biscuit rubs against my leg. "Don't worry. I'll take care of anyone who thinks to out you. Tongue is a sweet treat."

Nice. "Good boy."

"We don't need it to hide you for long, just long enough." Archer's head tilts to the side as he scours the sea of faces, and squeezes my hand. "Victor is famous for these types of parties. You sure this is Killian's handiwork?"

"I am."

Archer's eyes—so lovely, like freshly polished pennies— radiate anger as his smile evaporates. "Killian isn't going to come through for you. He's going to hurt you, again, and I'm going to have a hard time not killing him."

No. No more killing. "You were friends once. You know he's endured rejection, humiliation and loneliness."

Whoa. I'm defending him?

"I also know he plotted against me even after we called a truce," Archer says.

"Of course he did," I say, and Archer's brow furrows with confusion. Yep, I'm definitely defending Killian. "He's connected to Ambrosine, which means he's connected to an endless pit of paranoia, rage, envy, hatred, bitterness. I've gotten a taste of it myself. It's a miracle Killian didn't stab you in the back *literally*."

Realization dawns. With me, Killian did what he thought was right and turned to the person he once trusted most. The male he saw as a father figure and longed to impress. At the time, I was an unknown entity.

I have to forgive him for his betrayal, don't I? Face it. My distrust stemmed from hurt and anger that he chose Ambrosine over me, nothing more, nothing less.

Sow, reap. My harvest finally came in.

"I'll take care of Killian. You take care of Dior," I say. "I spoke with her right before you arrived, but she took off and I don't know where she was headed. When Killian searched the database for her home address, it was blocked. I'm sorry."

Determination and anticipation flare in those copper eyes, no hint of dread. This boy will not be giving up. Ever. "No worries. I'll find her."

I'm certain he will. "While you're doing your thing, we'll be herding the party into the Kennels." I give him a little push. "Join us when you can."

Biscuit brushes against my leg. "Leave the herding to me. Plus, I'll clear a path for you, Arch."

"You don't know your way—never mind." Who am I kidding? This super-dog can find any place, any time. "Thank you."

Biscuit takes a step forward, only to pause. He sniffs the air, frowns. "I scent two heavily armed guards coming this way. I'll take care of them and herd. I'm an excellent multitasker." Off he goes, his howl cutting through the cacophony of laughter.

Again, drunk people cry out, surprised to see a dog in their midst. Others complain about his "costume."

"Dior?" Archer gasps out. "Ten, I see her."

What? She's here? "Go."

"I'll cleanse her and meet you in the Kennels." He leaps forward and disappears in the crowd.

"Tenley." Lina's hand gloves mine. With a hard yank, she pins me to the wall.

I don't fight back. Yet. I remain aware of her other hand, hanging at her side, clutching a dagger.

"Please don't attempt to stab me, Aunt Lina." I'm not sure how I'll react. I don't want to hurt her.

She blinks, as if confused. When next she focuses on me, the confusion is gone, and her eyes are cloudy. "You're here when you should be there," she says, a new childlike tenor to her tone. Shivers of dismay move through me, and my stomach twists. "He's there when he should be here. If you don't work together, you'll both die. If you don't trust each other fully, you'll both die. Blocking him will only hurt you both."

Him...Killian? "You messaged me, Aunt Lina. Before this.

You said you were going to kill him." By killing me? "Why do you kill him? At the orders of your future husband?"

"Stop talking. Start listening." She snarls, clearly furious, and shakes me. "Help me help you. The darkness has to be chased away, Ten. We will all do what we must, or we will all fall down. Forever bound to Ambrosine."

chapter twenty-one

"It's not what you know that changes you; it's what you do."
—Troika

Ten

As the crowd surges in the right direction, thanks to Biscuit, people bump into me, driving me farther away from Lina. Her ominous warning echoes in my head.

The darkness has to be chased away, Ten. We will all do what we must or we will all fall down. Forever bound to Ambrosine.

The Grid hums with agreement, and my thoughts whirl. Okay, let's break this down. Darkness has to be chased away. By Light, only Light. *Light was always the answer.* Killian is bound to Ambrosine, the ultimate darkness. I'm bound to Killian, and my friends are bound to me. Other people are bound to them. Therefore, we're all bound to Ambrosine.

The bond must be broken.

Ambrosine must die. I was right about that, too. Upon his death, his people will be freed from their need for darkness. They can remain in Myriad if they wish, living their Ever-life on their terms, no longer forced to stay here because of an allergy to Light.

Flaws: Only Eron is strong enough to kill Ambrosine. Will he?

Do I want him to? I just cautioned my friends against killing.

Let's be honest. There's a big difference between Ambrosine and other citizens. Huge! Even if Ambrosine is defeated, he cannot be contained. He's too powerful. Also, he'll never abide by a truce. His words are never the same as his actions.

His end means a new beginning for millions. And really, his death won't be in cold blood, but an action born of this war. Because he *is* the war.

So, yes. Despite my speech to Clay, I am willing to help Eron kill Ambrosine. I doubt I'll walk away from the encounter, or even crawl. Ambrosine is evil incarnate, and his reign of terror must end. I'll *gladly* give my life to get it done.

Second issue. How deep is my bond to my friends? Strong enough to get them inside Myriad, but when I was injured, they were not. If I'm killed, will my friends die, too? Surely not. If I die, will I go to the Rest or Many Ends? Where will Killian go? Where will our friends go?

There are too many unanswered questions. Too many things that can go wrong. But then, there are tons of things that can go right.

Pounding footsteps echo in the distance, catching my attention. The sound of marching? Yes, oh, yes. Multiple men and women in multiple rows. An army is on the way.

We're being hunted.

I surge toward Clay and Raanan. We need to be at the head of the throng.

Pop, pop, pop.

The series of gunshots assails my ears just as I reach the others, and in unison, we duck. Chaos erupts. Panicked screams create a discordant chorus. However, one voice—Victor's—rises above all the others. Someone must have fed him ambrosia.

"Move to the walls and kneel. Those who refuse will be shot."

In unison, everyone stills. But it isn't long before one person after another is lining up against the wall and kneeling, as ordered.

I share a look with the boys, a moment of silent communion. We can't line up and kneel, and we can't *not* line up and kneel. But if we remain standing, we'll be easy targets.

We have to act.

Raanan takes the lead and throws a punch, nailing the Myriadian next to him. Clay pushes a group of guys, knocking them into each other.

"I'm sorry," I say, then trip the girl to my right. She falls into another girl.

Just. Like. That. A fight breaks out among the masses.

No, these people weren't being controlled. They were simply afraid of the speaker.

Fists fly. Legs kick. Obscenities darken the air, blending with grunts and growls. No one lines up, and no one kneels.

This is child's play, really, and proof that giving in to emotion isn't always wise.

Biscuit continues to urge the crowd onward...through a Stairwell, then another Stairwell, and there's nothing the army can do to stop us. We leave them in our dust.

Anytime the fight begins to dissipate, my group ensures tempers are roused all over again.

I duck, avoiding punches thrown my way. I jump over the legs kicked at me, until finally I reach the front of the throng, Clay and Raanan right behind me. There's no sign of Archer, Dior or Lina.

Biscuit leads us through another Stairwell and into a maze of twisting hallways. There are no patterns on the ceiling, walls or floor to help us navigate. Everything is the same. I don't know if we're going in circles or making progress. And I don't think Biscuit knows, either. His tongue is hanging out as he pants, his gaze darting from left to right, little whimpering sounds leaving him.

Our drunken followers begin to laugh, thinking this is a fun game.

I purposely cut my finger on the end of my sword, and wipe a bead of Lifeblood on the wall. A few minutes later, we pass the smear of Lifeblood, and I know. We *are* going in circles.

New plan. "Let's have a contest, guys. Sounds fun, right? Everyone stays where I put them. The person who stays put the longest, wins." The prize? My gratitude. But I keep that little gem to myself.

Cheers. Every time we turn a corner, I direct two people to stay in each hallway. That way, we know our next turn needs to lead to a hallway without people. It works! Finally thank the Firstking, *finally*—we exit the maze and enter the Kennels.

My relief is short-lived, replaced by horror. I remember the first time I saw this room. I'd wanted to vomit. This is my second sighting, and I still want to vomit. Bone torches light the cavernous room—flames dance at the ends of human remains. The floor is covered by pulled teeth and something akin to cat litter.

This is a nightmare come to life.

The scent of unwashed bodies, urine and filth pervades the air, stinging my nostrils. The walls are made up of cages, one cage stacked upon another. Inside every cage is a single person. Male, female. Young, oldish. Each captive has been stripped to their undergarments, just like I was. Whatever their crime, they are pallid, dirty and clearly starving, flesh hanging on bone. Their eyes are without hope. My heart utterly breaks for them and their plight.

Before my father bought and killed her, my mother spent time here. Killian has spent time here, too. His former Flanker, Erica, the one who tattooed him, is here still.

Behind us, gun blasts erupt. Screams of pain cut through the air. Bodies fall. Soldiers are mowing down their own people. Men and women, teen boys and girls, run in every direction, fear saturating the atmosphere.

Where is Archer?

Determined, I unsheathe my swords and work my way through the throng once again, this time in the opposite direction.

There. The moment I catch a glimpse of him, I'm stunned into immobility. He and Dior are holding hands, bright Light surrounding them both as he attempts to cleanse her of Penumbra. On his own. Without the princess's help.

First, he's turned himself into a beacon for Victor's crew. They haven't yet found us, but they will and soon. They weren't too far behind.

Second, if Archer isn't careful, he'll drain himself to death. Hit the point of no return, when an infusion of Light *can't* help him.

I don't have much Light to offer, but I'm willing to give the pair everything I've got. Except, with the shadows writhing inside me, I might do more harm than good.

No time to debate the pros and cons. Someone rams into me, knocking me down. Stars wink through my vision. Blinking, I jump to my feet—or try to. A stampede rushes over me, and all I can do is curl into a ball until the worst is over, using all of my strength to maintain my hold on my swords. They are special to me, and I won't give them up, not even to save my arms from the worst of the damage.

Ha! Every part of me sustains the worst amount of damage. No part of me is spared. Agony sears me. As my head swims with dizziness, a brutal roar blasts. The rampage stops, but it's too late. My bones are broken, my muscles frozen in protest. I can't move.

"Drink." Sweet liquid is poured down my throat.

Bones snap into place, and torn flesh weaves together. The pain is excruciating, but at least it's quick. I cough out a shredded piece of lung as I sit up.

Thank the Firstking, my swords are unharmed. Clay is crouched beside me, Biscuit in front of us, standing guard, forcing people to move around us.

"You good?" Biscuit asks, then snarls at a guy who stumbles too close. "I gots to know. Tell me!"

"I'm good, I promise. Thank you." Without my friends, I would have died in this realm.

Together we stand, or one by one we fall.

Beyond Biscuit, Raanan is fighting off a horde of guards, protecting...Killian! He's out of Victor's Shell and now in spirit form, but he's splayed on the ground, turning my relief to dismay. My injuries must have weakened him. However, my healing ensures his, and he lumbers to his feet.

He and Raanan work in tandem, guarding each other's backs while striking at the enemy. Their motions are fluid, graceful—and despite the violence meted against them, they are as gentle as possible with the opposition.

As I watch Killian safeguard my friends, the block around my heart begins to crumble. He meant what he said. He's fighting for me, and for us. He's putting our relationship first.

As soon as the last brick crumbles, the mortar nothing but

ash, the bridge between us opens up. Killian's thoughts and emotions flood me. Love. Determination. Anger directed at his people, who have turned against him. Concern for my well-being. But beneath it all...there is Light, stronger and brighter than ever before.

If *zero* is my curse word, *infinity* must be my exclamation of joy. So...sweet infinity! His shadows are gone and—

Like a river, his Light showers and floods me, and drowns *my* darkness. That part of me is dying. Killed by Light. Love. All the cruelties, all the insecurities, all the hatred, fury and paranoia. There's nothing left for them to feed on.

He and I...we are together, wholly, nothing held back.

—There you are. I've been so worried.—

His voice drifts along the Grid, and another upsurge of strength hits me, as if I've just ingested another vial of manna.

Love is Light, Light is love.

—I'm rememberin'— He goes quiet. Then a gasp flows over the Grid. *—I'm remembering every precious second with you. Before our bond and after. Meetin' you in Prynne. Bein' fascinated by your strength, courage and loyalty. Cravin' you more than air to breathe. Oh, Ten. I'm so sorry. I wish I could go back and change the things I've done.—*

He remembers. Because he did his part—trusted me—and I did my part, letting him back into my heart?

My eyes widen. Of course. His memories were never dependent on him. Not totally. We were joined. Two had become one. I had to trust him, too. I had to let my love for him overcome...everything. Just like he had to let his love for me overcome everything.

We are two halves of a whole. Complete together.

Joyous, I push my voice to him. *—If you could go back and*

change anything, we might not be where we are now, and we are right where we need to be.—

With one hand, he thrusts and parries a sword; with the other, he fires a gun. Around him, soldiers fall. —*You want me tae stop fightin', lass?*—

In the past, I told him not to put down his weapons. Today? —*Don't you dare.*— These people will go to Many Ends. I believe it more surely than ever. Troikans go to the Rest. Myriadians *must* go to Many Ends.

If spirits who experienced Second-death can leave the Rest, spirits who experienced Second-death can leave Many Ends.

Soon, I'll be in Many Ends, too. I'll guide everyone to the exit. Like Reed and Kayla, they will be free to choose their path. Stay in Myriad, or pledge allegiance to Troika. No need for court.

Hello, beautiful loophole.

While Trokian covenants are eternal, Myriadian covenants last only until Second-death. Ambrosine's choice. I wonder why. To sustain his lie about Fusion? Maybe shadows die at Second-death. Or maybe they move from the dead to the living. No matter the reason, if a person is not a channel of darkness any longer, they are no longer of use to him.

My mind is worked into a frenzy of questions and answers, probabilities and possibilities. Can the spirits inside the Rest be freed, as well? Not just one a year, but *all* of them? *If* they want to leave, that is. My guess? Yes. Eron could open a door... *Would* he?

As Clay helps me to my feet, I catch a glimpse of Lina, whose gaze is locked on Killian. She's fighting her way toward him. I stiffen.

"Guard Killian from my aunt," I tell Biscuit. "Without actually hurting her. If possible." He can zip across the distance in a blink. When he opens his mouth to protest, I add, "Keeping Killian safe keeps *me* safe."

My sweet, protective dog offers no arguments and bounds over. The number of soldiers fighting against us has dwindled, but I can hear a new thunder of footsteps in the distance.

"What next?" Clay asks me. "How do we get into Many Ends from here?"

When last I exited, I'd dived into a lake in Many Ends and fallen through the Veil overhead. Now I glance up, up, up. Zero! How are we supposed to climb into the sky?

—*We'll find a way.*— Again Killian's voice fills my head. He's reading my emotions, the impending sense of defeat.

"Look out!" Clay shouts.

A contingent of soldiers has slipped around Killian and Raanan, and is heading for Archer and Dior. I rush to meet them, swinging my swords together, creating a staff. As the metal arcs through the air, bolts of Light spray. The contingent falls, one by one. The group of men and women behind them simply steps over the bodies and fires different weapons at me.

I use the staff to deflect the bullets, but it isn't long before I'm clipped in the shoulder. Lifeblood leaks from the wound, and my motions slow. *Zero!* How much longer can we hold off this new army?

Once again, I need help. Scanning...scanning... My aunt has given up her quest to reach Killian. She comes up behind the next set of soldiers and pelts the group with a spray of automatic fire. More bodies fall. Or perhaps Lina never meant to hurt Killian? She could have shot him and Biscuit in a single swoop.

"The next round of soldiers will be the end of us," she calls, her gaze locked on mine. "Not because they'll kill us, but because they'll lock us away. If we're locked away, we'll lose."

Nausea churns in my stomach. "Clay, can you contact Clementine and transport back to Troika?"

"I don't know. She and Kayla are supposed to be waiting at the Eye, but since my arrival in Myriad, they haven't responded to any of my messages."

The Eye sees into the Land of the Harvest but not Myriad. Through it, Headhunters are able to monitor humans and Laborers, and pull Laborers out of dangerous situations whenever necessary—and no Bucklers have been engaged, of course.

"Get home however you can, then," I tell him, blocking the parry of another soldier. "You and the others. Gather the other Conduits. Make more. As many as you can. Guard the Veil of Wings in case the Myriadians bound to Killian think to risk—"

"Ten," Lina snaps. "It's time."

I hurry to finish my sentence. "The goal is Ambrosine's death." Everything hinges on that.

"Ten," Lina repeats.

I meet her determined stare. "How do we get into Many Ends?" I yank my staff apart to spray a new crop of soldiers with shards of Light, stopping their approach, buying us a few more minutes—seconds? "Do you know?"

"You are the key," she says, stepping toward me. "You have always been the key. You know what needs to be done, Ten. You *know*."

Suddenly I...do. The answer clicks. My number is up. I have to die.

I want to vomit. Linked to Killian, I'll kill him, too, but we'll appear in Many Ends, as planned. Because I'll hide my Light and let the shadows go free.

I reel, and there's no blunting the sharp edges of my shock, dismay and certainty. This. This is one of the reasons Eron supported my bond with Killian. This is the way inside Many Ends. Self-sacrifice. I give up everything—but I gain so much more.

The shadows will overrun me, but they'll lead me straight to Many Ends.

"If I do this…" I begin as sweat beads on my forehead.

"You will. Find the doorway, save the day. If the hills have eyes, everyone dies. To win the fight, you'll need Light."

Another rhyme. One that bolsters me. To win the fight, she said—that means winning *is* possible. I can do this.

I stop, my heart racing, and meet my aunt's gaze. "What will happen to the others? My friends?"

Torment darkens her features. "I don't know. Don't see. You just do you. Let them do them. All right? My husband and I will take care of the Secondking."

Someone. *My* Secondking. Take care…as in *kill*? "If you hurt Eron—"

"Who said anything about Eron?"

Oh, thank the Firstking. She's going after *Ambrosine*.

Grunting from exertion, Clay slays a male trying to sneak up behind us. "I won't leave until I know you're safe. So, let's get you to safety."

He has no idea what I'm planning with Lina.

A roar blasts through the sky. Gasping, I look up. Dragons. Ten of them. They fly overhead, their wings outstretched. More roars sound, loud enough to shake the ground. Then— fire rains.

People run for cover. Screams erupt. Streams of fire spray over buildings and Myriadians alike. Like the soldiers, the dragons are willing to sacrifice their people in order to kill me and mine.

Lina and I stay put. The rest of my team, as well.

—*Lass.*— Killian's voice rushes through my head. —*I'm with you. I'll always be with you. Even in this. Do what you must.*—

My gaze zooms to him across the distance. He's standing as still as a statue as people run all around him. Biscuit keeps him from being trampled, taking out everyone who attempts to get near him.

"Together," I say, even though he can't hear me.

"Together," he mouths.

Behind him, about three hundred yards away, are Victor and Javier. Other dragons unleash streams of fire to clear their path.

Almost too late…

Before I change my mind, I look to Lina. Tremors threaten to topple me, but I remain on my feet.

How far will I go for my realm?

All the way.

"Do it," I croak, and shove every ounce of Light into rooms in the Grid. My mind goes dark, but I remain aware. Shadows overrun me, as expected. They laugh with glee as ice crystallizes in my veins and wave after wave of evil bathes me.

I'm strong, there's no one stronger. Must prove my power.

Will take…everything! What's theirs is mine, and what's mine is mine.

Allow myself to be killed in order to save others? Never!

Does she laugh inside, thinking she's bested me? I'll turn her amusement to sobs.

"Do it now," I manage to push past clenched teeth. Before the shadows change my mind for good.

A moment later, a shot rings out and fire burns between my eyes.

TROIKA

From: M_V_3/54.5.8
To: L_R_3/51.3.15, J_A_3/19.37.30, S_C_3/50.4.13,
C_M_3/5.20.1, T_B_3/19.30.2, B_S_3/51.3.13, A_S_3/42.6.31,
J_B_3/19.23.4, S_J_3/62.5.5, M_P_3/45.10.9
Subject: What happened?

It's as if someone turned off a Light inside our realm. With it came a wave of weakness.

Light Brings Sight!
General Mykhail Vasiliev

MYRIAD

From: H_S_3/51.3.6
To: Z_C_4/23.43.2
Subject: What just happened?

Everyone in the realm just experienced a burst of strength. Why? And how can we do it again?

Might Equals Right!
General Hans Schmidt

PART THREE

Many Ends

chapter twenty-two

"Question everything. Take nothing by faith."
—Myriad

Killian

One second I'm standing on a battlefield, peering over at Ten,
who no longer glows. Anguish nearly fells me. I hadn't realized she glowed while inside Myriad until the Light inside
her was snuffed out. Shadows rise from her.

Then the space between my eyes burns. *Then* I wake up
sprawled across cold, hard ground. The scent of ash and blood
hangs heavy in the air.

Plagued by a sense of urgency, I jolt upright and scan the
area around me. A super creepy forest, trees knifing toward
the sky. Branches extend, tangling together, leaves shaking
as something moves beyond my line of sight.

Where am I? This can't be Many Ends. I expected fire and
brimstone. Torture. Although, I see no sign of Ten, and an
eternity without her *is* hell.

I pat myself down for weapons. None. Even my wrist cuffs
are gone. I'm left defenseless. Or at least, defenseless in the eyes
of others. Years of training have turned me into a weapon all

on my own. I'm wearing a black T-shirt and leather pants, the clothes I died in. *If* I died.

"Ten." My voice echoes. I wait, but there's no response. Next I try the Grid. —*Ten. Can you hear me, lass?*— Again, no response.

I focus on the Grid—

And suck in a breath. The Grid is gone. There's…nothing.

"Ten." I shout her name and wait for a reply, tense. The wind whistles, branches rattle, and leaves rustle, but there's no response.

My tension escalates, my hands balling at my sides. Where is she? Did she survive her aunt's shot? Part of me hopes she did, somehow, some way. I love that girl more than I love my own life, and I want her well. Even if it means I must live without her. Or die without her.

143, 10

I want her to have a full, long life, even if it doesn't include me.

On the flip side, I very much want that life to include me.

I know I don't deserve her. I've lived my life pretending to be everyone's friend—from my bosses to my targets—until the moment I had to make a choice: who could do me the most good, who could do me the most harm. I did everything in my power to make people love me, not just because I hoped to avoid the same rejections I suffered in my childhood, but because I wanted others to act against their own best interests in order to help me. That's how I've won so many spirits for Myriad.

Somehow Ten saw something good in me. She forgave me for my crimes. At the end, I felt her emotions, including more love than I have ever dreamed possible.

A blood-curdling scream cuts through the air. I'm rushing

forward before my brain registers I've taken a step. Branches slice my cheeks and dizziness swims in my brain.

As I sway on my feet, I slow. When I reach out to brace myself against a tree trunk, a thousand stings explode in my hand. Yelping, I jump back—and trip over a fallen branch.

Everything is working against me. This *must* be Many Ends.

From my perch on the ground, I blink rapidly until my vision clears. Of course, even then I'm not given a reprieve. The ground begins to shake, and the air thickens with dust.

Overhead, a plume of dark smoke mushrooms across the sky, and I tense. As the smoke dissipates...

No way, just no way, though I doubt my eyes deceive me. The smoke breaks apart and transforms into birds. Large, black birds with spiked beaks, skeletal bodies and wings that look to be made of sharpened bone and dipped in metal. Their claws are *definitely* made of metal.

As Ten would say: *Zero!*

One of the creatures catches sight of me and swoops down, down. With a squawk, it stretches its claws in my direction. Intending to collect me? What, I'm to be dinner?

Sorry. Not today. I grit my teeth and wait for it...wait... Now! I kick out my leg the moment the creature is within striking distance. Contact! Another squawk sounds. The creature soars through the forest, crash lands, and skids across the ground. I expect him to be down for the count, but he regains his bearings quickly and leaps into the sky.

As I climb to shaky legs, he circles overhead. Two friends join him, looking at me, projecting a single message: *You can run but you can't hide.*

Things are about to get ugly.

Thinking fast, I reach for a fat, fallen branch, but again, a thousand lightning stings explode over my hand like mini-grenades, courtesy of the tiny bugs that are crawling all over the wood.

My vision begins to swim all over again, leaving me defenseless. No, no. I've trained for this—trained in the dark.

Though my sight is compromised, I can rely on my other senses. I go still, listening. My ears twitch, detecting a *whoosh, whoosh* of wings. Wind brushes my face. The scent of rot... growing closer, closer...

I dive out of the way. A sharp sting agonizes my back, claws scraping my spine, but I'm moving too swiftly for the birds to grab hold of me. Thankfully, my vision clears as I jump to my feet. The birds remain low as they circle around me... and dart toward me.

Deciding to use my fists this go-round, I stand my ground. Ready...ready...

Just before contact, a thick branch comes out of nowhere, hitting two of the birds. New squawks. Hisses. I disable the third creature as planned, with a fist to the face. The bones in my hand crack, and pain floods me. Pain must flood the bird, too. It flops to the ground and struggles to straighten.

Another bird knocks me to the ground in order to grab its friend and return to the sky.

I roll to my back and blink in shock and relief.

"You okay?" My helper offers me a hand.

Ten! My heart leaps at the sight of her. She's not glowing, but she's not surrounded by shadows, either. She's alive, and she's here. Our connection is gone, but she's here. She's safe. Or as safe as possible, considering our location. Nothing else matters to me.

"I could be dyin'—again—and I'd be okay right now, because yer here. I love you, lass." I take her hand, but I don't stand. I pull her down on top of me. Breath gushes from my lungs as her slight weight settles atop me. I'm overcome, undone and overjoyed all at once. "I thought I'd lost you."

"Never. You're stuck with me. And stop apologizing. You died for me, Killian. I'd say we're even." She softens against me for a split second, and I luxuriate in the feel of our bodies pressed together. Then she places a swift kiss on my lips and climbs to her feet. "We need to reach the Tree of Life, and fast."

"Tree of Life?"

"Come on!" She grabs the limb and takes off.

I have no choice but to jump up and follow. Along the way, I snatch the limb from her grip, freeing her from its weight.

"Only step where I step," she says. "Okay? All right? The entire realm is a maze. There are invisible doorways. Pits, tricks and poisons. Monsters and disasters waiting everywhere."

Monsters that are worse than the birds? Wonderful. "So this is Many Ends?"

"Yep. Where happiness comes to die."

I reel. She was right. All along she was right about Myriad's connection to Many Ends. How it's possible, I don't know. How it's been kept a secret, though, I can guess. Ambrosine has always refused to host a resurrection. When Archer and I were friends, he told me it takes power from the Secondking to bring back one of his people. Power Ambrosine refuses to relinquish.

"How do you know where tae go?" She's been here several times before, yes, but I can see no marks to distinguish one path from another.

"I see the patterns. Raised stones and limbs every few steps, plus other tells—like glittery patches of air." She is panting now, the temperature rising. Sweat pours from us.

"Others are here?" I'm panting, too, the poisons I've already encountered still playing havoc with my systems. Without ambrosia or manna—or whatever I need now—I have no way to heal. Except naturally, of course, but who wants to wait for that?

"More spirits than I've ever encountered before. When the birds arrived, everyone took off in different directions. Some vanished through invisible doorways, some got grabbed by birds, some by gorillas. A few escaped, but I don't know where they ended up."

Gorillas? Invisible doorways? "Why did I no' appear in the same location as the rest of you? And how did you find me?"

She turns a corner and yelps as a branch slaps her in the neck. I snake my arms around her waist and spin her, taking the next lash against my back. *Ouch.* The bark bites into the wounds caused by the birds, and I grunt. Stars wink over my vision all over again.

Ten pauses, her gentle hands framing my face. Just for a moment. Gone far too swiftly. But in that stolen moment, I'm no longer in hell but heaven. She's all I see, all I know. Her blue hair lifts in the breeze, and her mismatched eyes regard me with an emotion I cannot name or feel. The bond... I frown. Like the Grid, it's gone, and a great sense of loss overwhelms me.

"Be careful, *baby*. Distraction kills." She leaps back into action, the moment broken. I remain close to her heels.

Baby. "I get why you hate the endearment. But shouldna you hate *lass*, too? It's just as common."

"Not for you. You hate your accent and fight it, but I make it slip out unbidden. Face it. You have no defense against me. What's not to love about that?"

Darling girl.

"And to answer your previous questions, I don't know why you ended up elsewhere. To find you, I followed the echo of your voice."

"Do you feel our connection, then?"

"Faintly," she admits. "I'm aware of the Grid, and our bond, but I can't quite get a lock on either one."

With a world-rocking roar, a gigantic ape leaps into our path. In unison, Ten and I skid to a stop. The ape swipes at Ten with a beefy arm, but I'm faster, leaping to the safety zone and taking her with me. When he swipes air, he issues another roar.

He's as wide as the trees, with a barrel chest. His arms and legs are the size of battering rams, and his teeth the size of sabers. But the worst thing about him? He has friends.

Six gorillas step from the foliage, revealing we're trapped in a tight-knit circle.

"Zero!" Ten gasps. "I led us straight into a trap."

chapter twenty-three

"Do not be led by opportunity. Be led by peace."
—Troika

Ten

I knew it before, and I know it now with far more certainty. The creatures of Many Ends have one goal: Destroy *everyone*.

The birds hope to carry us to their mountain, where they will feast on our organs, again and again. The screams…even now they assault my ears. The gorillas want to beat us into submission and, yep, feast on our organs.

The information came courtesy of Kayla and Reed during my last visit.

I've fought these gorillas before, but only one at a time. I've run from a big group of them, and if not for the lake— a lake that is nowhere near here, at least that I can see—they would have caught me. They can't swim. Or won't. In Many Ends, the lake is as dangerous as everything else.

"You see monsters every day. But you've never seen a monster like me." There's just enough contempt in Killian's voice to prove he means what he says. "I suggest you walk away. I'm out of mercy, only have wrath to offer."

He moves in front of me to act as my shield, and I'm grateful, I am, but there's no way to protect all of me at once. We're surrounded.

"When they attack, and they will, go for the throat, the only vulnerable part of their bodies," I tell him.

At least we aren't dealing with the monkey-spiders. (No relation to spider monkeys in the Land of the Harvest.) The creatures here have the bottom half of a toddler-size spider, with eight hairy legs tipped by ivory hooks, and the top half of a monkey with two heads. A nightmare and freak show rolled into one.

I could win the idiot of the year award, right? I mean, I *wanted* to return to this land and actively fought to get here.

One amazing development? The shadows no longer rule my mind. There isn't even a glimmer of darkness. As soon as I "woke up" in Many Ends, I opened doors inside the Grid, letting Light spill out, sending whatever shadows that remained fleeing. But it was then, that very moment, that my connection to the Grid and my bond to Killian faded.

Focus. I'm already cut and bruised from my trek to Killian, not to mention the fight I had with the spirits of soldiers who died seconds before and after me. Something I opted not to tell Killian. I'd rather he not get angry with the men and women, boys and girls we're here to save.

Save... The word rolls through my mind, reminding me of my aunt's newest rhyme.

Find the doorway, save the day. If the hills have eyes, everyone dies. To win the fight, you'll need Light.

The doorways. Okay, then. They are invisible...mostly. Glittering pockets of air lead to entirely new locations within Many Ends. If we go through one now, we'll be transported *away* from our new opponents. And we have to get away from the gorillas. We have to reach the Tree of Life. There's only one in the entire realm, and it produces…something.

Something akin to manna, maybe. Definitely not ambrosia, despite Many End's connection to Myriad. Whatever it is— I'm just gonna go with manna—the creatures here avoid it. Its leaves have the power to heal and strengthen us, and even protect us from the harsh realities of the landscape.

In Many Ends, there is sunshine and there is darkness, but both are warped. The sunshine is too hot, scorching every- one and everything in its path, and the darkness is too thick. In the cool shade, we can take time to heal, regroup and fig- ure out our next move.

Zero! There's no time to look for one of the doorways.

With a war cry, the gorillas converge on us, swinging their mighty fists.

Killian—

Dang him! He trips me, at the same time spinning me out of the way. As I crash into the ground, he meets round one with my branch, but the wood swiftly snaps in half.

I want to slap myself. I selected the branch because it was light enough to carry while we were on the move, but also because few insects were crawling along the surface. In Many Ends, the insects inject toxins meant to slow a spirit down for a second or two.

A single second can win or lose a battle.

Killian is fast, and he is methodical. He ducks when neces- sary and punches when the opportunity arises. So do I. I pop up, nail a gorilla in the throat, and dive back down.

At this rate, we're going to lose.

"Run, lass." Killian spins before shoving me to the ground, his body enveloping me. "Please." *Pop, pop.* He hisses, and I cringe. *POP.* The sound of his bones breaking.

Without our bond, his injuries are his own. That can be worked to our favor. But—

The realization hits me as hard as the gorillas are hitting Killian. He said please. Over *this*. To him, pleading for anything is begging for something.

Melting...

Focus! Right. But come on! As if I'll ever leave him behind simply to save my own hide.

Determined, I crawl between a gorilla's legs, escaping the circle of doom. Wasting no time, I jump on the back of the gorilla, jam my thumbs into his eye sockets and pop out both of his eyes. Cruel. Necessary.

He roars and raises his arms to beat at me. I hop down and swipe up the two pieces of the broken branch. Standing, I swing at another gorilla. *Whack, whack.* One slap of a branch after another. Impact jars *me*, not him, and I stumble back.

Slowly he turns to face me and give me a death glare. Without hesitation, I strike, jabbing the end of one branch into his throat. When he hunches over, desperate for air, I knock him in the side of the head with the other branch. He careens, toppling into the beast next to him. As that one turns, I jab him in the throat, too, with enough force to crush his windpipe.

Killian is forgotten, every gorilla concentrating on me. And why not? Killian is no threat, his face cut and bleeding, his body motionless as it sprawls on the ground, his hand sticking out between their legs—reaching for me?

Please, please, please be only unconscious, because I'm not sure where your spirit will reform.

"Cowards," I spit. "Takes six of you to kill two spirits, does it? You're *that* weak?"

Understanding darkens their eyes. So. Like the animals in Troika, communication is a skill.

Talents for their resumes: *Comprehends English, eats people.*
A twitch of Killian's fingers. He's waking up! Okay, okay.
Time to get this show on the road. Killian needs to escape
the circle, so, I need to keep attention away from him.

I twirl the branches and smile. "Well. Come on, cowards.
Show me what you've got."

Roars. Three of the beasts dive at me. At the last second,
I duck. They soar overhead, knocking into fellow soldiers.
As those soldiers protest, Killian yanks at the ankles of the
creature who remained behind to beat him, then pops to his
feet. Lifeblood soaks his face. His gaze is narrowed, his irises
fierce and glittering. Despite a wealth of injuries, he's never
looked more beautiful.

In a single, fluid move, he takes a gorilla by the neck and
twists, breaking the spine. Despite his own broken bones, he
kicks out his leg, punting another gorilla to the side.

I give the stumbling gorilla an extra whack, and a path
opens up. Killian limps my way, grabs my wrist and pulls
me forward.

"We need to find a doorway, fast," I pant, searching for
one of those glittering air pockets…searching…

As a chorus of roars sounds behind us, I spot what we need
and tug Killian in the right direction. Unsure where we'll
end up, we soar through a doorway—

Between one blink and the next, I'm with Killian and then
I'm alone, right back where I started. *Zero!*

I'm certain he ended up in the spot where I first found him.
If I go back for him—when I go back—we'll encounter the
same problems as before. I must be better armed. Problem is,
there's a lack of viable weapons.

In Many Ends, every inch, tree and creature is designed
to hinder the spirits trapped within. There are thousands of

discarded branches, each with sharp ends, but poisonous bugs crawl all over the best ones. There are trees with grooves all over their trunks, offering the perfect footholds, but poisonous sludge drips from each one. And let's not forget the fact that the leaves are like the Venus Flytrap, with razor-sharp teeth.

The air is dry, hotter than hot, my sweat doing little to cool me. Screams of anguish continue to fill the air, soon joined by wails of agony and moans of pain. A snakes slithers past me, then pauses to stick out its tongue and taste the air. Its *forked* tongue. At the same time, ember-bugs buzz around me; every time they touch me, I blister.

In the distance, a crack of thunder sounds, and I cringe. *Zero!* A rain shower will cool the air and drive away the insects and monsters—but every drop will burn like acid.

I need to—

Whoosh! Something hard slams into the back of my head, and the pain is excruciating. I stumble forward, barely managing to prevent a dirt kiss. Footsteps—*thump, thump, thump.*

Despite a bout of dizziness, I spin, and kick out my leg. Contact. My attacker grunts. He's a man—a spirit—not a gorilla. Probably one of the soldiers who died in battle today.

I swing my branch, forcing him to jump back. "Stop this," I pant. "To survive this realm, we've got to work together."

"I know who you are, and I'll never work with—"

A bird swoops from the sky, sinks its claws into the man's shoulders and hefts him into the air. Happens in less than a blink of time. I don't understand. Why was he grabbed but not me?

Oops. Spoke too soon. Sharp claws cut into my shoulders. A second bird. Should have known. I grunt, every muscle in my body clenching and unclenching as I'm lifted into the air. The branch falls from my grip and thuds to the ground.

As soon as we clear the tops of the trees, I scan the forest... there! My gaze is drawn to Killian, as if he's a magnet. He's perched at the top of a tree, insects crawling all over him, biting him, shredding his skin as he searches below. For me.

I won't be separated from him again. "Killian!"

Gritting my teeth against the coming onslaught of pain, I reach up to latch on to my captor's wing. His head whips around, allowing his spiked beak to scrape my hand all the way to bone. Through sheer grit and determination, I maintain my hold. He needs his wing, but because of me, he can't move it. Together, we fall. Limbs slap at my body, and leaves bite my face. By the time we land, I'm a mass of injuries, precious Lifeblood hemorrhaging from me.

This isn't a new development. Every time I've been here, I've bled.

But I take heart. Where there is blood, there is life. A spirit never dies. The very reason Reed and Kayla were able to leave this realm and join Troika.

There's hope for escape, and that hope gives me the strength I need to stand. My knees wobble, but I remain upright. The bird remains on the ground, unmoving.

I killed him?

"Ten." Killian bursts through a wall of foliage and yanks me into his arms. "Lass, I'm sorry. I'm so sorry I let you get away from me. Let's just burn this realm tae the ground and call it good, yeah."

He's more concerned with my pain than his own?

Focus! Lina helped me before; she'll help me now.

Did I tell you I died in the Land of the Harvest? I'm sorry I killed Killian.

I cried. You cried. I cried some more. My husband made it up to you. Light was the answer. Light was always the answer.

She killed me, which in turn killed Killian. We're in Many Ends, and we're going to save the damned. We're going to save our mothers and friends.

Lina's husband, whoever he is, will make it up to us.

If he makes it up to us, we survive this. *We survive this.* I throw my arms around Killian and kiss his lips, because I need to kiss him, and taste him, and connect with him, if only for a second. He kisses me back, a glorious meeting of lips and tongue, even teeth. A communion of souls.

Love spills through me. Love, Light. In the back of my mind, the Grid becomes more noticeable. As if finally hooked to a battery. A weak battery, but a battery all the same. Strength plumps my muscles. Joy eases the burden I hadn't known weighed down my shoulders.

Joy is as much a source of strength as love. It will hold steady when our circumstances roughen.

We're in Many Ends; our circumstances are definitely going to roughen.

Though I want to linger, I force my head to lift. Distraction kills; I must never forget. After all, Many Ends remains true to its name. The end of life as we know it. The end of safety and security.

"Where are you gettin' Light, lass?"

He felt it? His Grid must have sputtered to life, as well. "Love. My love for you, to be specific."

He beams at me, experiencing his own surge of joy, and my love—Light—only magnifies.

"Now come on," I say. "Let's find that tree."

chapter twenty-four

"When opportunity knocks, always opens the door."
—Myriad

Ten

Using Lifeblood—gotta use whatever is available—we mark tree trunks, to help us remember where we've been, and trek the woods. Avoiding gorillas, skeleton birds, monkey-spiders and ember-bugs requires cunning. We cover our bodies in sulfur-scented mud to better blend in with the landscape and also protect our skin from the too-harsh sun.

As we maneuver through trees, we're ignored, as hoped. And yet, I feel as if we're being watched. By another spirit? One of the many creatures? No, I don't think so, because my instincts aren't even close to razed or gearing for another battle.

I search and scan and examine every shadow thoroughly, but I find no sign of a tail.

Finally, blessedly, we reach the Tree of Life. And none too soon. The strength I acquired has already drained. Exhaustion has settled into my bones. I feel as if I've been in a car accident: battered and barely able to stand.

A quick exploration reveals we're the only two people in the area. What happened to everyone else?

Right on cue, a new chorus of screams assaults my ears, as if to say: *What do you think happened, dummy?*

All right, then. More people to save.

"I've never seen anythin' like this," Killian says, the words saturated with awe.

"I know." I've been here before, yes, but the beauty still takes my breath away.

With a trunk the size of a football field, and branches longer and wider than a freight train, the tree drips with colorful leaves. A thousand different shades of pink, purple and blue.

I pick a handful of those leaves, and thank the Firstking that none of the leaves have fangs. "Eat," I say, after handing half of my bounty to Killian.

I eat the other half, the taste sweet and the temperature cool. Absolute perfection. My wounds begin to heal, as expected, torn flesh weaving back together, fractured bones reforming.

My last trip here, the process amazed me. It amazes me still. The power! These leaves might as well be dipped in adrenaline and sprinkled with opiates. And they prove that even in the worst of times and the worst of places, we can have hope. Whatever the trouble that is plaguing us, there is always a way out.

Here, the scents of poison and sulfur are chased away by a fragrance perfumers would kill to bottle. Sweet, floral yet woodsy, earthy and clean, everything wonderful with no hint of taint. It's like all the best odors in the realms have been spliced together to create a delicious harmony of perfection.

"What is this stuff?" Killian asks. The cuts on his skin weave back together. Broken bones mend. Swelling fades.

"I refer to it as manna, though I suppose bread of life would be more appropriate, since it grows on the Tree of Life."

"It helps Troikans and Myriadians alike?"

"It does. Maybe because there are no Troikans or Myriadians here, all bonds severed upon arrival."

"Thank you for the food, and the explanation." He kisses the tip of my nose. "Now we need a game plan."

"Yeah, but we also need a breather. We've been on the go for months. No rest. No respite. It's time to recharge." Time to bask in our love, and the joy of being together, until we are an unbeatable unit, no matter what happens. I wiggle my brows at him. "Maybe do a little more of that kissing."

"Well. You *did* strengthen when I kissed you. What kind of man would I be if I left you in this weakened condition?" There's a husky, teasing note in his voice, that sends shivers cascading down my spine.

"True. Kissing and touching me is practically your *duty*. And we don't want you remiss in your duties, now, do we?"

"I'm willin' tae work myself tae the *bone*."

I nearly choke on a laugh. "I'll be disappointed if you don't." Up ahead, water flows from a branch, creating the perfect shower. I cast him a wanton grin and strip down to my underwear, his hot gaze cataloging my every move. "Catch me if you can," I say, and race forward.

He gives chase. And he *does* catch me. We fall into the water with his arms wrapped around me. Little moans of delight leave me as we surge above the surface.

Lightning fast, he strips and tosses his clothes onto a rock.

"This is our second shower together," I say. "Only this time you're not plotting my downfall."

He sucks in a breath as if punched.

EVERLIFE 397

"What?" I blink innocently, not letting my smile break free. "Too soon to joke about?"

"Forever will be too soon." He nips my lower lip with his teeth, then takes his time cleaning the muck from my skin.

I love having his hands on me.

When he finishes, I return the favor, lingering on his pecs and maybe kinda sorta the bulge between his legs. Not my fault. It's a big bulge. Like, really big. What, am I just supposed to ignore it? Impossible.

"Okay, playtime is over." He takes the leaves from my grip and pulls me under the flow of water. His chest presses against my back as he wraps his arms around my waist. He rests his chin on my shoulder.

The horse brand on his forearm is now as faded as mine. At least they haven't vanished. We are still in this battle.

"I'm sorry, lass."

I reach overhead to comb my fingers through his soaked hair. "You've got to stop apologizing...love." I try out the endearment, and breath hitches in his throat. Bingo. Found his new nickname. "Myriad taught you to rely on your feelings for every thought, action and situation, but they taught you wrong. You feel guilty, so you apologize, even though you've been forgiven. And even though your apologies are nice, they are basically a slap in my face, as if you don't believe I'm telling the truth about forgiving you."

"I'm—" He goes quiet, and I chuckle. His clasp on me tightens. "How can you forgive me? I hurt you worse than I've ever hurt another, and yet everyone else still harbors a grudge. And rightfully so."

"I just... I refuse to be an emotional bookkeeper, keeping a detailed account of the wrongs done to me. I choose forgiveness, even when and if I don't actually feel forgiving. Because it's not about what I feel. Like everything else, it's about what I choose. Do my emotions control me, or do I control my emotions? I decide. And really, like you, like everyone else, I've made mistakes. I like to think I've been forgiven, so, what I want for myself, I offer freely to others. Besides, love isn't about getting everything right. It's about being there for each other when everything goes wrong."

A moment passes in thoughtful silence, the stiffness leaving him. Then he kisses my ear, my jaw and the pulse hammering at the base of my neck.

He cups my breasts, then slides his hands lower...delving under my panties. "I'd say you are too good tae be true, but I'd rather spend my time enjoyin' you."

I mewl and purr as I writhe into his touch.

When my head begins to spin from the pleasure, I turn in his arms, facing him. My gaze snags on his plethora of tattoos. "I love these."

"Together they create a map of Myriad, as you once guessed, but they also mark where I hid my greatest treasures."

I already knew that, but his admission is like honey to my soul.

"Most of the items were stolen from me," he grumbles, "but I realized they weren't really treasures, after all. They never really mattered. I have you, and you are what matters most."

Melting...

He nuzzles my cheek. "Maybe I need to have an X inked over my heart. X marks the spot, and X stands for the numeral ten."

I laugh, delighted by him. "I never pegged you for a romantic. But I like it."

He lifts his head to gift me with a brilliant smile. "Seems

I've been buryin' my treasure in the wrong places. But that's about to change, yeah?"

A blush heats my cheeks. "You did not just say that."

"Oh, aye, I did." Grinning, he rubs against me.

I gasp with pleasure, and sink my hands into his hair. "We aren't always promised a tomorrow. The only guarantee we have is right now, and I'm not wasting another second. I want you, Killian." I want to show my husband the depths of my love for him, not just tell him.

I trust him with my future, so, I'm going to trust him with my body.

He cups my jaw, traces his thumbs over my cheeks. His pupils are blown, and his body is trembling as forcefully as mine. "Are you sure, lass?"

Very. "Kiss me." I lift to my tiptoes.

He meets me halfway, his lips pressing into mine. At first the kiss is as sweet as the air around us, gentle and wet, so wet, as the water continues to rain. An exploratory indulgence as we relearn and savor each other but it isn't long before sweet isn't enough. Our bodies are burning so hot the water droplets are steaming off our skin.

He is my first and last love, and he will be my first time. What could be more perfect?

His hands wander over different parts of me, driving my need higher. Until I'm aching, overcome—desperate.

Between panting breaths, I ask, "Can a spirit who has experienced Second-death impregnate another spirit who has experienced Second-death?"

As a human, I didn't have to worry. Not because I wasn't having sex, but because birth control is given to all menstruating females in the name of population control. To have a child, a couple must petition for the right.

"I highly doubt conception is possible here," he says, and I agree. "But if it *does* matter, we're good. I receive yearly shots in Myriad to stop my little swimmers. I've got three months tae go." He rubs the tip of his nose against mine. "Shall we continue?"

I nod. "Please d—"

He dives down, claiming my mouth before I can finish my command, sweeping me up in a brutal storm of unquenchable desire. Will I ever get enough of him?

He devours my mouth, giving and taking, giving and taking, sweeping me up in a riotous storm. Right now, we are the only two people in existence. Time ceases to matter. There is only here and now.

Blood rushes through my veins, a newly awakened river without a dam in sight. My heart races, and my limbs tremble with passion rather than weakness. I tingle and ache and burn and tingle and ache and burn and oh, I can't get enough of this boy.

We're dead—again—but I've never felt more alive.

He picks me up as if I weigh nothing and gently places me on a dry rock. He removes my bra and panties before settling on top of me. Skin to heated skin. Hardness against softness. Consuming need to consuming need.

The kiss deepens as his hands travel over me, kneading me, caressing me, driving me utterly insane. My tremors return and intensify. My blood turns to fuel, stoking my need higher. And higher. New mewls leave me, followed by moans, groans and pleas.

And he's just getting started.

Anywhere his hands travel, his mouth soon follows. He touches and tastes every inch of me, this husband of mine, and I'm lost, so lost, set adrift, and I have no desire to be found.

He is *my* treasure, and in his arms, I have everything I've ever needed. Love, joy, peace and hope. The foundation I will forever stand upon. The things for which I fight the good fight.

"I want this tae be good for you, lass, okay? All right? So you must tell me if ever you want me tae stop. I will stop, no matter how far gone we are. No questions asked. There'll be no pushing you for more, okay?"

I nod, because I'm past the point of speech. But that's okay, too, because he lifts his head to peer at me with radiant adoration, and I'm certain every bit of it is reflected back to him through my eyes.

In that moment, I'm so glad I waited, so glad he is my first, but had there been a thousand before him, the memory of them would have been burned away in the fire of our love.

When he claims me as his own, there is pain, but it's slight, and soon fades. I cling to him, my nails in his back, and lift my hips to encourage him. As he moves within me, kissing me, loving me, still giving and taking, I'm overwhelmed by the knowledge that we are one.

One heart. One mind. One body.

Afterward, as I cuddle against him, my cheek resting against his racing heartbeat, I can't help but look ahead to our future. After we save the spirits here, we can work with Eron to save the people of Myriad from Ambrosine. If Archer and the others haven't already done so, that is. We can live in Troika, as planned, without Killian having to go to court in order to defect, or even travel between both realms. But...

After his treatment in Troika, that may not be something he's willing to do. I'll understand. I won't like it, but I'll understand.

"You stiffened," he says. "Tell me why."

"Just thinking about what will happen after we rescue the damned. You know…where we'll live."

"We'll live in Troika, and visit Myriad if we so desire— and if the realm still exists, of course."

"Really? You'd be willing to pack up and move to Troika, even though you were treated so horribly?"

"You were treated horribly in Myriad, lass. The difference is, my people tortured you, and planned tae do worse. Yer people only locked me away."

This is true. "To be fair, my people might have tortured you if we hadn't been bonded."

"Doona care. I'm choosing Light. I'm pulling a Tenley Lockwood and forgiving those who have wronged me."

How much do I love this boy. "Thank you."

"Even before my memory returned, I'd begun tae like the Light."

I kiss his collarbone. "I'm sure the Light liked you, too. How could it not?"

He snorts. "The last time I had tae choose a realm, I picked based on hatred. Hatred for Archer, and his rejection of me. Hatred for the people of Myriad, determined tae prove tae everyone I deserved a family. This time, I pick for love—for you."

As I luxuriate in the beauty of his words, a new bond clicks into place. A *stronger* bond. I can *feeeeel* his love for me, more luminous than ever before, every shadow gone.

"The Grid," I say, and gasp. "It's so much brighter now."

"For me, too."

Love has won.

No matter what else happens, *love has won*!

"Killian," I say, grinning ear to ear.

He leans toward me, as if drawn to me, only to go still. We both go still.

He frowns. "Did you hear that?" he whispers.

In the distance, a twig snaps. For the second time.

I scramble for my clothes—zero! We left every garment on the other side of the waterfall.

Another twig snaps. The murmur of voices arises.

Incoming!

But will we find friend—or foe?

TROIKA

From: M_V_3/54.5.8
To: L_R_3/51.3.15, J_A_3/19.37.30, S_C_3/50.4.13,
C_M_3/5.20.1, T_B_3/19.30.2, B_S_3/51.3.13, A_S_3/42.6.31,
J_B_3/19.23.4, S_J_3/62.5.5, M_P_3/45.10.9
Subject: RIP Tenley Lockwood

I just received word. Tenley Lockwood has been slain inside Myriad, and she has not entered into the Rest. Because of her connection to Killian Flynn, she entered Many Ends.

Before his disappearance, Alejandro posed the question: What if she's right, and we're wrong?

I believe he was on the correct track. The girl needs our help. Let's offer our help.

Light Brings Sight!
General Mykhail Vasiliev

TROIKA

From: S_C_3/50.4.13
To: M_V_3/54.5.8
Subject: Worse is on the way

Forget Miss Lockwood. Penumbra is still spreading in the Land of the Harvest and Troika. Abrogates are loose. There's no way we can cleanse them all, even with our ever-increasing number of Conduits.

Also, Miss Lockwood's guardian hunted me down. After biting me for "daring to hurt the best human born in, like, ever," he demanded an audience with you, Mykhail. Well, an audience with whoever thinks Miss Lockwood is "right about everything, always."

I suggest you take the meeting. He claims we're all going to die if we fail to do everything he says.

Light Brings Sight!
General Shamus Campbell

TROIKA

From: M_V_3/54.5.8
To: S_C_3/50.4.13
Subject: Stay the course

I have a feeling the Abrogates are a distraction meant to divide our forces. You say forget Miss Lockwood; I say forget *the Abrogates*. More of our people are dead. Conduits we desperately needed. They are not in the Rest, but Many Ends.

The *source* of the shadows must be negated. And from whom do Abrogates receive their power? Their king. Remove the king, and victory will follow.

So, our first order of business is as simple as it is complex. Find a way to fill our trapped Conduits with Light. We can't take down a king of darkness without Light. They are Light. And before you argue, know that this instruction comes directly from Eron.

So how can we get our Light into Many Ends?
As for the dog, send him my way.

Light Brings Sight!
General Mykhail Vasiliev

chapter twenty-five

"In the end, you will have what you say."
—Troika

Killian

As quietly as possible, I crawl to the other rock to retrieve our clothing. I toss Ten her garments and dress in my own as quietly as possible. She does the same.

I will protect this girl with my life.

Of course, I should have known my Ten would climb from the rock, determined to protect *my* life. She's as fierce as she is beautiful, her loved ones always her top concern. And I am one of those loved ones. Me. Killian Flynn. She loves me with all her heart, soul and body. I'm still amazed, will probably be amazed for the rest of eternity. I'm not sure how it happened, only that it has; Ten told me so, and she never lies.

For the second time in my life, I understand the importance of hearing the truth and telling the truth. Had Ten lied to me even once—about something, anything, large or small—I might doubt her word now. But she never has, never will. Despite the consequences, she always tells me straight. Her word is as good as gold, no, better than, and from this moment onward, mine will be better than gold, too. I want her to experience the same trust in me that I have in her.

In trust, there's absolute peace and utter joy.

Ten moves to my side, and together we inch forward. I kinda sorta want to murder our intruders in cold blood. Interrupt my time with Ten and suffer. But I'll resist the urge. Barely.

I've never stuck around after sex, but this time I wanted to stick around more than I wanted to take my next breath. I wanted to hold my wife, enjoy her, bask in the pleasure we just shared. Pleasure unlike anything I've ever experienced.

Watching her come alive under my touch proved to be the great accomplishment of my life. So what that I wasn't wanted as a child. I'm wanted as a man—Ten's man. She is the soothing balm to every hurt I suffered in my past.

Muttering voices reach my ears, and I ball my fist, preparing to launch a sneak attack. Then the intruders come into view at last.

Ten gasps and rushes forward. "No, no, no. What happened? Why—how—are you here?"

Archer, Dior, Raanan and Reed swing around to face her. They are cut and bruised, their dirt-stained clothing torn. But Dior no longer appears sickly. I caught a glimpse of her as we fought our way to the Kennels, and shadows had filled her eyes and run through her veins.

Seeing Ten, Archer sprints to meet her halfway. The two embrace, and shockingly enough, I experience no hint of jealousy. Or maybe it's not so shocking. Ten is mine. Willingly, happily. Always and forever.

Archer looks up, and our gazes snag. We share a moment of silent communication: *I'm still not sure I like you, but I'm glad you're here.*

"How are you here?" she asks him again.

"After you died," Archer says, "our Grids got nailed by a total blackout. We were severely weakened, which allowed the Myriadians to slay us quickly."

Her eyes go wide, and she presses a hand over her mouth. "My fault. I'm so sorry."

Through our new bond, I offer words of comfort, and she casts me a thankful half smile.

"Hey, hey now. No apologies." He grins at her, saving himself from a...*chat* with me. No one makes my girl feel guilty about anything without severe consequences. "We planned to enter Many Ends one way or another to help you save souls. This just sped up the process."

"So you owe me your eternal thanks?" she asks, her tone now pure sass.

He snorts.

"Where's Clay?" She rises on her tiptoes to try and peek over Archer's shoulder.

Sadness glitters in his eyes. "Minutes after we arrived, he was taken by a horde of the ugliest birds in creation."

Tears well in her eyes and spill down Ten's cheeks. Tremors rock her. Then she lifts her chin and clears her throat. "Well. It doesn't matter. Nothing matters here. All will be well, everyone freed. We'll save him, along with everyone else. We *will*."

"We will," I agree. Nothing will stop us.

"Victor is here, too, but he was taken by a horrendous-looking monkey-spider thing," Archer says.

"Victor?" I demand.

Archer's nod is wooden, his teeth clenched. "I killed him before I died."

"What about Biscuit?" Ten asks, gazing around the garden as tension radiates from her. "Is he here?"

"No," Archer says, and she expels a relieved breath. "He made it out of Myriad."

"Thank the Firstking." She pulls from Archer's hold to hug Reed, Raanan and Dior, who she clings to longest.

"I'm so sorry," Dior says.

"I know," Ten replies.

"I never meant for him to—"

"I know," Ten repeats.

Him. They must mean Levi Nanne, a Troikan General, now deceased. Both girls loved and respected him, maybe even considered him a father figure. But he died trying to save Dior from Myriad and the horrible covenant I tricked her into accepting.

Guilt slithers through me, wraps around my neck like a boa constrictor, and squeezes. Our every action has a consequence. Not just for the people involved, but for innocents, as well.

Perhaps we can save Levi, too, just like we're going to save the souls in Many Ends. The Unsigned can leave this sub-realm. Myriadians should be able to leave, as well; we'll soon find out, one way or another. Ten thinks so, or we wouldn't be here. Troikan spirits can exit the Rest, absolutely, no question. Archer is proof.

In a perfect world, everyone escapes and becomes one big happy family.

Hey, stranger things have happened.

It's time I make amends with the family I already have. And these people are my family. They helped me when no one else would so much as spit on me if I was lit on fire.

"I'm sorry, Dior," I say. "I have no excuse tae offer for my past actions."

As her dark gaze finds me, shame claws at my mind. Because of me, this girl suffered greatly. She planned to make covenant with Troika and spend her eternity with Archer. Their love had been evident, even back then.

When Dior's father had a heart attack, I seized the opportunity to defeat my former friend. I told Dior I would ensure good ole dad walked out of the hospital, but only if she made covenant with Myriad right then and there—and made no adjustments to the contract I offered.

She agreed, and I did as promised, using shadows to convince the man he felt better. But the moment, the very second her father walked through those hospital doors, fulfilling my commitment, I took the shadows away. He died in an instant, the stress of his movements too much for his fragile body.

By then, it was too late for Dior. She'd already signed the worst covenant imaginable.

As a med student, she was supposed to help humans from both realms, and yet, her contract ensured she would face punishment every time she helped a Troikan.

Horrible of me, yes. At the time, I told myself I was saving Dior from Ambrosine's wrath. He'd wanted the girl killed so that he could use her against his unfaithful son. I made sure there was a reason to keep her alive: her continued torment. But I'd lied to myself. Back then, jealousy had seethed inside me. Resentment, too. Archer had left me behind, scarring me for life, and yet he got to enjoy his future? No!

Something in my chest tightens. I do not deserve Dior's forgiveness, but I lift my chin and repeat, "I'm sorry for everything I did to you. If it helps, I was banned from Ambrosine's presence for ensurin' yer torment rather than yer death, and placed under Madame Pearl Bennett's *care*."

"It doesn't help."

No, I don't suppose it does. My gaze moves to Archer. "I'm sorry." I mean the words with every fiber of my being.

Dior continues to peer at me, her stare unwavering as tremors rack her. "I want to hold a grudge against you, I really, really do. You used my dream of becoming a doctor against me."

"I understand," I tell her. Truth. Some mistakes you can't recover from.

"But I need forgiveness, too." She pulls from Ten to lean into Archer's side. "How can I withhold from you what I seek from others?"

Archer doesn't hesitate to wrap an arm around her waist. The two share a look so loaded with tension the air around them heats. The air around us *all* heats. Awareness crackles.

"You're *together* together?" Ten asks, fanning her cheeks.

Archer rolls his eyes. "We haven't had time to discuss all the details yet, Nosey, but thanks for inserting yourself into our relationship."

Ten pretends to tip a hat. "Anytime."

"If he'll have me," Dior says, "I'll stay with him always."

Now Archer beams, as bright as the sun. "Oh, I'll have you all right. Again and again and again…"

A rosy blush paints over her cheeks, and he chuckles.

Just like that, a small fraction of my guilt eases. Archer deserves a happily-ever-after with the girl he loves. Finally he's on the right track.

Reed and Raanan pretend to gag.

"Enough making me sick. Time for medicine." Reed pulls leaves from the Tree of Life and passes them out to his crew.

As everyone eats, gashes weaving back together, bruises fading, I twine my fingers with Ten's. Touching her isn't a compulsion but a necessity. To my delight, she melts against me and rests her head on my shoulder. The sweetness of her scent envelops me. But the best part? Her scent is mixed with mine.

Satisfaction and contentment shimmer inside of me, new and wonderful. Why did I ever want to resist her? Why did I even try? With her, I've always been doomed to fail.

"What's our next move?" Archer asks. His gaze moves from Ten to Reed, concern darkening his expression. "You guys are the only ones who have been here before."

"Before Aunt Lina killed me," Ten says, "she told me to find the doorway, and I would save the day. Check. Killian and I took care of that just a little while ago. Then she said something about hills having eyes, so everyone will die, and if I wanted to win the fight, I would have to use Light."

Reed pales. "The hills. With eyes."

"Uh, I've seen that movie," Raanan says, and shudders. "Spoiler alert. We're all going to die."

"I lived here for years, but never dared venture into the hills. For good reason." Reed rubs a fist over his heart, as if the organ is in the midst of a panic attack. "The screams you hear—they come from there."

If the hills are where spirits are being kept, well, that's where we need to be. Wonderful. "We've got tae get our hands on weapons."

"Weapons. Right." Nibbling on her bottom lip, Ten searches the ground. "Problem. There are no fallen branches here."

No branches, no weapons. And venturing outside this fantastical haven to search for branches would be foolish. Everything outside this area is covered in bugs and poison.

"No, there aren't. Nothing dies in this little paradise." Reed sighs. "And don't try to pull anything down. It doesn't work, only gets you slapped."

Slapped? As if the tree is sentient?

Sentient = aware. I scratch my jaw and say, "Why don't

we *ask* the tree for limbs?" The idea wafts through my mind, as if whispered into my ear by an invisible friend. The Grid? Maybe, but not the Grid I'm used to dealing with. Something is different.

Raanan laughs. "Aren't you adorable? Ask a tree? Afterward we can talk to the dirt."

"Well, why not ask a tree?" Dior spreads her arms wide. "I'm sure we've all had worse conversations with people."

Ten tilts her head to the side, thoughtful as she regards me. "Killian is right. The tree is alive, like all the others here. Hello, it even has a name. The Tree of Life. While the others do their best to harm us, this one willingly feeds us. I mean, we aren't bitten or poisoned when we take the leaves. So why wouldn't the tree give us more—if we ask nicely?"

"Why don't we have to ask for the leaves, then?" Reed asks.

"Because food is a necessity, and weapons are a luxury?" Ten hikes one shoulder in a shrug. "Because the Tree of Life doesn't want us using the limbs to hurt other spirits?"

Facing one of the massive trunks, she brushes her palms over the bark. "Please. We want to help the people here, not hurt, and we could use—"

Before she can finish her sentence, a branch lowers, reaching for her. The end curls around her fingers and turns her arm before stroking the warhorse branded into her wrist.

Limb after limb tumbles to the ground, and not a single one comes close to hitting us.

Reed gasps. "All this time..."

Our group goes silent, shock palpable. Then we begin whooping with happiness. The tree *is* alive and *is* aware and *is* willing to help us.

"Thank you, thank you, a thousand times thank you," I say. Other thanks follow. "Thank you muchly."

"You're the best."

"Owe you."

"Thanks so much."

"Thanks."

"You rock!"

Raanan is the first to sober. "We're not going to get far with a bunch of clubs. And that's all these branches are good for, considering none of us has a dagger." A limb still attached to the tree swings in his direction and whacks him on the butt.

Giggling, Dior flattens a hand over her mouth.

"Could it be?" Ten stares at a branch for a several prolonged seconds. "I mean, it's possible. Even probable. Even though it makes no sense."

She doesn't make any sense. "Could what be, lass?"

"Light is always the answer," she says, ignoring my question. She lifts the biggest branch and sits down. "I have an idea." With her eyes closed, she draws in a deep breath…wraps a hand around each end. Deep breath out. Tension soon lines her face, a sign of deep concentration.

"What is she—" Reed begins, and reaches for Ten.

I grab his wrist, stopping him. "Let her work."

His nod is stiff, but he drops his arms to his sides and presses his lips together.

Soon pinpricks of Light flicker to life at the ends of Ten's fingers, muted at first, but growing in intensity. Light she is somehow channeling. Light = heat. Heat = fire. Fire = change.

She rubs her fingers along the end of the branch and…yes! The heat creates a pointed tip. A spear. Or an arrow, if we can create a crossbow. I think that we can. My belt is metal, and we can unfasten each link to use as nails.

By the time she opens her eyes, she's drenched in sweat and

pale. I pick the most succulent leaves for her and do not relax until she's consumed each one, her color bright once again.

"Never thought I'd see Killian Flynn playing nursemaid," Archer mutters.

"I'm practicin' for later," I reply, deadpan. "When I'm naked with my lass."

Ten elbows me in the sternum, and I throw her a grin, all, *was it something I said?*

I rub the sore spot, and pretend to pout. "Baby, I was tellin' the truth, just the way you like."

Her snort delights me.

"Where did you get Light?" Raanan asks.

"Love is Light and Light is love. You have some, too. You all do." Her mismatched eyes gleam with anticipation. "Anyway, the tree showed me how my staff was created. One of its limbs was used, along with Light. Did you know that? About the staff, I mean." She directs the question at Archer.

He shakes his head, sandy hair falling over his forehead. "I had no idea. After I defected to Troika—" he casts me an unreadable look "—the Prince of Doves gave me the staff and told me to keep it close, because it would one day save my life."

The Prince of Doves has visited Many Ends? When? Why? How?

Did he somehow rescue someone here, without ever stepping foot in the sub-realm? But if he was here, why not rescue everyone at once?

I met him once. I was on assignment, and he simply appeared before me. He tried to convince me to defect to Troika. I mocked him, sneering at his offer. Truth is, as I'd looked into his sky-blue eyes, I'd never felt more inadequate. Plus, I genuinely believed he would regret his offer; I also suspected

he'd made it simply to throw me off my game. Which he did.
I'd been turned inside out, and failed to recruit my target.
One of my first failures.

Now, I've seen the Secondking of Troika through Ten's
eyes. He would never come here and leave spirits behind.
That's not who he is. He cares too deeply.

So. Someone besides Ten, Reed and Kayla managed to escape Many Ends, and take a branch with him. Or her.

Ten gasps, her entire body jolting. "Eron," she blurts out,
and everyone frowns. "Centuries ago, there was a bridge
between Troika and Myriad. Eron used to come here. He and
Ambrosine would meet with the Firstking under the tree's
shade."

So I was wrong?

Reed purses his lips. "How do you know this?"

"The tree." She pats the trunk. "Do you not hear him?"

"No," we all say at once.

Her ears twitch as she concentrates. "Reminds me of Eron.
A piece of Eron, maybe?"

I'm not sure if she's talking to us or to herself.

"Once the bridge burned," she says, "Ambrosine placed obstacles around the tree—the creatures, insects, doorways—and
built a barrier around them. What he didn't know until too
late—he'd created Many Ends, binding himself to the sub-
realm. Because he is bound, his people are bound."

Well. I wasn't wrong, not really. Eron *was* here, but not
while souls were being tortured.

"What about the Unsigned?" I ask. "Why are they sent
here alongside Myriadians who experience Second-death?"

Her eyes go wide. "Because there's no such thing as Unsigned. When the Firstking created the Land of the Harvest,
he gave possession of it to both of his sons. But Ambrosine

stole the deed. He owns the Land of the Harvest. If you aren't
bound to Troika, you are bound to him. Rather than welcome the Unsigned into his midst, he sends them here, as
punishment."

Dior rubs a hand over her breastbone, as if to ward off a
terrible ache. "How can Ambrosine be so cruel to so many?"

This, *I* can answer. "He feeds on the pain he causes." I've
seen it firsthand. As Zhi, Victor and Javier tortured Ten, I
watched him close his eyes and soak up her misery as if it was
his own personal brand of ambrosia.

"Well, it's time to take him down. Destroying this realm
and stopping the constant torment should starve and weaken
him." Ten links her fingers with mine and gives a comforting
squeeze. "Come on. We've got weapons to construct."

After we gather enough leaves to feed an army—gotta
keep up our strength—we sit, forming a circle around our
pile of fallen branches. I perch on Ten's right, Archer on her
left. Dior sits on his other side, and the two share a brief kiss.

I watch as everyone but Dior creates one weapon after another. Spears, bows and arrows. Daggers. Or more precisely,
shivs.

Noticing my lack of effort, Ten frowns and whispers,
"What's wrong?"

"I have no Light."

"Uh, that's not true." After positioning herself in front of
me, she flattens her hands against my temples. Her touch is
soft and welcome, and I have to swallow a moan of desire. I
want her again.

Who am I kidding? I always want her.

"Close your eyes," she says, and I obey—though it's difficult. I could stare at her forever, but it still wouldn't be long
enough. "Look. Look deep inside you."

Her voice drifts through my mind, rippling along the Grid. A Grid I see more clearly as I follow those ripples, deeper and deeper—

There! I spot a small Light, unimpeded by a single shadow. It is a flame that crackles in the heart of our marriage bond.

Joy explodes inside me, and the flame grows.

My eyelids pop open, and my gaze meets Ten's. She's peering at me, expectant.

"Well?" she asks.

I offer her a slow, secret smile as I lean toward her, intending to steal a quick kiss. Just before contact, a lance of pain renders me immobile. The Light has spread, burning away a thin film that covered a section of my mind. Not a section of memories, but...coming events? I tense.

The world around me vanishes, and I see myself staked inside...a nest? Warm Lifeblood drips on to my naked body. It comes from a tier above me. Another nest? My chest is cut open, several of my organs gone, but I'm still lucid as a skeleton-bird swoops down and pecks at my liver.

A scream bubbles in my throat, but I'm too weak to release it. And why bother screaming again, anyway? Help will never come. This will happen again and again and again—as it has already happened again and again and again.

Comprehension dawns. With it? Alarm. I'm not glimpsing my future. I'm seeing the present through someone else's eyes.

But whose? And why?

Besides my own, I've only ever seen through Ten's eyes, because of our bond. So... I must be bonded to this other person. But how?

More skeleton birds swoop down, devouring the rest of my—the victim's—organs. The pain is incredible. Agonizing. I'm not sure how much more I...can...

The world goes black.

"Killian! Killian, can you hear me?"

Ten's voice penetrates the fog in my mind. I blink open my eyes once again, and find her posed above me, those azure locks falling around my face to create a curtain.

Tears of relief pour down her cheeks. "Thank the First-king. I wasn't sure what happened… Had no idea how to help you…"

She eases me to a sitting position, and I see the others are gathered around me, and they appear to be equally concerned. Not only do I have Ten, I have…friends? Maybe. It's possible. Stranger things have happened.

I explain what I saw, and everyone expresses concern.

"What if you were seeing through…I'm sorry…the eyes of someone you know and love?" Ten asks softly. "Like Sloan. Or your mother."

The thought of either woman suffering nearly sends me into a tailspin. Deep breath in, out. "It's possible," I admit, a sense of urgency taking root inside me. "We need tae save these people. *Now*."

There's a slight vibration at our feet, and Ten frowns. "What was that?"

"Someone new has arrived in the realm," Reed says. "Or multiple someones. When I lived here before, my friends and I would venture outside the Tree of Life to aid any newcomers."

"I remember." She traces a fingertip along one of the spears she made. "You came for me. Have I ever thanked you?"

He pats her on the shoulder. "You have, but thank me again by agreeing that we shouldn't take the risk yet. We plan to save *everyone*, right, so there's no need to risk losing one of our group in order to save someone who might turn against us. We need to focus our efforts on getting to the hills."

Dior and Raanan nod in agreement. Archer thinks for a minute, then nods as well.

I bring Ten's hand to my mouth and kiss her knuckles. Such soft, warm skin. "I'll do whatever you think is best, lass." Anything but sacrificing her life for others. That, I will never do.

If eyes are windows to the soul, I can see the wheels turning in her mind. "We stay here," she says, her determination clear. "We're saving everyone. Whatever happens out there between now and then, it'll be okay. Everything will be okay."

Reed rubs his hands together. "All right. For the best chance of success, we should wait until the realm resets. And before you ask, it resets every twenty-four hours." He runs his gaze over each of us. "That means one of us has to be captured by the birds. On purpose. He—or she—will take a pocketful of leaves and drop them along the way, all Hansel and Gretel style. The rest of us will have twenty-four hours to follow the path and reach the final destination."

"How will we know when the realm resets?" Archer worries two fingers over the stubble on his chin. "And what does *reset* mean, anyway?"

"There will be a flash of absolute darkness. Just a blink, but one hundred percent noticeable." As he speaks, he arranges leaves and branches in a circle, recreating the sub-realm. "And it means invisible doorways will be moved, the hills will appear somewhere else—*everything* will appear somewhere else. Everything but the Tree of Life. It never moves."

A collective shudder sweeps over the group.

"When will the next reset happen?" Raanan asks.

Reed stares up at the sky—a veil of dark red water. "A few hours maybe? We'll need to be ready to go at a moment's notice."

I expect everyone to point to Dior or me; we're the Myriadians and we'll make the perfect bid food. But I should have known better. Everyone except the Myriadians jumps at the chance.

What is it with Troikans and self-sacrifice?

I'm pretty sure Dior's reasons for not volunteering are similar to my own. I want to be near Ten, need to protect her, whatever the cost. Dior has just been reunited with Archer, and will want to protect him, the boy she lost—because of me.

Not going to feel guilty anymore. Nope, not even a little. I've apologized. We've moved on.

"I'll go," Ten says. "Face it. I'm the best choice."

I scowl at her. No way. Just no way.

"Sorry, Sperm Bank, but *I'm* the best choice," Archer says, his expression pure stubbornness.

I've heard him use the nickname before. It used to send me into a rage. Today, I can only smile. She's *my* sperm bank.

Ten slaps my shoulder. "I know what you're thinking, perv."

"And I do no' regret it," I say, and press a quick kiss to her lips.

"Sorry, guys, but I'll be the one who's taken," Raanan says. "I've survived worse. You guys won't last *ten* minutes."

"What if we're all taken together?" Dior suggests.

"No." Reed shakes his head. "We could be taken in different directions or given to different creatures. One person. One trail. Trust me on this."

As they argue, I sit back and listen in order to better craft a defense against my worst nightmare: Ten's nomination.

Good thing. Ultimately everyone but me agrees that Ten should be the one to go. She has the strongest bond to us all, and she'll have the best chance of communicating with us if things go badly.

Though I'm screaming inside, I have no defense. Not that it matters. There's no way I'm letting her go, her organs an all-you-can-eat buffet for the birds. So. I make up my mind in an instant, and know what I have to do.

I expect half of me to balk, to express reluctance. Something. Instead, I'm eager. I owe Ten. Actually, I owe everyone here. If a life must be risked, it will be mine.

I wait as long as I dare. A mere hour and a half. Then I kiss Ten's cheek, stand and say, "I'm going tae stretch my legs." The unequivocal truth...if not the whole truth.

"What, you're not going to argue with us?" she asks.

"No." I'm not.

She appears pleased. "I'll walk with you."

"Stay. What if I have tae empty my bladder, eh?" Again, not a lie. A question isn't a statement. "I love ye, lass." She owns me, body and soul. Always will.

"I love you, too. Oh! Take this with you, just in case." She hands me one of the smaller branches with a pointed tip. The perfect makeshift dagger.

I accept, grateful, and anchor it behind my back, then hide it under my shirt. Catching a glimpse of my stomach, she wiggles her brows at me, all *I'm going to get me some more of that, just you wait*, before she returns her attention to the task at hand.

My heart is heavy as I walk away—stretching my legs as promised. I don't want to leave her, but I will do *anything* to keep her safe. When I'm out of sight of the others, I pluck leaves from the Tree of Life, and stuff as many as possible in my pockets.

When I reach the edge of the tree's shade, I see the armies of skeleton birds, gorillas and monkey-spiders waiting. Squawks, roars and high-pitched...giggles?...erupt. The birds flap their wings. The gorillas lick their saber teeth, and the monkey-spiders jump up and down.

My heart races, and tremors speed through me as I wait... wait...for the realm to reset. Then, it happens. A blink of absolute, utter darkness. There and gone, as Reed predicted.

The others will come looking for me, ready to send Ten to slaughter.

Chin high, I step forward. *Take me.*

One of the birds gets to me first, sinking claws into my shoulders and yanking me into the air. I hiss. And now... now time is ticking.

"Ten," I bellow. "Come find me."

chapter twenty-six

"In the end, you will have what you take."
—Myriad

Ten
A few minutes earlier

I love ye, lass.

Killian's words echo in my head as I continue planning with Archer, Raanan and Reed and stuffing my pockets with leaves.

Something about Killian's tone begins to bother me. Minutes pass as I await his return, tensing more with every second. Nine. Fourteen.

Every year, Valentine's Day is celebrated on February 14th. It's a day for romance and love.

I rub the words tattooed on my forearm, a new nervous habit, I suppose. *Loyalty. Passion. Liberty.* Loyalty to my realm, passion for the truth—and Killian—liberty for all.

The realm resets, which means I gotta go get myself captured, but there's still no sign of Killian. Until—

"Ten," he shouts. "Come find me."

I vault to my feet. "Killian?" What's going on?

A bird squawks, and a growing sense of dread has my gaze jerking up. Horror gut-punches me. *No, please, no.* But my eyes do not deceive me. My husband is hanging from a bird's claws. Despite the distance, my gaze locks with Killian's for a split second before he disappears in the dark storm clouds that are rolling this way.

A brilliant green leaf flutters from the sky, falling between branches to land on the ground somewhere in the distance. He's leaving the necessary trail.

"What's wrong?" Archer asks, but he reads the answer on my face, or maybe he senses my emotions on the Grid. "I should have known he'd want to steal all the glory for himself." He *tsks*.

I'd slap him silly, but I know he's trying to lighten the severity of my mood.

Trembling now, I strap on as many weapons as I can. "Let's go."

"Sorry, Ten, but we have to wait," Reed says.

"No way." I shake my head with so much force I'm surprised when my spine doesn't snap. "Earlier you claimed we needed to leave the second the realm reset. Well, it's reset. We're going."

"I didn't know there would be a storm—"

"In Many Ends, there's always a risk of a storm," I interject. "Killian risked his life for ours. We're going to do the same for him. And if a storm does appear, it could blow away his trail. We won't be able to follow. So we go now. Or I do. If you want to wait, fine, but nothing is going to stop me."

Peering at me, one of Raanan's dark brows wings up toward the arch in the center point of his hairline. "You give good pointers. And honestly, hanging out with you is never dull, that's for sure."

As the others strap on their weapons, I pat my pockets to double-check I have as many leaves as possible. Guaranteed, we're going to need sustenance and medicine at every turn.

Fear yanks me into a mental boxing ring, ready to go head-to-head. Over the last year, I've overcome so much and faced so many tragedies. Now, everything is about to reach the ultimate climax.

"Monsters know whenever a spirit has reached the Tree of Life," Reed says. "They'll be waiting for us."

"Feel sorry for them," I say. "They took Killian. Now they die."

I lead the charge, determination and menace in every step, a thousand thoughts rolling through my mind. In the Everlife, it doesn't matter how much money we made as a human. It doesn't matter if we built an empire, or collected rare items or convinced everyone of our special awesomeness.

Human = soldier in a war, whether we know it or not. It's what we do as a human that affects who we are as a spirit. Who we loved. How we loved. Who we helped. People matter, not things.

I made the mistake of coasting through my human life, floating on the waves of indecision, and because of that, I lost that life far too soon. Now, I'm a spirit, and even though I'm in Many Ends, I have what I thought I'd never have again: another chance. Another chance to live and love and help, and not necessarily in that order.

We reach the edge of shade offered by the Tree of Life, and, ready for us, our enemy steps into view. Too many monkey-spiders to count, and that's saying something.

"Where are the gorillas and birds?" Dior asks, and Archer wraps an arm around her waist.

"Probably followed after Killian. Fresh meat," Reed says.

"Even the creatures here are at war. The gorillas steal from the birds, the birds steal from the monkeys, and the monkeys steal from the gorillas."

"How do you guys want to handle—"

Raanan goes quiet as I swing my spear at one of the creatures. Contact! The wood nails my target in the face, and I gasp with shock. The monkey-spider explodes, but not into pieces. Into shadows. Those shadows blow away in a wind I do not feel.

"What the—"

"How did—"

"Do that again!"

We look at each other for a moment, and laugh.

Dior throws her arms around Archer. "We can do this!"

He's so large, and she's so small. They share a stolen moment of connection and perhaps even communion, and it's beautiful.

"When we get through this, and we will, we're going to celebrate. Hard. Until then, stay behind us," he tells her. "We'll need you if we're injured."

A very nice way of telling her 1) she'll slow us down and 2) she has no battle skill.

She flinches only to accept her lot with a nod, tenacity burning in her eyes. There's no changing what is, only what can be.

All right, then. We're as ready as we'll ever be. There's a clock in my mind, and it begins to count down to the next reset—when Killian's sacrifice means nothing.

Unacceptable! We will reach him, no matter the obstacles before us. I will not lose hope now.

"We attack on my count," I announce. "Three. Two. One."

In perfect harmony, we rush forward. Nope, spoke too soon. Dior hangs back, as requested.

Focus. One touch. That's all it takes to utterly destroy a monkey-spider. Which means victory should be easy as pie, but the creatures come at us en masse, desperate to rid us of our weapons.

Strike. Spin. Strike. Spin. I never pause. The moment I do, I'll be felled. Then Archer presses his back against mine, and Raanan and Reed take up positions at our sides. Together we slay one monkey-spider after another.

By the time the last one explodes into shadows, we're panting and soaked in sweat. Thing is, I know we're not even close to being done.

"Not a second to lose," Reed says. "Let's go."

We plow ahead and finally find the leaf Killian dropped. The first of many. It's a lovely shade of emerald, the only bit of color amid a sea of gray and black.

"What's that?" Dior points to a spot ahead.

I narrow my focus…and frown. A separate sea of black seems to be moving in our direction. It's—realization hits. It's an army of insects, and it is headed our way. Intermixed with countless bugs? Countless snakes.

Cold fingers of dread tickle my spine. I've dealt with my fair share of bugs. While locked inside Prynne Asylum, I lived with creepy crawlers and even ate them when Dr. Vans decided to starve me. Spiders taste like shrimp, and cockroaches taste like greasy chicken. Not exactly helpful information in this situation.

"We should go back to the Tree," Reed says, a tremor in his voice. "The bugs won't venture under its shade. We'll wait until they pass."

Hardly. They might not pass. "No." I am resolved. "If we go back, they could keep us trapped. Killian needs us."

"What do we do, then?" Dior croaks.

I...don't know. I don't how we're going to survive this. I'm used to having answers, but this...this is a little beyond my wheelhouse. "I need a minute to think."

"We don't have a minute," Raanan snaps.

"Shut up, just shut up for a second." How do you fight millions of tiny critters that can crawl all over you? You can't bat them away with a branch, or punch or kick them. You can't stop, drop and roll. You can't even outrun them because they form a wall in front of you in the direction you need to go.

"You guys listen to Reed and go back to the Tree. I'll let the bugs eat every inch of my skin, if that's what it takes, but I'm getting to Killian. If I die, I die. I'll resurrect somewhere in the realm, and I'll continue my journey." At least, that is how I think things work in Many Ends. When you die, you come back to life, but remain in the realm. Hence the name: Many Ends.

Great risk, great reward.

Loyalty, passion, liberty.

The warhorse will ride.

The bugs speed up, coming closer...closer still...

"I'm getting a little tired of you telling us to stay safe while you rush headlong into danger, Tenley Lockwood." Archer blows me a kiss. "You're not the only one who wants to save Killian. He was my best friend once."

He's right. "I'm sorry. I only hoped to save you pain."

"Pain is pain. Friendship matters more. We're in this together." He sheaths a branch behind his back and reaches for Dior's hand. "If we die, we die as one."

One heart. One soul. One body.

Together we will rise.

A trembling Dior accepts Archer's grip and reaches for Reed, the guy on her other side. Reed reaches for Raanan and Raanan reaches for me. We form a line, a wall of our own. Strength and love and Light flow between our joined hands. Heads high once again, we march forward...

So close—

We continue marching forward. Only a whisper away...

The bugs reach us at last. In a spilt second, we're covered head to toe. *Can't see...* Sharp stings register all over my body. Dizziness overtakes my mind, and my limbs quickly weaken. And yet, somehow, I remain on my feet. Marching forward, marching forward. And...

No, surely not. But...it's true. The bugs begin to fall off of me. Off of everyone—suddenly I can see. We're covered in red welts, but not bugs. Not any longer. They bit us...and they died?

Again, we're amazed.

"How—"

"Why—"

"What—"

"The Light," I say. "It has to be our Light." Death and life cannot coexist. Light = love. Love = life.

More confident by the second, we continue on, maneuvering through the bugs, unimpeded. Our hands drop to our sides and we spread out, though we remain in shouting distance of each other as we search for the leaves Killian dropped. We find the second and third and adjust our route accordingly.

As soon as we pass the last of the bugs and snakes, we pick up the pace. Running, running. Tree limbs reach for us, but we dodge and dive, avoiding capture. When we reach a darker part of the forest, however, thorny vines stretch from bushes, and those we can't dodge or dive. The thorns snag our clothing and embed in our skin.

As I pull at the vines, thorns prick my fingers, and I hiss with pain. Blood wells, and my fingers throb.

"Ten," Reed gasps out.

"I'm stuck," Raanan calls.

I don't... I can't...

A scream practically rends the air in two. My head whips to the side, and I groan. One of the vines is wrapped around Dior's throat, squeezing. The goal is clear: Take out the weak link to weaken the strongest.

Archer fights to escape the vines twined around his wrists and ankles, Lifeblood pouring from different wounds. "No!" he snarls. "Stop!"

I put every ounce of my strength into reaching the girl, no longer fighting my capture but allowing the thorns to rip through me... Lifeblood pours from me, as well.

Dior's knees give out, and she sags to the ground. Archer is there to catch her and ease her down. Finally, I reach her. Her eyes are open and locked on Archer, her lips opening and closing as mewls of pain escape.

"Save your strength, doc." He yanks at the vines around her neck, but they only squeeze harder, causing her eyes to bulge. "I'll get you out of this. I will. I—"

"Love...you." A final breath escapes her. Her head lulls to the side, those wide eyes dulling, staring at nothing.

"No. Don't you die. Don't you dare. I love you. We're going to make plans." Frantic, he feels for a pulse. He stiffens, his watery gaze lifting to meet mine, revealing a mix of rage, torment and sorrow in their copper depths.

"Archer—"

"No. This can't be. The monkey-spiders exploded. The bugs died. How did the thorns thrive when they touched us?" Even as he speaks, the thorns begin to wither.

When Archer realizes what's happened—too late, far too late—he looks up at the sky and roars with pain and rage and sorrow.

He must have left a spark of Light inside her when he cleansed her of Penumbra. Light = love, love = Light. Light is poison to the creatures here. She saved us. She gave up the little Light she had to save us.

"This doesn't matter," I say, but my chin trembles. "She's going to appear somewhere else in the realm, and we're going to save her. We're going to save them all." I won't believe anything less. "That's why we're here. We have to keep going. Okay? All right?"

"How do you know she'll appear elsewhere?" he demands. "How?"

"I just do." Because I have to. Nothing else is acceptable.

"Ten," he says, and his whole body shudders. Grief encompasses him, a dark cloud—a sign of another impending storm. "I just got her back. I just cleansed her of Penumbra. She was going to defect. I would have been her Barrister, and this time she would have succeeded. We were going to talk about our future, make things official. I love her. I've never stopped loving her."

Tears sting my cheeks. "I know you have every right to be upset. I know your pain." I know he failed to save her once before, dying when she needed him most, and he thinks he's let her down again. "But suck it up. Wallowing will get *us* killed. And we have to move on. Now fight!"

chapter twenty-seven

"Lies have no foundation. In a storm, lies will always fall, and
truth will always remain standing."
—Troika

Killian

At last. My "escort" reaches the infamous hills. Mountains,
really. Each one has been hollowed out, hordes of birds and
prey inside. Outside...

I shudder. The "eyes" belong to creatures I've never before
encountered. Small of stature with the fangs and the forked
tongue of a snake, the shell of a turtle upon their backs—shells
that are lined with bony spikes—and the arms and legs of an
alligator. But those eyes...they are neon red, watching me as
I soar overhead. Abject hunger sharpens the air, made worse
by the fetid scent of death saturating every burst of wind.

I watch as another bird flies by and drops an unwitting
victim to the creatures. What happens next...

Bile rushes up my throat, threatening to empty my stomach.

The creatures—monsters—react instantly, caught up in a
feeding frenzy, biting into the guy, ripping his limbs from
his body.

That is what Ten and the others must face. If she's harmed...
There will be nothing I can do about it. Not until I escape.
And I will escape. I must.

The closer we came to our destination, the louder the
screams became. Now that we're here, those screams are deaf-
ening. Millions of them clash in terrible disharmony, blending
with moans, groans and grunts. My ears ache from the assault.

I drop a leaf on the hill of my carrier's choosing, though I
wish I could keep it. For medicine, yes. But also as a weapon.
Something I've noticed: the animals and insects bolt away
rather than touch the leaves.

Unfortunately, I just discarded my last leaf.

We descend down, down, down into the depths of the
mountain. There's an uncountable amount of tiers—though
my sweet Ten will somehow find a way, I'm sure. Upon each
tier are equally uncountable nests. Inside most of those nests
are skeleton-birds that are feeding on their prey—spirits.

Myriadians I've met over the years. Myriadians I've watched
die. There are others, of course, so many others, but whether
they are Myriadian or Unsigned, I'm not sure.

My mother is in one of these mountains. One of these nests.
Ten's mother, too. Aunts, uncles and cousins I never knew.
Colleagues I lost in battle.

None of the victims notice me, too lost in their pain. For
most, limbs are missing. For some, bones have been picked clean.
Torsos are cut open, organs missing, just like the image I saw
inside my head. My gaze scans, searching for my mother. She—

I tense as my gaze collides with Sloan. She's here, trapped
inside this mountain. My stomach churns. She's awake, though
pieces of her heart are missing. One of her legs stops at the knee.

She opens her mouth to speak. Or scream. I'm not sure
which. Either way, she's too weak. No sound emerges.

The bird releases me. I tumble through the air before landing in a nest of my own, a single tier down from Sloan. In an instant, thorns stab and snare me. Black vines reach out to wrap around my neck, wrists and ankles, rendering me immobile.

A bird in the nest next to mine spots me, looks at his own meal—a little bit of muscle left on a skull—and decides I'll make a tastier treat. He hops over, but my captor dives into him, and the two fall from the tier. They plummet down, down, pecking and clawing at each other along the way.

I struggle against my restraints, old wounds bleeding more—faster. New wounds tear open, and weakness sets in. I do not stop. Thoughts of escaping, of doing everything possible to clear the way for Ten, drive me. Those turtle things... how can I force them from the hills?

"Killian." Sloan's voice. Weak, thready. "Don't fight... makes worse..."

Must!

Accepting abuse isn't in my wheelhouse. But all too soon, my captor returns. Though his skull possesses no eyes, he seems to stare straight at me, and he radiates hate and hunger.

He squawks with triumph at the sky—before using the tip of his beak to slice open my chest cavity and tear off a piece of my heart. The pain! A scream bubbles my throat, but I swallow it back. Screaming is too much like begging.

The bird takes another bite, and another. Not just pain, agony. Darkness closes in...welcome darkness...

I'm not sure how much times passes before my eyelids crack open, consciousness jarring me. One moment I'm blissful, lost in dreams of Ten, the next I'm aware of my throbbing head, and the torment wracking the rest of me. A chorus of sobs.

At first, my surroundings are blurry. *Blink, blink.* As my

vision clears, I look around with dry, burning eyes. My captor is gone. So are all the other birds. A welcome miracle.

I look at my body, distressed by the thought of what I might find. Elation sparks. My limbs are still attached, and bits of my heart remain. I'm only missing a kidney and a section of bowel.

Only. A near hysterical laugh escapes. How sad is it that I'm elated only a kidney and bowel were eaten?

"Killian."

A weak voice sounds from above me. Lifting my head proves difficult, pulling against the thorns still embedded in my neck, but I do it. My gaze lands on Sloan. She's leaning out of her nest, her skin ashen, her cheeks sunken.

"You died," she says, her lip trembling. "How?"

One of her tears splashes on to my forehead. "Long story." And I'm not sure I have the strength to tell it. "Where are the birds?"

"Yours retched after feeding from you and flew off. Nothing like that has ever happened before, and most of the others followed him."

I've been saved from round two of torture. But for how long?

"I wish I had a way to save you," she says, her voice breaking as if she's fighting tears. "No one has ever found a way. Some of these people have been here for decades."

Decades. Of this. What's sad is, I'm sure there are millions of spirits who have been here longer.

Will I be one of them?

No way. Ten has never let me down, and she never will.

"We're going tae be rescued," I say. "Help is on the way."

Hope glimmers in her blue eyes. "Ten is coming for us?"

"She is."

The corners of Sloan's mouth lift. "If anyone can save us…"

"She can. She will." I have faith.

MYRIAD

From: H_S_3/51.3.6
To: Z_C_4/23.43.2
Subject: Prepare your army

Also, prepare our Abrogates in Myriad as well as the Land of the Harvest. Troikan soldiers are headed this way. It's on like Donkey Kong!

Might Equals Right!
General Hans Schmidt

MYRIAD

From: Z_C_4/23.43.2
To: H_S_3/51.3.6
Subject: We have a problem, sir

I've just learned some distressing news. One of our subjects—Lina Lockwood, Tenley's aunt—has bonded to a Troikan General. He's the one we captured. Alejandro Torres. The two are now missing. How would you like me to proceed?

Might Equals Right!
Sir Zhi Chen

MYRIAD

From: H_S_3/51.3.6
To: Z_C_4/23.43.2
Subject: Forget them

There's nothing they can do to stop us. They're a distraction, nothing more. Proceed as commanded, and focus on annihilating the incoming army.

Might Equals Right!
General Hans Schmidt

chapter twenty-eight

"Some lies are more necessary than oxygen."
—Myriad

Ten

Time is running out. Energy, too. We've been following Killian's trail, without a single break, only pausing to fight when challenged by a monster, plant or insect. We win. Every time, we win, but every battle takes something from us. A little hope. A little strength.

I've been counting the minutes inside my head, and we are a mere two hours away from the reset of the realm. Aka 120 minutes. Aka 7,200 seconds. That means he's been with the birds for twenty-two hours. Aka 1,320 minutes. Aka 79,200 seconds. He could have been tortured and killed multiple times already.

If we fail to find him in time…

We can't fail.

I'm tense as we stumble this way and that. Trees hiss, and leaves snap their razor sharp teeth, but nothing else challenges us. Maybe word has spread. Try to stop us, die.

Up ahead, a lavender leaf glows. The next beacon. One more step closer to Killian.

I've pocketed every leaf he's dropped. When we find him, he's going to need an infusion of strength.

Urgency burns inside me, and I quicken my pace. The others follow without objection. Finally we make it out of the forest, and enter a clearing without trees. Ahead looms a dry and barren landscape, mist, and—I gasp. Mist clears, revealing hills. So many hills.

We did it!

With a whoop, we rush forward...only to stop when we're roughly five hundred yards from the first hill. What looks to be black tar is smeared over the ground. Thousands of... alligators? Kind of. There are differences. These creatures, whatever they are, form a circle around each of the leaves that lead to one particular hill.

"What are those things?" I ask, pointing to the creatures.

"Kayla and I used to call them land sharks," Reed says. "At the first scent or sight of Lifeblood, they erupt into a frenzy."

"Don't worry." Archer eyes the creatures as if he's hungry and could use a snack. "I'll distract them."

He wants to avenge Dior's death, and I understand. A good portion of his Light died with her. Now he hopes to join her, wherever she is. And she *is* somewhere. I will believe nothing less.

I reach out, take his hand, and squeeze. "You'll get her back, Bow. We'll find Killian, then we'll find a way to free the spirits."

"We can free the spirits *if* we figure out a way to do something no other ordinary citizen has done since the dawn of time," he grates.

"We've already done something no other ordinary citizen

has done," I remind him. "We are Troikans, and we entered Many Ends. And did you ever think you'd see Killian Flynn happily married? Face it. I'm a miracle worker."

One corner of his mouth twitches, some of his tension easing. "I never thought I'd see Killian Flynn married, period."

"And don't forget, Clay is in one of these hills, too. So is my mother. So is Killian's mother. I'm not going to rest until *everyone* is free of Many Ends."

"Don't forget we've got to pass through the creatures first." Raanan unstraps the two branches that are hanging against his back, places one end in the ground, then lets the other end fall toward our foes. "I think I have an idea about how we can do it—and survive."

The creatures squeal as they scramble out of the way to avoid any kind of contact with the wood.

Smiling now, Reed nods. "I get it. We walk across the branches. As we move forward, we drop another branch, then pick up the one behind us."

Giving him a pat on the shoulder, Raanan says, "Exactly, my friend. Exactly."

It could get us killed, but it could also maybe hopefully probably work. Really, what other choice do we have?

Find the doorway, save the day. If the hills have eyes, everyone dies. To win the fight, you'll need Light.

"So how do we blind these fiends?" I ask.

Raanan pops the bones in his neck. "Whatever the answer, I call first kill."

"We're running low on Light," Reed says. "We've got to have more."

Understatement of the year. The weaker you are, the harder it is to draw on love. We've been eating leaves from the Tree of Life, but we want to save as many as possible for any spirits we find.

"We're going to have to risk it," Archer says, his tone firm. "I'll go first. Ten and Reed will take the middle. Raanan will take the rear."

"Nope. No way." I shake my head, tendrils of hair slapping my cheeks. "Think about it. Weight has to be evenly dispersed across the branch. The two lightest take the ends, and the two heaviest take the middle, becoming our center of gravity and preventing us from tilting one way or the other. That puts me in the front, you and Rannan in the middle and Reed in the rear."

There's no reason to waste time debating my plan, and every reason to hurry. As my heart thumps against my ribs and sweat runs down my spine, I clutch my spear to use it for balance, draw in a breath and onto the "plank."

Every single creature eyes me like I'm some kind of tasty treat. Several even step closer while sharpening mental forks and knives.

My friends go still, and I know they're debating the wisest course of action.

"Wait," I say. *If the hills have eyes, everyone dies.*

Eyes...eyes...

Perhaps Aunt Lina meant...

Well, why not? Pushing my weight into my heels, I stab one of the creatures directly in the eyes. Jab, jab, destroying one peeper after the other.

The land shark squeals a high-pitched sound of pain as black goo sprays from the injured sockets. Other creatures leap onto its back, devouring every inch of it, even its bones.

Steady, steady. During the frenzied feeding, I stab three more land sharks in the eyes, causing *another* frenzy.

"Be ready. I'm stepping forward now," I say, fighting tremors.

As Archer steps up behind me and stabs two more creatures, I take my next step. The feeding continues. More goo sprays in every direction. The fetid scent of rot saturates the air. And the sucking, slurping, chomping sounds… I shudder.

"On three," I say. "One, two, three." Archer and I step forward, allowing Raanan to move on to the branch without tipping us over.

He stabs four of the creatures, and we motor forward a third time, allowing Reed to claim the rear of the branch.

Jab, jab. I blind another creature—and wobble. My thudding heart almost stops as Reed wobbles, too. Archer plants a hand on my shoulder, steadying me. He also plants a hand on Raanan's shoulder, and Raanan plants a hand on Reed's shoulder. We're a unit. A team. Balanced by each other. And surrounded by monsters.

Must stay calm.

"All right," I say. "We step forward, stab a land shark, then step again. I hope everyone's ready, because we're doing this on my count." No time to waste. "Three, two, one."

We step forward, stab the land sharks, then step again, as planned. For over an hour we repeat the action again and again. The only problem? We're at a point of total exhaustion, and we're only halfway to Killian's hill.

Reed wobbles, and though Raanan tries, he is unable to steady him. Features contorted with panic, Reed places one foot on the ground beside the branch. Just for a second, only a second. The land sharks rip into his ankle, removing his foot.

Falling, he screams. Raanan reaches for him while Archer reaches for Raanan, and I reach for Archer, but we're too late. Reed topples, and the land sharks instantly pounce.

His screams end as quickly as they began, his voice box gone—just like the rest of him.

I suck in a breath, and fight a wave of tears. My chin trembles. My heart aches, and bile burns my throat. I don't... I can't even process what... Such brutal, savage violence, rendered so quickly.

"We'll save him," I say, my mouth dry. This can't be the end for him. "We'll add him to our to-do list, and we'll save him." We must.

Archer scrubs a hand down his face. "How is he going to revive from that, Ten? Tell me. Please."

"He's a spirit. Spirits never die, and his Lifeblood wets the ground, even now. Blood is life. He'll regenerate." He must. This can't be the end of Reed. It just can't. "We'll save him," I repeat.

"If a spirit never dies, where is Reed now?" Archer spreads his arms to indicate the entire sub-realm.

"I don't know, okay? I don't know. But I don't have to know how manna works, either, and yet it still heals me. Every time. So zip your mouth and get your butt in gear." I wobble, and my stomach seems to drop into my ankles. When I steady, I clear the lump from my throat, and, with a gentler tone, I say, "I don't have all the answers. I never have. I only know I have to do this. I can't stop. I have to believe good will come from this or...or..." Or I will have no reason to motor on.

I've lost too much already.

"We gonna stand here debating something we can prove with action, or what?" Raanan demands in typical Raanan fashion.

He's right. I will prove the spirits in Many Ends can be saved, even spirits like Reed.

"Let's move." Only fifty-five minutes to go. Our destination is ahead, still so close, still so far.

Time continues to tick, and tick fast. We move forward together and stab the eyes of the land sharks in unison. Again. Then again and again.

Forty-one minutes. Symphony No. 41 is the last symphony created by Mozart.

Twenty-nine. The atomic number of copper, like Archer's eyes.

Thirteen. Apollo 13. Known by some as a successful failure. The rocket failed to land on the moon but much was learned in the rescuing of the crew.

Our mission will be a successful success.

Eight. Seven. Six. Five.

"How much time before everything resets?" Archer asks. Sweat pours from him.

"Four minutes, thirteen seconds." Will the hills switch places? Zero! What will we do then? We must be on Killian's hill.

"I don't care how tired you are, pick up the pace," Raanan commands.

I obey. Drawing from my love for Killian and all my friends, I find a reservoir of strength. At last we reach the desired hill, bypassing the land sharks completely. I'm trembling as I pick up the final lavender leaf.

What if everything we're doing is for nothing? What if we're stuck here?

Ugh! Doubts suck. I can't let them lead me—they'll take me down a dark path. Without hope, there is no Light. That means hope is a necessary weapon right now.

"What's next?" Raanan asks. "Are we supposed to go through or over the hill?"

"There are no caves that I can see." Archer wipes sweat from his brow. "So, we go up."

Great. "Makes sense, since we're dealing with birds." My muscles burn and strain, my entire body trembling as we trudge up, up. My lungs feel as if they're melting.

Four words keep me motivated. *Save Killian. Save everyone.*

"If we have to fight anything, we're going to lose," I rasp. "I'm almost tapped out."

Two minutes.

"Leaf," Archer says.

Left with no other choice—if we want to win—we each consume a leaf. The last we'll allow ourselves. Our supplies are running low, and what remains will be passed to Killian and the others.

"Wait. You know what I don't hear? Squawking," Raanan says. "Maybe the birds are gone. But why leave?"

With the new boost of strength, we increase our pace. But we aren't yet all the way up when the entire world goes black. I gasp and stumble, rendered blind as another reset takes place. What will we find when—

The darkness flees, revealing an island littered with hills, surrounded by water rather than tar and alligators. Water as far as the eye can see, surrounding the hills.

If we'd been any lower, we would have drowned.

Dread. Dismay. This is *the* lake. The one with the portal into the Kennels.

Carnivorous mermaids swim beneath the surface. But okay. This isn't a bad thing. Our portal home is a dive away.

Did Lina time my death, so that I'd be on the hills when the lake appeared around them?

I'm still on my knees, gripping hunks of grass and dirt. Realization. We're still positioned on Killian's hill!

"Come on." Heart hammering, I right my position. "We need to reach the top before the birds come back."

chapter twenty-nine

"As long as there's breath, there's hope."
—Troika

Ten

Raanan reaches the top first, only to rear back, nearly falling down the side of the hill. As every muscle in his body seems to clench, he drops to his knees. The color drains from his cheeks.

"What is it?" Archer demands. He reaches the top next—

And has the same reaction.

My stomach churns. What do they see?

"Help me," I plead, stretching out my arm.

Archer's eyes are pools of shock when he faces me. He takes my hand and hoists me to the top of the hill. A ledge. The inside of the hill has been hollowed out and—

Air wheezes between my teeth. There are thousands of nests, each one occupied by a person or two. Or really, the remains of a person or two. Moans and groans assault my ears.

I can't… I don't…

Where is Killian?

The scents of rot, punctured bowels and shredded bladders

reach me, and my stomach stops churning in favor of heaving. I lurch forward to vomit. Bye-bye precious leaf. And so, so, *sooooo* sorry, person underneath me.

"We were right. No birds." Raanan's words blend with the anguished chorus.

I wipe my mouth with the back of my hand and call, "Killian? Where are you?" What horrors has he endured?

A terrible pause as I wait, hoping, praying. What if his final leaf blew away from another mountain? The right mountain?

Finally I hear a weak and broken, "Lass."

One word. Only one, but still my heart leaps. My gaze scans...

Oh, please, no. Killian is sprawled inside one of the nests, his chest cavity split down the center, exposing muscle, bone and multiple organs. I press a quavering hand over my mouth. Hot tears well in my eyes, spill down my cheeks; I feel like I'm crying rivers of acid.

"Just hang on, love." My voice trembles. "We're going to..." What? We've come so far, and Killian is down there, helpless. He needs me now more than ever. *All* of these people need me, but I don't know what to do.

I glance at Archer, who is scanning the nests in search of Dior, just in case she reawakened here. I glance at Raanan, who is chalk white, staring at someone I've never met. I glance at the multitude of other victims. My gaze lands on a girl I don't recognize—

I inhale sharply, my horror magnifying. I *do* recognize her. This is Sloan. Once luxurious blond hair is now tangled, caked with...things, and thinned out; she has bald spots, where birds have picked her scalp clean. One of her eyes is missing. And one of her legs.

She's in worse shape than Killian.

Mouth drier by the second, I call, "Hang on just a little longer. We're going to free you." How? *How can I keep my word?*

A sob escapes her. Hope and relief glimmer in her remaining eye.

"Miss Lockwood." A feeble voice catches my attention. "Please. Help me."

I study the mass of faces…and find Dr. Vans, the former leader of Prynne, and once my greatest tormentor. Hatred pricks me, attempting to worm into my mind and heart, but I resist. Hatred = darkness. Darkness = weakness.

Bitterness will not poison me. Not again. No more shadows, please and thank you. I will do the right thing. Save one, save all. I can't pick and choose.

Squawks sound in the distance. Stiffening, I whip around and spot large black clouds in the distance. No, not clouds. Birds. They are returning to their nests.

Panic showers me with ice, determined to slow me. Ruin me. "They're coming." And there are too many for three lone—exhausted—Troikans to fight.

"We're in no shape to challenge them," Raanan says. "Especially on their home turf."

Archer squares his shoulders. "We have only one weapon capable of keeping those birds away. Our Light."

Searching the Grid…searching…on the lookout for any rooms where extra Light might be stored. I find none, and my chest tightens. No Light, no hope. No hope, no victory. I call on my love for Killian and the others, but I'm tapped out. So weak.

I try to open one of the doors in the Grid, just in case, but none of the knobs will turn. I'm locked out?

—*We're here, Miss Lockwood, and we're ready. Open your link to Killian, then your link to your fellow Troikans.*—

The voice overtakes my mind, familiar and welcome. General Alejandro Torres. He's alive, and he's...here, in Many Ends? But... I'm not bonded to him like I am to my friends.

—*What do you mean, you're here?*— Though I'm speaking with Alejandro, I keep my gaze on the birds. Closer...

—*I'm inside Myriad with your aunt. We're bonded. It's a long story best told when we have time. The other Generals are outside of Myriad. According to your guardian, Ambrosine planned to flood our Grid with shadows, weakening us. Now we're going to use the Secondking's plan against him and flood the Myriadian Grid with Light. The citizens will be weakened, my soldiers will enter the realm, and the final battle will be waged.*—

Too much information to process, every bit startling. What strikes me with the most force? Alejandro is the General my aunt married.

Shock demands answers now, now, now, but he's right. Later is better. Time is short, and this is everything I've wanted, wrapped up in a satin bow. This is help. Except, if the General is wrong, or this is a trick, I'll expose everyone I love to Myriadian shadows. Exactly what I fought to prevent during Javier's torture.

Closer still...

"Guess we have no other choice." Raanan's tone is resigned, as if he knows he's going to die but plans to go down swinging. "Get ready to engage."

There's no time to think this through. I didn't trust my team before, and it cost me dearly. I won't make the same mistake again.

"Don't fight, just trust me." I grab both Archer's and Raanan's hands. "Concentrate on your bond to me while I concentrate on my bond to Killian."

"If we stand here," Archer says, "we'll be—"

"Please," I beg, and then I decide action is better than words. I close my eyes and do as promised, concentrating on my bond to Killian while dropping my shields.

Whoosh. One of the doors springs open of its own accord. That exact moment. Light floods me. Light from the people of Troika. Not just Alejandro and the Generals—so bright, nothing brighter—but Laborers and Leaders, Headhunters and Messengers, too.

My aches and pains vanish. Amazing warmth invades every inch of my body, then spills from me into my friends.

"Too much," Raanan grates. "Too much for us to contain."

I've experienced this before, when I cleansed Dior of her first case of Penumbra, only on a much smaller scale. "As Conduits, we have the power to share. So share it! Now!"

Just. Like. That. Light explodes from our pores. We're lifted off our feet, held suspended by magnificent rays of Light.

We soar, shining, shining so brightly, empowered by Light, by love. We are warhorses, each of us, ready for battle, refusing to give up, even when the odds are stacked against us.

Nothing is impossible for us. Victory is ours. Victory will always be ours.

As quickly as the Light hit, it disappears. We collapse to the ground.

Panting, I blink open my eyes. I'm flat on my back, staring up at a bright Light that isn't coming from the boys. No, it reminds me of a sunrise in the Land of the Harvest. For a moment, I imagine children playing in the streets, laughing together, ice cream melting in dirt-smudged hands.

Sitting up gingerly, I survey Many Ends and a fresh dose of shock saturates my cells. The birds are scattered on the ground—dead. Mermaids float atop the surface of the lake—

dead. The hills are gone, the land flat, millions of people lying all around me. Missing limbs and organs have been replaced. Everyone is healed and whole!

Archer and Raanan remain at my sides. With a cry of happiness, we launch at each other and embrace. Tears pour down my cheeks.

Other people stir, realization quickly settling in. Then cheers ring out.

Spotting Erica, the girl who gave Killian his tattoos, I push through the crowd. "Have you seen Killian?" I have to yell to be heard.

"No, I'm sorry." Eyes stark, she throws herself against me. "Thank you. Thank you, thank you, thank you."

"How did you get here?" I ask, pulling back. Business first. "Last I heard, you were in the Kennels."

"After you and Killian bonded, all of Killian's allies were gathered together and slaughtered, so he would have no one to rely on but Ambrosine."

"Ten? Lass?"

Killian! Joy causes every cell in my body to dance.

He and Sloan maneuver around a group of girls. Too far. I run as fast as I can, and hurl myself into his waiting arms.

He buries his face into the hollow of my neck and breathes me in. "You did it, lass. You did it."

"*We* did it. All of us, together."

"The others? They made it?"

"Only Archer and Raanan." Fighting concern for their fates, I take a moment to breathe in my husband's peat smoke and heather scent. "But the rest are still alive, somewhere in this realm." They must be. "Have you seen Clay, Reed or Dior? What about our mothers?"

"Not yet, but—"

Shake, shake.

We frown at each other as the shaking only intensifies. Overhead, dirt and debris begin to rain from the veil.

"I think Many Ends is crumbling." Archer comes up behind me. "If we remain inside…"

I think I understand. This sub-realm grew to accommodate new arrivals. Now, because of the Light, it knows the residents will be leaving. Many Ends is shrinking.

No telling what will happen next. "Get everyone to the water," I shout. "It's our only way out."

chapter thirty

"The more you care, the more you'll worry."
—Myriad

Killian

We urge the crowd into the lake, but there are millions of people present, spread out over the crumbling landmass left by the hills. Millions of others have already disappeared in the water—those who did not end up on a piece of land when the bright Lights faded.

We're ignored, and I'm not surprised. We're trying to make everyone in the entire realm do the same thing at the same time. Impossible. Most people run *away* from the water as the shaking intensifies, screams of panic erupting.

Ten, being Ten, starts *shoving* people into the water. Archer, Raanan, Sloan and Erica follow suit. Everyone who enters disappears beneath the surface, as if sucked below, and yet the dead mermaids continue to float without interruption.

"Sloan, Erica," Ten says, shouting to be heard. "The crowd will need a guide on the other side. Jump in, and help them find their way out of Myriad. And they need out. There's going to be a battle. Troikan troops are going to invade. Let's get the innocent to safety."

Sloan doesn't hesitate. She obeys, slipping under the water.

Drawing in a deep breath, Erica trails after her.

Those of us who remain...what are we going to do?

I'm not sure why I caved to worry. Where there is Light, there is a way. Vivid beams shine from above, sweeping people up, hundreds, thousands at a time, and carrying them to the water.

The glorious sight of such brilliant illumination leaves me reeling.

As I track Ten's movements, acting as her personal guard, I realize the beams are tracking us—those who entered Many Ends to free the damned. "Charge through the crowd," I call. Whether she heard or not, I can set an example. I fling myself into the masses, and Light accompanies me, picking up everyone around me.

"Dior!" Archer sprints away, desperate to reach his girl.

She's just as desperate to reach him. The two slam into each other and cling, as if the other could float away at any moment.

"We were right! We were right! She came back to life." A smile dawns on Ten's beautiful face, making her brighter than the beams. "Killian, she came back to life!"

A smile dawns on *my* face. Despite the obstacles, opposition, betrayals, doubts and uncertainties, she never gave up or let circumstances dictate her decisions.

Though Many Ends is crumbling, its monstrous protectors are defeated. The condemned are free. Death has lost its victory; the grave has lost its sting.

The collective sense of panic fades as more and more people are carried to the water, and relief takes hold. Those who aren't picked up begin jumping into the lake on purpose.

Archer returns with Dior at his side. Behind the couple are Reed and Clay. Ten embraces our newly revived teammates, her smile unwavering. Joy radiates from her.

When there is no one left, the Light coasts over us and lifts us off our feet. I take Ten's hand as we are eased into the water. Thankfully the putrid liquid never reaches us. We're caught up in the eye of a storm, Light our air and peace our shield.

We come out the other side—the Kennels—without a blip of trouble, and are placed on our feet. Cage walls surround us.

I hate this place. I've been confined myself a time or twenty, and the experience is scarring. Freedom is gone, your reputation in tatters. Humiliation is the soup du jour.

But the past is the past. I don't care what horrors I've suffered, as long as I have Ten by my side in the present, and the future.

"The cages are empty," she says.

She's right. The doors swing open. "Why is no one scramblin' tae climb up or down tae escape?" The masses from Many Ends are gone, as well.

Sloan and Erica stand a few feet away, but though they are armed and ready, they have no one to direct.

"The Light carried everyone away," Sloan says.

"Burned through the locks on the cages, too," Erica says. "Even the prisoners were carried away."

"Where'd they go?" I demand. Troika? The Land of the Harvest? Simply outside the Myriadian borders?

The girls share a look before saying in unison, "I don't know."

Boom!

We are thrown to the ground. Impact jars me. Spots wink

before my eyes as air heaves from my lungs. Several of my
bones break, and pain consumes me, but I scramble over to
Ten, who fell beside me. She's injured, but as quickly as the
wounds appear, they heal.

I cup her face the way I like to do, and drink in this girl I
love so dearly. "Are you all right, lass? Tell me true."

"I'm fine, I promise." She kisses me before she stands and
helps me do the same. The color in her cheeks deepens to a
rosy pink until she's glowing, so bright I should probably—
but won't, can't—look away. "Now to deal with Ambrosine."

"We can do it, too. We can do anything." The brightness of
her Light might be more than I'm used to, despite our bond,
and it might pain me even now, but it also strengthens me.
As interconnected as I am with her, my life is hers. Her life
is mine. Together, we are stronger.

$1 + 1 = 2$. The easiest problem with the simplest solution.

The vibrations we felt inside Many Ends bleed into Myriad,
rocking us on our feet. Or perhaps they originated here. Will
the entire realm crumble?

In the distance, a storm of darkness approaches. Thick black
clouds. Writhing shadows. The echo of a thousand screams.
In the center is Ambrosine. Drawing closer and closer. Wind
whips at his hair, the strands tangling around his face. He is
dressed in black leather and gold armor, many of his medals
hanging at odd angles.

"You!" His voice booms like myriad claps of thunder all at
once, and it sounds as if there are other voices trapped inside
his—each one crying for help.

I cringe as I whip around, but scowl as I meet the narrowed
gaze of my once beloved king. Rage and power radiate from
him. I feel the first wave of that power as it tries to send me
to my knees. Gritting my teeth, I resist.

Archer, Dior, Clay and Reed line up behind Ten in a show of support. I remain at her side, and I dare anyone to try to move me away from her.

"You did this." Ambrosine extends an accusing finger at me, perhaps Ten. Perhaps both. Violence charges the air. "You, who are *nothing*. *No one*. You think you have the power to defeat me? A mistake. The last one you'll ever make, I assure you. You entered my realm, but you will not leave it."

Behind him stand Leonard, Victor, Hans, Javier and Zhi, as if they are part of some Varsity All-Star team of evil. A growl reverberates low in my chest. After every terrible thing these men did to Ten, a savage need to lash out invades every muscle in my body. My hands fist, and I brace my legs apart.

There *will* be a battle today. Nothing can stop it.

I'll take no prisoners.

Leonard holds a dagger in each hand. Victor is no longer inside a Shell. Somehow, he's fully healed. Maybe Ambrosine is responsible. The effort could have cost him valuable energy.

Hans is young, fresh in his teens, full of overinflated pride. Zhi is wearing armor, just like his king. As if he hasn't lost every bit of his battle skill by spending centuries behind a desk.

A grinning Javier stretches out his arms.

Will wipe the floor with that smile!

Shadows spray from his fingertips, like poisoned gas, and coil through the air. Denials screech inside my head as they zoom toward Ten. *Must protect my wife, whatever the cost. My beautiful, brave wife. Her life matters more than my own.*

Leaping, I move in front of her—

Only to fly backward as I collide with the darkness.

As I crash land, Ten stretches out her arms, and Light explodes around her, bright enough to make my eyes water.

Light and shadow collide, shaking the entire realm. If I'd been standing, I would have fallen like everyone else. Both Javier and Ten flinch, but remain on their feet.

The Light manages to chase away some of the darkness behind the Abrogate—revealing untold men and women, boys and girls climbing to their feet.

Myriad's brand-new Varsity All-Star team?

"Now," Javier commands through clenched teeth.

The crowd mimics Javier. Arms stretched. Shadows summoned.

Anger chews me up, but dismay spits me out. The urge to pick up a dagger and just start slashing is fierce. I'd like nothing more than to take out each and every Abrogate. And they *are* Abrogates. Probably the ones from the warehouses I overheard Ten talk about. This group wasn't here when we first arrived.

Hurting the people determined to harm your loved ones feels good...for a time.

Wait. Plan. What is best for my *team?* "I need tae take them out, Ten?" The words are meant as a warning, but they emerge as a question. If I act, death will reign. Exactly what my girl doesn't want to happen. Is there another way?

A groan of exertion escapes her, and my hands clench. The shadow-wielders might be new and inexperienced, but they are powerful, and they are bombarding Ten with darkness. Clearly! Sweat sheens her face, and strain pulls at her mouth. Her arms tremble.

She's so strong, so determined. Seeing her weakened like this hurts *me*. How can I help her? What can I do?

Archer, Clay and Reed surround her, close their eyes and... impart their Light to her? The beams brighten, and the Abrogates waver. Color begins to return to Ten's cheeks.

Relief threatens to wipe me out. But I can't take a single moment to bask. The Abrogates must be stopped for good. Before my wife is harmed irreparably.

A war cry brews in my throat as I launch forward once again. I quickly pick up the pace, running. Sprinting. Yes, yes. I can do this. I can help Ten without compromising our goals.

Ours. Not just hers. I'm in it to win it.

Winning = saving those we can.

Light explodes through my veins as I dive at Javier, intending to take him out first. Noticing me, he tosses a shadow in my direction as if it's a javelin. That shadow nails me in the chest. Pain! My heart stops as I fly backward. Another crash-landing steals the air from my lungs, but I don't care.

What is pain in the face of victory?

Back on my feet, I start sprinting again. This time, I attack multiple Abrogates from the side. Like pins hit by a bowling ball, rows collapse. Different *clinks* reach my ears, and I grin a cold grin. I know that sound. Fallen weapons. Where is... there! The glint of a sword.

As my numerous victims lumber to their feet, sheer grit propels me to a sword. I swipe up the weapon, race forward, and fall to my knees—as I slide forward, I start hacking.

Screams of pain mingle with bellows of shock. Bodies pile around me, and Lifeblood pools. I purposely hobble the Abrogates rather than rendering a single death blow.

But mercy sometimes comes with a cost.

They continue reaching out, casting shadows. Hurting my girl.

Rage packs its bags and moves in to my chest, breathing for me. It is a fire that burns. Smoke fills my lungs, my nose, even hazes my vision. My heart wants to jump out from behind my ribcage and rest at Ten's feet.

I will save her, and if need be, I will not be nice about it. If my hand is forced, I will unleash pain like these Abrogates have never seen.

Mess with Ten, suffer.

Then, a miracle happens. Logic supersedes emotion. I am no longer Myriadian, controlled by what I feel. I am Ten's man.

My rage cools as logic tells me I do not have to be worked into a foaming-at-the-mouth lather to unleash pain. I gave these Abrogates a chance. They chose to continue harming Ten, as well as others. Now they will be disabled.

Calm but focused, I hurry to my feet. The sword is an extension of my arm as I work my way through the crowd, removing arms, hands and even legs. Painful blows, but if the Abrogates get help in time, not fatal.

A blast of darkness suddenly slams into me. Agony sears me as I'm hurled through the air. I crash land in front of Ambrosine, and skid backward. The sword flies from my vise-grip, and I curse.

Down, but not out. I will prevail.

My former Secondking glides toward me. *Bring it.*

Biscuit, Deacon and Clementine appear in a blaze of glory, just in front of me, carried on a beam of Light, stopping him.

I grin. Backup has arrived. Now the party can get started *right*. Biscuit will tear in to anyone who threatens his charge.

Then a Troikan General shoves through the crowd of Abrogates, no one able to stop him. I recognize him. Alejandro Torres. At his side is—I tense. Lina Lockwood. Ten's killer. *My* killer.

I don't know whether to take her out or thank her.

Can we bring home this victory?

My gaze finds Ten, and my heart constricts. She's on her

knees, color gone again; any second she might fall flat on her face, and the realization devastates me.

At least the shadows slither back, as if they, too, are weakening.

Ten's head bows. Then, she goes still, and I think my heart stops. The shield of Light fades.

Biscuit gallops to her side, licks her face. "You get strong now, hooman. Now, I tell you!"

Deacon and Clementine take up posts of defense behind her. Lina crouches at Ten's left, and Alejandro at Ten's right. I'm grateful that they're helping her, but she's my wife. Mine to protect. I'm willing to give my life for her, again and again and again.

Panic drives me to her side. I push the General aside and link my fingers with Ten's. She's trembling. There's only one thing she needs. Something I can give her. My Light. What I have left, anyway.

Willingly. Gladly.

Gratefully.

I push the beams across our bond, and there are no obstacles to impede the transfer. Color returns to her cheeks once again, and the sweat on her skin dries. Relief makes me light-headed.

All of us, we are loyal to this girl. Passionate about her safety. Because of her, we are free.

Loyalty, passion, liberty.

Love.

"Myriadians." Trembling with rage, Ambrosine points at Sloan and Erica. "Return to your family, or suffer the fate of the Troikans."

He calls his own people by their realm? I grind my teeth. "What are their names?" I call. "Do you know even one?"

The response is immediate, and snapped. "Names mean nothing."

For years I loved this man, and wished he had been my father. He never cared about me, or any of us. "I'll take that as a no." My tone is dry and prickly but inside, I'm seething.

"I am no longer Myriadian," Sloan announces. "I hereby pledge my allegiance to Troika forevermore."

"Troika has my allegiance, as well. Now and always." Erica nods, certain. She's a true friend I once treated poorly, but never again. Honest friends, those who are loyal to the end, are priceless. I can't afford to lose one.

Think! If we have any chance of winning this, we need to take out Ambrosine. To take out Ambrosine, we need...

Time to figure it out.

I can buy us time.

But first, I'm prompted by the Grid to say, "Come up with a way to cull Ambrosine from his Abogrates, and negate his powers."

"Okay, sure thing," Raanan retorts. "Not like that last task is utterly impossible."

One of my brows arches. "For Troikans, all things are possible, right? But go ahead. Refute your realm's campaign promises."

A muscle jumps underneath his eye. Silence.

Yeah. Didn't think so.

"Killian." Ten lifts her head, an action that seems to require more energy than she currently possesses. "Know what... planning. Will find...another way. Don't endanger yourself."

Her voice sends a thrill through me.

Trying to protect me, even now? I caress her cheek, luxuriating in the softness of her skin before I stand. I'm doing this. "Hey, Ambrosine," I call, my use of his name a dig at *his* pride. "Remember me? Or should I reintroduce myself. I'm Killian Flynn, yer doom." Nothing mocks a super villain quite like B-movie dialogue.

He inhales sharply in a clear attempt to control his temper. "Even if Myriad falls, Miss Lockwood will die this day. This time, she will not come back."

Must keep him talking. "You can't stop us. You can't stop her."

"We already have, you just don't know it." He smiles now, smug. "Javier found a way through her blocks—you."

No, not in this lifetime. But even still, unease takes a swing at me.

Unease has claws. I flinch.

The new Abrogates look to their king, unsure, and he offers a clipped nod.

What are they going to—

Shadows invade my mind in a burst, and a new surge of pain follows, my temples throbbing. I'm quaking as I clutch my head, my forearms pressing against my ears, my fingers weaving together in back.

Fury burns through me. Fury and fear. So much fear. What if they *can* use me to harm Ten?

Sweat pours down my temples.

Can't yield. Not for a second. Again and again, I've watched Ten battle her fears. Most people cave, never realizing they were already defeated the moment, the very second, they stop fighting. I will not stop fighting. Not now, not ever.

As dust rains from above, I drop to my knees. A shadow springs from the Secondking, wraps around my neck and yanks me across the way, until I'm kneeling directly in front of him.

What did Ten say? Light is love and love is strength. I focus on my love for my wife and fight my way back to my feet. I'm panting, sweating, agonized. My teeth are clenched so tightly I fear my jaw will snap.

"Ambrosine," Archer calls from behind me. No longer does he refer to the male as his father. "Stop this."

"Never," the Secondking replies.

"Killian?" Archer again. "What do you want me to do?"

I remember the days when we fought side by side. Then the days we fought so hard to hurt each other. Now, he's willing to risk his life to help me?

Trust. Loyalty. Honor.

Love.

They take the broken pieces inside me and help weld me back together again. Giving me the strength to say, "Let him continue." *Must find a way to use Ambrosine's plan against him…* "I'll win." A taunt.

A taunt that reaches its intended target. Eyes flashing with fury, Ambrosine motions Javier over.

The Abrogate steps in front of me, flattens his hands on my temples, and sends his darkness whisking through my mind, an ice-cold gale force I struggle to resist. Because, at long last, I see the shadows for what they really are: bondage.

These shadows do their best to tempt me, even as they barrage every barrier I erect. ***Let us in…will make everything better…all your pain will go away…earn respect…***

Panic feels like a thousand needle pricks against my skin. *No, no. Fight!* So often Myriadians have claimed the Troikans are slaves to their rules, but all along, the opposite has been true. We served the will of greed, nothing more, ignoring the plight of others. We waxed poetic about luxury and frivolity, taking what we wanted, when we wanted, citing might equaled right. To us, the weak deserved their lot.

Today, I'm the weak one. I need help, but my fellow kinsmen won't lift a finger in my defense. A bitter laugh sounds inside my head. Ten warned me this day would come. She said the weak do not stay weak and the strong do not stay strong, there's a constant ebb and flow, and we need each other to survive it.

With a cry from deep in my soul, I push the shadows and their ice away from the Grid, away from Ten and Troika.

I am part of Troika.

I might have shared what little Light I had with Ten, but there must be more. The *source* of my Light, buried deep, deeper...yes! In this cold, oppressive darkness, a pinprick of Light beckons...

I jolt. It is my connection to Ten, and Javier hasn't touched it. He can't. It's too bright, too pure.

A smile blooms. Like a heat-seeking missile, I focus on the flames, stretching out my hand...

Knowledge comes, cutting through the shadows to glide across the Grid. *Light* comes.

Once I thought Myriad had an intractable hold on me—but *I* was the one holding on to *Myriad*. No longer. I let go without a beat of hesitation. Let go of my past, hurts and fears. A heavy weight lifts from my shoulders. A weight I never knew I carried.

I grab hold of my future with Ten, allowing the Light to grow, spread and deepen. Warmth pervades, melting ice. Love for my wife expands. She is my life, the reason I breathe.

Javier grunts, and begins to shake. His grip on me loosens, but I latch on to his wrists, maintaining contact. *Will use their plan against them...*

The Light continues to expand, filling me...and spilling into Javier. He goes quiet and still, then collapses. Dead? Perhaps. I expect satisfaction, but feel resolute. His actions, his consequences.

Where will his spirit go, if he breathes his last? Many Ends is nearing complete collapse.

I open my eyes…and reel, the rest of the world coming back into focus. The Kennel cages have fallen over. Paths have been formed over the ground, where soldiers fight. Troikans versus Abrogates. Sword against sword, Light against dark. Ambrosine hovers in the air, held by a cloud of shadows, watching as a battle rages.

Ten lies on the ground, motionless, guarded only by Biscuit.

Panic returns, those needle-pricks sinking ever-deeper.

I don't know why she's out, and I'm not. What happens to one no longer happens to the other? I can only guess the reason. Before, we were two halves of a whole. Now? We are two wholes linked together. Rings connected and inseparable.

I just want her healthy and whole. Will do anything to ensure her safety.

Urgency sets my feet on fire. I run, shoving my way through the combatants to drop to my knees and gather Ten close. Her eyes are closed, her body boneless. Trembling, I scramble to check for a pulse…a pulse I cannot find.

No! No, no, no. A heart can be restarted.

Her heart *will* be restarted. Here. Now. No other outcome is acceptable.

"Tell me what happened," I demand, easing her back to the ground. Verging on hysteria, I pound a fist in the center of her sternum. Again. Again. And again. "Live, Ten. Do you hear me? Live!"

Without her I can't… I won't…

"She tried to get to you," Biscuit says between sobs. "Ambrosine hit her with more darkness than she could withstand. Make her breathe again, Killian. Please."

Hands just over her heart, I begin compressions. One, two, three. All the way to fifteen. Tears blur my vision. I check for a pulse. Nothing. Begin compressions again, doing everything in my power to push Light into her.

Light. My Light. She fed me what remained of her Light, didn't she? To save me from Javier. *Put my needs before her own.*

Argh! I want to scream, rant and beat everyone in the vicinity. She dies, we all die. "You come back tae me, Tenley Flynn. That's an order." Whatever I plan to say next gets clogged in my throat.

Darkness, darkness, all around her, enclosing her…so thick, too thick, but I refuse to give up. I push and push and push, my Light draining… And yet, *I'm* not drained. The other Conduits are feeding me Light even as they engage in combat. Feeding Ten, too?

A hard hand settles on my shoulder. Leonard Lockwood. Before I can strike, he gasps and stumbles away from me. His knees give out, and he collapses. The Light too much for him? Good!

Suddenly the brightest Light of all explodes from the Veil of Midnight, mere feet away from Ambrosine. In the center, a being appears. A being I've only ever seen in holograms.

Eron, Prince of Doves. Wind blows around him, and lightning flashes under the surface of his skin.

Relief fills me. He will save Ten in ways I cannot.

The battle stops abruptly, Abrogates rushing to one side of the battlefield, Troikans to the other. The Myriadians do not rush to offer their support to their Secondking, but to hide from Eron.

Archer, Deacon, Sloan, Erica, Clay, Reed, Clementine and Raanan race back to Ten's side. My family. My...friends?

"Eron," I call. "Ten needs yer help." *I* need his help. I need this beautiful lass now and always.

His blue, blue gaze finds me. The corners of his lips lift slightly, and he gives me a barely perceptible nod.

Relief spills from me. Ten will be all right. I know it. *I know it!*

This is the faith she's always had in the man. The being. I understand now. No matter how bad circumstances seem, things can get better.

"The time has come at long last," Eron says to his brother, voice booming. "While you punished your people, I've taught and empowered mine, waiting for a group willing to sacrifice everything to brave the darkness and save the damned, no matter the risk to themselves."

"They might have saved the damned," Ambrosine growls, "but they doomed themselves."

A smile of pure joy spreads over Eron's face, and in that moment he's so beautiful that it actually hurts to look at him. "What has Father always told us? There is no power stronger than love, and the greatest sign of love is giving. Giving is sacrifice. One after the other, my people have died to save yours. Now they will be reborn—and your reign ends." With barely a pause, Eron shouts, "Shine. Shine now."

Light explodes from each of us, including me! Beams soak into Ten, and she stirs in my arms. When she moans, her eyes blinking open, my heart leaps for joy. She lives!

Most Abrogates run away, screaming in pain.

Ten's mismatched gaze clears of any fog, and questions me: *What's going on?*

I lean down to place kisses all over her face and whisper,

"You're alive and well. Everythin' is going tae be all right. Your king is here." *Our king.* "I think we're about tae witness the showdown of the ages."

Above us, Eron and a trembling Ambrosine face off.

"Take your people and go." My former Secondking shakes his head in denial. "Leave my territory. You do not wish to fight me, Eron."

"Oh, but I do. Father wishes to rebuild the bridge between realms. Without your shadows, Myriadians will be unharmed by Light. They may choose to enter Troika, or stay here. I have no quarrel with your people—only you."

Ambrosine grows pale but swiftly rallies. Pride will do that—trick you into thinking you are better than you truly are. "There cannot be new life without blood and *sacrifice*, just as you claimed. If you want my people, Prince of Doves, you must die for them."

Eron lifts his chin, refusing to back down.

But his brother isn't done. "Our entire court system is built on a single principle. A toll must always be paid. A life for a life. A king for a city. Would you and your father prove yourselves unjust, rebuilding the bridge without the proper blood sacrifice? And after so many of our people have willingly died for the chance to help someone else defect to another realm. Someone who is, in essence, an enemy at the time."

Your father. Every day of my life, I've yearned for a family of my own. Yet Ambrosine has disavowed his own flesh and blood, as if they mean nothing to him.

"You want my life?" Eron spread his arms wide. "Very well. Take it."

"Oh, brother. I will. With pleasure." Ambrosine unsheathes a sword and, with a shrill war cry, launches at his brother, who is prepared, meeting the sword with one of his own.

The two propel into the air, twirling this way and that, their swords clanging together so quickly that my eyes cannot keep track. I see blurs, yet I'm still amazed by the show of strength, skill and speed.

Ambrosine will lose. I'm certain of it. As certain as I was that Ten would live. Our choices dictate the conditions of our life. Even faced with pain and death, Ten has always done what she believes is right. And more often than not, she's put others first. My former Secondking never has.

What Ambrosine and his minions do not understand? This war has never been about gaining the upper hand, or destroying the other realm. This war has always been about love. When you deal like with like, return pain for pain, you've *already* lost.

Ambrosine lost day one. Today's battle is simply the manifestation of it.

His people do not yet comprehend this truth. The Abrogates who opted to remain behind join hands, probably thinking to aid him. Darkness soon rises from them, a mist that wafts on the breeze to envelop the combatants. Eron's movements slow, and Ambrosine laughs with glee.

"You're only fighting the inevitable, brother," Ambrosine taunts.

"Killian," Ten says, and gulps. "We must help our king."

In that moment, my heart swells. I love her a thousand times more. She trusts me to help, not hurt.

I tug her to her feet, my hand clinging tightly to hers. "Together," I call.

We join hands with the others, forming an unbreakable link. Love floods me. *Light* rises from us all and spreads, chasing away the darkness.

When our Light reaches Eron, he stops altogether, rather

than speeding up. He hovers, his head thrown back and his
arms spread, as if he wants…no, surely not. Confusion pokes
holes in my triumph, and my brow furrows.

A life for a life. A king for a city.

The words reverberate inside my head, and I gulp.

"He's got this," Ten says.

Ambrosine closes in, maneuvering around the Light, and
swings his sword—

Eron doesn't move.

Ten and I shout in unison. "No!"

Shock jolts me. My stomach collapses into itself. Metal
slicks through Eron's throat. His head detaches and falls to
the ground. His body isn't far behind, the Light under his
feet vanishing.

Thump. THUMP.

Another denial from Ten, blending with a chorus of denials from every other Troikan. I open and close my mouth,
my mind unable to compute.

We…lost? The greatest Secondking is dead?

Ambrosine won? *Evil* won?

No. No! Absolutely impossible.

But in the space of a heartbeat, our Light goes out. *All*
Light. There's nothing left—except darkness. I'm left cold,
and empty. Nothing but a shell.

chapter thirty-one

"Leverage the pain of your past to ensure a brighter future."
—Troika

Ten

"No," I cry. I can't... I don't... Shock and horror trap my thoughts in an endless loop. I can't... I don't...

I can't... I don't...

I shake my head, and wires get rerouted. *I can't process the ramifications... I don't know what to do.* Darkness hangs heavy in the air, blinding me as a cacophony of protests and cheers assault my ears. The temperature drops, ice seeming to grow over my skin.

"This can't be the end," I whisper. "Darkness can't be the winner."

All hope is gone? We fought, and we lost, so go home and lick our wounds? I give my head another shake, the ends of my hair slapping my cheeks.

This simply cannot be. Light has to win. Light chases away darkness without fail. And, and, and we've sown love. Now we reap love. That's how things work. Spiritual laws are never broken. Never!

Killian's hand tightens on mine. Right now, he's my only anchor in a terrible storm. "Eron must have had a reason for acceptin' the beheadin', lass. Trust him."

"He just…he can't be dead." We did everything right. Where is Ambrosine? I can't see him—can't see anything. Is he hovering beneath the Veil, gloating about his victory?

A sob splits my lips. We risked our lives to save the people being tortured in Many Ends. Not just those we know, or those related to us, but strangers. We had Light on our side. We worked together. We stood as one. One spirit, one soul, one body. Surely we aren't going to be punished for our sacrifices.

"Spirits never die," Killian reminds me. "This is no' the end."

He isn't just hopeful, I realize. I hear certainty in his tone. He truly believes we will see Eron again. That belief spurs mine, warming me inside and out. Eron would never do anything to harm his people. Whatever he did, he did for our good.

There is no power stronger than love, and the greatest sign of love is giving. Giving is sacrifice.

Suddenly a burst of fireworks explodes through the sky, revealing Ambrosine in the same spot as before. His people are on the ground, staring skyward, watching the show. My father, Victor, the remaining Abrogates. Even Javier. But I can hardly bring myself to care. The starburst is the most magnificent, glorious display I've ever seen. Streams of sparkling light more dazzling than the Northern Lights in the Land of the Harvest. They cause the burst of other Lights, lighting up Myriad from the inside out.

"I'm hooked to the Troikan Grid." Awe drips from Killian's voice. "There are no shadows, only Light."

"We don't need to go to court?" Eron let his brother kill him outright…for this?

—*He did not kill me, Mighty Ten. Spirits never die. I am… I am. I was and I will always be. Though I lost my physical form, I have gained a better place in the Grid. I remain a part of my people.*—

Eron's voice flows across the Grid, and a gush of surprise laughter escapes me. He *is* alive. —*You could have bested Ambrosine. You could have found another way.*—

—*You've been to court. You know there is only one way. You know every court case is paid in blood, the most precious commodity for human and spirit alike. Only a king's blood could pay the price for countless Myriadians and Unsigned. Now they have a choice: defect or stay. Either way, they have been given a new start, without the influence of Ambrosine's shadows. At least for a little while.*—

I gulp. Such a beautiful exchange. Eron's life for ours. For all. Only love could make such a sacrifice. —*Are you saying Ambrosine will rebuild?*—

—*Myriad has been dealt a devastating blow, but yes, Ambrosine will rebuild. The difference is, any Myriadian who later decides to defect to Troika may do so, without ever having to go to court. No one else must experience Second-death. That is what we fought for, and that is what we won.*—

—*But what of peace?*—

—*With our actions this day, we've extended an olive branch. Some will accept, some will not. We can only love them all, and strive for better.*—

Deep breath in, out. So badly I longed for peace. But I do understand what he's saying. I cannot force others to comply. I can only do what I know is right. —*And what of humans?*—

—*A choice must still be made. They must choose Troika or Myriad. My people will continue on, winning souls.*—

Here's hoping we can fight for souls without actually fighting Myriadians.

"Do you guys see what I see?" Archer asks, awe dripping from his tone. "Or am I imagining my dream scenario?"

I'm drawn out of my head—and gasp. A section of the Veil of Midnight has been parted to reveal a breathtaking bridge that glimmers with all the colors of the rainbow. A staircase descends from each side, branching into multiple staircases midway, the ends reaching every Gate and Stairwell in the realm. As if the bridge has many arms open wide in welcome. *Come to me.*

Anyone can climb to the top at any time.

Side rails rise into a magnificent bejeweled arch, with four pillars acting as anchors. Two on each side. Those pillars end in razor sharp points, as if to ward off any aerial threat.

"No!" Ambrosine rams his big body into the bridge, but the massive structure holds steady.

Contact must weaken him, because he tumbles from the sky, his shadows unable to catch him. He crash-lands, his bones breaking, the resounding pop echoing through the Kennels. The foundation at my feet quakes, and drops of water rain from the crimson Veil. As if the realm is crying tears of blood.

One by one, the Myriadians around us collapse, just like their king. Javier, Victor and my father stay down, writhing in pain. Victor curses me, as if his pain is my fault.

My father reaches for me. "Ten...help..."

Help? He can't be serious. Only one day ago, this man slashed my mother's throat in front of me, hastening her Second-death. And he laughed about it!

His throat should be slashed!

Ugh. *Who are you?*

Resentment is not my friend. Resentment heralds hate, and hate heralds bitterness. Ambrosine was the epitome of bitterness, and I won't be like him.

I don't have to like my father. But. If there's a chance he has seen the Light, or will see the Light, can I really turn him away? Resolute, I make my way toward him, then crouch at his side.

The closer I get, the more I see glee glimmering in his eyes. I slow my pace. He reaches for me with one hand, as if beseeching me...and tries to stab me with the other.

Reflexes well-honed, I raise my arm to block. I'm about to launch a counterstrike when Killian appears at my side and stomps on my dad's wrist.

Leonard bellows with pain and outrage. I won't refer to him as "my dad" or "father" ever again. He is neither of those things.

He hasn't seen the Light. He might not ever see the Light. Even now, he thinks to betray me.

Any other time, my heart would have grown heavy. Today, the Grid—Eron—shines too brightly, a soothing balm to my soul and more of a father to me than Leonard ever was. I did my part. I tried to help. I can walk away with my head high.

"Goodbye, Leonard," I say, the words unlocking invisible shackles I've worn since my birth. Part of me held on to the memory of a doting father who used to carry me on his shoulders. But no longer. I'm free. "You have to live with your mistakes. And probably die with them, too."

Where will his spirit go, now that Many Ends is gone? Or will he be sent to Many Ends anyway?

The Grid provides clarity. Myriad is not destroyed, nor is Many Ends. They have simply been reset. Shrinking, as I guessed.

Leonard curses me, spewing hatred. Tuning him out—his words mean nothing to me—I stand as Killian draws me away.

"We can no' stay here, lass," he says.

Ambrosine is gone, I realize. He left his people behind. Water falls from the Veil of Midnight faster and faster. "I know."

Biscuit bounds over, tangling around my feet, his fur soft against my skin. "Eron told me this would happen. He said to tell you to leave the dark ones to their darkness. They will reap what they have sown. Everyone else is to cross the bridge and enter Troika."

Cold drops of water splash my face as Killian leads me toward the nearest Gate. "This way."

Our group follows. As soon as we enter the Gate, we come to a fork. A dark path, and a lighted one. We step toward the Light. A second later, we're standing in Troika. A manna field surrounds us, one that hasn't been touched by bombs or darkness. Or perhaps it *was* touched by bombs and darkness, but repaired itself like an injured spirit.

I spin, counting my friends. Killian and Biscuit. Archer, Dior, Reed and Clay. Raanan and Clementine. Lina, General Alejandro, Sloan and Erica. Deacon. We stare at each other for just a moment, and then we're hugging. A group hug driven by shock, joy, sorrow for Eron's beheading, and incredulity.

My smile is so wide my jaw aches, my heart an erratic drum in my chest. It's over. For now, the war is over, and Troika has won. Light—love—has won.

"Well, I was wrong about one thing," I say. "I thought killing Ambrosine was the answer."

"I did, too," Alejandro replies, "but your aunt instructed me otherwise."

Speaking of... "How did you two end up bonded?"

He grins a satisfied grin. "I was captured, tortured and she set me free. Then she convinced me that the only way to win the war was to bond with her."

Lina fluffs her hair, her eyes brighter than I've ever seen them, no hint of cloudiness. "I'm irresistible."

As he chuckles, I marvel. The two barely know each other, and yet their affection for each other is palpable.

"Neither one of ye experienced trouble because of the bond?" Killian asks.

"I'd already faced my madness, and won," Lina says.

I kiss Killian's cheek before focusing on Dior and Reed. Curiosity gets the better of me. "What happened to you guys in Many Ends, after you were killed?"

A shudder racks Dior's small body. "I woke up in an ember-bug hive. They burned me to death, and I woke up in a sea of alligator...things."

"I kept dying and reawakening in new places, too," Reed says with a shudder of his own.

"Enough chitchat—about you." Biscuit bounces around my feet. "I did so good. I showed the Generals where you were in Many Ends, and they listened good enough to head for Myriad to shine their Light through the Veil of Midnight, because I'm smart, and I knew you'd win. I knew it! And don't worry. I guarded your brother with my life, and when I left, other animals ensured his safety. I'm sure he's pooping his diaper without a care."

I laugh, so happy I could burst.

Kayla appears in a beam of Light, bright and beautiful. Dawn is beside her. The two girls race over to throw their arms around me.

"It's over," Kayla sings. "It's really over." She laughs, then leaves me to go embrace Reed.

"Thank you for your service to our great realm." Tears glimmer in Dawn's eyes. "Many Myriadians—or rather, *former* Myriadians—have arrived, my father among them. I missed him, and you brought him back to me."

"I had a great team. And really, I only did what—"

"Do *not* try to be humble right now," she interjects. "You led a great team. You fought to get inside a place others feared."

Shrug. "Okay, then. I rocked the heck out of it."

"Good girl." With a laugh, she moves off to search for anyone with injuries that might need tending.

I spot—no way. I spot Marlowe Dillinger! A beauty inside and out.

Our gazes collide, and her jaw drops. We rush to each other and embrace.

The last time I saw her, she was hanging from the end of a rope inside Prynne Asylum. She killed herself to escape the horrors of abuse the guards inflicted. I hated myself for failing her. So badly I wanted to save her.

Tears stream down my cheeks. "I'm so glad you're here."

"Me, too. Oh, me, too."

"How did you—"

"Clay spotted me and brought me over."

"Well, thank the Firstking for Clay!"

We chuckle together.

She takes me by the shoulders and squeezes. "Thank you. Thank you for entering Many Ends and giving us a way out."

"I had a great team," I say. I'll say it again and again, because it's true.

Clay joins us, and Marlowe throws her arms around him. Do I detect a spark?

Cue my eyebrow wiggle.

The Generals arrive next and each pauses to pat Alejandro on the back for a job well done.

"I did nothing." He inclines his head in my direction and smiles. "We won, because love is Light, and sacrifice is love."

I come face-to-face with General Ying Wo Li and go still. Hope unfurls wings inside me. "I was told you died and moved on to the Rest."

"I did," she says, "but the Secondking Resurrected everyone for the final battle."

That...makes sense. He said he was building his army, biding his time. While Ambrosine's people suffered in Many Ends, Eron's people learned from their mistakes in the Rest and prepared for a better future.

Archer once told me he got to replay his entire First- and Secondlife, discovering where he went wrong and what he could have done better.

"Did you miss me, Miss Lockwood?"

Levi's voice hits my awareness, and I squeal with happiness. When I find him in the growing crowd, I go weak in the knees with joy. Grinning, I fight my way toward him. More people arrive with every second that passes. Animals, too. Even dragons! They fly overhead, roaring with...pleasure? Maybe. I think they're smiling.

They hated the dark?

I wonder if they sprayed fire over the Myriadians because they were ordered by Ambrosine, not because they craved destruction?

Well. Hugs, hugs, for everyone! This just gets better and better.

"I did miss you," I tell Levi. "Perhaps. A bit. And the name is Mrs. Flynn."

"And me?" a woman asks. "Did you miss me?"

My gaze zooms to Meredith, my gorgeous grandmother. Then I'm wrapped up in her arms, tears blurring my vision. My chin is trembling so forcefully I have trouble speaking. "Yes, yes, a thousand times yes."

Beside her are Hazel and Steven. With a laugh, they join us. Tears spill down my cheeks. This is the best reunion of all time.

Next I find Elizabeth Winchester and her boyfriend, Claus. I hug her, and though I've never met him, I hug him, too. The two are glowing with happiness.

Luciana steps forward and—shocker! She bows to me. "Thank you, Miss Lockwood. I mean, Mrs. Flynn. Thank you for everything you did for us, *all* of us, despite our behavior. We—I—should have treated you better." Her gaze strays to a man I've never met but know, through the Grid, as General Orion. He clutches a fine-boned woman against his chest. Sadness, then acceptance, radiates from Luciana. "I should have done a lot of things differently, and going forward, I will." Her gaze shifts to Killian. "My apologies and thanks to you, as well, Mr. Flynn."

My eyes widen at the respect in her tone. Another miracle.

Shamus steps forward next, clutching a sword in his newly regrown hand.

I lift my chin, gearing for a fight.

Instead of taking a swing at me, however, he performs a bow to rival Luciana's. "You have my thanks, Miss Lockwood. Without you, we would not have had a way to invade Myriad and free the spirits trapped inside Many Ends."

Killian wraps his arm around my waist. "The war might be over, but our efforts are no'. Many Myriadians will choose tae remain in their realm and help Ambrosine rebuild."

Their realm, he said, and I smile. I'm full of smiles today. To him, Troika is home.

"They will not be harmed," Shamus says. "You have my word. If ever they wish to come and live in Troika, they may. If not..." He shrugs. "Always their choice. We will help them rebuild to the best of our ability."

This is better than I ever hoped, more than I ever dreamed. "What about Killian's mother? My mother?" Where are they?

"Already found." The crowd parts as Princess Mariée steps forward. Light halos her as she waves her arm, motioning to two women who stand together.

For a moment, my mind whirls with questions...about the princess. Eron has merged with the Grid. At least, that is my understanding. Will he ever take bodily form again? Will he and the princess be able to wed?

The Grid, as always, provides the answer. Once things are settled in Troika, Princess Mariée will be joining him in the Grid. They *will* be married. Happily ever after.

"Ten?" My mother, who is holding my baby brother, Jeremy, inches toward me, hesitant. Beside her is a woman I've never met, who is wringing her hands, clearly nervous.

"Mom!" I rush forward and she rushes forward, and we meet in the middle, throwing our arms around each other, careful not to smush Jeremy.

He wiggles and giggles as we pass him back and forth, neither one of us wanting to let go of him or each other.

—*Love my Ten.*— His beautiful voice fills my head.

—*Love my Jeremy.*— Always.

"Oh, my sweet girl. Thank you." Mom cups my face, kisses my cheek and drinks me in with her gaze. "Thank you for forgiving me. Thank you for freeing me. Thank you for helping me reunite with my baby. Thank you for *everything.*"

Once again tears burn the backs of my eyes. "I can't take all the credit."

Her gaze strays to Killian, and her smile grows. "Oh, trust me, I know." Then she wiggles her brows. "Your husband is quite handsome, isn't he."

My gaze strays to him, too. I watch as he and the other woman approach each other warily. She has dark hair, like Killian, and the same dusky skin tone, though she is far shorter and very slender.

The two stare at each other for a long while. They've never actually met. Not as two adults anyway. But I think their hearts recognize each other. They must. With a sob, the woman dives into Killian, and he shuts his eyes to hold her and savor.

My tears spill over, raining down my cheeks. Out of everything that's happened, this might be the best.

Killian's lids open, and he meets my stare, as if he sensed my gaze, even amidst his happy reunion.

—*Lass.*— Emotion coats his voice.

—*Don't you dare thank me again.*— I try for a stern expression, and I'm pretty sure I fail. —I *owe* you *thanks.*—

—*You owe me nothin'.*—

—*And yet I'm willing to give you everything.*—

The corners of his lips curve upward. —*That, I will accept. Gladly.*—

In the ensuing days, many changes are made in Troika. The realm expands to accommodate the new additions, homes are built, and welcome parties are thrown. Former Myriadians are allowed to go back to their realm, and many do. Including Dr. Vans. We let them go without protest. They want to rebuild, and so they shall.

As for Troikans, more Conduits are made every day. In fact, it's practically an epidemic. Light continues to spread.

Dragons fly through our skies at all hours of the day and night. They've caused no trouble. In fact, they've helped us. They've used their fire to burn away what remained of the bomb debris.

Like the people of Myriad, they'd been bound to Ambrosine. The Secondking used the creatures to intimidate and control, and forbade them from interacting with the realm's citizens.

Now they are free. And I think... I think they are happy.

Happy is all I want for everyone. Those who remained in Myriad. Those who came to Troika. Troikans. Those in Troika who have decided to move to Myriad.

Yes, we've had large groups pack up and head for Myriad. And I'm glad! This is what I wanted. Peace between Troika and Myriad. Freedom. Every citizen's right to choose a path without censure. Love and respect for each other, whatever our differences.

I only wish I'd gotten to spend more time with Killian these past few days.

He's spent the bulk of his time with his mother. He's even gotten to meet other family members he never knew about. Oh, and he helped Erica get settled in Troika.

Once, I would have been jealous of their relationship. No longer. I know where I stand with Killian. That boy is crazy about me. He loves me more than life.

He's mine, now and always.

And really, he can't be blamed for our time apart. I've spent the bulk of *my* time with...well, everyone else. My mother and brother. My grandparents and great grandparents. Lina and Alejandro. Archer and Dior. Deacon and Sloan. Reed and

Kayla. Raanan, Clementine and Levi. Clay and Marlowe—and yes, they are a couple!

And let's not forget my sweet Biscuit. He's always by my side.

But, oh, I miss Killian something fierce. Word of his exploits has spread faster than the speed of Light. Mainly his willingness to sacrifice his life for the sake of our realm. No joke, he went from being one of the most hated men in the realm to one of the most beloved, forgiven for all his past crimes.

Archer and Dior had their talk, and they are officially together. I've never seen the two so happy. Thankfully Bea approves of the relationship, and she's agreed to guard both Archer and Dior.

And there are more happy couples among us! Sloan and Deacon are dating, and they couldn't be any cuter.

There are also soon-to-be couples. Raanan has been sniffing around Erica, and I'm expecting him to win her over any day.

Like she really stands a chance against his charm. Everyone who ventured into Myriad and Many Ends to save the damned has been awarded a new title: the Exalted. With each of our promotions comes our choice of any future assignments. Of course, we're also given new homes and great wealth, two things Leonard Lockwood wanted in both of his lives. The things he could have had if he'd made better choices.

Killian and I are moving in together, along with our guardian animals. Yep, he got one, too. A female poodle named Zoey.

Zoey, as it turns out, is the baddest dog on the block. She can take down a grizzly, guaranteed.

Biscuit pretends to disdain Miss Zoey, but danged if he doesn't secretly love her.

Even though we have a home, we haven't spent much time in it. Not simultaneously, at least. We've been too busy. I miss him the way I'd miss a limb, which is why we are going on a date this evening, after he helps his mother move into her new apartment.

I helped my mother move into her new home yesterday. Jeremy is living with her, and she tells me he's more trouble than I ever was. The scamp! Their guardian animals—a lion and jaguar—are now valued members of the family. I invited the entire group to stay with Killian and me, but Mom was adamant that "newlyweds need time alone."

I'm trying.

—Where are you, Killian?—

The doors swing open, and he strides into the foyer. Our eyes meet, and he gives me the sexiest grin of all time. A grin reserved strictly for me, making my insides melt. "I'm right here, lass. At yer service, always and forever."

"Twenty-two seconds late." I glide closer to him, over-come by love and heat—so much heat. "I should punish you."

"How about you kiss me instead?"

Excellent plan. I kiss him hard and deep, pouring myself into the communion of lips and souls. By the time we part, we are both panting.

His eyes sparkle. "I was goin' tae ask if you missed me, but I can guess the answer."

"Oh, I've missed you, all right. The war is over, we're on vacation, and you haven't been seeing to my needs."

He arches a brow. "I have no', now, have I? Well, it's time I do so." In a single fluid motion, he sweeps me up into his arms and begins to climb our winding staircase, as if I am as light as air.

I laugh, filled with joy and Light. "I'm not sure how little ole me ever won Killian the Untamable."

"You breathed, lass. I often wonder how sexy ole me ever won the fiercest female in the history of ever."

Aw. Could he be any sweeter? "So you're happy you married me?"

"The happiest."

"You're not—yet," I say, and kiss his neck. "But you will be. Take off your clothes."

His pace increases, and I belt out another laugh. Never, in all my wildest imaginings while I was trapped inside Prynne Asylum, desperate to escape, could I have predicted I would end up here, with Killian. But through the darkest moments of my life, I finally saw the Light, and through the deepest depths of my pain, I found great pleasure.

Life might not go the way we think we want, might even lead us through dark nights and across stormy seas, but we can't give up. The only sure way to fail is to quit. We are Lights of the world, and we must keep fighting for what is good and right—we must keep fighting for love.

Me? I'll fight till the day I experience Second-death.

One day, though, my battle will come to an end, and I'll move on to the Rest. Like Myriad and Many Ends, the Rest has been reset.

By the time I go, the world I leave behind will not be the world I was born into.

I want to leave a legacy of strength, hope and Light. I want what was once my mess to become a message—people matter. Whoever they are, wherever they come from, whatever they look like or believe, they are worth something. They are precious.

Life is precious, and I don't want to waste a single second.

★ ★ ★ ★ ★